Fran O'Brien established McGuinness Books with her husband Arthur McGuinness for the purpose of publishing her novels to raise funds for LauraLynn House Children's Hospice at the Children's Sunshine Home, in Foxrock, Co. Dublin.

Her first four novels – *The Married Woman, The Liberated Woman, Odds on Love, Who is Faye?* have raised €113,000.00 in sales and donations for LauraLynn House. Fran and Arthur hope that *The Red Carpet* will raise even more funds for the charity.

Also by Fran O'Brien

The Married Woman

The Liberated Woman

Odds on Love

Who is Faye?

THE RED CARPET

FRAN O'BRIEN

To Carol & Marilyn
love Fran
& Arthur.

McGUINNESS BOOKS

McGUINNESS BOOKS

THE RED CARPET

This novel is entirely a work of fiction. The names, characters and incidents portrayed in it are the work of the author's imagination. Any resemblance to actual persons, living or dead, events or localities, is entirely coincidental.

Published by McGuinness Books,
15 Glenvara Park, Ballycullen Road,
Templeogue, Dublin 16.

A catalogue record for this book is available from the British Library.

ISBN 978-0-9549521-4-3

Cover artwork by Mary Cahalan Lee (PIXI)
career Irish artist – www.pixi-art.com

Typeset by Martone Press Ltd,
39 Hills Industrial Estate, Liffey Bridge, Lucan, Co. Dublin.

Printed and bound in Great Britain by
CPI Cox & Wyman, Reading, RGl 8EX.

www.franobrien.net

For all our family, friends and clients who support our efforts to raise funds for LauraLynn House Children's Hospice at The Children's Sunshine Home, in Foxrock, Co. Dublin.

Jane and Brendan McKenna have been through every parent's worst nightmare – the tragic loss of their only two children. Laura died, aged four, following surgery to repair a heart defect. Her big sister Lynn died less than two years later aged fifteen, having lost her battle against Leukaemia – diagnosed on the day of Laura's surgery.

Having dealt personally with such serious illness, Jane and Brendan's one wish was to establish a children's hospice in memory of their girls. The hospice will offer community based paediatric palliative respite and end-of-life care in an eight bed unit. There will also be support and comfort for parents and siblings for whom life can be extremely difficult.

Now LauraLynn House has opened at last, and Jane and Brendan's dream has become a reality.

ACKNOWLEDGEMENTS

As ever, our very special thanks to Jane and Brendan, our dearest friends.

Thanks so much to all my friends in The Wednesday Group who continue to give me such valued critique. Many thanks especially to Muriel Bolger, who once again edited the book for me, and thanks also to Vivien Hughes, who proofed the manuscript – both of whom are so generous with their time – it means everything to me.

Many thanks to both our families, friends and clients, who continue to support our efforts to raise funds for LauraLynn House.

Thanks to all our friends at the Farmer's Markets in Nenagh, Killaloe and Thurles for their friendship and support for the charity.

Thanks also to Martone Press – Yvonne, Martin, Dave, Deirdre and Kate – who help with the final production of the book in so many ways.

Thanks to our printers CPI Cox & Wyman.

Many thanks to Mary Cahalan Lee – Pixi – whose original painting was used for the cover of the book. We really appreciate her generosity.

Thanks to all at LauraLynn House at The Children's Sunshine Home.

Thanks to Craftprint, Irish Distillers Pernod Ricard, Ballygowan Natural Spring Water, Superquinn, Tesco.

Many many thanks to Kevin Dempsey Distributors Ltd., and Power Home Products Ltd. for their generosity in supplying product for LauraLynn House.

And in Nenagh, many thanks to Walsh Packaging, Nenagh Chamber of Commerce, McLoughlin's Hardware, Cinnamon Alley Restaurant, Jessicas, Abbey Court Hotel, Irish Computers, and Caseys Service Station, Toomevara.

Many many thanks to all at Cyclone Couriers – especially Mags – who continue to support us by delivering the books free of charge to shops all around the country. We really appreciate their generosity.

And to my darling husband, Arthur, whose love and support makes this possible.

My mother went away

No beginning and no end **on my birthday**

You go around and around one moment she was there

There's no escape and the next she was gone

When you're eight It was my fault.

No Beginning and no end I hasn't been able

You go around and around to blow out all the candles

When you're eight There's no escape

There's no escape When you're eight

You go around and around No beginning and no end

No beginning and no end You go around and around

When you're eight There's no escape

There's no escape *No beginning and no end*

You go around and around

PROLOGUE

Amy opened the velvet covered box, and sifted through its' contents. So many things she had kept for sentimental reasons - photographs, birthday cards, letters, examination results, gymkana rosettes and much more. Some she would take with her to Dublin, others she would have to leave behind.

It was difficult to decide, but the first thing she picked up was the photograph of her mother. Dressed in a beautiful red dress, Maxine posed for the cameras at the Academy Awards on the night she received the Oscar for Best Actress in the film *Dry Landscape*.

It was years since Amy had looked at this photograph, forced to keep it hidden away, like the memories of her mother, Maxine. She kissed her image and put the photo into her wallet so glad now that she could look at it whenever she wanted and leave secrecy behind.

*

PART ONE

1983

Chapter One

Beverly Hills, LA, late afternoon –

For six year old Amy, life was all sunshine. In Hollywood, it was the excitement of the film studios, of being on location, as she played a role in her latest film. Home always seemed to be filled with people who drank champagne. The men had deep voices and thumped each other on the back when they met. The women giggled as they gathered around the pool, swanning in bright designer bikinis.

Amy put on her sunglasses and the picture in front of her softened, a slight greenish tinge on everyone now. She wondered did they notice that their suntans had changed colour. She smiled to herself and giggled. They couldn't see her and she liked that. To be able to spy on them was exhilarating. The undulating ripple of conversation flowed upwards but she couldn't hear what anyone was saying. She pushed the sunglasses up on to her head and the brightness was back. Now the blue water in the pool sparkled even more as they dived, throwing up high sprays which caught the light like diamonds.

'Hi Amy.' Doug wandered towards her perch among the wide branches of the tree.

She stared at him, suddenly aware that she shouldn't be out here. She was supposed to be learning the lines for her part in her Dad's film – *Dry Landscape*.

'Honey, why don't you come and join us in the pool?'

She shook her head.

‘Come on, don’t be shy, I’ll help you down.’ He put out his hand. He was tall. His face at the same level as her own.

‘Amy, what are you doing up there?’ Her Mom suddenly appeared. The expression on her beautiful features didn’t auger well. She was cross, and there were little creases at the corners of her full lips.

Amy climbed out of the tree. It wasn’t sensible to disobey her Mom particularly when she was entertaining.

‘I’m sorry, Doug, Amy should be inside,’ she said.

‘Don’t send her in, Maxine,’ he grinned, ‘we were going swimming.’

Her mother gripped Amy’s hand. ‘Say goodbye to Doug.’

Maxine hurried Amy through the garden and into the house and the child had to run to keep up with her pace.

‘Maria, where are you? Maria?’ Maxine called out as she entered through the patio doors into the living room.

‘I am here, señora.’ A plump dark-haired woman appeared.

‘Go and study your lines, Amy.’ Her mother let go of her hand. ‘How’s the lunch going?’ she addressed Maria.

‘The caterers have everything ready.’

‘Good, I’ll just check the tables.’ She disappeared in a swish of pale turquoise chiffon.

‘You want some juice, pineapple?’ Maria asked.

‘Yea, please.’

It was poured into a glass and handed to her. ‘Now, while we are serving you stay here, chica.’

Amy sipped the cool drink and thought about learning her lines. But that didn’t appeal so she finished the juice and ran around to the back of the house where their Labrador pup was lying asleep in his kennel. ‘Wake up, Joey.’ She stroked his fur and he immediately climbed up on her knees licking excitedly. ‘Where’s your ball?’ She searched around and found it. They played together and in her enthusiasm, her dark hair, carefully tied by Maria in bunches, worked its way loose. She flung the ball high in the air and the pup jumped to catch it in his mouth, and immediately rushed back to her to start all over again. No-one came near and eventually she lay beside him and slept, her arms wound around his neck, the two exhausted.

'So this is where you're hiding.' Laughter woke her up.

She stared up at Doug, confused, raising her hand to her eyes against the sunshine.

'Why don't you come for a swim now, the pool is free.'

She shook her head.

'Come on, you know you like swimming in the big pool, I've seen you watching us.'

She clung tighter to Joey, who raised his head.

'No.'

He put his hand out. Joey growled.

'Hey, Joey, quiet, it's only me,' Doug raised his voice.

Joey growled again.

'OK, OK.' He put his hands up and stepped back a little.

'Amy?' Maria appeared from the house, bustling, wiping her hands on a towel. She stopped when she saw Doug.

'Hello Maria,' he smiled at her.

The angry voices of her Mom and Dad were the first thing she heard when Maria came to wake her the following morning. It was five o'clock and she had to be at the studio in an hour.

'Come on, chica, we'll have some cereal and then you can have a shower and dress.'

'What's wrong?' she asked, her pert six year old face worried.

'Nada,' the Mexican woman assured.

'He's directing the next film I'm producing,' her father said. 'We'll be seeing a lot more of him, I guess.'

'I told you I don't like him, and lately he always seems to be around the place.'

'You didn't always feel like that. I thought you and he were almost an item at one stage, I was jealous,' he laughed.

'Don't be ridiculous. Why didn't you tell me he was directing?'

'It's none of your business.' His voice was louder.

'Of course it's my business.'

'Don't question me.'

'I will if I want,' she screamed.

There was the sound of movement, a thumping, shuffling sound. A door banged. Amy's dark eyes were riveted on the door. She was afraid. Unsure who was going to hurtle through. But no-one appeared. After a moment she looked down at the Frosties and slowly brought the spoon to her mouth. She held it there for a few seconds and then slowly lowered it again. She wasn't hungry any more.

Chapter Two

'You'll have to make an effort. I didn't get you this film role because I wanted to be humiliated,' John shouted. It was a never ending rant.

'I'm good, I know I'm good,' Maxine said softly.

'You're the best of a bad lot, but you have a standard to keep up, and you're not doing that, you're nowhere near the Parker family standard.'

'That's something you've created. Sounds like a car or something.'

'That's right. I created you. Don't you realise that?' he barked.

Without a word, she stood up from the coffee-table, settling the fall of the black silk robe as she walked away. She was tall and slim, with shoulder-length blonde hair. In that graceful lilting movement the robe flipped open to reveal long suntanned legs.

'How dare you ignore me.' He followed her.

She stopped at the door. But kept her head averted.

He grabbed her shoulder and whirled her around to face him.

'Don't you realise that I have my reputation to think of?'

'And I have mine, it's just as important.'

'Might be to you, but it's not to me. My reputation is what brings in the money.'

'I don't need your money,' she retorted, her dark eyes edged with thick lashes.

‘So you’ll provide everything we need, will you?’ he said, grinning, a sarcastic twist to his full mouth. He was a handsome man, John Parker, and tall too, a good head above Maxine.

‘If necessary.’

‘Wouldn’t leave much for designer clothes, or beauty treatments? And don’t forget Amy.’

‘There would be enough.’ She was defensive.

‘You saying you can do without me?’

She lowered her head.

‘I’ve given you everything. Everything,’ he raised his voice again.

‘I’ve made my own life, right from the beginning. I’ve worked hard, and I’ve been rewarded,’ Maxine said stubbornly.

‘You came from the worst part of Dublin, not the most salubrious of backgrounds. Dragged up by a couple of aunts. You don’t even know who your parents are.’

‘I’ve put all that behind me.’

‘Maxine Howard is a fabrication.’

‘I am Maxine Howard.’

‘You’re what I made you.’ His tone was sarcastic.

‘You’re revolting.’

‘Am I?’ He stood up and moved swiftly towards her. She stepped back, but wasn’t quick enough, and he was there beside her, his arm darting forward to hit her sharply on the side of the head. She cried out and fell to one side, grabbing on to the back of a chair to keep herself upright. She pressed her hand against the affected spot and squeezed her eyes shut, standing in the same taut position.

‘That’s just to remind you never to speak to me like that. Have you got the message?’

She nodded.

‘And don’t worry, you won’t ever have to manage without me.’ His voice softened unexpectedly. ‘I’m not going to leave you. I’ll always be there for you and Amy.’ He put his arm around her and pulled her close. ‘Oh baby, baby, why do we squabble like this? You know how much I love you.' He pulled her chin up and kissed her lips hard. 'Why can't you be more careful of what you say, you never think before you speak. When I say that you're not good enough in the part, that's the truth of it, and there's no arguing.' He stared down at her. There was a red mark on her pale chin where he had pressed his thumb.

Her shoulders drooped even more.

'Now, let's go through a few of the scenes and see if you can improve your delivery.' He picked up the script and flicked through the pages.

'I don't feel up to it now. It's late.'

'You need to rehearse, you can't go into studio tomorrow and not know where you're going wrong.'

'Look, I promise to do better, I'll make a special effort. Just let me go to bed, I need sleep, otherwise I'll look terrible,' she appealed to him.

'Just give it a few minutes.' He shook the script in front of her face.

'It's all hours, come on,' she coaxed.

'You're a stubborn bitch.' The script slid across the marble tiled floor and he marched out of the room.

Maxine did try harder. Aware of John in the background, watching, noting. They were doing more takes of the scene which was a dramatic meeting between two lovers. Normally, she found this type of scene easy to play, but in this film the actor was an attractive dashing guy, who had already made a pass at her. Because of that she felt he was taking more pleasure in their love scenes than he should. She knew exactly what John had meant last night. He was right. She had held back. Afraid to show her emotions in case her leading man mistook her excellent acting for some depth of feeling that didn't exist.

Now, caught between the two of them, and because the fear of John was the stronger, she performed as well as she ever had, throwing herself into the scenes with all the ability she could muster. The actor reached for her and she let herself go. Soft. Pliable. Her slim body sank into his and their lips touched sensually as the passion they were supposed to portray grew out of control. Now she didn't know whether this was real or not. Her heart thumped. Her pulse raced.

'I love you,' he whispered, pushing her gently along the length of the couch, reaching to lift her skirt.

She ran her fingers through his short fair hair. Aware this was someone new, someone different. That his skin was soft, and firm, his fingers gentle, a question out of the blue then, an unwelcome question. Could she love him? This person. Whom she didn't know at all really. She looked into his ardent blue eyes. Could he love her? Was he genuine? Or did he amuse himself with all the women who played opposite him.

'Cut!'

It was a successful take. The director was really pleased. She looked around for John, but couldn't see him. She was disappointed then. Something in her needed his approbation.

'How did I do today?' she asked that night as they lay in bed together.

'It was almost too real.' He picked up the book he had been reading the previous night and slowly removed the bookmark from the page. John was a very methodical person. Everything had its' place in the house. In his office. In the car. The bathroom. The kitchen. The garage. The list was endless.

'Does that mean I played the part? She leaned into him, and put her hand on his arm, pushing up the sleeve of the pyjama jacket. She stared into his eyes willing him to look at her. 'John?' There was no response, his eyes concentrated on the lines of text before him. She put her arm around him, and pressed her lips on his smooth suntanned skin. Now he wouldn't tell her. Because she wanted to know. It was his way of getting back at her.

John and Maxine had estates in Beverly Hills and Malibu along with the other stars of Hollywood. You came by invite only. Luxurious cars with tinted windows shot in and out very fast through electrically controlled gates. Helicopters landed and took off. Security men with radios checked who came and went. They patrolled the grounds and kept out undesirables - paparazzi, fortune hunters, and tourists, who hung around outside when the celebrities were in residence.

They entertained lavishly. This particular evening the dinner table was arranged with silver, cut glass, orchids and candles. Maxine wore electric blue silk and smiled at the people around her. They were all in the film business, and it was important for John to keep them at his fingertips. Everyone was talking about *Dry Landscape* - the film they were shooting at the moment. A tense drama with psychological twists and turns.

'It's a good script,' someone commented.

'Definitely an Oscar contender.'

'When will you wrap?'

'I guess in another month or so. We're almost there,' John said, smiling.

'And within budget?'

'Just about.'

Everyone laughed.

'Anyone else for wine?' John nodded to the waiter and the glasses were immediately topped up.

The buzz of conversation continued.

'How do you feel about the film, Maxine, you're playing the lead?' Someone to her left asked.

'I love it.' She played with the dessert in front of her, using the fork to chase one of the chocolate dipped strawberries around the dish. Finally pinning it against the sugar coated glass and sinking the prongs of the little fork into it. For some reason she noticed the juice of the fruit ooze from the pinpricks and ran her tongue along the inside of her lip, her taste buds sharpened. She popped it into her mouth, enjoying the delicious flavour.

'Of course you do, *Dry Landscape* is your best film yet,' the director slid his arm around her shoulders.

They smiled and nodded agreement.

'This film is going to be a big success with Maxine starring. Break all box office records.'

There was a ripple of laughter.

'What's next?'

'We start shooting my new film in three months,' John announced.

'Will Maxine star?'

'Of course,' he brushed his lips with a white napkin.

'Where is the location?'

'Ireland.'

Maxine looked down the length of the table at him. To say she was surprised was an understatement.

There was a babble of excited chat. Everyone enthralled about the idea of shooting in Ireland.

'How wonderful,' the people closest to him expressed their delight.

'Maxine is going home.' John's smile was wide and he seemed very pleased.

'You never mentioned it before,' Maxine said later. 'I saw nothing about Ireland in the script.'

'I deliberately had that omitted.'

'Why?'

'Because the final decision about location hadn't been made, and as we only pulled the whole thing together a few days ago, I didn't want to put your hopes up.'

'Where exactly is it?'

'Connemara.'

In her mind, she had an image of undulating green landscape, stone walls, ruined cottages.

'I always wanted to bring Amy there.' She grew dreamy.

'She isn't going to be enamoured with the west, what d'ye bet?' he laughed.

'How long is the shoot?'

'Five or six months.'

'Is there a part for her?'

'No, not this time.'

'She could go to school there.'

'Maybe.'

'She doesn't learn very much at the studio classes. I've always wanted her to have a good education. Now this is her chance.'

'I thought we might buy a house. Have a base there.'

'Yes, that would be wonderful.' She was unbelievably happy.

'I knew you'd be glad about it, I love surprising you, darling.' He put his arm around her and drew her close.

Chapter Three

Amy watched and waited until the storms abated. She couldn't differentiate between a major row and a minor row. The tension was the same. It whirled around her like the way clouds suddenly scudded across the blue sky, black edged, threatening. She held her breath. The words which passed between her mother and father were unintelligible usually, but the anger which fuelled them was all too apparent. At times like this she shrank into herself, waiting until the air lost that pressure which warned of an explosion. But these days, the rows were continuous.

'Are you ready, Maxine? I don't know what you're doing down here in the kitchen? This is Oscar night, and we can't be late.' John appeared in the kitchen dressed in his tuxedo.

'I wanted to spend some time with Amy, she's just had her dinner.'

'Mom made me chilli con carne,' Amy said, smiling.

'What do we pay Maria for?'

'You know I like to cook for Amy sometimes.'

'Not when we're going out to such an important event.'

'We're just finished.' She rose.

'Then hurry up, I don't want to be late, this evening of all evenings. There are some very important people going to be there.'

'I must get ready, pet.' She kissed Amy on the forehead, and hurried upstairs.

'And you get to bed, it's late,' her father vented his anger at Amy.

She was suddenly frightened.

He prodded her shoulder with his finger and forced her towards the door and out into the hall.

Reluctantly Amy lifted one foot after another up the stairs. She hated going to bed. I'm a night person, she would say to herself. Her mother was a night person, or so she said. What exactly that meant was something vague and unknown. She opened her bedroom door but waited for a moment to see if her father had followed to kiss her and say goodnight. Sometimes he patted her on the head, and she liked that tingle on her hair. She always associated it with a smile on his face when she could cuddle up to him and know that he loved her. But he didn't come up tonight.

She picked her teddy up, hugged him and stood staring out the window. People still walked on the white sandy beach and there were even a few swimming in the crashing waves. She wished she could swim in the sea as well with her Mom and Dad. But that never happened. When they stayed in the house on the beach at Malibu Maria sometimes took her for a walk but she could only swim in the shallow pool either in the pool room or the garden, whichever, but never in the blue waves. The soft fuzziness of teddy's head on her cheek was comforting and a longing swept through her. She wanted to be out there with those people. Moms, Dads, and kids, all together.

'Amy,' Maxine rushed through the door, wearing a beautiful silver dress, the skirt swirling around her like a satin ribbon. 'Goodnight, honey, sleep tight.' She held her close.

Amy could smell her mother's perfume waft around her and felt the warmth of her body through the thin fabric of the dress.

'I'll see you in the morning, pet, don't forget to read over your lines with Maria before you go to sleep.'

'Maxine,' John's voice drew nearer. A warning there.

'Must go.' She held Amy's face and kissed her on the lips.

Amy closed her eyes for a few seconds.

'Night.'

When she opened them again Maxine was just closing the door behind her. Amy stood there licking her lips. The taste of her mother's lipstick was nice. She went to the dressing table and stared at herself in the mirror. There was a trace of pink on her lips and she spread it with her tongue. Did she look like her mother, she wondered. Her reflection told her no. Maxine was blonde and she was dark. She was disappointed. Now she would never be a movie star like her Mom. There were tears in her eyes.

'Let us have a bath and then to bed.' Maria came in.

'I have to read the script.'

'Then we will do that, sit up on the bed.' She picked it up from the locker and handed it to Amy.

'I think I know it.' Her face was serious as she flicked the pages and found the one she wanted.

'Then it will only take a little time.'

They went through the scene.

'Tomorrow is the scene with the horses. That's my favourite.'

'You will be riding?' Maria's seemed surprised.

'No, the other actors will be doing that, the horses are too big for me,' she giggled.

'I am glad.'

'It's on a ranch, and the man who plays the lead is my uncle and I come to visit,' she explained, 'and there's a woman as well, and they have two kids who are my cousins.'

'I like this movie,' Maria said.

'So do I.'

'Now tell me your lines.'

Amy went through them.

'You know the lines for the actors as well?'

'I have to.'

'So you could play the other parts?'

'I can play all the parts,' Amy said, smiling.

Chapter Four

Maxine had grown up in Dublin in the care of her Aunts Nuala and Bridget in Ringsend. Their house was filled with books. In every room of the house. A mad mix of paperbacks. Thrillers for Bridget. Romance for Nuala, with curled edges and an occasional broken spine from over-use. Maxine liked history and lost herself in the worlds of long-dead civilisations.

They raised her strictly. Insisted she study hard at school, and stay on until she was eighteen. Nuala and Bridget had great hopes for her, often talking of their cousins who worked in the film studios in Hollywood.

'Mike will get you a screen test, he promised me,' Nuala would tell her. 'Do you remember him?'

Maxine nodded, and smiled. 'He's really tall, isn't he?'

'It seemed like that to you at the time I suppose.'

'When I heard he was working in Hollywood, then I decided I wanted to go there too.'

'You have the looks and you can act too. That part you played in the school musical was wonderful.'

'Where is my mother? Did she go to Hollywood?' Maxine asked one day when the subject came up and the talk expanded, which only happened if the sisters were in a particularly garrulous mood.

'Yes.' Bridget was always first in. 'Mary always dreamed of that.'

'Was she in the movies?' Maxine asked.

'That we don't know, lovey.'

'Maybe I might meet her out there, I often wonder about that. Do you know where she lives?' Maxine asked.

'Is that pot boiling over?' Bridget rushed into the kitchen followed by Nuala and they fussed over the piece of ham or whatever else it might be, the conversation forgotten.

Maxine always thought her mother had to be a movie star. She had gone to Hollywood and made it big. She was beautiful. Maxine could see that in the photo they had. And like Mike, she had to be there too.

'Was there a row or something?' Maxine would ask.

'She was the wild one in the family. Always longing to be off and doing her own thing.' Bridget was the most talkative. Filling in little details which Maxine soaked up and kept in her diary. To be read over and over in the quiet of her bedroom at night.

'What about my father, did he go with her?'

The question always had an explosive effect on them.

'Was that thunder and lightning?' Bridget would immediately rush to the window and peer out anxiously.

'Cover up the mirrors quick.' Sheets were procured and appropriately draped while they waited for the flash which sometimes never came.

'It's moved off, thanks be to God.'

'But the sky is blue,' Maxine would say.

'Means nothing, it can still happen, could be a storm over the city, that's all it would need. I remember a man was killed by lightning. He was sheltering under a tree.'

'And a chimney was cracked.'

'And a house went on fire.'

And on and on.

There were always enough stories to take their mind off the question which had innocently started it all.

But as Maxine grew older she knew exactly what was going on. Her aunts didn't have answers to her questions. Or wouldn't tell. Or couldn't tell.

Once the results of her Leaving Certificate were announced, and she had received honours in all of her subjects, the plans were put into action. Mike was contacted. He would sponsor her. They picked up forms at the US Embassy and completed them carefully, going over each line again and again before finally writing in the information requested. Her Birth Certificate was produced by her Aunt Nuala. It was a long time since Maxine had even looked at it, and then had been so young the information hadn't meant anything. Now she noticed that her father's name was noted there - Thomas Cullen.

'So that's my father's name?'

Bridget and Nuala looked at each other.

'Why am I not Cullen then?' Maxine demanded.

'She didn't want to have anything to do with him. She hated him,' Bridget said.

'Why was that?'

'We don't know, lovey.'

'Where is he?'

'He left before you were born.' Nuala patted her on the shoulder.

'He was a bastard,' Bridget burst out.

'Don't speak like that in front of Maxine,' Nuala admonished.

'Why not? It's true, isn't it? Time she knew anyway. Too many secrets in this house.' Bridget took off her glasses and began to clean them vigorously with her handkerchief.

'We can't tell her everything.' Nuala's voice was soft, placating, and there were tears in her eyes.

'Why not? I'm grown up now,' Maxine said.

There was silence for a moment.

'Tell her,' Bridget insisted.

Nuala was in tears.

'It has to be done now, there's been too much time lost,' Bridget was agitated.

'I want to know, whatever it is,' Maxine reached for Nuala's hand.

'I am - your mother,' Nuala whispered.

The words slipped out almost unnoticed. Maxine wanted her to repeat them but was afraid to ask, as Nuala was in tears again.

'So many years we wanted to tell you, but we had to stick with the story. Couldn't let anyone know,' Bridget said.

Suddenly they were all hugging each other, murmuring endearments amid floods of tears. Not much sense made out of what they were saying. It was later when they talked. Nuala and Bridget explaining the story of how the sisters had to keep up a facade that Maxine was their sister Mary's daughter. She had supposedly given her child to the sisters to raise before she had emigrated to the US.

'I met Tom at the library. He was nice, wasn't he?' Nuala looked at Bridget for affirmation.

'If you like the type.' Bridget sniffed.

'He was good-looking and fun, I liked that best about him.'

'But he was unreliable, and he liked to roam, you have to admit that,' Bridget said bluntly.

'He was so handsome, women just gravitated to him, he couldn't help it.' Nuala held Maxine's hand.

'Fairy-story.' Bridget began to stack the tea dishes on the tray. Noisily.

Nuala gave her a sharp look. 'You wouldn't have minded him yourself.'

'Not my type.'

'You were just jealous.'

'Was not. I tried to tell you what he was like but you weren't listening,' Bridget bristled.

'Bridget, Nuala, will you stop?' Maxine intervened.

They looked at her, guilty looks on their faces.

'Tell me what happened, I want to know.'

It took hours for the whole story to be told. Maxine heard the detail of Nuala's first meeting with Tom. How she fell in love and thought he was going to be the man in her life. She couldn't resist him and when she discovered she was pregnant, was full sure that he would immediately rush her to the altar.

But Thomas Cullen didn't respond the way she expected. Sheer horror was the best way to describe his reaction when she announced the news.

'What?' he stared at her, his dark sallow complexion growing ever paler.

'We'll have to get married.'

'Married?'

'And it better be soon before I start to show.' She put her hand over her stomach and smiled.

'I'm not getting married,' he muttered almost under his breath.

A rush of emotion seared through Nuala.

'Did you think you could trick me into marriage by producing a sprog?' he scowled. His features changed. Ugly now. The sensual lips drawn down. The eyes which had promised so much were full of hate.

The words hit her with a thump, and her lungs felt like they had been punctured, all of her breath sucked out. She couldn't speak, devastated.

He left her there in Bewleys in Grafton Street with her cup of coffee untouched in front of her. She stared down through a mist of tears. At the brown surface of the table. The milk jug half-full. The cubes of sugar in the bowl. The cake stand laden with creamy cakes. She reached to pick up the cup and sipped. Just to do something. So that people wouldn't notice her distress. There were voices all around her. Conversations about other lives. Clinks of cups on saucers. The thumps of trays being stacked by the waitresses. The hiss of the boilers. Footsteps walking past. Doors opening and closing.

'Is this chair free?' someone asked. A hand on smooth dark wood, a beige cuff, the wisp of a silky blue scarf. A damp umbrella.

She nodded.

'You don't mind if I join you?' She sat down. 'Such a day, so busy in town, and that rain, I'm exhausted.' The rest of the beige coat came into view and filled the space where Tom had sat a few moments before. Nuala had an urge to scream 'you can't sit there, he'll be back any moment'.

The waitress came over and began to clear the table. Tom's cup disappeared. Thc last thing he had touched. With it went the sound of his voice. His tall broad-shouldered presence. All she had left were memories.

Chapter Five

Nuala took the blue suit out of the wardrobe and laid it on the bed. She was nervous, but excited too. Maxine and Amy would come to Dublin tomorrow, and since Maxine had phoned it had been one mad rush.

'I'll do my lemon Madeira, and make some tarts, and I'll have to give the garden a facelift too.' Bridget stared pensively out through the window, hands on ample hips. 'Is John coming?' she asked, following Nuala into the kitchen.

'Maxine didn't say.'

'I hope not.' She took the big mixing bowl from the press.

'Why?'

'I want them all to ourselves.' Bridget picked up a framed photo of Maxine and Amy which stood on the window sill. Then she took a handkerchief from her sleeve and rubbed the glass. 'What's the film about?'

'Don't know, didn't ask. Not interested to tell the truth. Makes no difference to me. Or to you either. Wouldn't be worrying yourself,' Nuala was already making notes on a piece of paper.

'Will we get everything done in time?' Bridget sat down, her hand on her chest.

'Of course we will, the place isn't that bad.'

'I don't know,' she stared around her worriedly.

They did get it all done, but the night before Maxine's arrival, Nuala had to suggest to Bridget that she might go around to see the doctor.

'Your breathing seems a bit uneven.'

'It's nothing,' Bridget snapped. 'I don't want to be shunted off to hospital just when Maxine's coming, I couldn't bear not to see her.'

'That won't happen,' Nuala assured. Bridget had a heart condition, and the fact that she was considerably overweight didn't help.

'I'm not going,' Bridget began to get even more upset.

'You're getting all het up, and there's no need for it.' Nuala left it at that. She hated to argue. Normally they got on well. But each respected the idiosyncrasies of the other.

'I'm not going to be able to sleep a wink tonight,' Bridget confided as they had their supper. 'Do you think we've covered everything?'

'Oh yes, I think so,' Nuala looked around.

'I'm so looking forward to tomorrow,' Bridget said as she cleared away the dishes. She hummed a tune. 'They're coming at twelve?' she asked.

'Yes, twelve.'

'I'll lock up, you go to bed.' Bridget took the tray and went into the kitchen. She couldn't relax, and continued to clean and tidy although it wasn't really necessary. But just as she turned the key in the back door, she pressed her other hand against her chest. Pain caught her breath. She squeezed her eyes tight shut. Tears welled up. She bent over, and a few seconds later she collapsed on to the floor.

Upstairs Nuala heard the crash and rushed down.

'Bridget, what's wrong love?' She gently patted her cheek but noticed the cold clammy feel from her skin and had a terrible sense of foreboding.

'I'll get the doctor, no, the ambulance, I'll ring, I won't be a minute.' She rushed into the hall.

Chapter Six

Maxine, John and Amy were staying in a hotel in Clifden while looking for a house. It was early May. A weak sun glimmered through cloud. It was exactly the weather John and Doug wanted for their film *A New Day*. Misty mornings and rainy evenings could be used to set scenes and give them that exact quality they needed to portray the story of the Irish Famine and the hundreds of thousands who emigrated to the US in the mid eighteen forties. Maxine had been very enamoured of the idea of playing in this film which portrayed the history of the Irish people. In the final cut there would be sequences which needed to be shot at sea, as well as at studios in Hollywood.

Most of all Maxine was over the moon to be back in Ireland after so many years, and was looking forward to going to Dublin to visit Nuala and Bridget, and introduce them to Amy. But the phone call from Nuala in the early hours of the morning changed all that.

'What? Dead?' John barked.

'The doctors think she may have had a heart attack. It was very sudden, just before she went to bed. They have to do a post-mortem, Nuala is terribly cut up about it,' Maxine explained tearfully. She was very upset, and found it hard not to lose it altogether.

'So what does this mean?' John didn't seem to be particularly concerned about Bridget, but was more annoyed that he was being discommoded.

'I'll have to go, to be with Nuala.'

'How long will you be away? You were only going for one day.' Anger began to build up.

Maxine could see it in his eyes.

'I'll need more time now, don't you realise that Bridget has died?' She dabbed her eyes with a tissue.

'But we're shooting, we can't spare you.'

'Nuala's all alone, it's going to be so tough on her, and there's the arrangements to be made, I'd like to help if I can…' she gabbled.

'For God's sake,' he muttered impatiently.

'OK, I'll go as planned and come back in the evening, then return for the funeral when it's organised.'

'If you must,' he grumbled. 'And try and get yourself under control, we can't have you looking like that, you're a mess.'

'Why did Auntie Bridget go to heaven when she knew we were coming?' Amy asked.

'She didn't know that was going to happen,' Maxine explained. 'I'm sorry she's not going to be there. But we'll see Nuala, and that's going to be lovely, she's looking forward to meeting you.'

Maxine had to make a big effort to hide her desolation that Bridget had died, very much regretting that she hadn't come back before now. In the early years in Hollywood, she didn't have the money, succeeding in only getting bit parts on which she barely survived. Then she had met John at a cocktail party. A larger than life character who liked her looks and immediately saw her playing a particular part in one of his movies.

It was the beginning of her new life, and within a few short months she had married him. He had called their relationship the perfect partnership. Love of each other and love of career. It could only bring success. And he was right. One blockbuster followed another. Her name was on everyone's lips. She was immediately recognised wherever she went. She was famous, at last.

But over the years John had become a controlling force in their marriage, and she had let him dominate her. Now there were times when she felt that she followed behind him, a silent shadow.

Drawn away from the superficiality of an actor's life, Maxine was catapulted into reality with a jolt. Death was something which hadn't visited her before. She couldn't sleep that night, only dozing for short spells of time, to jerk awake suddenly as a memory pushed itself into her mind. Scenes of the past, her childhood days, were painted so graphically that she might actually have been there. Maxine, come in for your tea or dinner or bed. The twin voices alternated. Do your homework. Go out to play. Let's go shopping. We're going to buy you a new outfit, jeans, sweater, shoes, whatever she wanted. It was a simple childhood. Maxine only realised that now. An utterly happy time. But her aunts always worried about the future. Would they have enough money to give her everything she needed? That big question dominated, as did a myriad of little ones scattered into their daily life. What if it rains tomorrow? What if we're late? What if we're short of flour? What if we don't find it? All the what-ifs that children don't understand. But there was always utter certainty about everything in Maxine's mind. Nuala and Bridget's what-ifs flew across her mind like the slipstream behind an aeroplane.

Maxine had to use Pete, their chauffeur, to do the driving while in Ireland, and asked him to drop them off a little way from the house. She wore a dark grey suit, and had put on a large pair of sunglasses. But no-one here recognised her. There was hardly anyone around, just a couple of kids kicking ball. But the house was the same as ever. It was home. She rang the doorbell. Her heart thumping, her hand holding Amy's tightly. Her first view of Nuala was through a mist of tears. She embraced her. So glad to be here at last.

They cried, and talked, and cried. While Amy was looking at cartoons on the television, Nuala went over the events of the evening before in hushed whispers. Maxine wanted to help in some way, but there was nothing she could do, except listen.

Very little had changed in her home. The furniture was the same. The photos on the mantle, and above all, the collection of books. If anything, there were even more now. Piled on the floor. In boxes. On top of the side-board. Under the table. They seemed to have taken over.

'Where is Bridget now?' Maxine asked.

'At the hospital. She won't be released until the post mortem is done.'

'So we can't see her?'

'No, they'll let us know and then we can talk to the undertaker.'

'Let me make those arrangements for you.'

'No, no, it's all done. Bridget was very particular about that, we both were. We discussed the readings with Fr. O'Sullivan, and decided which funeral parlour. We'll have three cars, and after Mass she'll be buried in Glasnevin. We have a plot there.'

'I can't believe you have everything arranged,' Maxine was horrified.

'When there's only the two of you living together you have to look to the future.' She lowered her voice. 'I know this sounds strange, but you should discuss your wishes with John.' She patted Maxine's hand. 'Now I'm making tea for us, and do you think that Amy would like some lemonade?' She got up to put on the kettle.

Later the doorbell rang, and it was the first of a succession of callers to express their condolences, and as Nuala said later with a twinkle in her eye, who wanted to meet Maxine again. To her surprise she remembered quite a few of them, particularly those girls with whom she had gone to school.

'You're so famous, and us here surrounded with kids,' Tricia laughed. She had been her best friend in secondary school.

'Maybe it's not all it seems,' Maxine smiled.

'Go on with you. All that money. And knowing those fabulous people. Tell us who you know? Brad Pitt, George Clooney, Richard Gere and who else?

'I've met Richard Gere.'

'What's he like?'

'He's a lovely guy.'

'Oh wow. Do you know I have a photo of you that appeared in "Hello" magazine. You were walking up the red carpet at the Oscars.' Karen pulled it out of her bag, and showed it to her.

She laughed. It was really nice for her to meet all the neighbours and friends again, but sad too, because of the loss of Bridget. Now here in the sitting room of home, her life in Hollywood grew ever more distant, and she felt more like the Maxine Howard who lived in this house than she had in years.

The funeral took place three days later. Maxine and Amy travelled to Dublin again. It was the same church where all her life she had attended ten o'clock mass each Sunday, and went to confession in a dark velvet space on a Saturday. Fr. O'Sullivan was much older now, shrunken, a harmless old man. But in that confessional of long ago he assumed a different character. There he was a frightening ogre. With a smell. A warm body aroma. With bad breath like he had just eaten his dinner.

Some members of the family showed up, but she only vaguely recognised a couple of her relations. Nuala and Bridget kept to themselves, and had very little contact with their family. People shook her hand. Murmured their condolences. Sorry for your trouble. She fumbled through it. Visualised Bridget inside the coffin. White marble-like face. Eyes closed. Lips compressed. Chubby double chins which always sagged when she was asleep. Then a sudden fear that she might not be dead. Panic swept through her. She looked at Amy who stared up at the priest. Her face white too but gladly alive. She rested her hand on the shoulder of the pink jacket. Amy's eyes met hers. She smiled and received a smile back, and moved slightly closer to her daughter.

At the graveside, Maxine tried not to lose control. She didn't cry easily. That had been drummed into her by Nuala. Amy pulled at her jacket, and she bent down to her.

'Is this like when we made a hole in the garden and put my bird *Cheepie* in a little box,' Amy whispered. 'And we put flowers there because he had gone to heaven?'

'Yes sweetheart, it's like that.'

'Do you think Auntie Bridget liked my flowers?'

'Of course she did.' She wrapped the small hand in her own and squeezed.

'I'm thinking of leaving Amy here with Nuala for a few days, it would be so nice for her to have company,' Maxine said to John when he phoned later.

'Did I hear you correctly?'

'Perhaps over the weekend and I'll come back for her then.'

'On no account. You never know what might happen.' His sharp response cut through her.

'You're being unreasonable. It's quite safe, I grew up here,' Maxine tried to persuade him.

'No, Maxine, I want both of you back here immediately.'

'Please John?' She hated to beg, but on this occasion made an exception.

'I said no, and I mean it. You're holding up the schedule and, as you know, every second costs money.'

'We'll come tomorrow,' she said slowly. It was so hard to argue with John. She could never put her side. He just wouldn't listen.

Chapter Seven

They moved from the hotel into a rented house which had been extensively renovated, with an option to purchase if it was suitable. Just a short distance along the coast from Clifden, it stood overlooking the wild Atlantic, and Maxine was very much attracted to the area which had something magical about it.

That first evening, they sat on the patio a little way from the main crowd, late evening sunshine casting long shadows across the grass.

'I love it here, John.' Maxine raised her glass. 'Let's toast.'

He raised his and their glasses clinked musically. 'To Ireland.'

'To home,' she said, smiling.

'The landscape looks great on film, *A New Day* will be our biggest success yet.'

'Let's buy this house, it will be our getaway home,' she suggested softly.

'Yea, why not,' he agreed.

'Thank you darling,' she kissed him. 'This means so much to me.'

'You know I just want to keep you happy, babe,' he said with a wide grin.

'I want to spend as much time as I can here, and we can choose a school for Amy, somewhere she will get a really good education.'

'Suppose that's important,' he sipped his glass of wine, and stared out over the sea.

'I don't really like the idea of a boarding school, but now we'll have somewhere to come home to, and we can see her often. And maybe we'll get a dog for her, remember we promised?'

'Yea, sure.'

'A Labrador, the same as Joey. She'll love it.'

He didn't reply.

'What do you think?'

'Go ahead.'

He was in amazing good humour this afternoon, and she couldn't believe her luck that he agreed with everything she suggested.

Maxine made enquiries about a boarding school for Amy.

'What type of place is it? I hope it's not too religious,' asked John.

'No. The educational record is good, and there are a lot of activities provided.'

'I'm having second thoughts, I don't know whether I want to send her to school or not.' John response was abrasive.

Maxine wasn't sure whether she wanted it either. Other people would be closest to Amy, leaving her out on the periphery of her daughter's life. Would she have to get to know her six-year old again? Children forget. Someone had once said that to her. Would Amy forget her? It was a ghastly possibility.

But there was another reason for her decision. The director, Doug, was too friendly. Just that. Too friendly.

Amy's reaction to Slade College – their final choice - was amazing. She loved it. As Maxine guessed, the most exciting part of it was the working farm and stables. Suddenly, it was all arranged. Amy would stay for a couple of days each week, and get to know everyone during the last few weeks of term. Then it would be easier to go back in September.

Maxine bent down on her hunkers, and zipped up her red jacket.

'Don't be fussing over her,' the gruff tones of John drifted down.

'You'll be back tomorrow then?' There was a sound of loss in Amy's voice.

'No, Tuesday, Amy, didn't we say?' He patted her on the head.

She looked up at him. 'You're sure?'

'Of course we are.' Maxine kissed her and slowly stood up.

Amy's hands reached up to clasp hers and John's as well.

'All ready now?' The teacher in charge of the junior school was a young girl, and Amy had already taken to her. 'Now we're going to go over to the farm to see the ponies, and we can give them their lunch, they're very hungry.'

'What do they eat?'

'Hay and we might give them some apples as well. Say goodbye to Mum and Dad now.'

'Bye, pet.' Maxine kissed her again and gave her a quick hug.

'Bye, poppet,' John said jovially. 'You go on and get acquainted with those animals.'

The following forty-eight hours were the longest in Maxine's life. She had never been without her child before for such a long time and she missed her dreadfully. They continued to shoot the film as the weather was just right, but her mind imagined all sorts of eventualities befalling the pupils at the school and Amy was right there in the thick of them. Accidents. Fire. Sickness. Maxine's mind was a carousel of evil portent.

But when she picked her up, Amy was full of excitement. 'My favourite pony is Kitty, and I brushed her hair and took her for a walk, and I love the dogs too, and I saw them milking the cows and the sheep have cute woolly coats, I have a friend now, her name is Patricia and Ann my teacher said I could learn to ride Kitty next time.' Amy rattled on as they drove away. 'Can I come again soon?'

Maxine nodded, her heart clenching.

'When?'

'Next week.'

The house had an open door policy as did their homes in Beverly Hills and Malibu. Some of the crew stayed with them instead of in local hotels, and Doug, the director, was always around.

Amy was staying the full week now at Slade College and seemed to love every minute of it. Maxine had never got used to her absence, and as time passed, she wondered was she alienating her daughter altogether because of a crazy notion that someone watched her with an unhealthy interest?

'Is Amy coming back this weekend?' Doug sauntered into the dining room.

'Yes.' She nodded, barely glancing at him while continuing to re-arrange the flowers on the table. The caterers had done all the work but she always liked to cast a final eye over things.

'I miss her around the place,' Doug smiled. The tall Texan, hands pushed into the pockets of his blue jeans, stood just that bit too close to her.

She stepped back to look beyond him, but said nothing.

'She's a sweet child. So much fun. Knowing her always makes me regret not having a family of my own.'

She wished he would go away.

'Maybe I could go along when you visit her?'

'No.' The retort was sharp.

Surprise sent his eyebrows up and he stared questioningly at her. 'Why not?'

She stared back thinking that he had a nerve to even ask such a thing.

'We want her to settle, too many visits are disturbing.'

There was a pout of disappointment on his lips. He shrugged. 'Maybe later?'

She watched him and felt as if she was in a dark place. There was a growling out of the depths. A terror without a name.

Chapter Eight

It was a good day. Bright. Blue-skied. Scudding white clouds. Not too much wind but enough to fill the sails and send the yacht cutting through the sea. It was a large vessel and extremely comfortable. They had sailed out of Killary Harbour. The next part of the shoot would be at sea and they were getting their sea legs before they began. Some of their group crewed, others relaxed with a glass of wine, determined to enjoy themselves. And Amy was home from school.

'Maxine, come pull this rope,' John called.

She walked up the deck. Just slightly unsteady.

'Here, this is what you do.' He showed her how to tie it off.

She managed to do it the way he wanted. 'You've never seemed that interested in sailing, yet you really enjoy it,' she said.

'I spent my early youth on the water, now I realise how much I've missed it,' he laughed.

'Mom!' A call from further along caught her attention.

'Be careful,' she yelled at Amy who was leaning over the side.

'I saw a fish. Look, down there.'

'The sea is full of fish, but you don't want to fall in. How would we catch you?' she laughed, enjoying this unexpected day out.

'I have my life jacket on.'

'Still, you must be careful.'

'Another rope, Maxine, come on,' John called. 'This is supposed to be a lesson, you have to learn something.'

Maxine enjoyed sailing. One of the few on board who didn't have some feeling of queasiness by the end of the day. Maybe it was because John kept her busy tying ropes, or because she was watching out for Amy. She was just so relieved that there wouldn't be a problem with seasickness when they filmed at sea.

As they disembarked, Maxine couldn't see Amy. She had been with John a short time before, but when they stepped on to the quayside, he was alone.

'John, where's Amy?'

'Thought she was with you.'

'I saw her with you a few minutes ago.'

'Maybe she's with the crowd, they're walking over towards the cars.'

'You check with them and I'll go back on board.'

She was already clambering up the gangway.

'Amy, Amy? Where are you?' she cried out, running along the deck. But the yacht was empty. She went into the engine room and back along the other side. Looking everywhere. Becoming more and more frantic with worry. John was walking along the quayside and she called to him. 'I can't find her.'

'Maybe she's gone in one of the cars, they've already left.'

'No, she'd never go without me, I know, Amy?' she screamed.

'Mom.'

She whirled around, and almost lost her footing when she heard her voice.

'Where are you?'

'We're down here.' Amy appeared up a ladder from somewhere.

'Who's with you?'

'Doug.'

Maxine put out her hand and helped Amy up. 'Where were you?'

'We thought we'd check out below,' Doug said, grinning.

'I told you to stay away from ...' she burst out.

'Mom, there were such cute little windows.'

'Come on, your Dad's waiting for us.' She grabbed her hand and hurried her along the deck and down the gangway.

When they got back, she put Amy to bed and sat beside her on the bed pensively.

'Read me a story, Mom?'

'Which book would you like?'

'The one about the caterpillar and the ladybird.' She pushed herself up on the pillows.

Maxine flicked through the pages. 'Where were we?'

'Start at the beginning again.'

She stared at the first line, but looked down at her daughter's expectant face, and hesitated.

'My love.' She stroked Amy's hair gently. 'You would tell me if anyone did anything to you which wasn't nice?'

'What does that mean?'

'If Doug touched you.' Maxine's heart hammered.

Amy looked puzzled.

'You mustn't let him close to you, and always tell me if he puts his hand on you, that's very important, you must tell me.' She took her hand and held it tight.

'Why?'

'He just might.'

'Do you not like Doug?'

'No, my love, I don't like Doug, and I don't want you to like him either.'

'But he's nice.'

'No, Amy, he's not nice, that's what I'm trying to say to you.'

'Dinner's being served.' John came into the room, shrugging into a navy blazer. 'Are you ready?'

'I've to change.' She stared into the wardrobe trying to decide what she would wear this evening.

'Chop, chop.' He clicked his fingers.

'I have to talk to you.'

'About what?'

Her stomach was sick. This thing had erupted inside her again, with all its' awful portents.

'Amy.'

'What about her?'

'This afternoon.'

'Really, Maxine, there isn't time for this, tell me later.'

'No, I have to tell you now,' she insisted.

'Well then?'

'Amy was with Doug.'

'Yea, on the boat, I know, I was there.'

'He's shown an interest in her, wanted to go over to the school, and there were other times too - I noticed different things.' She felt confused, and knew she wasn't making sense.

'What are you on about?' He moved closer to her.

'Can't you understand what I'm saying?'

'No, you're not making any sense.'

'But I know it, I feel it in here.' She thumped her chest.

'What?'

'He's always around.'

'He's directing the film, for God's sake. You'd expect him to be around.'

'He always seems to want to be close to Amy.'

'Are you suggesting that he might ... are you crazy?' he exploded.

'Yea, I am.'

'He's a good friend of mine, I've known him since college. How can you make such an accusation?'

'He'll have to go. He shouldn't be around children.'

‘And you expect me to stop shooting, and ask him to leave on the basis of a whim? What about contracts? Do you want me to jeopardise the film and be in court for years?’

‘He’s not going to argue if he thinks we know what goes on in his mind. God knows what he intends to do. He could kidnap her and keep her for himself, I can’t bear the thought of that, I can’t bear it, get rid of him,’ she screamed.

‘That is not going to happen, such a thing is preposterous.’

‘But what about Amy? She’s in danger.’

‘You need to see a doctor.’

‘I do not. I know what I know.’

‘I’ll arrange it.’

‘Don’t. I won’t go.’

‘It’s what you need. A prescription for something.’

‘Stop arranging things for me.’ She was suddenly frightened.

‘I only do things for you because I love you, honey, you know that.’ His voice softened. He was smooth. As ever, in control. ‘Baby, don’t get upset. But get this thing out of your head. It’s all imagined. He’s a really good guy, Doug, I know him. You can’t accuse him of something like that, it’s dangerous. Just get your head together before we go down, I want to hear no more of it.’

‘There’s nothing wrong with my head.’

‘I didn’t mean literally, honey,’ he said, smiling now. ‘Come on, get ready, I’m hungry.’ He put his arm around her shoulder, and kissed her.

Chapter Nine

The film was in post production now. They were back in LA. Amy was approaching her eighth birthday, and was still attending Slade College. She had been home for Christmas and Easter vacations, and Maxine had travelled to Ireland to see her as much as she could. If she wasn't in Clifden, then at weekends Amy stayed with Nuala. In May Maxine decided that she would fly home to see Amy for her birthday, and hoped to persuade John to come along as well.

'Yea, we could spare a couple of weeks at this point, need a break,' John agreed. 'Maybe Doug might come over, and a few other people, we'll have a party.'

'I'd rather we went on our own, just you and me,' she reacted immediately.

'We'd be bored stiff, you looking at me and me looking at you, can you imagine?' he said, laughing. 'No way, forget it. Do you want me to go crazy altogether?'

'It doesn't have to be like that.' She felt hurt. He could be so dismissive at times.

'You know I'm a people person, I'm no good on my own.'

'You won't be on your own, I'll be there, and we'll take Amy out of school for a couple of weeks, it won't do her any harm. And it's her birthday. It will be really cool.'

'I'd like to be there for her birthday, but I'm not going on our own, I need company.'

'Maybe just a couple of people?' she ventured hopefully.

‘I’ll put out the word,’ he said. ‘There’s plenty of accommodation at the house and locally for whoever wants to come.’

‘Do you have to ask Doug? You know how I feel about him.’

‘Maxine, I thought we’d finished with all that nonsense?’

‘No, it’s not finished. It will never be. I have to protect Amy.’

He stared at her. His eyes cold. ‘I’ll ask who I please. If you don’t like it then too bad.’

‘But it was my idea in the first place.’

‘Maxine.’ He leaned his head back, and gave an exaggerated sigh. ‘You’re going on and on about this, when are you going to quit?’

‘I’m never going to do that.’ She stood up, arms twisted around herself tightly.

‘And I’m never going to lose my friendship with Doug because my wife is hysterical.’

Maxine left it at that. She was fighting a losing battle, which was no surprise to her. But in the end, they did go on their own. Doug couldn’t spare the time, neither could the others they invited.

Maxine was happy that there were only herself, John and Amy together in Clifden. But John came under duress really, only because Amy’s birthday happened to occur on the last day. It would be such a change. To have no security. Drivers. Minders. PR people. All such a big feature of their lives. Now she planned for them to spend time as an ordinary family. She was going to cook and clean and take care of them as any wife and mother would do.

Their nearest neighbours, farmers Sean and Brid, had looked after the property for the previous owners, and they kept them on. Sean looked after the extensive gardens but now in this month of May Maxine wanted to spend some time there herself. To give life and put her mark on this place. The gardens in

Beverly Hills and Malibu were beautifully manicured by the gardeners, but there was a wildness here which she loved.

The loss of Bridget was hard and she still hadn't got over it. She phoned Nuala regularly and went to Dublin to see her a couple of times during their stay. She was managing quite well and loved having Amy spend each weekend with her. To see her granddaughter so frequently had given her a new lease of life.

Their last day was Amy's birthday and Maxine was going to cook her favourite dinner - spaghetti bolognaise. She had baked a birthday cake the day before. She spent the morning packing and cleaning the house and then changed into her old jeans and a sweater and went out into the garden. As she worked at the planters near the kitchen door she heard Amy's voice from the living room.

'Dad, come for a walk,' Amy begged. 'Joey 2 wants to go to the beach.'

'I have to read through these.' John was leafing through the pile of scripts on the table.

'Please?'

'Amy, I can't.' He stopped to read a page.

She sidled around behind him, and leaned over his shoulder.

'Is it a good story, Daddy?'

'No, there's none of these good.'

'What's our next film?'

'I haven't decided yet.'

'Am I going to be in it?'

'You're at school now.'

'But I could do it in the vacation.'

'There wouldn't be enough time.'

'You never come to see me at school.'

'I'm very busy, Amy.'

'Then I have to come to see you on the set.'

'You can do that during the summer.'

'Can I?' She wrapped her arms around him.

'Yea, yea, now go and annoy your mother instead of me.'

She wandered through the kitchen and out to where Maxine was working on the patio.

'Can I help?' she asked her mother, eyeing the flower pots.

'Yea, sure, when I make a hole in the soil you put in the little flower.'

'That's cool.' Amy picked one up.

'First I'll put in some water and then you can go ahead.'

Amy carefully put it into the earth and pressed it in.

'Now another.'

They worked together. The sun came out from behind drifting clouds. Maxine sat back on her hunkers, and pushed tendrils of hair under the scarf she wore. 'It's so beautiful here, isn't it Amy?'

'Yea Mom, it is.'

'I'd like to live here all of the time, wouldn't you?'

Amy nodded. 'And then I could have my own horse and lots of other animals.'

'You could.'

'Do you think that will happen?'

'Maybe, but it won't be soon, our work takes us all over the world and we have to give up some things to follow our careers.'

'I want to be a vet when I grow up. I decided the other day. Joey 2 had a thorn in his paw and Sean helped me take it out.'

'A vet is a very good profession. But you'd have to study hard at school.'

'I know.' She nodded seriously.

Maxine handed her another plant and she put that into its' place and tucked the earth around it. Her little hands softening the fine brown granules.

'And I'd prefer you to be a vet rather than an actress.'

'Sometimes I'd like to be acting again, it was fun,' Amy giggled.

'But see how we live. We have three homes, I'll admit, but how long do we stay in any one of them?'

'The girls at school think it's great to be an actress. They all think you're beautiful. Some of them even asked me for your photograph. But I only have the one with the three of us together so I can't give that to them.'

'People imagine our lives are amazing, but they don't always understand how it is for us,' Maxine said, smiling.

'No, we can be lonely.'

Maxine looked at her daughter. Astonished to hear her say such a thing. It was hard to imagine she was only just eight. But it was the truth and she left it like that. 'Yea, we can.'

They fell silent then, continuing to plant the flowers in the large planters on the patio which spanned the width of the house.

When they had finished, Amy helped Maxine to put everything away, and then they took Joey for a walk. As they approached the shore, the wind whipped up. Amy held Joey on the lead. The Atlantic waves crashed in and rolled across the golden sand, white foam at their tips, lengths of the frothy stuff left shivering in the breeze as they retreated again. She released Joey and he ran in and out of the water.

Amy scooped up some of the foam in her hands and laughed as she showed it to Maxine. Then she ran further on and picked up some iridescent shells which she pushed into the pockets of her jacket. 'I'm going to put these in the garden.'

Maxine followed and they collected some more. Then they threw off their shoes and socks and danced among the waves in their bare feet. Screaming as the waves thundered in and they were forced to run back, their jeans wet. Maxine picked up a stone and skimmed it across the water as it receded. It jumped three times.

'Try it,' she encouraged Amy. 'Find a nice flat stone.'

Amy picked up one and threw it, but it disappeared into the water. 'I can't do it.' She was disappointed.

'Watch me.' Maxine flicked another stone which leapt across the water.

Amy tried again and again, and finally managed to make the stone take two leaps.

'It needs practice,' Maxine laughed, as her stone leapt four times.

On the way back, they stopped to build a sandcastle. A really big one with walls, turrets, and a moat.

'It's beautiful.' Amy smoothed a tower which was in danger of collapsing. 'It's a pity Dad isn't here, do you think the castle will stay up until later. He might come then.'

'It may, but the tide could come in further and wash it away.'

Amy stared at her handiwork sadly.

'You can always build another for him.' Maxine kissed her.

Chapter Ten

'Let's put up the birthday balloons,' Maxine suggested to John while Amy was over at the farm with Brid and Sean.

He grunted, but didn't take his eyes off the papers he was leafing through.

'Are you going to help?' Maxine brought the steps out from the cupboard under the stairs.

'I really haven't time.'

'But it's hard for me to reach.' She hated having to ask for help.

'I'm sure you'll manage,' he grunted.

Maxine compressed her lips, and moved the steps to the position she wanted. She had already blown up the balloons, and now tied them together in a bunch, attached a piece of adhesive tape, and positioned them around the house.

Everything was ready when Amy came back, all excited when she saw them.

'Darling, Happy Birthday, it's time for your party.' Maxine kissed her.

'John, dinner's ready.' Maxine put out the plates of spaghetti on the big wooden table in the kitchen. There was crunchy bread she had made herself, and a big bowl of mixed salad. The birthday dinner was special. The house looked really festive. Amy wore her new red dress, and her dark hair was tied up with red ribbons. Maxine opened a bottle of wine for herself and John, and Amy was allowed Coke as a treat.

'John?' She went into the living room and found him speaking on the phone, and she mimed 'hurry up', and returned to the kitchen, where she sat down at the table beside Amy. 'We'll just start, Amy, Dad will be in soon.'

He came in after a few minutes, but stood by his chair. 'You've started without me.'

'The meal was getting cold.' She took a cover off his plate. 'Yours is fine.'

'Dad, it's lovely,' Amy twisted long strings of pasta into her spoon.

'I'm sure it is.' His expression was grim.

'Will you have some Parmesan cheese?' Maxine held out the bowl. 'Salad? Bread?'

'We had a lovely day today, Dad, and we made a great sandcastle, I wanted you to see it but Mom said that the sea would wash it away. If I build another one tomorrow, would you come down to see it?'

'No, we're leaving tomorrow.' He picked at his food.

'It won't take long, just a few minutes, please?'

He shook his head.

'If I go down to the beach early I can build it in the morning and then you can see it before we go.'

'I said no.'

Her face was crestfallen. She looked at her mother. Pleading.

Maxine shook her head. Then stood up and began to clear away the plates.

'Now we'll light the candles on your birthday cake. This will be the best part.'

John drank his wine slowly.

She struck a match and lit each one. Then turned around and approached the table carrying the cake, the candle flames wavering.

'Happy Birthday to you, Happy Birthday to you, Happy Birthday to Amy, Happy Birthday to you. Three cheers. Hurrah.

Hurrah. Hurrah.' Maxine's was the only voice singing. She put the cake down in front of Amy.

'Now it's time to blow them out. You have to make a wish, but don't tell us what it is, otherwise it won't come true.'

'I'll keep it a secret,' Amy whispered.

'Take a deep breath,' Maxine warned.

Amy's eyes squeezed shut as she blew. But when she opened them again there were still two candles burning.

'Try again,'

She leaned over the cake and blew again until the last one was extinguished.

'Hurrah, hurrah!' Maxine clapped and reached to kiss her. 'And now a present for a birthday girl.' She took a box from under the table and handed it to Amy who opened it excitedly to discover a beautiful doll inside.

John finished his glass of wine, and poured another. He hadn't got involved in the business of the birthday cake.

'Isn't she cute Mom, thank you, I love her.' She kissed the doll's face, and then Maxine, and ran around the table to John.

'Give her a kiss, Dad, she wants a kiss.' She held the doll to him.

'She doesn't want a kiss from me,' he grunted.

'Yes, she does, go on, kiss her.' She held the doll close to his face. But he raised his hand and pushed the doll out of his space, and it tumbled on to the ground.

Amy wailed and picked it up. She cradled her, in tears now.

'Why did you do that, John?' Maxine asked.

'Are you blaming me?' He was belligerent.

'She's fine, Amy love, there's nothing wrong with her, give her another kiss. Your doll didn't feel anything.' Maxine stroked the doll's blonde hair.

'But I did.' Tears drifted down her cheeks.

'Now we'll have to give her a name. What will we call her?'

'I don't know,' she whispered.

'What about Angelica, an angel?' Maxine persuaded.

A suggestion of a smile played around Amy's lips, and she nodded.

'Right, that's decided. She'll be Angelica. Now sit up and we'll cut your birthday cake.'

John said nothing.

Maxine picked up the knife and cut through the soft sponge layers.

'Would you like a coffee?' she asked John.

'No, I wouldn't like a coffee,' he shouted. He flung the empty wine glass across the room where it splintered against the wall.

Maxine and Amy's eyes were riveted on the pieces which littered the floor.

'I don't want anything at all.' He lifted the plate and the cake sailed up into the air. Cream and sponge disintegrated and clung mostly to Maxine's dress. A large blob shivered on her hair. And there were smaller spatters on her face.

Tears filled Amy's eyes. Cream splashed on her dress as well. She looked frightened.

'Go to bed, Amy,' her father ordered. 'Bed,' he repeated loudly.

She struggled down off the chair, carrying the doll and walked backwards towards the door. 'It's not my fault,' she whispered.

She turned to twist the door handle, slowly went outside into the hall and climbed the stairs.

'Why do you always blame me for things? The doll fell. It was an accident. She let it slip out of her hand.' He attacked Maxine as she tried to clean the remains of the cake from her face with a napkin.

Her hand shook. She couldn't quite see through the mist of tears.

'You threw the doll on the ground deliberately,' she said slowly.

'I did not.' He banged on the table with his fist and the dishes shuddered.

'You did.' She wasn't going to let it go this time. 'You spoiled Amy's birthday, and now she's gone to bed all upset. You must say you're sorry. Go up now and say it, otherwise she'll cry all night.'

'Don't tell me what to do.' He moved around the table. His height overshadowed her.

She wept openly now. The tears trickled through the spots of cream on her cheeks. 'You don't care about us. We're nothing to you. I'm just someone to act in your films. To make money for you.' She stood up.

'How dare you,' he hissed. And his hand swept across her face.

The strength of the blow threw her off her feet and her headlong fall was finally stopped by the couch. 'You bastard.' The words were spat at him. She had never been so angry. He had hit her before, but usually chose a part of her body which wasn't visible to the rest of the world. She always forgave him in the past. It wasn't worth making an issue out of it, their lives were so closely interwoven. But now suddenly she hated him because he had upset Amy on this so special of days. Maxine felt certain that her daughter would never forget it.

She stared up at him aware that they had passed the point which mattered. The balance was unstable and she didn't think they would ever get back to where they were a few minutes ago. In that short time the die was cast.

She rushed past him up the stairs and into Amy's room. She lay curled up on the bed, still wearing the red dress.

Maxine opened the wardrobe door and began to drag clothes off the hangers.

Amy sat up, the stains of tears still on her cheeks.

'We're going, come on, quickly now.' Maxine pulled her jacket from the wardrobe and put it on her.

The door was pushed open. John stood there.

'We're leaving,' she said, and went straight towards him carrying the suitcase, her hand in Amy's.

'Where?'

'That doesn't matter. You'll be glad to see the back of us, no doubt.'

He put out his hand and grabbed her arm. 'You're not going anywhere.'

'Yes, I am, and I'm taking Amy with me.'

'Never,' he growled. His fingers tightened around her bare skin, and stopped her rush. 'Let her go.'

'No.' She tried to push past him, but he blocked her way.

'Amy, get back into bed,' he yelled.

'Mom?' Amy cried.

'Let her go,' he ordered Maxine.

'We are leaving you,' she said.

He dragged Maxine through the door and she lost her hold of Amy.

'Don't hurt Mom,' Amy whispered. 'Dad, please don't.'

The door closed with a bang, and Amy was left alone.

'I don't know what you're at, Maxine.' He threw her ahead of him down the stairs. She lost her balance and stumbled.

'I can't take any more, John.'

'You're not leaving me.'

'I am.'

'C'mere.' He reached out, grabbed her hair, and hauled her back with a jerk.

'Let me go,' she screamed.

He pushed her up against the banisters and slapped her across the head.

She was almost stunned.

'Get downstairs, into the sitting room, go on, get down.' He twisted her arm behind her back and pushed her ahead of him.

'You're hurting me, stop John, please?' Her shoes slipped on the carpeted stairway, and she almost fell, but managed to escape his grasp. She reached the hall and unsteadily ran across it to the front door. She turned the handle and went out into the driveway where she stood looking back at him with her arms wound tight around her body.

'You come back into the house or I'll beat you until you're black and blue. Then you'll know all about it,' he roared.

There was a bark from the dog who had bounded around the house towards them.

John reached her and swung his broad hand across her face again. She turned from him and half walked half ran down the avenue.

'Maxine, get back here,' he shouted and hurried after her.

She could hear his footsteps following behind on the gravel, but managed to reach the gate before he caught her. She swung through it followed by the dog. In the shadows of the narrow country road she forced herself to go on. Her breathing was heavy and she had no energy, her legs barely able to support her.

'Maxine,' John shouted.

He was closer now.

Then, suddenly, everything went black.

Chapter Eleven

It was still dark when Amy awoke. She was lying on top of the bedclothes wearing her jacket on top of her birthday dress. 'Mom?' she called softly, but the house was silent. She sat up. 'Mom?'

There was a sudden noise outside. A strange noise. She pushed herself out of bed and moved slowly across the room to the window. She looked out. There was someone in the garden. Near the trees. She wondered was it her Mom. She moved her face closer to the glass. After a moment it fogged up. And with her fingers she rubbed a hole and stared though it at the person who was digging in the garden. The light shone out from the house and she could see that it was her Dad. She was puzzled, and wondered what he was doing out there in the middle of the night. But, suddenly afraid that he would see her, she ducked down under the sill below the window, and crept back to bed.

The following morning, John opened her bedroom door and called her. 'Amy, get up now. We'll have to get you back to school.'

'Where's Mom?'

He didn't reply. 'Have you got your school clothes sorted?'

She nodded. 'Mom packed them yesterday.'

'Have your shower, get dressed and come down for your breakfast. Quick as you can now.'

'Where's Mom?' she asked again.

'She left early to go to Dublin. To see Nuala.'

'Will I see her before I go back?'

'No, I'll be meeting her at the airport.'

Disappointment was etched on her face.

'Chop chop.' He went downstairs.

She still wore the red dress and took off her clothes in the bathroom.

It was a while later when she appeared in the kitchen, wrapped in her robe.

'What kept you?' John barked.

'I can't reach the shower.' She sat down at the table and poured milk on her cornflakes.

'For God's sake,' he groaned, hunted her back up, and switched it on.

'Is it too hot?'

He tested the water.

'Get in there, I've to catch a flight this afternoon,' he reminded. 'So hurry up.'

Eventually she was ready and John started the car.

'I haven't said goodbye to Joey 2,' Amy said suddenly.

'There's no time for that, he's in his kennel.'

'But I have to say goodbye to him.' She ran around the house and he followed her.

'He's not there.' She searched among the shrubbery around the kennel.

'I forgot, I took him to the vet, Sean will collect him later.'

'What's wrong with him? Is he sick?'

'He just had something wrong with his paw, needs a little job done on it.'

'Is that where he hurt it before?'

'Yea, that's right.'

'But he wasn't sick yesterday.'

'No, it was just this morning, early.'

'Can we go see him?'

'No, there's no time, you can see him next time you're home, he'll be well then. Now get into the car Amy, this instant, I've had enough of this.'

She climbed in, and sat staring out the window, her expression gloomy. 'I didn't say goodbye to anyone.' Tears filled her eyes.

Chapter Twelve

Maxine had been flown by helicopter to hospital in Dublin. She lay in a cubicle in ICU. Her eyes were closed. There was a deathly white pallor on her face shadowed by blue purple bruises. She was in a deep coma, a life support machine helping her to breathe.

John had telephoned Nuala a couple of days after it had happened. He explained that he had to go back to the States and wondered would Nuala visit. Would she visit? Nuala couldn't believe that he would even ask her such a question, and that he had waited such a long time before letting her know what had happened.

She went immediately to see Maxine, finding it very difficult to control her emotions when she saw her daughter lying there. She had asked John about Amy and how she was taking the news of her mother's accident. But he said abruptly that she didn't know about it. And he didn't want her told.

'But it might do Maxine good if Amy came to see her,' she suggested.

'I will decide when to tell her. So don't open your mouth.'

She was intimidated by him, and said no more. She wanted to visit Amy but couldn't leave the hospital. In those first days she slept in a chair beside Maxine, only leaving to rush home to eat, change, and hurry back later. She wanted to be there when her girl woke up. She had to be there.

Sitting by the bedside Nuala talked of their life together when Maxine was young, and of her growing up before she went to live in LA. And about the wonderful career she had ahead of her. Nuala would sing to her too. Old favourites. Always hoping to trigger something in her girl's mind which might cause her to wake up.

John arrived back a few days later.

'I'll keep an eye on her, you don't need to be here all the time,' he was dismissive of Nuala.

'What's going to happen, is there anything the doctors can do?' she asked tentatively.

'It's just a matter of time, hopefully she'll come out of it.'

'What about America? The doctors there might be able to do something?'

'No, I think she's getting good care here, makes no difference where she is. They don't give a good prognosis.'

'They've been doing tests I know, during the week, scans and that sort of thing.'

'The medics may decide to turn off the machine.' His words were terse and without any emotion. As if he was a doctor himself. Just reporting a fact.

She didn't say anything for a few seconds. Her heart somersaulted inside her chest. The blood rushed from her head. Her legs felt weak.

'What?' she whispered.

'The scans of the brain show that there is no activity now.'

'But how do they know that for sure? Doctors are not always right. People have come out of coma after years. They simply cannot tell.' She gripped the Rosary beads in her hands tightly.

'They know,' he said bluntly.

'But surely it's all in God's hands. Maxine will wake up, I know it, I feel it inside, she will, surely you believe that too?'

'I can only accept what they say. They are the professionals. It's their job.'

‘But what about miracles? The spiritual. All that unknown area. Maybe she hears everything that’s going on and simply can’t respond?’

He shook his head, a look of impatience on his face.

‘Maybe she’s trying to tell us things but we’re not listening. Can you imagine what that must be like? Such frustration. Put yourself in her place. Imagine, John, you can do that surely, someone like you?’

‘I have to accept the medical advice.’

‘I can’t believe what you’re saying. It seems so callous,’ she hesitated for a few seconds. ‘No, maybe that’s too harsh, it has to be terrible for you too.’

‘It is.’

‘Then we have to give her every chance.’

‘She would never want to live like a vegetable. We’ve talked about it. We decided that we would both want to be released from such a life. It has no quality. So really I’m only doing what she would want.’

‘She said that?’ Nuala sank into a chair. No strength left.

‘It is mere existence. Would you like to be in that position?’

Tears drifted down her cheeks. She didn’t wipe them away and could taste the salt on her lips.

She collected Amy from school the following Saturday morning, and they took the bus to Dublin.

‘I talked to your Mom, she sends her love,’ Nuala said when they arrived at the house. She put the key in the door and pushed it open.

‘Is she very busy?’ Amy struggled out of her backpack and jacket and threw them on the couch. ‘Where is Pickle?’

‘She’s out the back I think,’ Nuala picked up the jacket and hung it in the cloakroom with her own coat.

Amy peered out the kitchen window. ‘There she is, look, sitting on the window sill.’

‘She knew we were coming.’

'Honey, come in,' Amy whispered.

Nuala opened the window and the cat immediately straightened up, and delicately put a black velvet paw across the wooden frame.

'Hello, Pickle.' Amy put out her hand and gently caressed her head, stroking the shining black coat. Pickle responded by pushing herself closer to Amy and purring. She gathered the cat in her arms and held her close.

Nuala watched Amy but in her mind she constantly argued with John. Trying to think of new reasons why he shouldn't allow the doctors to turn off the machine. She was like someone in a debate.

Nuala couldn't accept the possibility that Amy would be left motherless. Or that Maxine might spend the rest of her life in a hospital bed, being fed through a tube, bathed, turned, medicated. Her mind took her on to another level. Perhaps there was something in what John said. Her darling girl might not want to exist in such a state. I must be positive, she thought. I refuse to accept what they say. I won't.

She took Amy to the circus that evening. Her granddaughter was enthralled. The animals her particular favourites. The horses. And the gentle slow moving elephants.

The trapeze artists swung high above them.

'Do you think they could fall?' A worried whisper.

'No, they're much too good. But there's a net there, see, if they fall they won't be hurt.'

She nodded. Dark eyes staring upwards following the swing of the girl above who wore a sparkling costume which glittered in the lights. She twisted her legs around the ropes and swung downwards. She swayed back and forward. The man dived and caught her, and they moved together magically. The audience were silent. Faces turned upwards.

After that the relief of the clowns again made everyone laugh. They did their tricks, fought among each other, turned somersaults, ran in and out of the audience. Amy laughed out loud, loving them.

It was over all too soon.

'I'd like to come again, can we?' she asked as they walked home.

'When the circus is here.' Nuala took her hand.

'When will that be?'

'Next year.'

'That's a long time away.'

'It won't seem that long.'

'Maybe Mom and Dad will come with us, wouldn't that be cool?'

'Yes, that would be lovely.' Nuala nodded, a lump in her throat.

Nuala took Amy back to school on Sunday and after that went straight to the hospital, anxious to see how Maxine was. Praying that God might have answered her prayers and that she had improved. But when she walked into the ward, she was to be disappointed. Maxine lay in the same position. Prone. Eyes closed. Obviously still in a coma.

It was always busy in ICU. Noisy too. There was tension in the hurried attention of the staff, all of the patients here fighting for their lives. In Maxine's cubicle, the heart monitor beeped. Tubes carried liquids; food and medication in; bodily fluids out. Everything happened automatically.

Nuala sat by the edge of the bed and reached for Maxine's hand. It was cool. The skin soft, and smooth. But there was a purple bruise, and swelling where the needle pierced. She wanted to pull it out and ease the pain it caused, and kiss it all better like she used to do when Maxine was a child.

She spoke to her then, told her all about Amy and the weekend, going over every detail about the circus and what they had to eat and drink and what Amy said. And how much they both loved her.

John arrived.

She wasn't too happy to see him there.

'I'm heading back to LA in the morning.'

'Were you talking to the doctors?' she asked.

'They think it's time to turn off the machine.'

'But can't you say no? She might wake up at any moment.'

'And be unable to speak, or see or hear?'

'It mightn't be like that.'

'It will be,' he said tiredly. 'So there's no other option.'

'Wait a little longer, give it a week, please - for me,' she begged.

'Well, I'll discuss it with them and see what they say.'

She experienced a sudden warmth towards him. She went back to the bed. Took a scented wipe from a box and pressed it gently against Maxine's face and hands. Then carefully she rearranged her blonde hair, tidying strands which had drifted forward. To do these little things for her daughter, so small and insignificant really, seemed crucial and justified her presence there.

Chapter Thirteen

John watched Nuala tend to Maxine. Such loving gestures were something with which he wasn't familiar. His own parents had moved among the aristocratic set of Boston. His elder brother, Brian, and himself were left in the charge of a nanny for their young lives, and then tutored privately. His mother was beautiful, his father handsome, and they lived in a large house outside the city. John Parker Senior had inherited great wealth from his father who had struck oil in Texas. The endless stream of riches meant that his father had time to dally with writing, painting and travelling to oversee his various business interests.

On his death, both sons had inherited equal shares of the business. But John had sold his to his brother, and used the money to produce films.

Nuala spoke to Maxine, while gently cooling her skin with a wipe. 'This will refresh you. I know you like lavender. Remember the lovely bush we had in the garden. It was under your bedroom window and you loved the scent.'

He sat there. Really anxious to leave but unable to do so.

'Maxine, did you say something?' Nuala leaned closer to her. Holding her hand tight, hoping for a tiny response. But there was nothing. She continued talking. 'Tomorrow I'm going to bring in some books. The old ones you used to love - *David Copperfield, Little Women, Anne of Green Gables* - they're just a few but if I read a little it might take you back, remind you of how it used to be.'

When John met Maxine Howard at a cocktail party he had already made a name for himself in Hollywood, and was immediately captivated by her gentle personality, so very different to the other actresses who hung around him hoping for a chance to audition for a part in one of his films. He had already been married, and divorced, and had a son and a daughter. But he had no interest in his children. He made a very generous settlement to his wife, and forgot about them. After that failure, he had vowed not to marry again, but he asked Maxine to be his wife within months of meeting her although there was a ten year difference in age between them. She hadn't said yes immediately and her shy refusal had made him even more ardent. She would be his wife. He told her more than once, until finally she said yes.

He was drawn back to the present again by Nuala's soft voice.

'I hate this awful hospital gown, but I'm sure you'll be able to wear one of your own soon. Your fingers look so bare without your rings, but John is keeping them for you.' She stroked her hand.

John loved Maxine in his way. Like a possession - a piece of art for which he had made a bid in an auction. Now that delicate porcelain figurine had been smashed beyond recognition. He had created Maxine Howard and made her into the great actress she became. But in that transformation he had lost the person with whom he fell in love. Slowly she had drifted away from him, like there was a mist of rain between them.

'I have to go now,' he said.

'Hold my hand tighter if you can hear me, just use your little finger, I'll be able to feel it, my darling, even a gentle squeeze will do,' Nuala murmured.

'Nuala?' John spoke again.

'I'm just waiting for her to let me know if she can hear me,' she whispered.

A wave of anger spread through him. Why was it Maxine could even annoy him from such a distance. She wasn't going to bother waking up for him. Maybe she didn't want to. The thought caused a puzzled discomfort inside. He looked down at her. She was like a child, her face serene, dark lashes shadowed her cheeks. Skin and lips pale without her usual make-up. The bruises were fading and she was still beautiful, but different. He didn't know her.

He returned to LA where they were doing the post production. In the theatre he sat and watched the portion of the film which had been edited. Maxine glowed on screen. Her eyes wide, moist, emotional. Her voice evocative. She played a role. Maybe he only knew her in that way. Who was this woman he had lived with for eleven years, who had given him Amy? The only one of his children he loved. He hadn't told anyone that Maxine was in hospital. And so far the paparazzi had been kept at bay. John was intensely private, and hated the thought that people would gossip about him.

'Those scenes might improve when the music is laid against them, I thought we might look at the earlier sequence which has the score rough-mixed in. It's about twenty-eight minutes running time,' Doug said. 'We've got it set up, we're ready to roll.'

The supervising editor pressed the cue button.

John didn't reply.

'Hey, are you with us?'

'Yea, go ahead.' He nodded.

The lights dimmed. The music caught the swell of the waves and the film cut to the billowing sails of the ocean-going vessel. It was a scene on board ship between some of the people heading for America. Maxine wore a nineteenth-century costume which was not revealing, but she had a sensual quality about her. The tone of her voice was poignant. There was something very special about Maxine and he had a sudden sense of terrible loss.

'The piano and uilleann pipes work really well together,' Doug murmured.

The music swept John away, to a hospital bed, to a sleeping woman, a shadow of the vibrant smiling person on the screen. Suddenly, he wished he could leave, but that would have required an explanation. He let the film roll until the screen grew dark. The lights went up in the auditorium.

'Well, what do you think?' Doug asked.

'Good,' John said.

'Is that all?' Doug seemed astonished.

'I'm happy with it,' John added.

'Any criticism?'

'No, it all seemed to run seamlessly and the music reflected the drama, yes, seamlessly.' His remarks were vague, and he couldn't summon up any enthusiasm.

'Maxine was wonderful,' Doug said, grinning widely.

'Yes.'

'How is she?'

'Fine.'

'Will she be back soon?'

'I'm not sure, Maxine feels she is at home in Ireland. I don't know if she will ever want to come back here,' he said.

'Maybe I'll take a trip over.' Doug stood up, grinning.

'As you know, I've been back and forth, but I guess I have to make decisions, and there's a lot to be done with the film yet.'

'When will we launch?'

'As soon as we can.'

'We should be nominated for the Oscars with any luck.'

'And get our money back.'

'Hundred-fold.'

'There's a lot of talk about it already in some circles.'

'I know, I've heard.'

'What's next?'

'I don't know.'

‘That’s not like you, you’re usually planning the next film way before we get to this stage,’ Doug laughed.

‘I’ve been going through scripts, there’s nothing.’

‘Maybe you should take a break, do all of you good, Maxine too, spend some time together.’

‘I like to work, you know that,’ John said, slightly tetchy.

‘Sometimes it’s important to take a back seat for a while, refreshes the mind, and you come at it again, rejuvenated.’

‘No, that’s not the way I do things.’ They walked outside into bright sunshine.

‘Will I ask around for scripts?’

‘No.’ His retort was razor-sharp.

‘Ok, ok, don’t mind me.’ Doug shrugged.

John said nothing, but he wondered what Maxine might do if she did recover. Would she tell the world what had happened? Would his reputation be destroyed, and his name splashed all over the headlines - a wife beater?

Chapter Fourteen

Nuala waited outside the ICU until the nurses had finished giving Maxine a bed bath and changed the linen.

'How is she?' she ventured when they ushered her inside again.

'She's holding her own,' the dark-haired nurse smiled.

'Do you think she'll come out of the coma?' She asked the question although she didn't expect an answer. They never told her anything. They were vague to the point of nothing. It drove her insane.

'We're not sure,' the other one said, keeping her eyes averted.

'Keep doing things that will remind her of the past. Sometimes it does trigger a reaction.' The nicer of the two suggested. Her voice soft. Gentle. They lifted Maxine back on to the pillows. Checked that the various tubes were properly connected, read her blood pressure, made a final inspection of the monitors and left.

Nuala went back to the bedside. She took Maxine's hand again, stroking her skin. She murmured to her. She didn't know what she said exactly, it was just words, like a prayer. Maybe God would listen. He was the only one who could help. It would have to be a miracle for her girl to get out of this place of imprisonment, populated by uniformed nurses and white-coated doctors, and all those other people who came in and out during the day. Maxine was serving a sentence here, and Nuala didn't know when she would be granted parole.

Nuala picked up one of Maxine's favourite books when she had been a teenager. It was *Little Women*. She turned a page and began to read aloud.

She remembered a day when she read this story to Maxine when she was a child. She was about thirteen years old. It was a Sunday in winter. Hailstones rattled against the window with a staccato beat. The wind gusted erratically. The orange flames of the fire roared up the chimney and threw out great heat.

Maxine cuddled up beside Nuala on the couch. 'It's so sad. What happened to Jo after that?'

'Well, she wrote the story and sent it to the Professor.'

'She loved him, didn't she?'

'Yes, Maxine, she did.'

'Did you love someone like that, Auntie Nuala?'

'Yes, I did.' She turned another page slowly.

'Who was he? What was he called?'

'His name was Tom.'

'Was he nice?' The child smiled up at her. Her dark hair curled around her pretty face.

'Yes, he was.' She stared across the room pensively.

'Where is he now?' Maxine drew circles with her finger on the open page.

'I don't know now. Let us read some more.'

'No, don't read it, just tell me the story about Jo. I like her the best.' She ran over to the fireplace and stretched on tippy-toes to look into the mirror which hung over the mantle.

'I don't like my face,' she sighed. A whispering sadness.

'Don't be silly, you're beautiful.'

'Jo didn't think she was beautiful.'

'Beauty is inside a person, not outside.'

'But you can't see inside.'

'It's what you see in the eyes. They are the gateway to the soul.'

'What does that mean?'

'It's hard to explain exactly, but you'll understand some day.'

'Do you think I'll be clever enough?'

'Where do you get all those questions?' Nuala smiled.

'I don't know.'

'I'm exhausted answering them.'

'Tell me more of the story, please?' Maxine tucked her arm through Nuala's and leaned her head on her shoulder.

Nuala was back in the ward. She closed her eyes and took a few deep breaths. She needed to stay on top of everything for Maxine's sake, and for Amy too.

Chapter Fifteen

John flew in at the weekend and filled the small space with his strident personality. Nuala felt small and insignificant in his presence, and her relationship with Maxine was changed. Somehow, by being there, he was taking control, and she was losing her, just a little bit at a time, but losing her all the same. Nuala touched Maxine's slim arm, needing to bring her into their circle. She was a person with a mind, a heart, a soul. Don't ignore my girl. She shouted in her head. But compressed her lips, afraid to let the words out.

He didn't speak. In the busy ICU, the sound of the machines was like another entity. He didn't touch Maxine.

How could he be so cold? Nuala thought.

'I'll be meeting the medical team soon. Do you want to sit in?'

It was the first time he had suggested this. And she was suddenly grateful to him. 'Yes, I'd like that.'

'I'll call you,' he said, exiting the cubicle.

She stared after him, then turned back to Maxine. 'John will be back soon, don't worry, he's just going to see the doctor,' she murmured.

A little while later, John reappeared through the curtains and motioned with his head for her to come outside.

'I'll be back in a minute, pet.' Nuala kissed Maxine. Then she stood up. But delayed, reluctant to face whatever lay ahead, but it had to be confronted so she straightened her shoulders and followed John down the corridor into an office.

The consultant sat at a desk, his eyebrows knitted close together in a frown. Two other doctors stood to one side and murmured words which she couldn't understand. The air was thick with unasked questions. These are the men who will make the decision. These are the men who think they are gods. Maxine should be in here with us, she thought. Panic sent her heart into overdrive.

Nuala turned back to the door, but it had been closed by John. She felt like a captive bird, wings beating against the bars of the cage. She imagined Maxine getting up from the bed, suddenly well.

'Won't you sit down, Nuala?' One of the doctors pulled out a chair.

'I don't want you to take her off life support. She's going to wake up, I know it,' she appealed to the consultant.

He looked at her. 'I'm sorry. She's not responsive,' he said.

'There's no hope, Nuala,' John said.

'There must be hope,' she whispered.

'Take some time to say your goodbyes, there's no hurry,' one of the doctors said.

She stood up. John held the door open. She walked back down the corridor and into Maxine's cubicle. She sat by the bedside again, and took her hand.

She stayed there. All that day. All that night. John came and went but she took little notice of him. When he came in he just stood there, looking at Maxine, but said nothing. She prayed. Endless murmuring, counting time, seconds, minutes, hours. Eating into what was left of her darling's life.

The darkness of the night slowly receded and the dawn light sent delicate fingers of brightness into the room through the venetian blinds and competed with the permanent artificial light. It was planned for this morning. Nuala couldn't get her head around it. She tended Maxine even more carefully today.

Combed her hair. Creamed her face, arms and hands, slowly, tenderly. After that there wasn't much more she could do.

John arrived around nine, and the medical team followed. They stood in conversation. But Nuala did not hear what they were saying. Her mind was somewhere else. Back in time to when Maxine was a child. To be brought up living a lie, only to discover who her mother really was when she was a grown woman. It was only now Nuala regretted the decisions she had made all those years ago.

'Nuala? The doctors are going to switch off the life-support now.' John bent down closer to her, his voice low.

'Shouldn't Amy be here?' Tears trickled down her cheeks.

'It would be too upsetting for her, it's better this way.' John was firm.

'I want her here, she should be able to say goodbye to her Mom.'

'No.'

'But why not?'

'Because I have decided against it.'

'Please?' her voice broke and she bent her head.

A chaplain arrived. An elderly man, kindly, wearing a white shirt, roman collar, grey trousers and a purple stole around his neck. He came over to her and took her hand. His palm was soft, and his touch gentle. She liked him. He carried a small vessel containing holy oils. Then he shook John's hand and went over to Maxine. He made the sign of the cross over her, blessing her. Saying prayers, and anointing her with the oil on her forehead, her eyes, her ears, her mouth, her hands, her feet. It was a cleansing. She was prepared now to enter heaven.

The doctors busied themselves. Doing whatever they had to do.

'No,' Nuala cried.

They took no notice of her.

'She may continue to breathe on her own, we don't know,' the consultant said.

'You think it's possible?' Nuala whispered, hopeful. She drew closer to her. Listening carefully. Like she used to do at night when Maxine was a tiny baby. But now her breathing was noisy. Her lungs under stress.

The doctor listened to her chest with his stethoscope. Another checked her blood pressure. A nurse came in. Nuala wanted to scream. She couldn't get close enough to Maxine.

Her breathing became more laboured. Nuala knew by the sound that she couldn't last like this.

'Help her,' she begged.

The nurse stood close, a hand on her shoulder. 'It won't be long now.'

In a matter of minutes the hoarse sound began to diminish, slowly, whispering away to silence. An uncanny eerie silence.

'Maxine?' Nuala reached for her. Gripped her hand. The needle for the drip had been removed. Only the bruise was visible. The monitor was still attached. Intermittent bleeps indicated her heart rate. Nuala brought Maxine's hand to her lips. Kissed away the bruise.

Suddenly the bleep stopped. And after a terrible few seconds, it began again at a slow uneven pace. Nuala stiffened. Could hear her own heart thump. 'I wish I could be in her place,' she murmured. 'It's not fair. She's too young.'

The nurse patted her shoulder.

Silence again for a few agonising seconds. Then the halting bleeps began again, bleep - bleep - bleep - and then a whine which went on and on.

How could she tell Amy?

Chapter Sixteen

The funeral was private. John and Nuala were the only people in attendance. He didn't want anyone else there.

'What about Amy?' Nuala asked.

'She's too young.'

'She must be told. She would want to be here. I know her. She's a sensitive little thing.'

'She's my daughter, Nuala, and I've decided to handle it this way.' He was caustic. 'I will tell her myself.'

She was silenced. To suffer her grief alone.

He said to come to his hotel and they would go on from there to the mortuary in a limousine. But in the early morning she phoned and said she was already on her way. He didn't seem concerned one way or the other.

The coffin stood in front of the altar. She knelt to pray. The last few days had been appalling for her. Barely able to eat, or sleep, she had existed in a numb world of disbelief.

John arrived just before the undertakers and the hospital chaplain. The same man who had given Maxine the Sacrament of the Sick said Mass and prayed over the coffin.

Nuala had brought a bouquet of flowers. As Maxine was to be cremated, John had insisted there was no need for flowers. But Nuala refused to listen. On the coffin a lone garland for her darling. Bright, colourful, red roses, white daisies, yellow chrysanthemums, blue forget-me-not, tied with pink ribbon. Her girl had a right to so much more. Music, song, flowers. Friends and family saying a few loving words about her from the altar. It ought to have been a celebration of her life. And most of all, her daughter should have been there. Nuala was sure that it would be something Amy would always regret.

The cremation was equally forlorn. They watched as the coffin disappeared through the curtains. Nuala stood still. Her hands clasped together. She heard a choking noise. Unsure whether it came from herself or not. Her head felt light and she pressed a tissue against her lips, praying she wouldn't be sick. Maxine was gone now.

John asked her to join him for lunch at the Shelbourne Hotel where he was staying.

'I couldn't eat, but thank you.' Nuala was surprised at his invitation.

'I'd like you to come, keep me company.'

She hesitated for a moment, but then agreed. If she was to see Amy again, she would have to keep up some relationship with John. And she wanted to be there when he told her about Maxine, that most of all.

They sat in the sumptuous restaurant, and he tucked into a well-done steak with all the trimmings. He ordered an expensive bottle of red wine but she refused. Her choice from the menu was grilled sole and really she could barely manage to eat the large piece which lay on the plate.

'Will you go down to see Amy?' she asked, just after coffee was served.

'Yes, today.'

'Can I go with you? I think she's going to be very upset.'

He stared at her, his eyes considering.

She sipped the coffee.

'Yea, I guess you could.'

At the school, he suggested that she wait in the car. He would bring Amy out. She sat there, feeling helpless. She couldn't imagine how the child would react to hearing the news about her mother. Totally out of the blue. The shock would be unimaginable. She wanted to be in there with her, to put her arms around the poor mite and hold her close. To show her how much she loved her. She got out of the car, trying to think of some excuse which would get her inside. The evening was cold. A heavy cloudy sky pressed down upon her. Girls in chatting groups walked in and out of the large rambling school building. It was the end of the day. Screams came from a hockey pitch hidden by the trees. The thumps of tennis balls echoed from the courts.

'Auntie Nuala.'

She turned quickly to see Amy running towards her followed by the teacher Ann. She stretched out her arms and as Amy crashed into her, she swung her around, unable to speak.

'Dad is waiting for me, and now you're here as well.' She held on tight to her.

Nuala put her hands around her face and kissed her.

'Come on, let's find him,' Ann smiled and led the way into the school.

John was surprised to see her arrive into the sitting room with Amy. She could see it on his face.

'Is Mom coming?' Amy asked excitedly.

'No. She's not with us today.'

'Will you come over to the stables to meet my pony, and maybe I can ride for a bit, and you could hold the reins, and you can meet the dogs too,' she smiled.

'Not today, Amy, I'm sorry,' his voice was soft.

'Why?' Disappointment flashed across her face.

'Because there's something we have to talk about, honey.' He put his arm around her shoulders.

'What?'

'It's about Mom.'

'Where is she?'

'She's been in hospital - she had an accident.'

Her face crumpled, and tears filled her eyes. 'Is she sick?'

'Yes, she is.'

'Can I go to see her, now, please?' She jumped up.

'No, you can't.'

'Why?'

'Because she isn't there any more.' He hugged her.

'Where is she?'

'She's gone to heaven.'

'But she didn't tell me she was going.' Tears dribbled down her cheeks.

'I don't suppose she knew.'

'But she could have phoned. Auntie Nuala do you know why Mom didn't phone?' She appealed to her.

Nuala moved closer and put her arms around her. 'Mom has gone to live with Baby Jesus.'

Amy stared at her, her mouth quivering.

'She didn't get better and he asked her to live with him.'

'Is she coming back?'

Nuala shook her head. She was finding this very difficult and tried hard to control her own tears.

'Will I see her again?'

'You'll see her in your dreams.'

'I want my Mom,' she cried out loud.

She clung to Nuala, sobbing hysterically.

After a time they managed between them to persuade her to go down to the stables and talk to her horse, and the other animals. Amy told them all about Maxine. A heartbreaking story about a sick mother who had gone away and wasn't coming back. The simple child's version of what had happened helped Nuala a little that day. But it didn't ease the loss of her darling girl whose life was quenched out like the bright flame that it was.

PART TWO

1987

Chapter Seventeen

Beverly Hills, LA, early evening -

Amy sat with Joey in her usual place under the tree. She had had a swim in the small swimming pool earlier and now watched the adults as they lay on loungers around the patio, or swam in the main pool. The sun shone brightly and the umbrellas were pretty in shades of blue and white. Waiters served champagne and canapés to the crowd.

She pulled a crumpled card from her shorts pocket, unfolded it and stared at it. There was a big ten on the front, and lots of coloured balloons.

"*Dear Amy, hope you have a very happy tenth birthday. With lots* of *love from Auntie Nuala. xx*" At the back was written a special little note, and she read that again. "*Thank you for your letter, it was lovely to hear from you. I hope you enjoy the summer and that you are happy. Write soon and tell me all your news. Take care. Love. Auntie Nuala.*"

She had read it more than once since receiving it a few weeks ago, and had already given her letter to Maria to post. But she had to be careful. Maria had warned her about that.

'Your Dad is not happy that you write, you remember the first letter he tore it up.'

'But I want to write to Auntie Nuala.'

'Si, that is good, but it cannot be often.'

Amy glanced at her watch. It was almost time to go for her riding lesson. They had their own stables, and trained a string of race horses. She rode her own horse, Dancer, as often as she could.

Deborah walked in her direction. Amy stuffed the letter back into her pocket and shrank into the shrubbery, but Deborah didn't notice her. She wasn't looking for Amy, it was John she was searching for. Amy had seen him go into the house but wasn't going to tell her. She was her Dad's new wife - her stepmother.

She climbed out of the tree and followed her. She had something to ask her Dad as well. She opened the door of the television room. Deborah and John were standing very close and he was kissing her. Amy closed the door again.

Maria was at the counter chopping vegetables for dinner. Amy threw herself against her and clung tight, arms around her ample body. 'What is it, chica? You are playing a joke on me?'

Amy hugged.

'Don't hold me so, I cannot breathe,' she smiled and held on to Amy's hands.

Amy didn't let go.

'What is the matter? You are crying?' Gently, she managed to lead Amy over to a chair and sat her down. She knelt in front of her and wiped the tears away with her white apron. 'What is it you cry about?'

Amy snuffled.

'She was kissing him.'

'Who?'

'Deborah.'

'So what is wrong with that?'

Her head drooped. 'My Mom is the only person to kiss my Dad.'

'Deborah is your new Mom.'

'No, she isn't.'

'Your Dad loves her. They are married now. Don't you remember the wedding was in Canada when they were on location for the last film?' Maria patted her on the cheek.

'He loves her more than me and he doesn't love my Mom any more either.'

Maria laughed out loud. 'You are his special one, he loves you since you were a tiny baby.'

'No, he doesn't. He takes no notice of anything I say,' she grumbled. Her feet, in pink sandals, swayed back and forward, occasionally hitting the leg of the chair.

'You are imagining things, chica, he loves you, I know it.' Maria pressed a hand on her chest. 'In here, I know. I think maybe you will have to get used to Deborah. She is a nice person. I know she is trying to make a place for herself in this family,' Maria explained.

'But I don't want her to be in this family.'

'Dad has decided that she should be.'

Amy stood up, a frown on her face. 'I'm going to tell him that I don't want her here, he'll see then and tell her to go.'

'Amy, chica, that won't happen, I tell you, they are in love. She is Mrs. Parker now.'

Amy slumped.

Chapter Eighteen

Deborah grew more and more irritable. She complained a lot. The house was full of tension and arguments flared up out of nothing. They were in post production now on their last film, and she had plenty of time to herself.

'Baby, you're really good in this movie, it's going to be a great success.' John kissed her.

'I didn't like it,' she grumbled. 'You'll have to find a better part for me next time, I want to be somebody really special, so that I'll win an Oscar.'

'What are you talking about? You're the star and we may well be nominated. You're just being negative, my love.'

'I must have a drink, what'll you have?' she asked John, as she poured herself a vodka and tonic.

'I don't want anything now.'

'I don't want to drink alone.'

'You'll have to, there's no-one else here.'

'Come on, don't be a spoilsport.' She walked along the edge of the pool unsteady in her high white stilettos.

'Be careful. You could fall,' he warned.

'Stop bullying me. Don't do this. Don't do that. You'd think I was a fucking child. We've one in the house, isn't that enough?'

He didn't reply, just stared across the manicured gardens, the colourful flowers, the greenery, and the waterfalls which poured down into the blue pools. He seemed to be somewhere else.

'Why don't we send her to boarding school?' she asked.

'She's an actor - there may be a part in the next movie.'

'You could get some other kid to play the part.'

'I don't want another kid,' he objected.

'It would mean so much to us. She'd be out of our way. We could lead our own lives without interference. There are plenty of schools she could go to. What about that one she went to in Ireland?'

'When Maxine died I took her out of there.'

'She could go back.'

'No, I want her around.'

'Why?'

'Because she's my daughter.'

'She's my daughter too, well step-daughter, so I have some say in what she does.'

He didn't reply.

'Dad, Dad?' Amy appeared and ran towards John.

Suddenly Deborah lost her balance and slipped into the pool with a scream, her glass flying in the air.

'I told you to be careful.' John went over to the edge and reached in to help her out.

She continued to scream and splashed about in the water.

'Stop that racket, Deborah. Grab hold of my hand.'

She went under.

'Swim, Deb, come on, just a couple of strokes. Anyway, you're in the shallow end, stand up.'

She surfaced again. Gulped water and yelled in a strangled voice.

'I'm not going to dive in to pull you out, so you'll have to make an effort to get out yourself.' He bent down and held out his hand.

She made an effort to swim towards him, and their hands somehow clasped and then parted again, then clasped and held.

'I've got you.' He pulled her along towards the ladder and finally she managed to climb out and collapsed on a lounger, coughing and spluttering. He wrapped a robe around her shoulders. 'Come on, honey, stand up and put this on.' He helped her.

'I'm a complete mess, look at my hair and my make-up.' She burst into tears. 'And it's all your fault.' She rounded on Amy. 'Rushing out here and shouting.'

Amy stood there. Silent. Her dark eyes frightened.

'Debs, go upstairs and change. Don't forget we've people coming at six,' John said.

'What am I going to do in this state?'

'Women,' he sighed dramatically.

'Men!' she retorted, struggled into the towelling robe, and disappeared upstairs.

John came up a little later. 'Why are you lying in bed?'

She pushed her face into the pillow.

'Deborah, get up.'

She shook her head.

'All your friends will be here. You invited them.'

He sat down on the edge of the large bed. 'Darling?' He kissed her.

'I want you to send Amy to school. She's driving me mad. It's her fault I fell in the pool, and yours too.' She began to blubber again. 'I was so scared.'

'I'm sorry.' He reached for her hand.

'That's easy for you to say.' She snapped her hand out of his.

'Honey, just forget about it will you, I've said I'm sorry haven't I, isn't that enough for you? Now the guests will be wondering where you are, so you'll have to pull yourself together and get ready. Will I send Maria up to help you?'

'Tell them I'm very ill.'

He stared at her, exasperated. He never could win with Deborah.

Chapter Nineteen

'Dear Auntie Nuala, thank you for your letter. I don't know when we will come to see you as Deborah is very cross all the time. She is going to have a baby. And I will have a brother or a sister. Could you come over here. It would be cool. Love. Amy. xxxx"

That letter had so little in it, and yet so much. Nuala knew that John didn't want Amy to stay in contact with her, and wondered whether he even knew that her granddaughter wrote to her. Maria was instrumental in receiving and posting letters, and Nuala was grateful to her. She knew Maria and Amy were close, although she had never met her. But in the time Amy had been at school here, Nuala had heard enough about Maria to know that she was a woman who loved her granddaughter, and would look after her. Now that Deborah was pregnant, she prayed that Amy would not be pushed out on the periphery of the family, as all the attention was given to the new baby.

She thought of Maxine, suddenly emotional. The loss of her daughter never left her. It hovered in the back of her mind and swept back without warning at the most unexpected moments. Then, she was distraught, reliving the days and nights she spent at the hospital, those last hours of her life. So much bereavement. First her sister Bridget and then Maxine. And now she had lost Amy too, whipped back to live in LA by her father.

In the year which followed the empty days passed slowly and her heartbreak never eased. Time will heal, friends told her, but she didn't find that to be true. In her case, some days she felt she could face out into the world. On others, she wouldn't go outside the door.

To fight her way out of that darkness she had begun to reorganise the collection of books which filled the house. She wanted to remember Bridget and Maxine. Which books they had enjoyed most. Even touching them brought back those special memories.

Gradually she started to categorise. Hard backs. Paper backs. Romance. Thrillers. History. Biographies. Poetry. These were only some of all the genres of books which packed the shelves. She told herself it was worth doing. The collection was valuable. Someone might want it one day.

She had little contact with her own family, and doubted if they would have any interest. She couldn't imagine that Amy would have any interest either. She lived a different life in LA. While Nuala had never been there, she pored over travel books and read up on that part of California. Read and re-read books about Hollywood. Her cousin, Mike, who worked in the film sbusiness had died some years before, and contact between their families had diminished to Christmas cards.

Eventually Nuala's work was finished. Or nearly finished. She realised that it was something which could never be complete. However much she thought that the last book had been placed in its correct position on a shelf there was always a question hovering. Was this book strictly a biography? Into which genre did it fit? She grew frustrated. This collection had its own volition.

Now she was back to those long endless days. It was into the second year since Maxine died. She had to force herself to face out into the world. One Monday, she got up out of bed early, dressed in her best clothes, and went to Mass. It was important to start the day well. Then she went down to the day centre where the elderly received care.

'I was hoping to offer my services,' she told the woman at reception. 'I have some free time and I need something to do.'

'Have you any particular hobbies that we might poach?' she asked with a grin.

She wasn't sure what to say.

'What do you do in your spare time?'

'I read.'

'Ah, a bookworm. We have a library here, maybe you have some books you might be able to donate, we're always looking for new titles.'

Nuala felt suddenly intimidated. She had an image of home. Every space available occupied by someone's words. They had never loaned out their books. Neither Bridget or herself were prepared to lose even one. Only if there happened to be two copies then perhaps, but they could never take that chance of giving their only copy to someone else. It would be like giving a part of themselves away.

'I don't have very many,' she told an outright lie.

Chapter Twenty

'Oh my God, I look ghastly.' Deborah stared at herself in the mirror.

'You're beautiful, my love.' John put his arm around her. 'A woman expecting a child is at her most beautiful.' He kissed her.

'I'm huge. And I can't walk properly. I waddle. And how will I ever get back my figure? Tell me that?'

'Once baby arrives, honey, you'll tighten up in no time, a few exercises is all it takes.'

'It's all very well for you, men don't have to endure this.'

'Not much longer to go,' he said gently.

'Five more weeks,' she sighed.

'And I'll be with you all the way.'

'And then the section. I'll be cut open,' she grimaced.

'You could have it naturally.'

'And go through all that pain?' She tied up her long blonde hair. Then sat down at the mirror and began to put on her make-up. Smoothing on various layers of moisturiser, toner, foundation, slowly moulding it into the shape of her classic features. For her eyes, she used shades of soft grey, combined with silver, mascara, eyebrow pencil. She finished with blusher and lip gloss.

Deborah went into the dressing room, and stood staring into the wardrobes which lined the room. 'What am I going to wear?' she wailed loudly. 'I hate the maternity clothes, they're shapeless, I'm shapeless.' She ran her hands over her bump. 'He kicked, or maybe it's she, feel it, John, here, quickly.' She walked back into the bedroom and stood beside him. He put his hand on her bump.

'It's always amazing, every time I feel it,' he murmured, with a smile. 'You're something else, you know.' He put his arms around her and held her close. 'Now baby, concentrate on getting ready, we don't have a lot of time left.'

'But I can't find anything to wear.' She burst into tears.

'How can that be? You've masses of clothes in your dressing room.'

'I can't find anything, and now I've ruined my make-up.'

'No you haven't, just dab your face dry and re-do your lipstick, but dress now.' He patted some after shave on his face, and swished a clothes brush across the shoulders of his dark jacket.

'But I can't fit into anything,' she wailed loudly.

'What about the black dress you wore the other night?' He flicked through the rack of evening dresses.

'Can't wear that again,' she snapped.

'Who's going to notice?'

'Everyone. I can't be seen twice in the same outfit.'

'What about this one?' He chose a red satin dress.

'Don't like it. Makes me look too big.'

'Or this?' he took out a deep purple and held it up against himself and grinned. 'What do you think?'

'Looks good on you, but then you don't have a bump this size.'

'I give up.' He hung it up again and went back into the bedroom.

She pulled out a cream dress, stood before the mirror with it draped over herself for a few seconds, then threw it on the couch. She chose another, a blue silk, but it was consigned to the couch also. Then a grey, a black, a green and another and another. So it went until the pile on the couch trailed on to the floor.

'What am I going to do?' She waved her hands in the air.

'Darling, you're beautiful, no matter what you wear, you're stunning. And I love you.' He stood in the doorway.

'How can you say that?'

He looked puzzled and shrugged.

'You're a man, you couldn't possibly understand. It's how I feel inside.'

'I know, I know.'

'I'm not going.'

'Debs, why not?'

'Because I don't want to. In fact, I'm not going outside the door until the baby is born. Until I can get back into my own clothes, not these misshapen bags.'

'What?' he exploded.

'I'm staying in the house. I'll have no contact with anyone except you my love, and of course, Maria.'

Deborah and John had a suite at the top of the house for their own use. Amy had her own bedroom, and spent all of her time with Maria in the living area downstairs.

'So I'll have to go on my own then?' John asked quietly. He never liked to argue with Deborah. She could fly off the handle at the slightest little thing, so he was careful, always anxious to keep her happy.

'Do you have to?' She had a look of a lost child. 'Can't you stay with me?'

'There will be a lot of money floating and I need investors for our next film. The last one didn't do so well at the box office, so I'm putting everything I have into this next script. I can't afford two flops.'

'I'll be so lonely,' she pouted.

'I won't be late, honey.' he kissed her.

He went downstairs into the kitchen where Amy worked on her school homework at the table.

'Are you going out, Dad?'

'Yes.'

'Maria?' he called out.

'Si señor?'

'Would you keep an eye on Deborah. And maybe Amy might run up and see if she wants anything before you go to bed?'

Amy nodded.

'Do I have to?' she asked Maria after John had gone.

'Your Dad asked you.' Maria emptied the dishwasher. It was a state of the art kitchen and had only recently been installed. Maria was still trying to get used to it. The house had been completely renovated by Deborah over the past few months although Amy had insisted that her bedroom remain untouched. There had been a nice quarrel between them over that. But she had stood her ground and Deborah had finally given in.

'She will only complain if I go up. She says I never do anything right.' Amy sucked on the end of her pen.

'No she won't.'

'Yes she will.'

'If you are sweet and smile at her she can't say anything to you.'

'Makes no difference.'

'You must be sympathetic for her, chica, it is difficult to have a baby.'

'She's always been the same.'

'She will be different when the baby comes.'

Amy made no response.

'Do you know where babies come from?' Maria asked.

'Of course I do,' Amy snapped.

'And where?'

'From the mom's tummy.'

'Do you know anything else about it.'

'I know all of it. It's the same as the horses, and once I saw a baby foal being born.'

'If you want to ask me any questions I will try to answer them.'

Amy nodded.

Maria gently introduced the subject of sex. She couldn't imagine Deborah sitting down to tell Amy the facts of life so as the birth of her baby came closer, Maria made a point of giving her various bits of information. It was an ideal opportunity. She had been concerned that Amy should know something of life, it was important.

Maria loved Amy. They were very close. She was like her own child, and she was fiercely protective.

Chapter Twenty-one

Back home, Nuala wandered through the rooms, stopping occasionally to run her fingers along the spines of the books. Bright covers and titles jumped out at her and drew her mind back to the time when she had first read that particular one. She pulled one out and flicked through the pages, loving the smoothness of the cover and the paper with that thick velvety texture. It was a book of short stories by William Trevor, an author she enjoyed. Her eyes swept along the lines of text. His descriptive powers took her into the place inhabited by the characters. As she read, the germ of an idea began to grow in her mind. Something which almost frightened in its' audacity.

She was shy by nature. Never one to stand up and speak her mind. Now a sudden recollection took her back to that day in Bewleys all those years ago. She had arrived first, and just managed to find a table in the packed restaurant. Raincoats hung wetly. Umbrellas stood against the walls or lay on the floor, threatening to trip up the unsuspecting waitresses. Bags of shopping were pushed under chairs. The air was warm and sticky. Tom was late, but she was happy to see him. Nervous, but joyful too, when she told to him that she was going to have a baby. Smiling as she explained to him how wonderful it would be to have a child together, sure that it would be a bond between them. He had told her he loved her and that she was the only one for him, inferring that they would be together at some future date.

But his furious reaction to her news had shocked her and she hadn't the courage to try to persuade him around, to make him see that he had a responsibility to this child also. That's where she had made her mistake.

She forced the memories away. She was different now, and knew that she could take this idea and make it work.

A few weeks later at the community centre day room, she sat down on a chair on a low dais. The maintenance man had arranged a mike so that she could be heard clearly by everyone.

There was quite a crowd there, men and women, and they cheered when she came in. She sat down, and took the book out of her bag. Her hands smoothed the shiny cover as she gathered her courage to speak.

'I'm Nuala, and today I'm going to read you part of a short story. It was written by William Trevor, and I'm sure some of you have heard of him, and perhaps have read him before.' She looked around, and one or two hands shot up. 'I hope you won't be bored hearing it again, but it's a really good story and you should enjoy it regardless.'

There was a murmur of anticipation and then quiet.

Nuala took a deep breath and began.

Chapter Twenty-two

The birth of the baby was all arranged. Deborah would go into the clinic and the following day would have a section. But it didn't happen like that.

Alone in her room one evening, and waiting anxiously for John to arrive home, she felt a sudden sharp pain and screamed out loud. No-one heard her cry, as Maria and Amy were outside in the garden feeding Joey. The pain was followed by another and another in quick succession. She was doubled up for a few minutes, but then as the pain eased she reached for the phone, and pressed the button for the kitchen. Holding her finger on it, until the pain pierced through her again, and she was forced to release it.

'Oh my God, John, John, the baby's coming,' she screamed out loud. 'Maria, help me.' She curled up in a ball, the pains continuous now.

Amy looked up. 'I heard somebody crying, Maria, did you?'

'No.' She patted Joey on the head.

'There it is again.' Amy walked around the side of the house.

'What you hear?'

'I think it's inside.' She went into the kitchen.

'It is Mrs. Parker.' Maria ran through the living room, into the hall, and up the stairs, followed by Amy. She stood outside the door of the suite for a few seconds then knocked and opened it.

There was an immediate cry of someone in extreme pain.

She went through to the bedroom. 'Mrs. Parker?'

All formality disappeared when she saw Deborah writhing on the bed.

'The baby's coming, Maria, now, help me, please?' Tears ran down her face.

'I will phone for the doctor.'

'It's coming now, help me.'

Maria lifted the phone.

'Now,' she screamed.

'Amy, you ring security and get them to phone the paramedics.' She handed the phone to Amy who did as she was told.

Maria went closer to the bed. 'Pardon me, Mrs. Parker.' She pulled back the sheet.

'I think the baby's out,' Deborah cried.

'It is so, si, si, I can see the head. You must push more now so that the little one is born. Amy, you get me some towels and tissues quickly.'

She brought white ones from the bathroom.

'Push, push, Mrs. Parker, only a little now, the baby he is coming, the head is out, and the shoulders, si, it is your baby here, I have his little legs, and it is a boy, relax now, I will look after him.' She wiped his face with a tissue, lifted him and gently tapped his back until he began to cry.

'Give me my baby,' Deborah reached for him.

Maria wrapped the baby in a towel, still attached to the cord, and handed him to her.

The doorbell rang.

'Amy, let in the paramedics.' Maria quickly placed clean towels over the soiled sheets.

Amy ran downstairs, and opened the front door. She could see the paramedics outside with the security man.

'The baby is here already, it's a boy, and he's so cute,' she said, but they had already passed her and gone on upstairs.

'I can't believe what happened, Maria, I saw a baby being born, just like the foal, although he was much smaller,' Amy smiled.

'I cannot believe too, chica, I have not seen a baby born before, but to touch the little one, so warm and soft, it is wonderful.' She held Amy's hand and squeezed it. 'And he is your brother, do you know that, well, your half brother.'

'What is a half brother?'

'Because Deborah is not your mother, but your Dad is your blood, so this new baby is only half blood.'

'What is his name?'

'Your Dad and Deborah will give him his name.'

'I wish I could choose it.'

'It will be a nice name, si,' Maria laughed. 'And we will love him.'

'When will he come home from hospital?'

'In a few days.'

'I love him already.'

'We will see him grow bigger every day, and he will learn to walk, and talk, and you can look after him.'

'I can give him some of my toys.'

'Chica, he will get many presents,' Maria cleared the table.

'I can't wait to see him.'

'Your Dad will take you into the hospital I am sure.'

'When will he be home?'

'I do not know, my pet, but you will have to go to bed soon.'

'Let me wait up longer.' She threw her arms around Maria's neck and hugged her.

'It is late now.'

'Please?' she begged.

'I'm sorry, chica, but your Dad might not be pleased to find you up so late.'

'But this is a special night.'

'Tomorrow will be a special day too.'

Amy had to wait until her step mother came home to see her half brother again.

'Oh, I am exhausted, I'll have to rest,' Deborah said the moment she came in the door.

'Maria, will you see to Harry,' John carried the baby in a basket.

'Of course I will, he is so beautiful,' she smiled at the sleeping baby.

'Don't wake him, he'll start screaming again, and I can't take it.' Deborah went upstairs with John.

Maria brought the baby into the kitchen and went looking for Amy who was outside. 'Chica, quickly, the baby has arrived, come see.'

'He's so cute.' Amy stared into the basket at the baby who was covered with a blue blanket.

'Let us not wake him,' Maria whispered.

'But I want to talk to him.'

'Later, chica, later.'

'I can't wait.'

Maria put the basket on the couch.

'I'll sit here and watch over him.' Amy stared down at the baby. She wanted to touch him. His little lips opened and closed every now and then. His perfect fingers curled and uncurled.

'Don't wake him,' Maria warned.

'I love him,' Amy smiled.

Suddenly he began to cry. Screwed up his eyes and waved his hands about.

'What's wrong?' Amy was worried.

'He is hungry, I will make a bottle for him.' She busied herself at the counter, heating one of the bottles she had made up earlier.

'Can I feed him?'

'We have to be very careful, he is so very small. But you can watch what I am doing.' She lifted him out of the basket, and sat with the baby cuddled in her arm. 'Now, baby Harry, this will make you feel better.' She gently pushed the teat into the pink mouth, wide open now as he demanded to be fed.

John appeared in the doorway. 'Maria, you're feeding him, good, Deborah is resting.' He seemed distracted, and ran his hand through his greying hair.

'Si, señor, he is a very good baby.'

'You have everything you want, diapers and all that kind of thing?'

'Si, do not worry, señor. There will be no problem.'

'We'll look after him, Dad,' Amy smiled at Harry.

Chapter Twenty-three

Life changed completely once Harry had arrived. Motherhood didn't suit Deborah. She couldn't cope with the constant round of feeding and changing, particularly at night. So Maria took care of Harry, helped by Amy.

'I'll never be a size one again. Look at me. So much flab. I'm disgusting to look at,' she complained.

'You are even more beautiful, Debs, come here to me,' John stretched out his arms.

'I think I'm going to have some surgery, I have to get rid of this floppy stomach.'

'You don't need to go down that route yet honey. You've plenty of time.'

'You don't understand, how will I fit into my clothes again?'

'Why not work out some more?'

'I have been doing that, four or five hours a day, you just haven't been here to see what I'm doing. My trainer keeps me at it, don't you realise?'

The baby began to cry.

'There he is again, I don't think that child ever shuts up, what keeps him crying so much.'

'Maybe he's hungry, any child of mine has to have a big appetite, and he's going to grow up into a fine hunk of a man,' he laughed.

'You feed him then,' she retorted.

'I don't have your gentle touch, he won't appreciate my large hands.'

She went into the nursery and stood looking down into the crib. The baby was three months old now, but still awoke during the night demanding a feed. She lifted him, and went across to where she had a bottle warming. Maria made them and brought them up regularly. She wandered back into the sitting room and sat beside John.

'He's looking at you, he recognises you. That's your Daddy, Harry.'

John grinned.

The phone rang. He took the call. 'It's Doug, he's arrived. Why don't you bring the baby down when you're ready.'

'No, I want some time to myself, I can't enjoy the night if I have to look after him,' she snapped.

'I'll come back up for him when you're finished feeding,' John said.

'I'll have to change his clothes then.'

'You always change him after he's been fed.'

'I'll have to be even more fussy,' she frowned.

'He's got enough clothes, a whole dressing room full, just pick something simple.'

'I'll see how I get on, by the time I've got myself dressed and made up there won't be time for him.'

He stared down at Harry who was contentedly sucking. He brushed the pink cheek with his fingers, and smiled. 'Come on Debs, I want to show him off.' He left the room.

Impatiently, she rocked the baby from side to side. 'Come on, finish the bottle. Hurry up.'

He threw up.

'For God's sake, look what you've done. Dirty boy. And you've gone and got it on my jeans as well. Disgusting. And you smell too.' He began to cry. She wrinkled her nose. She rang the intercom phone connected to the kitchen.

'Maria?'

'What can I do for you, señora?'

'The baby threw up all over me, can you come up and sort him out, I've no time, have the guests arrived?'

'Si.'

'Is he all right?' Amy asked.

'He just needs a change.'

'Give him to me, I'll bathe him first.' She took him and kissed him, and he smiled at her and chuckled. Waving his hands in her face. 'There's nothing wrong with our little pet, he just brought back his bottle.'

'I'll fill his bath.' Maria hurried out.

Amy lifted Harry into the warm water. He immediately started splashing, water going everywhere.

'He loves his bath, si?' Maria tickled him.

'Maria, where are you?' John and Doug came into the kitchen. 'Can you get some more white wine from the cellar and put it on ice. We may need it later.'

'We are bathing the baby, señor.' She appeared.

'What's the baby doing down here?' They stood in the doorway. 'He was sick, and Maria brought him down,' Amy explained, washing him with a sponge.

He smiled up at John.

'He's a cute kid,' Doug splashed water on him.

'I'm washing him,' Amy said.

'Let me hold him,' Doug put his hands into the bath.

'No.' Amy spoke sharply. 'He's wet.'

'He wants to come to me, I'm Uncle Doug,' he grinned.

John handed him a towel and he lifted Harry, letting him lie on his chest.

'Your jacket will be soaked,' John warned.

'I don't care,' Doug smiled.

'Give him back to me, I want to dry him properly, he might get a cold,' Amy said.

'Amy, don't speak to Doug like that.'

She blushed.

'Apologise.'

She hesitated and bent her head.

'Amy,' John's voice was hard.

'I'm sorry,' it was barely a whisper.

'Hey boy,' Doug grinned down at him.

'We'd better get back to the guests,' John said.

'I think I'll take baby in to meet everyone,' Doug turned to follow him.

'He's not dressed,' Amy said. 'Deborah won't be happy if he's not wearing anything.'

Suddenly, he looked doubtful. 'Maybe not, see what you mean.'

'I'm going to put on his diaper, and dress him now.' She took a step nearer Doug. 'Give him back to me.' There was an edge in her voice.

Slowly he handed him to her.

'Fancy having one of your own, eh Doug?' John laughed.

'Yea, I envy you, man.' He wiped the collar of his navy jacket with a white handkerchief.

'So this is where you are.' Deborah appeared. Dressed in a full length black dress, with her hair and make-up perfect. She waved her hands, diamonds glittering. 'Shall I bring everyone else in here? Is it all happening in the kitchen? Come on guys, let's party.'

Chapter Twenty-four

Amy loved Harry. Her brother brought a new dimension into her life. During that first year, her horses and dogs slipped into second place and the baby assumed the most important position in her world. It suited Deborah for Amy and Maria to look after her child and really she only took a slight interest in his day to day life.

The biggest occasion was his first birthday. Malibu was turned into a magic fairyland for children. Amy brought him outside and held his hand as he took a few hesitant steps. Then she let go and he stood alone. Smiling dimples in his chubby cheeks. He waved his arms. Swayed. And sat on his bottom. She put him back on his feet again and they walked a little further. But as yet he wasn't going to try those few footsteps alone.

Deborah and John took him out to meet their friends as they arrived. But they grew tired of him and handed him back to Amy a little later. She was glad to have him and took him to see all the entertainments. Amy really enjoyed watching the jugglers, magicians, and musicians. It was a wonderful day. She put Harry down for a nap later, and when he awoke, she changed him again. As he stood up, he made a tentative movement towards her. It was just a few steps but he managed it. An unsteady rush, hands outstretched, a wide smile on his face.

'Harry, you walked on your own.' She clasped him in her arms and hugged him tight.

Maria was thrilled when he repeated his few steps for her.

'We will not tell the señora.' Maria combed his hair.

'Why not?' Amy was puzzled.

'It is something she should see herself. Let him walk towards her later and then she will be happy. Perhaps when they will light the candle on the cake.'

Amy nodded. But a dark shadow crossed her heart. Out of the past a dim memory of candles on a birthday cake. She had done something. It was all her fault. She shivered, put her arms around Harry and held him close. He always made her feel better.

On the main table, there was a large iced birthday cake, made in the shape of a train, on which was placed a white candle. Everyone gathered around and the musicians played *Happy Birthday*. Such a special day needed something to celebrate and he had done that already when he took his first steps alone.

Deborah held Harry close to the cake. 'Come on, kiddo, let's blow out your first birthday candle.' She showed him how it was done, and he made gentle efforts to imitate her. A cameraman recorded the events of the day. Deborah posed with John and Harry for photographs.

'That's my boy,' John laughed.

Amy smiled, her hands clasped behind her tightly. She was bursting to tell her Dad about Harry taking his first steps, and when the candle was blown out, she pushed forward.

'Look after him, Amy, will you?' John lifted him down.

'We have a surprise for you.' Amy held his hands.

'What is that?' John asked.

'Just wait, Dad.' Amy took him along the patio for a short way, and then ran back to where Deborah and John stood. 'Come to me, Harry, come pet.' She bent down on her hunkers and called him. He slowly took a step, and then unsteadily he made his way towards her.

'My God, John, he's walking,' Deborah squealed.

'What a day to do it,' John grinned widely and reached to lift him. 'Let's see you do that again.' He set him on his feet. 'Now walk to Mom, Harry.'

There was a murmur of anticipation from the crowd of people standing around. Even a little applause.

'Harry, I'm here, Harry.' Deborah waved at him to come towards her.

'Go on boy,' John encouraged.

He looked uncertain, and then began to walk slowly. But it was in Amy's direction he went.

'Over here, Harry,' Deborah encouraged. 'Come to Mom.'

His face crumpled. He stood unsteadily and tears began to dribble down his cheeks.

'What's wrong, baby?' Deborah asked.

He cried louder, and reached out to Amy. She gathered him up and comforted him.

'Give him here to me.' Deborah reached to take him from her. 'Why didn't you come to Mom, baby?' She jiggled him about and he wailed.

'He'll do it again, don't worry, Debs,' John reassured. 'Later, he's just tired now.'

'But I wanted to see him walk to me first,' she complained. 'Not Amy.'

Harry continued to cry.

'Amy, get Maria, will you?' John asked. She nodded and ran.

'Where's Harry?' Deborah asked Maria when they came inside after everyone had left. 'Hope he isn't still crying,' she grimaced at John. 'Keep us up all night.'

'No, he is sleeping.'

'Good, I'll check in on him.' Deborah went upstairs, and after a moment or two they heard a scream.

'What's up, Debs?' John followed her.

'Harry's not in his crib.'

'Señora, he is sleeping with Amy, I forget.' Maria opened her bedroom door.

'What?' Deborah stared at the two, cuddled up together in her bed.

'Thanks be to God, thought for a minute he'd been kidnapped.' John laughed.

'We'll take him back to his own room.' Deborah went closer to the bed.

'Leave him, he'll only be disturbed,' John said. 'It's too late at this stage.'

'I don't wasnt him sleeping with Amy, he's to be in his own crib, if he wakes he won't know where he is.'

John sighed. 'We could be up all night, have you thought about that?'

'That won't happen,' she snapped, pulled back the duvet and lifted him.

He immediately screamed, and Amy woke up. 'Harry?' she cried.

'Sshhh, stop crying,' Deborah held him close to her and hurried out of the room.

'Dad?'

'Go to sleep, Amy.' John closed the door.

'Should have left him where he was,' John grumbled.

'He spends too much time with Amy. Even walked to her tonight and wouldn't come to me. I'm his mother, John, she's only his sister.'

'She looks after him, what's wrong with that? And she loves him.'

'He's too attached to her.'

'Ridiculous.'

'I'm going to get a nanny.'

'You know I don't want that.' In the bed, John shifted himself up on his elbow.

'He needs better care.'

‘We can’t have a stranger looking after him.’

‘Don’t go against me, honey, please? Our son is growing up now and needs the best of care. Maria and Amy can’t give it.’

‘He’s doing fine.’

‘And I want to send Amy to boarding school, she’s too wild.’

‘But there might be a role for her in the next film,’ he objected.

‘She needs a good education. Discipline. When we’re away on location God knows what she gets up to.’

‘Maria keeps an eye on her.’

‘She can wind Maria around her little finger.’

‘That’s true.’ He lay his head back on the pillow.

‘So that’s arranged, thank you, my love.’ She put her arm around him and hugged close.

Chapter Twenty-five

Amy was angry with Deborah. She felt that Harry was being taken away from her. This nanny person would look after her brother. Whisper to him when he cried, kiss him when he fell and rock him to sleep when he wouldn't settle. This woman would do all those things which Amy did. She waited nervously, not sure when this woman would arrive into their lives. Every time she went out to school, she gave Harry a special kiss, praying to God that this person wouldn't have arrived when she returned.

'When do you think she'll come?' Amy pestered Maria.

'I do not know, Amy.' Maria was always busy. Today she was ironing Harry's freshly washed clothes.

Amy watched her and felt a sense of loss. She wouldn't be dressing him again. The nanny would do that. And she would wash his hair. And comb it. And put him to bed. And tuck him. in. Tell him stories and kiss him goodnight. And she wouldn't be here.

She felt that Deborah had betrayed her. She was sending her away from Harry, the person she loved most in the world. She wondered if she should try to explain that to her. But knew instinctively that it would be impossible to get close to Deborah. She was always somewhere else and had no interest in what Amy might have to say.

'I wish I didn't have to go to boarding school. I want to be here with Harry and you,' she said to Maria.s

'You are growing up now.'

She walked around the ironing board and stood close to Maria. Breathing in the scent of steam from the iron. She touched a pair of cotton trousers which had already been folded. The texture of the blue striped fabric was smooth and cool.

'He will forget me.'

'No chica, you will see him in the vacation.' Maria picked up another shirt.

'But he'll have grown up then and I won't know him. And he won't know me.' Her voice was low. She moved closer to Maria.

'Watch the heat, it will burn you,' Maria warned. 'And don't stand so close to me.'

Her voice came from a long way above. So far away Amy felt lost. Everyone had abandoned her. Even Maria didn't understand.

PART THREE

1995

Chapter Twenty-six

Bridewell College, San Francisco, early morning –

The light glimmered around the edges of the window shade and Amy was instantly awake. She turned in the bed and closed her eyes hoping for a few more minutes of sleep. But it didn't happen, and she found herself thinking about all the work she had to do. She was playing the lead in the college production of *Romeo and Juliet.* Renowned for the achievements of its' drama students, Bridewell tackled some of the most challenging pieces of theatre and Amy revelled in the opportunities.

At eighteen, Amy was tall. Five foot ten inches, and slim. She sat on the floor cross-legged and meditated for a while. She murmured a mantra. It helped her start the day and would clear her head for what she must do to absorb the part of Juliet and go back to medieval times when a girl and a boy loved each other against all the odds.

She wondered would her father come to see her performance. He said he might if he could spare the time. He had just finished shooting his latest movie and that usually meant his whole life was put on hold until post production was finished. Not that it changed things very much. Amy was out there on the periphery of his life. Home was somewhere she went to in the vacation.

She wasn't close to her stepmother. They sparred with each other constantly, and her father always supported Deborah. It was her stepmother who had persuaded her father to send her to boarding school when she was ten years of age and arrange for the nanny to look after her brother Harry for those early years of his life, before he too was sent to boarding school. She had never forgiven her.

When she was home she spent a lot of time on her own. If she wasn't riding or looking after her horse, Dancer, then she retreated to her old tree overlooking the pool. If her parents were home she watched what was going on hidden among the thick green foliage. Even Harry didn't know about her hiding place. If they were away, she explored around the house. Climbing down into the cellar when Maria wasn't around. It was full of dark shadows, with long cobwebs stretching from the ceiling over old bottles of wine which lay on the shelving which lined the walls. A very valuable vintage collection apparently, according to her father.

Often she would climb the back stairs which led up to the upper floors. The attic was full of old dusty furniture, picture frames, unused crockery and a myriad of other bits and pieces. The afternoon light slanted through the circular window in the eves which had coloured glass in the design, creating a delicate rainbow in which dust motes sparkled. There was a musty smell of old things and she revelled in the knowledge that she was hidden in this forgotten place and no-one knew where she was.

Up here she could read her books.

And dream.

And know she wouldn't be blamed.

For anything.

It's not my fault.

The old rant came out of the past to haunt.

Back in the present again, she rang Maria. 'Just checking in to see how you are down there?'

'It is all well, you want to talk to Harry? He has been home for the weekend.'

'Ame, I've got a new puppy, his name is Toby, and when are you coming home to see him?'

'At Christmas.'

'Must go now. Bye.' He put down the phone.

So like a boy, she thought.

She still wrote to Nuala. Their correspondence was now more frequent as she had freedom to receive and post her own letters. She felt almost closer to her grandaunt than her own father. Always drawn back to Ireland, that place she had been happiest.

'Amy?' Her bedroom door burst open and her best friend Cindy rushed in. 'We're late for rehearsal, Juliet, got your lines off?'

'Guess so,' Amy laughed.

'Let's make tracks, you know what herr direktor Bartley is like if anyone is late. Hey, great news, my Dad said I can go to Trinity College in Dublin to study when I graduate,' Cindy said excitedly.

'What?'

'I didn't think for one moment that he'd agree, although his grandparents were Irish so that probably made a difference. Do you mind doing lines with me this evening?'

'Yea sure,'

'Why don't you think about Trinity too?' They went into the rehearsal room.

'You're late,' Bartley yelled.

They grabbed two chairs and sat down.

'We're starting at Act Two, Scene II. Romeo, Juliet - ready?'

Amy leafed through her script to find the page. There was a long pause and the sound of Bartley's pen tapping on his script.

'First line, Romeo,' Bob grinned at Amy and began to speak.

"He jests at scars, that never felt a wound,
But soft! What light through yonder window breaks?
It is the east and Juliet is the sun!"

He paused.

Amy loved the play. The language. The tragedy. Everything she had went into the lines. She was Juliet. She loved Romeo.

"Romeo, Romeo! wherefore art thou, Romeo?
Deny thy father, and refuse thy name:
Or, if thou wilt not, be but sworn my love,
And I'll no longer be a Capulet."

She meant every word she spoke.

Acting took her out of her life, and into another. A parallel universe in which she existed. There were no rules in this place. Here she could forget the longing for home as she played other people, and lived their lives.

They worked through the scene until it was finished and they were free to chat together over coffee.

Bob sat beside her and smiled as he moved closer to her. She liked him, he was a popular guy with everyone.

'Fancy going to the movies on Saturday night?' he asked, his voice low.

'Once it's not one of my father's films,' she said, grinning.

'It's science fiction, Spielberg.'

'Sure.'

He covered her hand with his briefly.

Cindy noticed that and pushed her with her elbow. 'Thought you said you'd no interest in Bob?'

'We're only going to the movies,' she defended.

'Yea, yea.'

'You'll have to leave him behind when you go to Dublin,' Cindy said, teasing.

'Who said I'm going to Dublin, my father will never let me go, as for Deborah, you can forget it altogether if she gets involved.'

'You're going to college anyway, so it may as well be there.'

'I'd love to study in Trinity, and my grandaunt lives in Dublin, I haven't seen her in years,' she said softly.

'Haven't seen who in years?' Bob asked.

'My grandaunt.'

'The one in Ireland?'

She nodded.

'I'm hoping to persuade Amy to study at Trinity College with me,' Cindy explained.

'Lucky you, I have to do medicine, my father won't have it any other way,' Bob grimaced.

'You'll make a good doc,' Amy said.

'It's not what I want.'

'At least my father is in the same business, but it's theatre I love as opposed to film. That could be just as big a problem,' Amy admitted.

'Have we a modern day *Romeo and Juliet* theme here - two people who feel they can't do what they want,' Cindy added. 'So you should fight for it.'

'You don't know my father,' groaned Bob.

'Or mine,' Amy grinned ruefully.

As expected, her father didn't manage to make it to any of the performances of *Romeo and Juliet*, but Amy had every intention of asking him about Trinity College when she was home for the Christmas vacation. Put it to him in such a way so that he couldn't possibly refuse her.

'Dad, I've got an idea.' Her voice sounded high-pitched and she swallowed to clear her throat.

John sat in his black leather armchair, engrossed in *Screen International*.

She pulled up a chair and drew closer to him. 'I'd like to study drama next year.'

'You're an experienced actor, why would you need to study?' He didn't look at her.

'I want to.'

'Talk to Deborah about it.'

'I'd prefer you to make the decision.'

'She makes all the decisions, as you well know.'

Amy felt she was losing him as his attention fastened again on to the article which he had been reading.

'I want to study in Ireland, at Trinity College.'

'Trinity?' His eyes alighted on her this time, and his grey eyebrows disappeared into his hair which drifted untidily on to his forehead.

'Yea. I'm half Irish anyway. And I'll have Cindy for company. I must go to college somewhere, so it might as well be there. And Auntie Nuala is in Dublin too, please Dad, say yes?' She spoke in a excited rush.

'I'll have to think about it and talk to Debs.'

'She won't care,' Amy flashed, 'whether I go or not. She has no interest in what I do.'

'That's not true, Amy, she cares very deeply about you.'

'How could you say that?'

'Debs loves you.'

'She doesn't love anyone but herself.'

'What do you mean?' Deborah's voice echoed behind them. Floating into their space. A gross interference to Amy. She wanted to shout at her to go away and leave them alone. But compressed her lips to keep those words from bursting out. Her white teeth gripped the soft pink skin. Her fingernails bit into the palms of her hands. Tears threatened.

'Amy feels you don't love her,' John said smoothly.

Deborah opened her mouth and closed it with a snap. 'Of course I love you, Amy.' She strolled across the room. 'I missed my soaps earlier, I'll catch them now.' She sank gracefully on to the leather couch and turned on the television.

Amy pushed her hands into the pockets of her blue jeans, and stood awkwardly.

'I want to go to college in Ireland.' Amy took her chance.

'What?' Deborah's head jerked in her direction. 'Not if I have any say in it.'

‘You know I want you to join me in the company, there are some very interesting roles out there,’ John said.

‘It’s live theatre I want, not screen. I want to see my audience, feel their response, whether it be good or bad,’ she tried to explain.

‘I could get you some parts on stage, no problem.’

‘I don’t feel competent enough for the professional theatre yet.’ She felt she was losing her grip. He seemed to have an answer for everything she said. Sitting there. So arrogant.

‘You’re very competent, more than most I see on set. I haven’t bothered you while you were at college but now I want you.’

‘But if it’s not what I want?’

‘You’re saying you’re not keen to work in my movies?’ He was putting it very carefully. Boxing her into a corner and making her feel so guilty.

‘No, it’s not that exactly. I just want to study the art of drama, all aspects of it. Maybe I’ll never perform, I could teach perhaps if I get a good degree.’

‘So the bright lights of Hollywood don’t interest you?’

‘Didn’t do any good for my mother.’

‘You’re mother was a star. She loved it all. The openings. The glitter. The success. Walking up that red carpet. Who wouldn’t?’

‘Tell me about her. So that I can remember,’ she begged.

‘I don’t want to talk about it.’

‘No-one ever tells me anything.’

‘These things are better left unsaid.’

‘What are you two going on about,’ Deborah interrupted.

‘Nothing, Debs,’ John said.

‘I’m talking about my mother,’ Amy was defiant.

‘Oh Maxine, the wonderful one. No-one can equal her achievements,’ Deborah laughed.

‘You’ve equalled them a million times over, baby,’ John reassured.

She turned back to the TV.

There was an awkward silence.

'You'll think about it, won't you?' Amy addressed her father again.

'Yea.'

'I'll have to find out the procedure for application.'

'I suppose you'll expect me to pay for it?'

'Everything with that one costs money,' Deborah muttered. 'You're always telling me to watch my budget, what about her?'

'The company isn't performing as well as it did in the past. The last couple of movies haven't done well at box office, you know that. You could describe them as flops.'

'Don't you dare say that. I starred in them. They were great successes,' Deborah retorted.

'Financially, they were a waste of time.'

'Then maybe you should choose decent scripts.'

'If I could find them.'

'What about this one? I'm brilliant in it. Everyone tells me that.'

'It has a bit of tension, and the fantasy of discovering another world under New York should appeal to the masses, but whether it'll turn a cent remains to be seen.'

'I'm telling you it'll make millions at box office,' she turned up the volume of the television.

Amy felt pushed aside. That always happened. John and Deborah's conversation inevitably swirled out of control into something else, and whatever she had been talking about was forgotten. She was very disappointed.

Amy and Harry walked the beach with the dogs on Christmas mornng. Joey was growing old now but still had the energy to enjoy a run, although he couldn't really keep up with the gambolling pup, Toby. The sunshine sparkled on the blue sea, the waves thundered on to the golden beach, a gentle breeze cooled the hot sun.

Amy picked up a stone and skimmed it across the water, laughing as it took five leaps before the next wave thundered in.

'Show me how to do that.'

'You have to practise.'

'Where did you learn?' He grabbed a stone but it just cut through the water and disappeared.

'It was a long time ago,' she remembered that last day she spent in Clifden with her Mom, when they had skimmed stones. A rush of tears moistened her eyes but she brushed them away, picked up a suitably shaped one and followed Harry. They spent the morning on the beach and returned tousled, windblown, to find that some of the family had already begun to arrive.

'There you are.' Maria wagged an accusing finger at them. 'Your Mom has been looking for you, but better clean up and change before she sees you.'

It was at the end of the Christmas lunch when John mentioned her name in conversation with her Uncle Brian, her father's elder brother.

'Amy is trying to persuade us to let her go to Dublin to study, but we don't want to lose her. I'm looking for a suitable role for her in my next film.' He glanced along the table towards her.

'That would be wonderful, have you approached a college yet?' Brian smiled at her. 'Going to follow in your father's footsteps and study at Oxford?'

She shook her head.

'What's your first choice?'

'Trinity College, Dublin.'

'I'd give my right arm to go there,' Brian said, with a grin.

'My friend has already applied and is waiting for a response.'

'We can't let her go so far away, she's too young,' John interrupted.

'If you want to go, Amy, then you should. You're a grown woman, and it is a wonderful opportunity,' Doug cut in.

'More champagne?' John indicated to the waiter to replace the glasses with fresh ones.

'Tell Amy she can go, we can find someone else for the film,' Doug said.

Amy listened, astounded.

John didn't reply.

'Let's make a toast to Amy then.' Brian raised his glass.

'I'll second that.' Doug followed his example.

'Well, John?' Brian looked at her father.

'I don't know.' He shook his head, a confused look on his face.

'Go on, let the girl spread her wings,' Doug said, grinning at Amy.

He hesitated for a moment or two, then raised his glass. 'OK, you can go, but I want you back here ready to shoot a film as soon as you have your degree.'

'Thank you, Dad.' She stood up and kissed him, Brian and Doug as well. 'I can't believe it,' she smiled broadly. 'Such a surprise.' She could hardly believe that Doug, in particular, had supported her.

'To Amy!' They raised their glasses again.

Chapter Twenty-seven

Amy travelled with Cindy to Dublin a couple of months later. Their applications to take the Bachelor in Arts in Drama and Theatre Studies were made, and now they had to attend for interview before securing their places. It was exciting for both of them, but particularly for Amy to be back in Dublin again after so many years and most especially to see Nuala.

She was waiting for them at the airport, and Amy was shocked to see how old she had become, although she said nothing. Nuala had always been slight but now was even more frail. Still her straight grey hair was cut fashionably, and she wore make-up and an attractive outfit of navy trousers and a beige jacket. The girls were whisked by taxi to Ringsend, and it was emotional for Amy to see again that house, and remember where her Mom had grown up.

In the sitting room, the cat Pickle sat at her usual place on the back of the couch. She stared at them suspiciously, but there wasn't a move out of her. The green eyes were like jewels in her head. The black fur glistened.

'Pickle?' Amy called her name and went closer. Her tail flicked.

'You can never tell what she's thinking,' said Nuala. 'Enigmatic, I'd call it.'

Amy held her hand out towards her. But still she made no move except to slowly move the black tail. 'Pickle?' she said softly and ran her finger along her head. 'Don't you remember me?'

'How long has it been?' Cindy asked.

'About twelve years.'

'It's an elephant who never forgets, not a cat,' she laughed.

'I remember you could do anything with her, drag her, pull her, kiss her, and she let you. If I tried any of that, she'd sharpen her nails on me immediately. But be careful, Amy, she's an old lady now like myself and cranky with it,' Nuala warned.

'I'll take a chance.' Amy lifted her, murmuring her name over and over. To her delight, the cat purred loudly and curled over her shoulder.

'Do you know, I think she does remember.' Nuala was astonished.

Tears moistened Amy's eyes.

'I was so sorry you never came back to Slade College.' Nuala admitted.

'So was I.'

'You have grown up, and you have such a look of Maxine in your eyes and your expression too,' Nuala said softly. She stared at her.

'Do I?'

'Oh yes.'

'I thought I was more like my Dad.'

'In colouring, but in all other ways you're so like your mother.'

'I'd love to go down to Clifden, it always reminds me of Mom. It was the last time we were together.'

'When are you going back home?'

'We're here for a week.'

'Then let's go one of the days.'

Amy wandered through the front hall of the large house, which was still looked after by Brid and Sean who lived on the adjoining farm. But it was a silent, echoing place. As if it was waiting for someone. For Amy, the years rolled back. She was eight years old again. She could hear echoes of voices in the distance. Mom? She went through to the kitchen followed by Nuala and Cindy. Her hand on the door handle, cool, smooth, so familiar. She went inside. Expecting to see her mother there. That last time so clear in her mind. The party. Spaghetti Bolognaise. Birthday cake. Candles. The doll. The cake tossed in the air because she couldn't blow the candles out. That was the way she remembered it. But she questioned it now. Was that really how it was?

'There were always people in the house when we were shooting here.' She led the way into the large drawing room. The furniture was still the same, upholstered in rich burgundy brocade. The high windows, dressed with drapes of gold silk, looked out over the sea, and in between mirrors reflected the room and enhanced its size. 'I don't know what I expected, but I'm almost surprised things haven't changed.'

'It's a beautiful house, so full of character and charm, Maxine loved it,' Nuala said.

'Yea, she was always so happy here.' Amy put her arm around her grandaunt.

'It's an amazing place,' Cindy seemed equally blown away by the beauty of the house.

They settled in, planning to stay one night. Brid had made up the beds and picked up some provisions for them.

It was a cold blustery day, but they enjoyed facing into the wind all the way along the sandy shore.

'I'd love to swim.' Amy turned towards the crashing waves.

'I wouldn't put a toe in this icy water,' Cindy laughed. 'It's like the Arctic.'

'Dad never allowed us to swim in the sea. Someone forbids you to do something, you always want to do it.'

'And you were a girl who knew her own mind,' Nuala reminded.

'I hope so.'

'Now you're away, you can do what you like, we can do what we like,' Cindy laughed.

'Try and be sensible girls, I don't want to be your chaperone and feel I must report back.'

'Nuala, you wouldn't do that?' Amy gazed at her, horrified.

'Anyway, we're not going to do anything we shouldn't do,' Cindy added.

'Of course not. We're paragons of virtue.'

Nuala looked at them, a knowing smile on her face.

Their time spent in Clifden was wonderful. It was Spring, the weather sharp and crisp. The sun shone, and the sky was blue, and Amy knew that she was meant to be here. To be in Ireland. She was half Irish, after all. And Maxine's half was strong.

Chapter Twenty-eight

'What do you think of this outline?' John pushed a sheaf of pages across the desk to Doug.

'Is this another crime thriller?'

'With a bit of fantasy thrown in. It seems to be popular these days and I want to get back into the swing of things, the next film has to bankroll.'

'Have you shown it to Deborah?'

'No, I wanted to get your opinion first,' he muttered. He had worked night and day on various outlines. So tired of what was sent to him. 'We have to find that *je ne sais quoi* - that unknown quantity which was there in our earlier films, when ...' He stopped suddenly in mid sentence, and took a gulp of whiskey.

'There has to be something which brings you into the soul of the story, to understand what makes the characters tick,' Doug murmured.

They were silent.

'Will Deborah play the lead?' Doug turned the pages.

'I don't know yet. I wish Amy would agree to do it.'

'Deborah won't be happy if she's not given the lead.' Doug read through the outline, reluctant to say anything until he had reached the climax. For many years, his association with John had taken him to the heights of success, mostly due to John's unfailing eye for a good film script in which Maxine starred. Was it Maxine who had taken them all to the sun? Were they just hanging on to her talented coat tails? When she died and disappeared out of their orbit, in many ways Doug had died too.

The last few films in which Deborah starred had been decided flops. He took his mind back to the plot of this outline. It was banal and he wasn't looking forward to imparting that fact to John.

'If only Maxine was still here she'd play this part so well,' John said softly, and took a deep pull on a cigarette.

Doug was startled. It was as if John had read his mind.

'Do you remember those days.' John stared up at the ceiling, and blew smoke rings.

Doug nodded. 'This isn't her type of film.'

'What do you mean?' there was a hint of grating anger in John's voice.

'She was never into the strictly thriller genre. All of her films had a serious dramatic story. Love. Loss.'

'This is a dramatic story,' John retorted.

'But you don't have Maxine,' Doug's words hung between them, and he continued to read for a few minutes.

'Well?' John's bark interrupted his concentration again.

'So far so good.' He turned a page. 'It needs a lot of work.'

The door opened. 'Dad, have you seen Ame, we're going riding,' Harry's childish voice echoed.

'I'm here,' Amy came up behind him. 'Come on, kid.' They turned to go.

'Amy.' Her father called her.

'Yea?'

'Would you have a look at this outline?'

'Sure, whatever.' She shrugged.

'There could be a part in it for you.'

'But you know I'm hoping to get a place in Trinity, and I have to finish this year in college.'

'We could film in the vacation, before you go, that's if you get a place. The timing would be just right. If it took us a bit longer you could forget about this year and go next.'

She stared at him. 'But I don't want to do that.' Shock flashed across her face.

'Why the hell not?'

'If I get offered a place I have to grab it.'

'Honey, you'll love the role I'm writing for you, this is a great chance.'

'What about Deborah? I thought she was playing the lead?' she asked tentatively.

'What about her?' Deborah appeared in the doorway. Her blue jeans hugged slim hips, and her augmented breasts left nothing to the imagination through the silky top she wore.

'We're just talking,' John said vaguely.

'So fill me in.'

'It's this next film, I thought Amy might play a part.'

'Which part?' She gave her a venomous look.

'There's a couple of possibilities.'

'Don't forget I'm playing the lead.' She flounced across the room.

'Yea sure.'

'At the stage we're at now, I don't see us starting to shoot for at least six months, so that will definitely clash with Amy's college plans,' Doug said.

'But the outline is finished.'

'There's a lot of work to be done on it before it will be a finished script.' It was the first time he had given his opinion.

John looked up sharply. A frown creased his forehead.

'Amy can't play a part in the movie then,' Deborah smiled.

'Let's go, Ame?' Harry said.

'Hold on, Harry,' John waved at him.

'Aw Dad,' he whined.

'You stay until I say you can go. Sit down.' John ordered.

Harry did as he was told, a look of rebellion on his face. Amy stood, arms folded, sulky.

'I'll have the outline finished in a day or two, and the script writer will have a screenplay back to us in a matter of weeks,' John explained.

'I still feel that Amy should have her chance to go to Trinity if she gets it, it's a once in a lifetime opportunity, and if she has a role in this film then she might never take it up,' Doug said.

Amy stared at him. Surprise etched on her face.

Doug winked at her, so glad he was able to do something for her. Usually she kept him at such a distance he often felt she hated him.

'She has no experience,' Deborah said.

'It's the beginning of her adult career, I want Amy in this film.' John was adamant.

'Well, if she's in it then I'm not.' Deborah stood up.

Amy said nothing.

'But Debs, you're playing the starring role.'

'Don't care.' She shook her blonde curls.

'God, I'm surrounded with stubborn women,' John groaned.

'Let it go, John, we'll stick with the original plan, and then everyone will be happy,' Doug said, smiling at Amy.

John sighed.

'Right, decision made,' Deborah looked at the diamond studded watch on her wrist. 'I'm meeting with Ivan now, I'll have to bring him in here. Can you give us some time?'

'Who's Ivan,' John enquired.

'You must know Ivan, honey, he's my interior designer.'

'Oh that ponce! What do you want with him again?'

'I'm making a few changes to the house.'

'Again?'

'Yea, I'm bored with the decor.' Deborah was sulky.

'But it's just been a few months since the last refurb was finished,' John burst out.

'There are certain rooms that need a major job done, in particular Amy's.' She looked at her, triumph in her eyes.

'No, my room's fine,' Amy said.

'Dad?' Harry was impatient.

Deborah wandered around the large room. The walls were lined with bookshelves, an amazing collection of leather bound books on every subject under the sun. They were Maxine's books. She was the only person who had ever read them, no-one else bothered, although Doug enjoyed to browse among the various authors and had occasionally borrowed one.

'Debs darling, please don't touch this room. There's not much you can do. Books can't change their colour,' John implored.

'We could put them into storage, you never read them anyway.' She took one off the shelf, opened it, and blew along the open page. 'Thick with dust.'

'Of course I do. Anyway, this is a library and a library always has books.'

'I'm changing it into an extra dining room, we need one when there's a crowd staying.'

They took no notice of Doug. He was like a member of the family and he loved that anonymity. Deborah could literally hang John out to dry when she wanted to get her own way.

'What do you think, Doug?' Deborah asked, suddenly pulling him into the conversation. She could occasionally force him to take sides, the way it was in most families.

'I like the library, it has a certain character about it.' He went with his own intuition, although he felt he had said enough for today already.

'A dining room is a practical need.' She sat down on the wide arm of the brown leather couch, discomfited. 'I thought you two would be delighted with the idea.'

'To have such a library is wonderful, and now that John is writing it seems appropriate.' He couldn't explain exactly what was in his mind. But this room had been Maxine's creation. Her chosen volumes were especially bound. It was a tribute to her.

Deborah looked at John. Her fingers traced the button depressions in the leather.

'You understand what Doug means?' John asked.

'Of course I do, honey,' she murmured. 'But I had an overall plan and a library doesn't fit.'

'Can't you just forget about this one room?'

'Where will I find space for a dining room?'

'Somewhere else.'

'You're as bad as Amy - but I'm doing up your room this time around so you'll have to put up with it.' She stared straight at Amy, a sarcastic grin on her face.

'Don't you touch a thing in my room,' Amy was angry. 'I'll keep it locked.'

'You're having no input. Ivan will be doing the design. And we'll have no locking of doors in this house.'

'Dad?' Amy appealed to John.

'If Amy doesn't want her room done, why do it?' John barked. 'It's only going to cost another arm and a leg and probably doesn't need it anyway. She hardly spends any time there.'

'That's true. I'm only home for an occasional weekend. There's no need to do it.' Amy was unrelenting.

'Well, if you insist on having her room left as it is, then you'll have to give me the library. Which way do you want it?' Deborah stared down at him, and smiled.

John sighed and nodded.

Doug watched the play between them, and almost laughed. He knew John would have to give in, whatever way Deborah worked around it.

She smiled. 'Now, I need all of you out of here.'

'Let's go, kid.' Amy crossed the room to the door, and they left quickly.

'But we're working,' John protested again.

'It won't take long,' she cajoled.

'Don't commit to anything, we'll have to discuss the budget. The last refurb cost millions.'

'So what?' She was getting annoyed again.

'We have to watch our expenses.'

Doug was surprised to hear John's sudden aggression. He didn't usually argue with Debs in that manner. Doug had agreed to take a twenty-five percent stake, and the other backer the same, but he knew that John had to raise the balance and that he had put up some of his property as collateral against the loan. A very risky move.

Chapter Twenty-nine

To Amy's delight, both she and Cindy secured their places on the Drama and Theatre Studies course at Trinity College. It was such a challenge for them both. On the degree course, the students studied the skills of the theatre historian, analyst and practitioner. The lecturers were all people with vast experience of the theatre.

The girls had rooms at Trinity Hall and made many friends, most especially Babs and Rachel. They enjoyed life and tried to see as much theatre in Dublin as possible. It was a vibrant city, and they spent many an evening with their friends in the pubs listening to Irish music. Amy had never enjoyed herself so much before.

Best of all, she really enjoyed the course. Which combined academic lectures, and workshops in actor training, direction, design, and many other aspects of theatre. She had already decided that she would specialise in acting, and was particularly interested in the work of Synge and Beckett.

Both Amy and Cindy planned to go home for Christmas but Amy was disappointed when her father called and suggested that she shouldn't bother. They were shooting right through the holiday, and would only break for Christmas Day. He had been adamant.

'But I was looking forward to going home and seeing everyone,' she said. 'You know how much I love Christmas.'

'I know, I know, but I explained to you how difficult it is at the moment, we're under a lot of pressure to get the movie finished. You of all people must understand how that is.'

'Yea, I know.'

'I'm sorry, honey. Truly I am.'

'But I won't be able to give you your gifts.'

'You can bring them next time, now I must take another call.'

'But when will that be? When are you finished filming?'

'Not sure, it's taking too long already. Now, you have a Merry Christmas and we'll talk again soon.'

He was gone.

She talked with Harry. He was only concerned with horses, dogs, football, basketball - ten year old boys tell you very little about anything else. Christmas didn't really figure, except the presents he would receive.

'What are you giving me?'

'I'm sending it.'

'What is it?'

'You'll know when you open the package.'

'I can't wait.'

'It won't take long.'

'You're not coming?'

'Sorry, no.'

Her gifts for them were packed up and sent by courier.

The atmosphere of Christmas in Dublin was infectious but there was also a mix of happiness and loneliness. Amy could be trapped by sudden longing for home at unexpected moments. Particularly as she wandered with Nuala through throngs of people in the crowded streets. In and out of the stores, all bright flashing lights and glittering baubles, red, gold, silver. Children's faces excited, wide-eyed, Santa Claus, angels, reindeer, carols, crackers, plum pudding.

But Nuala made Christmas very special. They went to two pantomimes - *Cinderella* and *Aladdin*. On Christmas Eve they attended Midnight Mass and visited Nuala's family on Christmas morning.

'How many in your family?' Amy asked, as they walked the relatively short distance.

'I've two sisters, both widowed now. Their families always get together at Christmas.'

'How often do you see them?' Amy asked, with the innocence of youth.

'Not very often. There was a row between us years ago, and we've never repaired it. But I proffer the olive branch every Christmas at least. I hear nothing else from them the rest of the year. I don't get in touch either so it's hard to know who's at fault,' Nuala explained.

'What was the row about?' Amy was curious.

Nuala didn't reply at first, but then looked straight at Amy.

'I became pregnant although I wasn't married,' she admitted slowly.

'Was that a problem?'

'It was one hell of a problem in those days. People took sides and it split the family.'

'How sad.'

'Yes it was. Particularly when some of the family never saw my baby,' she hesitated for a moment. 'I've wanted to tell you for so long, but I didn't have the courage. Your Mom, Maxine, was my daughter.'

Amy stared at her, shocked. 'Oh my God,' she burst out. 'That makes you my grandmother!'

Nuala nodded.

'I can't believe it. Why didn't my Mom tell me? Why didn't you tell me?'

'We agreed to keep it a secret.'

'I wish I'd known before now.' Tears moistened her eyes. She reached for Nuala and they held each other close.

'I'm sorry, I should have told you.' Nuala's voice was muffled.

'My grandmother.' Amy whispered, pulled away and stared at Nuala. 'I always thought you had a look of my Mom, now I know why.'

'We were quite alike,' Nuala said, smiling.

'It's so cool. Now I have a grandmother,' Amy exclaimed, and hugged her again. 'I never knew Dad's parents, so this is amazing. Does he know?'

'No.' Nuala shook her head.

'We must tell him.'

'I don't know whether he would be interested,' Nuala hesitated.

'I'm sure he would.'

'Remember he didn't want us to keep in touch when you were young.'

'He's changed now.' Amy refused to believe that it could be otherwise.

'I'd prefer if you told your Dad face to face, instead of on the phone or in a letter, so maybe wait until you see him?'

'Sure, it's just that I'm so happy I want to tell everyone immediately.' Amy hugged Nuala.

'I love you to bits. Just remember that. You're the only person who matters to me.'

There was quite a crowd at the house. It was noisy and rowdy. Everyone seemed in good form. They were offered a drink, but declined, and accepted tea.

To Nuala's surprise, her sisters, Kathleen, and Joan, were unusually friendly.

'And who is this beautiful girl you have with you?' Kathleen asked.

'This is my granddaughter, Amy.' She just came out straight with it, but could feel her heart hammering with tension as she held Amy's hand tight.

‘Your granddaughter?’ Joan looked astonished.

‘Yes, Maxine’s daughter.’ She knew both of her sisters were aware that Maxine was her own daughter, although the fact had never been referred to in the past.

Kathleen had nothing to say, although it was obvious that she was equally surprised.

‘You know that Maxine was a famous actress, and Amy grew up in LA. She’s doing theatre studies at Trinity,’ Nuala gabbled nervously.

‘Amy will have to meet the rest of the family, this is really nice, such a Christmas present, come along with me.’ Kathleen took her hand and they disappeared through the crowd.

‘You should have brought Amy over to see us before this.’ Joan said, looking after them.

‘She’s only been here a few months.’

‘There’s been a lot of time lost over the years.’

Nuala nodded.

‘We don’t see enough of you either.’

Tears suddenly moistened Nuala’s eyes.

‘I was the youngest sister and didn’t know what was going on but there were others in the family who felt very strongly,’ Joan admitted.

‘It was the times.’

Joan turned and threw her arms around Nuala. ‘Forgive me.’

It was amazing. In a matter of minutes, all of the bad feeling which had existed within the family had disappeared. Nuala felt so happy she couldn’t believe it was happening, and had to go searching for Amy eventually.

‘I’m meeting all the family, it’s so cool,’ she smiled.

Nuala had never seen her granddaughter so excited.

‘And so am I. There are relations here I haven’t talked to in years.’ She hugged her.

'And everyone is so friendly, they all want to know about Mom and the films she made. They're going to try and find them on the net.'

'Nuala and Amy, I want you to stay for dinner, there's plenty for everyone and I've set two extra places.' Kathleen fussed.

'Thanks so much, but our turkey is already in the oven,' Nuala explained.

'Can't you drop back and turn it off?'

'Well...' Nuala didn't know what to say.

'No, no, I'm putting you under pressure. There'll be another crowd around tomorrow, a lot of the younger nieces and nephews. So come then. That would suit Amy too. They'd all love to meet her. About two o'clock?'

'That would be really nice, I'm looking forward to it.'

As Nuala and Amy walked away from the house they linked arms closely. 'That's all because of you. Suddenly it's like as if all the bad feeling over the years never happened,' Nuala said.

'I'm so glad I'm here.' Amy hugged closer to Nuala.

'This is the best Christmas I've ever had,' Nuala smiled.

'Me too.'

After they had finished their own delicious dinner, Nuala asked Amy to come upstairs with her.

'I want to show you these.' She opened a press on the landing to reveal piles of notebooks, the years written on the spines with a black pen. 'My diaries go back to when I was a girl and I have Bridget's diaries as well which sometimes deal with the same events from a different point of view. That can be quite interesting.' There was a twinkle in her blue eyes. 'And I want you to have them all when I pass away.'

'Don't mention that, I hate the thought of it.' Amy shivered.

'I'll be around for a long time yet.' Nuala chose a notebook, and handed it to Amy.

'That's the year I was born,' she exclaimed, and opened it. She flicked to her birthday and read aloud. *Today, my first granddaughter was born. Seven pounds, six ounces. She is to be called Amy. She has dark hair and eyes. I'm looking forward to receiving a photo soon so that I can see how beautiful she is.* The entry was written in Nuala's careful hand.

'Everything I have will be yours, Amy,' Nuala explained. 'The house, the furniture, and all the books too. I've made my Will, and my solicitor has the papers. There's an envelope in the top drawer of the dressing table with the details. All you have to do is to go to him and he'll arrange everything for you. And, by the way, there's a nice sum of money salted away.'

'Salted?' Amy laughed.

'Banked to be precise. Your Mom sent us money every month and we never wanted to use it, or had the need of it, thank God. So it's still sitting there if you ever need it.'

'I wouldn't like to take it, my Dad gives me an allowance. My friend Cindy has to help with her expenses by getting a job next semester. Her Dad doesn't want her to think money is too easy to come by,' she giggled.

'Does your Dad ever mention that?'

'Never says anything. He's so preoccupied most of the time I guess he doesn't take any notice of what Harry and I are doing.'

'I can't say I know him at all, the only time I met him was when your mother died,' Nuala said softly.

'Tell me what happened? Dad won't speak of it. I just know it was my birthday. We were so happy.'

'It's good to remember your Mam like that,' Nuala smiled.

Memories had been sparked by the conversation with Nuala. 'We spent the day on the beach and Mom baked a birthday cake,' Amy whispered. Images flashed into her mind. Her Mom's smile. A sudden shout. The candles flickering. A doll. Amy's face was suddenly pale.

'Are you all right?' Nuala asked.

Amy nodded.

'What's wrong? Tell me about it.'

'I don't remember it all properly, it's mixed up, I wish I could get it straight in my head.'

Nuala ushered her downstairs.

'Tell me what you know, Nuala, you were there.'

'No, I wasn't.'

'But you must know. Something happened. I'm sure of that. But I just can't recall.'

Chapter Thirty

'But I don't want to have another baby,' Deborah shrieked, staring down at her body.

'I can't say the timing is perfect, this being first day of principal photography, but I'm happy, babe.' John kissed her. 'We'll shoot your scenes quickly and then you'll be free, or maybe we'll make a change of plot - your character could be pregnant. What about that idea?'

'No way. I don't want to appear on screen looking like that. Anyhow it's not the movie that bothers me.'

'It will be wonderful to have a sister or a brother for Harry and Amy.'

She broke away from him, stared into a mirror and inspected her face. 'I can't afford to let myself put on one ounce of extra fat, not with all the work I've had done, and the money I've spent.'

'You're even more beautiful when you're pregnant, my love, you know that,' he assured her.

'What do you know? Like most men you haven't a clue what it means. And remember what happened the last time. It was horrendous, and I had to endure the birth without any medication or help. I can't go through that experience again. In fact, I refuse. Never again.'

'It won't be like that, Debs, we'll make sure of it.'

'And don't tell anyone I'm pregnant, I don't want anyone to know, especially Harry and Amy.'

Deborah was very worried. She ran her hands down her body, which was flat and curvy in all the right places. This wasn't part of the plan. How could she have let it happen? She had been so careful, taking the pill every day at the exact time, and insisting that her new lover, Brent, must use a condom. She couldn't have this baby, and most of all John couldn't discover about the affair. Although there had been others over the years, he had never found out.

'Brent darling, we'll have to be extra careful, we can't have the paparazzi spotting us, taking a photo and splashing it all over the front pages.' Deborah moved closer to him in the large bed and kissed him.

'Don't worry, pet,' his velvet tone reassured. 'I'm looking after you.'

'Brent, I want to wake up every morning with you,' she whispered. 'I love you so much. What am I doing with an old man, he could almost be my father.' She wound her arms around him. 'Then when we're together it won't matter who sees us. Let's swim,' she whispered, and they slid off the bed and pushed through the white voile drapes which softly drifted in the breeze.

They walked on to the golden sandy beach. Together they stepped naked into the warm aquamarine sea and swam leisurely, turning on their backs and drifting. 'This is perfect.' She stared up at the clear blue sky above.

'You are so beautiful, my love.' He kissed her, his lips soft, and they clung together, arms and legs entangled as they treaded water.

'Pity we have to leave, I'd love to stay on for another day, but we're shooting tomorrow,' she murmured, her fingers massaging through his short dark hair.

'I have to work tomorrow too.'

She gave a disappointed mew, and suddenly wondered would she leave John for Brent? Although he protested his love he hadn't actually suggested they divorce their present partners and settle down together. He already had three children and she couldn't imagine he would want any more. But was this child even his? It could also be John's. Deborah had no problem keeping them both spinning with her need for sexual gratification. Brent thought all his birthdays had come at once. John had to make a valiant effort to keep up with her demands, which ensured he never suspected there was another man in her life.

Now this was an unexpected set of circumstances with which she had to grapple. Why now? She groaned. Her body would become hideously distended as the baby grew. The last time she had got her figure back quickly but she had been much younger and the hard work she put in with her personal trainer had proved worthwhile.

This time her body wouldn't respond as well and might never be a size one again. But to her surprise, she hadn't suffered from morning sickness yet, in fact she was amazingly well and was able to continue shooting the film, choosing the scenes in which she was involved before her pregnancy began to show.

But time began to run out and she could see that a decision would have to be made quickly or else it would be too late. On the pretext of needing a break she checked into a clinic. A luxurious place on the coast where her every need was granted. At a price of course. Deborah had been there before for the work she had done on various parts of her body and knew that the doctors would be able to deal with the problem. She told John she needed complete peace and quiet.

John was really pleased with the thought of fathering another child. It cemented his relationship with Debs and confirmed his masculinity. They were making good progress on the tight schedule of the film, and he hadn't minded Deborah taking a break.

'Sure baby, you go right ahead, but come back soon, I need you here.' He saw her off at the airport. They still had their private jet but he wondered for how long as he watched it soar into the air, a silver streak which consumed a massive amount of money.

But when she didn't appear back within a few weeks he grew worried, and his phone calls became more frantic.

'Debs, surely you must be feeling better by now?' He found it increasingly difficult to hide his irritation. 'When are you coming back?'

'I don't have a problem anymore,' she said.

'That's cool, honey.'

'But I'll still need more time.'

'What? We've practically shot every other scene in the film now, and have re-written yours to incorporate a pregnancy so you needn't worry about that. Just get back here as quickly as you can. I've missed you terribly.'

'You can go back to the original script,' she said.

It seemed to him a rather blithe light-hearted remark, and he couldn't understand what she meant. 'But we had to pay the script writer to do it, and made other changes too, honey.'

'You didn't think I'd appear on screen looking like that?' she giggled.

'What do you mean?'

'I'm not pregnant any more.'

He said nothing for a moment. Only his breathing betrayed his shock.

'Debs?' he uttered her name in a long-drawn out sigh. Disappointment hurtled through him.

'It was the best thing,' she said.

'You had an abortion?' He couldn't get his head around it. It was too big. Too much for him.

'Yes.'

'When?'

'In the first week I was here. It was straightforward. Everything went well. So you've nothing to worry about.'

'How could you say that? I've lost my child.'

'It wasn't a good time.'

'That's not reason enough to take a life,' he glowered furiously.

'There is no point looking at it like that now, it's over, and I'll be back soon.'

'I don't care if you never come back,' he shouted, his voice echoed through the room, and he flung the phone against the wall and watched it fall to the floor in pieces.

Chapter Thirty-one

When John arrived at the studios at six-thirty in the morning, there was a sudden crisis. All the crew had gathered together, and John and Doug were faced by the Assistant Director.

'We need to know exactly what's happening with Deborah. The scenes which still have to be shot have a pregnant woman playing in them, but now the woman will have had the baby if we don't get on with it.'

There was a silence. The large group of people waited on what John had to say. Feet shuffled. Heads turned. Eyes glanced at each other in expectation.

'I'll call a meeting for tomorrow morning when we will have the exact schedule sorted out with the script writer.'

'What about today?'

'I can't do it.'

There was some very loud grumbling.

'Doug, we need to talk.' John turned and left the room.

John stood and stared out the large plate glass window of the office. The walls were covered with posters of the various movies in which he had been involved over his career. Photos of award ceremonies, lavish parties, film premieres and other gatherings.

'Deborah's not coming back,' he said bluntly.

Doug's heart sank.

'I don't want her.'

'Why?' Doug asked the question not really expecting a full explanation. But to his surprise he got exactly that.

'She killed my child.'

Doug was silenced.

'Not only that, it happened quite a while ago, so she could have been here weeks ago.'

'What's going to happen?' Doug asked. 'I've been looking at the figures and I don't think there are enough funds to keep going anyway.'

'What about the completion bonds?' John grimaced.

'They're all fucked up now because it doesn't look like we'll be able to complete.'

'The accountants were on to me yesterday.'

'Why didn't she let you know about it before now, particularly if she had no intention of completing the film?'

'Don't ask me. She does her own thing. Always has. And I've been a fool to let her away with it.' He turned back to Doug. Pain quite apparent in his eyes. 'I was happy about that baby.'

Doug was surprised to hear John speak so candidly. It was the first time ever.

'I've a meeting with the accountants at ten-thirty this morning.'

'Will I call in the rest of the team?' Doug asked.

John nodded despondently.

They had a hard-hitting meeting over the next few hours going over the parameters of how they could finance the future of the film. But they had lost too much time and there wasn't enough money to continue. The accountants brought in the legal people and they got down to the real meat of it. The company was bankrupt. Some monies had already been paid out but no-one had received the full amount contracted. So John, Doug and the other backer lost control. The bank was the main creditor. Doug and the other investor had a small hope of receiving some of their money down the line if the film was ever finished, but John was out there in unknown territory.

Chapter Thirty-two

Deborah reached for Brent. 'I've been dreaming about this,' she whispered as she wound her arms around him and they fell back on the bed.

'My love, I've missed you.' His lips touched hers, warm, moist. She responded. Her fingers trailed over his skin, and he moved slowly at first, but their movements grew more intense as they made love and all in a rush, they reached orgasm. The pleasure only lasted a short time for him but for her it was something which continued to take her to greater and greater heights.

'Wow, that was something else, darling.' She kissed him. They lay together in a sleepy doze but it wasn't long before they made love again, and again as the afternoon sun lowered in the sky. Sometime later sheer exhaustion caught up and they drifted to sleep.

Later, they ate on the patio. Lobster. Prawns. Delicious salads, washed down by sparkling white wine. She watched him. He was neat, precise, and ate slowly, using both a knife and fork, a napkin always to his hand. She liked these things in him. He had grown up in Australia and moved to the US in his early twenties. His accent was a mixture of the two countries. Today, he wore a linen shirt and shorts. The white stark against the deep tan of his body.

'We've so much to talk about, now that I'm going to divorce John,' she said excitedly, only playing with her food.

‘That’s a big move. Are you quite sure about it?’ His blue eyes held hers. They seemed to be saying something to her which she couldn’t quite grasp.

‘Of course I am.’

‘You’ve only just made the decision based on one row?’ He seemed surprised.

‘I know him so well. He won’t forgive me for what I’ve done.’

‘Surely if he loves you?’ With his fingers he pushed a blonde curl away from the corner of her eye. It was a possessive move, gentle, a you’re mine message there.

‘He hates me now. He wanted that child.’

‘You can have another.’

‘I don’t want any more children.’ She was absolutely certain about that.

‘You didn’t tell him how you felt until now, why?’

‘It never came up. We had Harry. And Amy. That was our family.’

‘The perfect family,’ he smiled. ‘Deborah, everything about you has to be just so perfect.’

‘Just like you, Brent. Your clothes. The way you make love. Everything you do is so measured. I love that in you.’

‘Two relationships only work with me for a short time. I cannot sustain a double life.’

‘Then shed one.’

She waited until the very last touch of his lips, always hoping, but he said nothing.

She was devastated. She had thought that announcing the divorce would spur Brent on to make a declaration that he wanted to be with her. Certainly she had not disappointed on the sexual side of their relationship. Indeed, that was the most vibrant part of it. All about consummation. Eating. Drinking. Making love. The secrecy added that extra zest. John had provided what she needed for many years but the initial excitement of living a high flying life with him had palled. She deliberately dallied with other men, the thrill of discovery paramount.

It was only now that she wondered whether John would agree to a designer divorce. She had certainly given him a terrible blow. But he had always been accommodating with her, giving her whatever she wanted, money no object until now. When she had done the last refurb, Ivan had the most wonderful ideas, but John had baulked at everything he suggested as being over the top and too expensive. But she knew it really wasn't about the money, it was because John just didn't like Ivan. In particular, the *piéce de rèsistance* - as Ivan put it in his wonderful broken English - was the white marble salon or living room as John insisted on describing it.

'No-one else in California will have anything like this.' Ivan waved his hands in the air.

'No-one else would be mad enough to spend so much on such a monstrosity,' John had muttered. But he had gone along with the plan to keep Debs happy.

She checked out of the clinic the following day suddenly worried that she might have pushed John over the edge. His mood had darkened the longer she had stayed away, and she thought that might affect her own plans. Now she needed a seamless divorce which would ensure that she would get a very good settlement. It seemed only fair to settle half of his estate on her. And the houses in Beverly Hills and Malibu.

But Deborah was independently wealthy. Astonishingly, John was unaware of this. Her father had been in retail when she was a child growing up in Wisconsin. The family were now billionaires, running a chain of stores around the country, and her brothers had inherited the bulk of the estate on her father's death. Deborah had only received what she had felt was a relatively paltry amount in his Will. But that fund had been carefully managed by her investment brokers. And its' value had increased over the years. It was a very well kept secret. She had a clever mind underneath the rather flighty personality and was highly manipulative too. The only reason she had married John had been to further her career in Hollywood. He had taken her to places she would never have reached on her own.

She flew back to LA, and took a taxi from the airport. The house was quiet. Not a sound could be heard. She wandered around admiring Ivan's work. She loved it. This was her favourite refurb ever and above all she wanted to stay here. This had to be her house. Hers and Brents.

Suddenly the thought of Harry and Amy sprang to mind. She had not included them in her plans for the future. Had almost forgotten them, so caught up in everything which had happened. She went upstairs. In her room, she showered and changed. John wouldn't be home until later and she would have a chance to devise a scheme and decide how she would approach him.

Chapter Thirty-three

It had been a long stressful day for John. The gates were opened by the security man and the silver limousine swept up the long tree-lined drive and drew up in front of the steps.

The chauffeur opened the door for him. He stepped out and stared up at his home for a moment. Situated on The Summit it was a large, neo-classical house. Originally built in the nineteen twenties and owned by a number of stars since then. His shoulders slumped and he was aware that within a very short time he might lose everything he possessed to the banks and be forced to walk down these steps and out the gates. The car disappeared around the side of the house to the garages, and John could see the sweep of the elaborate gardens in front of him, and thought again how beautiful it was.

The bank had put in their legal people and accountants and were assessing whether or not it was possible the film could be saved. It might not be as long as originally planned but perhaps could be made into home box office. What had been shot to date might yet be useable.

But his own personal situation with the bank was very bad. He had foolishly put up his homes in Beverly Hills and Malibu, his vintage car collection, wine collection, art collection, anything he possessed, as collateral, and now these would be sold. He came inside and immediately poured himself a drink. He needed it. As he stood by the bar, the glass held to his lips, Debs came into the room. She looked as beautiful as ever, dressed in a white suit with black trim. He stared at her.

Neither spoke for a moment.

'So you've come back?' he asked.

'Yes.'

'Bit late now.'

She looked puzzled.

'Have a drink? I'm having one. Better grab it while it's there.'

'I'll have a vodka and tonic,' she said.

He nodded towards the bar but made no effort to get it for her.

She poured it herself. Added tonic and ice. Swirled it around and took a sip from the glass.

'I'm sorry about everything.' She wandered across the room towards him.

'Sure you are.' He was sarcastic.

'Truly, I am.' She sounded contrite.

'You know what you have done?'

'Of course I do.'

'I don't think so. The movie has collapsed. We've been forced into bankruptcy. Some of the crew are talking about taking civil cases against you.' He was enjoying this. 'Your contract is with the company, not me.'

'What?' She sank on to the couch and gulped the vodka.

'The re-writing and the footage we shot to change the plot to a pregnant women cost a lot of money and as time lengthened without your return it looked as if it would never be finished. You wrecked the project. You, who should have known better, a person with so much experience of movie-making floated off without a thought for all the other people involved.'

'I never thought that such a thing would happen.'

'You knew the budget was tight.'

'You've always said that. Nothing different. How was I to know?'

'Our homes are probably gone too, so maybe there will be nowhere to live.'

She was shocked.

'We can find a new place together.' She reached out to him, touching his hand.

'Look Deborah, I think we've come to the end. I've heard rumours recently about you and some guy, so I think you should just take off with him. I've been given some months by the bank to vacate. I don't know where we're going to go. And what about Amy and Harry, they have their lives ahead of them, do you give a damn?'

'Of course I do.'

'They can't live on nothing.' John stood up and flicked through some papers which were spread on the table. I think we should just agree to divorce. Do it as cheaply as possible. Each pay our own legals.'

'I will not,' she shouted. 'No way.'

'I know about the other men in your life. I believe the latest one even called on you at the clinic.'

'How do you know all this?'

'Doesn't matter. Just say I do.'

'John, why don't we try and finish the film. I have a contract.'

'I think that's null and void now.'

'But surely it could be finished, I'm back now, I want to do it.' Her eyes filled with tears, her mascara was smudged.

'I've been a lapdog where you've been concerned, Deborah, but I've had it now,' he said bluntly.

'John, I've been stupid, I know that.'

'What about this guy, where does he fit in?'

'There's no-one, John,' she smiled. 'How could you think I would hurt you like that? You know you're the only man for me.' She came towards him, the glass held in her hand. Her attitude teasing. She licked what was left of the pink gloss on her lips as if she was hungry. 'I love you.' She leaned closer to him. 'Love me, John, like I know you do.'

'I can't, anything I felt for you is gone.' He turned from her.

'Just because I stayed too long at the clinic?' She positioned her hands on her hips, and swaggered.

'No, because you killed my child, that's even if it was mine to begin with,' he muttered.

'I did it for us.' She ran her hand along his arm.

'What do you mean?'

'I knew things weren't going well financially, you needed another success, if I wasn't available then it would be more difficult for you.'

'We were managing to work around it.'

'It was going to prevent you from doing what you wanted. Believe me. So I took the decision. Took the responsibility. I didn't want you to shoulder it. Don't you see, my love?'

'You could have talked to me about it.'

'I hadn't the courage. I felt guilty.'

'Yea, because maybe that other guy was the father.'

'I don't know where you got that from?'

'It was said to me. An impeccable source.'

'Do you believe everything you hear? This is tinsel town, John,' she shouted.

He was taken aback. He hadn't wanted to believe it. 'It still doesn't change things, you took the life of a child.'

'Don't you think I feel bad about it? I'm the person who went through the procedure. My baby was taken from me. Torn from my body. It's a terrible experience. It's against nature. I shouldn't have done it. I must have lost my mind.' She reached to kiss him. 'Forgive me.'

He looked away. 'I can't.'

'Why not?'

'It goes against everything I believe in. Against God.'

'But God forgives.'

'He doesn't forgive murder - I don't forgive murder,' John said bluntly.

Suddenly, guilt swept through him and he said nothing more.

Chapter Thirty-four

Amy was just into the third semester at Trinity and loving every minute of her time in Dublin. One night her father called. They chatted for a few minutes but then he fell silent.

'Is something wrong?' she asked, somewhat puzzled, and stared at Cindy, who was standing beside her.

'I'm sorry to say there's a lot going on with us at the moment, but the main thing is that we've gone bankrupt, there isn't enough money to continue with the film,' John said slowly.

She was silent, unable to believe what she was hearing.

'And I don't know if I can cover your fees for Trinity next year, so you mightn't be going back in October.'

Her initial delight at hearing from him changed to horror.

'You'd better come home when term ends and hopefully I'll have found a new place for us by then.'

'You've no money left at all?' She couldn't get her head around it.

'We're broke.'

'What about Deborah and Harry?'

'Deborah and I are getting a divorce.'

It was the most puzzling conversation she had ever had with her Dad.

'How's Harry?' she asked.

'Haven't told him yet, I will wait until he comes at the end of term.'

‘Will he go with Deborah?’ Her question was hesitant. She could barely get her mind into working order, or form a sensible response. She didn’t really care about Deborah but the thought of Harry going away would be heartbreaking.

‘I’ve said to Deborah that he’d be better off with me but in a divorce case, however amicable, the child could be asked by the judge which parent he wishes to live with, so I don’t know what will happen.’

Amy’s heart plunged. ‘And Maria?’

‘She knows nothing yet. But we couldn’t let her go , so she’ll be with us in the new place, wherever it is. Something will be arranged for the rest of the staff. I hope you have some of your allowance left?’

‘Yea, some.’

‘Watch your spending, I don’t know when I can send you some money.’

They talked some more, but then he had to go.

She put down the phone.

‘What’s up?’ Cindy asked her.

She shook her head. Quite unable to form words which would explain what her father had just said. She stared into the distance. Her heart pulsated, and she was unable to breathe. She pressed her hand to her throat, and suddenly didn’t know where she was.

‘We’ve no money left.’ She burst into tears.

‘Here.’ Cindy pushed a tissue into her hand.

‘There’s nothing at all.’

‘It can’t be all that bad, he’s probably exaggerated it.’

‘I don’t know.’ She shook her head.

‘Why don’t you call Deborah, see how she is?’

‘They’ve split up.’

Cindy was silent.

Later, when she had got herself under control, Amy phoned Harry at the appointed time in school.

'I'm on the football team, we're playing a game at the weekend, I'm at quarterback.'

'I hope you win.'

'We will, we've beaten them before.'

He was full of it. In Harry's life nothing was more important than sport.

'I get to ride a lot and I've a new horse, she's a bay and great over jumps, she's called Fano. When are you coming to see me?'

'I don't know Harry, you know I'm in Ireland and that's a long way away.'

'You didn't come for Christmas.'

That was an accusation.

'No, I stayed with Nuala. Dad was very busy. Did you enjoy your day?'

'Yea, send me some more stuff from Ireland.'

'What would you like?'

'I don't know, what do you have there?'

'I'll choose something.'

'When will it come?'

'It will be a surprise.'

Nuala and Cindy were both very upset to hear the news about the divorce, and their financial problems. And it was all they could talk about.

'It will break my heart to leave and not come back, I'm so sorry, Nuala.' Amy put her arm around her shoulders.

'Maybe something can be arranged,' Cindy said, hopefully.

'I don't know.' Amy was still tearful.

'Don't you worry, we'll make sure you'll be back in October, take my word for it,' Nuala reassured.

Amy managed a smile.

'What time are you due into work, girls?'

'Seven,' they said together.

'Better get your skids under you.'

The girls both worked in an Italian restaurant on Nassau Street a couple of evenings a week and also on Saturday night. Antonio's was a very busy place and they were kept on their toes serving tables until late. Amy would have worked more hours if she could to earn some extra money, but now she had to study for the exams, every spare moment was spent in the library, revising.

'I've been checking up on your mother's money, and there is more than enough to pay your college fees, and living expenses until you qualify. So you can stop worrying. Now's the time to study and pass those exams with flying colours,' Nuala said, when they talked the following day.

'I don't want to take that money, it's yours, Mom gave it to you to spend on yourself,' she protested.

'Your mother would have given it to you first if you needed it, and don't you think that she would be happy to see you use it now. I'd say she's smiling down at us and is delighted.' Nuala kissed her.

'You sure?' It was hard for Amy to be convinced.

'That money was put away for the rainy day. Now it's arrived, and we've got our umbrella.'

With the exams finished, the girls immediately got down to planning their summer trip. First they would go to London to earn some money, and then to Paris, Rome and on to the Greek Islands.

Then Amy dropped a bombshell.

'I'm not going on the trip, girls, I want to hang on to the job at Antonio's. He'll take me on full-time for the summer, and then I can go back to part-time next year. If I go away, there's no guarantee I'll have a job when I get back, and to spend that much money on a trip would be crazy, I have to keep every penny I earn.'

'But it won't be the same without you,' Babs said. And the others agreed.

'What if we all put something into the pot to cover you?' Cindy suggested.

'I couldn't take your money, girls, anyway, it's really about keeping the job,' Amy said.

While she tried to explain to the girls exactly why she couldn't go on the trip, she wasn't able to understand it herself. How her father had arrived at bankruptcy was a mystery. They had always been so wealthy. Money never a problem. Anything needed in the family was available immediately. Their homes were palatial. They had servants. Security. Drivers. They mixed with people who moved in the same circles. They didn't know what it was to be without money.

The girls headed off to London, and Amy moved in with Nuala. While she would have loved to go with them another part of her was happy to spend time with her grandmother.

Together they worked on the garden, and planned to give Amy's room a new look.

'I think you're a bit past pink and lilac now,' Nuala laughed. 'What about creams and beiges, they're fashionable shades.' She pulled out a colour chart. 'We can get a painter in.'

'Let's do it ourselves.'

'Would you trust me up on a ladder at my age?'

'You're a very sprightly seventy-three.'

'But I don't want to break anything. If that happens I'm bunched altogether,' she laughed

'If you get in a man, then maybe I can help him?' Amy asked.

'No man is going to want a girl under his feet.'

Amy looked disappointed.

'It will be hard enough to get him to do a decent day's work, and there will be plenty for us to do, so don't worry, you'll be kept busy.'

John was surprised to hear that Nuala could cover Amy's college fees. 'She can put her hand on that amount of money? I guess she must have had a good job,' he said doubtfully.

'Yes, and they always saved their money - for the rainy day - that's what she says,' Amy added. Maxine had been adamant that John shouldn't be told about the money she had sent over the years. That was between mother and daughter. 'Have you bought a new house yet?'

'Harry, and I, and Maria, are moving in with Doug for a while. Why don't you come over for the summer? I might be able to cover the flight, I'll try.'

'No, I'd prefer to stay here.'

'Why not take a break for a few weeks?'

'Must keep on my job.'

'I'm surprised you've that much sense in your head.'

'But I thought we were broke?'

'You're right, we are. We're just lucky to have a friend like Doug, even though we have cost him a lot of money already. He's lost a packet on the film.'

She found it hard to be enthusiastic about the idea of living with Doug, and was relieved that she had an excuse to stay here.

Chapter Thirty-five

Deborah sat in her lawyer's office. Looking particularly beautiful in a black Versace suit, the jacket revealing a deep décolletage, her long tanned legs crossed at the knee, a ridiculously high stiletto dangling from one foot.

'It doesn't look good.' Her lawyer, Thomas Kurthoss, said slowly. A rather grim expression on his smooth features.

'I was so sure I'd take him to the cleaners,' she fumed, sorry now that she had pushed things to the limit with John. She should have played a waiting game. Been more certain of Brent before she had made any move.

'There's nothing left.'

'I've put so much into those homes. Ivan only did a refurb last year on Beverly, it's out of this world,' she pouted. 'And we were planning to make further changes. You've no idea what a disappointment this is to me.' She dabbed a tiny square of embroidered silk to her eyes.

'There may be something down the line if the film can be engineered into a viable entity.'

'But what about those civil suits against me? John seemed to think it was possible someone might take a case and win out.' Deborah's sharp brain had covered every angle.

'So far I've received no documents, so I wouldn't worry, they probably think it's a waste of time, trying to get money out of you at this point. If John's gone down, so are you,' he said, grinning. 'That's as far as they are concerned.'

‘Have you examined my own portfolio?’ She changed the position of her legs. She quite liked her lawyer.

‘It’s looking OK, I keep in touch with your broker. Property values aren’t what they used to be but your rents are coming in so you’ll still have an income from those.’

‘I’m worried.’

‘You’re worth a considerable amount of money, Deborah, so you don’t have to worry unduly about benefitting from John’s estate.’

‘That’s all very well for you, but my money is my own, something no-one else knows about, particularly John. And I might add it’s our estate, Thomas, mine and John’s.’ She corrected him, becoming slightly irritated. ‘And it’s my entitlement.’

‘Sure, yea,’ he stared fixedly at the files spread out in front of him.

‘And I don’t want the world to know I’ve got zilch from him.’

‘Now what about your children?’

‘Amy’s not my child, and anyway she’s grown up and studying in Ireland.’

‘But you will have to receive maintenance for her.’

‘I’ll let John look after her, she’s his.’

‘And Harry, will he stay with you?’

‘He’s at school. I’ve only a month before the bank takes possession of the houses so I’ll have to move into an hotel and that’s no place for a ten year old boy, he’d drive everyone crazy.’

‘What does John say?’

‘He wants the kid, feels it would be better for him.’ She picked up her large black handbag and searched in it. After a moment she found a gold compact, opened it, and examined her face in the mirror, refreshed her lips with a colour brush and snapped it closed. ‘But I mightn’t let John have him, he is my only child - my trump card.' It seemed to indicate a decision made.

'So you're going for custody?'

'I probably will, but I'm not sure.'

'What are the child's feelings in all this?' He made some notes on the pad in front of him on the desk.

'I don't know. He's away at school. It's usually John who phones him. I don't have a lot of time.'

'Have you talked to him since the break-up?'

'No. I don't even know if he's aware of it.'

'I see.'

'I'll have to get my life together. Is there any chance I'll get anything from the sale of the houses, after all they're half mine, and I created them.' She leaned forward, closer to him.

'To be blunt, no. But what about the property in Ireland?'

'I wouldn't be bothered living in that desolate place on the edge of nowhere. Nothing but wind and rain all the time.' She stared at him, eyebrows arched.

'It could be sold perhaps, and there may be some residual for you in that.'

'Where has my mind been? I'd almost completely forgotten that the dump might be worth something. Get on to that, Thomas, immediately.'

She left his office and took a cab to downtown LA, telling the driver to take her to a quiet restaurant a little off the beaten track and not one of her usual haunts. She was ushered to a corner table at a window and she ordered a vodka and lime and sat sipping, occasionally glancing at the gold watch she wore on her wrist.

'Sorry, my love, I was delayed.' Brent arrived and kissed her. 'Mmm, you smell delicious,' he murmured.

'Chanel,' she smiled coyly.

'My favourite.' He sat opposite.

The waiter came over and handed them large menu cards. Brent chose a bottle of wine.

'What would you like to eat?' he asked.

'I'm not very hungry, maybe a salad.'

'Me too, with some protein on the side,' he laughed, and ordered a steak with all the trimmings.

'I've missed you,' she mouthed a kiss.

'And I you, but it's been really hectic. Have you found a home yet?'

'I'm waiting until we can choose one together.' She ate a little of the salad with a fork, and sipped her drink.

'Deborah, that's a big move.'

'I know, and that's why I don't want to rush it. It will be our first love nest.'

'We haven't reached that point yet.' He cut into a rare steak with a sense of purpose. 'And I think you should talk to a realtor.'

'When are you going to make a decision about us?' We're so good together, you know that,' she pressed him.

'I know we are, but there is still the matter of my wife and children.'

'I think you still love her, whatever her name is. You've never told me what that is or the kids' names either, and I haven't pushed it, although how it doesn't slip your lips occasionally I don't know. I wonder do they actually exist at all?'

'Deborah,' he smiled. 'Don't be ridiculous.'

'And if they aren't real then maybe you're just fooling around with me all this time, and one of these days you might just disappear out of my life.' It was something which floated in the back of her mind. An insidious suspicion that he wasn't what he seemed. That his whole life was a fabrication.

'How could you say that?' He covered her hand with his.

The waiter came over again.

'Is everything OK?' he enquired.

Brent nodded.

She waited until the waiter was out of earshot and continued on. 'I never meet any of your friends. We hardly ever go out. This is as public as we get, a dingy place like this,' she was building up.

'I'm disappointed that you should think so little of me.' He still continued to eat, obviously enjoying his meal.

'Doesn't stop you chomping away.'

'I'm hardly going to let this delicious food grow cold. It wouldn't be edible then.'

'And that would be a tragedy, I suppose,' she hissed.

'It has to be paid for either way,' he said, grinning.

'That's gross, how could you.'

'Deborah, where's your sense of humour?'

'I didn't think we were telling jokes.'

'Have you heard the one about the?' he sipped some wine.

'Oh you!'

'Deborah, I never promised that we would move in together.' He grew suddenly serious. 'When we met, we were both married, and there was no question of either of us being available. We dallied. It was wonderful. Exciting. And you are amazing in bed. Haven't I told you that?'

'But I'm available now.' Tears filled her eyes.

'And I'm not.'

'But you could be, if you wanted to,' she pouted.

'We'd never survive in a permanent set-up.'

'Of course we would, it would be fantastic. Imagine waking up every morning with me beside you, I love you, do you understand that?'

'What I need, I have.'

'What does that mean? You said I was the best ever.'

'And you are, in certain ways, but for everyday living I need something more stable.'

'Are you suggesting I'm not stable?'

‘I want a woman at home to look after my kids, not to have them stuck in some boarding school.’

‘I’m an actor, Brent, that’s the way it is. For everyone in my business.’

‘It’s not for me.’

‘So love doesn’t mean anything to you?’

‘Love?’ he smiled, and kissed her fingertips.

‘Yea, I love you, you love me, sort of thing. The way it should be.’

‘Love means many things.’

‘What does that mean?’

He shook his head. ‘I think we’ve come to the end, Deborah, it’s obvious I’m just not for you.’

‘You are for me. You’re just exactly the sort of person I want.’

‘It’s been really good, Deborah, but let’s say *au revoir*. Maybe we can meet again at some point in the future, but I don’t want to hold you back, you need to carve out a new life for yourself.’ His blue eyes were warm.

‘At some point in the future?’ She imitated his sharp accent.

‘Yes.’

‘You want everything, don’t you?’

‘Perhaps, who doesn’t?’ He sipped his wine.

‘You’re not getting any more from me, so slide along in tandem with your little woman who looks after the house and kids.’ She stood up, grabbed her Gucci handbag and exited the place at speed.

Chapter Thirty-six

'Look man, if the bank won't cover you any longer, then tell me what you're going to live on?' Doug asked.

John didn't reply.

'What about your art collection?'

'All included in the legal inventory, as is the botched film,' he muttered.

'You were very foolish, it wasn't worth putting everything you have into one film. I hadn't realised that.'

'I was so sure that the film would be a big hit.' John was morose.

'I have a proposition. Let me lend you some money. I've made a lot over the years and it's all thanks to you.'

'I don't want to take your money.'

'It's only a loan, look at it like that. I'll put your name on one of my credit cards, so you can use that account. The bank can't touch it.'

'Bastards. And I've given them millions over the years,' John grumbled.

'And there's something else. As a special favour, I want to support Amy and Harry, pay for their education, everything they need.'

'No, thanks, you've been generous enough. I'll manage to sort out Harry, and Amy tells me Nuala has enough money to pay for her course, and she has got herself a job as well.'

'What kind of job?' Doug laughed.

'In a restaurant, waiting tables.'

'I don't think Amy should have to work, and the aunt mustn't use up all her money either, let me help.'

'No, she was adamant. Mind you, I wouldn't mind her coming back, we might find a suitable script for her, it could be her adult debut, and get us back into the business. But she won't thank me for that, she's loving her time in Dublin.'

Doug would have given anything to help Amy and Harry. It would be like saying thanks to John for all he had given him over the years. Vacations, parties, dinners, and so many other family get-togethers to which he had been invited. John had given him a family. Being unmarried, and with no permanent woman in his life, this was something he didn't have. Doug had made a lot of money on previous films and he had it now at his disposal. He really valued John's generosity and this was the first opportunity he had to make retribution.

'Maybe I'll send Amy some money?' Doug suggested.

'I'm going to look for a script. Something to suit a young woman. A love story. Simple,' John said excitedly.

'Do you think she'll agree to come home?' Doug suggested.

'Maybe I'll try to write a rough outline, but I'll put the word out anyway.' John was already enflamed with the idea, and pulled a pad towards him on which he jotted down some thoughts. 'There's bound to be plenty of scripts out there.'

'What do you think?' Doug asked.

'I think it's a great idea.'

'About the money?'

'You mean investors?' John's forehead was furrowed with concentration, and he bit his lip anxiously.

'No, about Amy.'

'It will be all about Amy, I can see her already in the role. How about a modern consumer driven *Romeo and Juliet* theme?' He quickly sketched out a rough story board.

'I meant about sending her some money,' Doug explained, trying to get through to John who was already in the midst of his next film.

‘We could shoot it in Italy, in Verona, where the original *Romeo and Juliet* story was set, with an operatic background. That would be fantastic, we might do the rich poor thing, I can hear the music. Perhaps we might set it against the second world war, how about that? Give us that contrast, the exotic against the horror. I can feel the beats. We need great music and a screenwriter who can produce a dramatic plot, this is going to be something, I can feel it in my bones.’

Doug gave up. Suddenly uncertain. John wasn’t listening to him.

‘Why did I let her go? I was crazy. And I promised she could finish her degree, it’s four years and we’re only through the first year. Can you think of any way we could persuade her back, Doug?’ John rounded on him.

‘You won’t have discharged your debt for about three years so the timing is right. I don’t think it would be fair to Amy to ask her to come back.’

‘But she doesn’t need to learn how to act, she has a career just waiting for her, she could be an amazing success, do just as well as her mother, as beautiful and talented too, what the hell is she doing over there, can you tell me?’

‘She wants to study. There’s more to her course than acting, it has a very wide scope, literary, cultural, historical, it’s a marvellous opportunity, you never know what she might achieve.’

‘But she could have fame, and money, the sky’s the limit.’

‘She’s young, and wants to make her own way.’

‘But chances don’t wait for you. They have to be grabbed, otherwise they’re gone.’

‘Don’t forget your debts,’ Doug reminded. ‘You have three years.’

John was suddenly quiet.

‘It’ll take quite a while to set it up. Hone down the outline. Get a decent script. Storyboard. Chose a scriptwriter who will have fire in his gut and really want to do this film. Find backers.

Choose a cast. And we should take our time. The last film was a rush and look what happened in the end? When we have everything in place Amy will be back to shoot. Let her enjoy her time over there, she's only young once.'

'I'm heading towards old age by the minute. She has her whole life ahead of her.'

'Don't be selfish, John.'

'I'm not being selfish, I only want to produce a great film, to be at the top again, where we used to be.'

'You'll be there again, man, up with the best of them.'

'Yea, sure I will, sure.' Suddenly that hyper mood of earlier seemed to have died.

'Let's go somewhere, take a trip, you'll feel better,' Doug suggested.

'We should go back to Clifden, great fishing there, better than here.' John watched the sea, searching for signs of a shoal.

'It's been a long time.'

'They were good days.'

'Yea.'

'The house could go as well, although it wasn't part of the security given to the bank.' John was morose. 'That's the only piece of property left. I have to pay Deborah off and she's pushing for half.'

'What's the market like in Ireland.'

'It's good, improving all the time.'

'Why don't I buy a percentage from you and then you can pay her with that. Then I could use the house occasionally?' Doug suggested.

'You'd do that?'

'Glad of it.'

'You never cease to amaze me.' John had a wry smile on his face.

'I'd love an interest in Clifden. It would feel like home, especially since Maxine loved it so much and all of us had such good times there.'

‘I reckon that might sort things out,’ John mused.

‘It takes the pressure off you.’

‘You can have everything I have, Doug. You’ve been more than generous to me and this offer gets Deborah off my back.’

‘Why don’t we go over as soon as Harry is home. Are Sean and Brid still caretaking?’

‘I’ve told them I might be selling and that I wouldn’t need them any longer. I felt bad about that, the few dollars I pay them isn’t much but they work hard. Still Sean has insisted on keeping the gardens in order. He’s done so much work on it over the years he said it would break his heart to let it go wild. I think they’re still doing everything they did before the bankruptcy thing without any pay. They’re great people.’

‘That’s decent, isn’t it, I always liked them.’

‘Salt of the earth, guess you might say.’

‘We’ll sort them out, can’t be working for nothing. I’m looking forward to going back already.’

‘Yea, let’s do that,’ John grinned and slapped Doug on the back.

Chapter Thirty-seven

Amy was togged out in the black shirt, trousers, white bow tie and large black apron all the waiters wore at Antonio's. It was tough work, on her feet from about six in the evening to all hours, but Amy didn't mind. There was always a great buzz in the place, a long queue of people waiting for tables, kept happy in the bar with generous platters of calamari or other tasty finger food, and atmosphere was provided by the jazz group playing in the alcove.

Most nights she was almost the last to leave, with just Antonio and his sons Sergio and Giuseppe, forced to go home eventually only when Antonio called a taxi.

'Everything can be done tomorrow, cara, you are not supposed to be working all night. Go now when I say. The taxi is waiting.' He would embrace her then, kissing her on both cheeks affectionately, and wait at the door until she was driven away.

She kept in touch with the girls who were still working in London trying to make some money for their trip, and she was envious of the great time they were having, without her.

One summer night about two o'clock, she began to flag, uncharacteristically longing to put her head down and sleep. But there was still quite a number of people in the restaurant, drinking champagne and wine, ordering coffees, liqueurs. That was when it happened. One man moved his arm just as she put down a coffee pot in front of him. Suddenly, it tipped over. The top opened and the hot liquid spread across her hand. She screamed with pain and stood there helplessly, holding her hand in a napkin. Sergio appeared at the table within seconds, and immediately rushed her into the kitchen, turned on a tap and made her hold her hand under the stream of cold water.

'I'm so sorry, Sergio,' she mumbled.

'Don't worry, cara, I think we will have to get you to hospital. These burns need attention, phone an ambulance someone,' he instructed.

'I don't want to go to hospital,' Amy wailed, only now beginning to realise what had happened.

'You must,' Sergio insisted.

The concerned face of the man who had knocked over the coffee pot appeared in the doorway of the kitchen.

'How is the girl who hurt her hand?'

'We must send her to the hospital,' Sergio said.

'I'm really sorry, it was all my fault. I turned around and knocked it over.' The young man seemed very upset, his dark eyes worried.

'You are all right, not injured?' Sergio asked.

'No, I'm fine thanks,' he dismissed the suggestion.

'You would like some more coffee, champagne perhaps?' Sergio ushered him back into the restaurant.

'Antonio has already brought some, but to be honest I think we've all had enough for the evening, it was a great night, thank you.'

Antonio appeared in the doorway, his chubby face flushed, mopping beads of perspiration which stood out on his face with a large napkin. 'Amy*, come stai?*' He put his arm around her.

'I'm not too bad, Antonio,' she sniffled, still holding her hand under the icy water.

He took the napkin, wiped her eyes and pinched her nose like he would do to a child.

'The ambulance is here.' The young man appeared in the doorway, followed by two paramedics. They checked her out and put her sitting in a wheelchair.

'I can walk,' she argued.

'And pass out on us,' one of the men said with a grin.

'I'm not that bad.'

'I'm sure you're not, but I'm afraid we're going to have to insist.'

'Cara.' Antonio kissed her.

The streets were quiet at this hour of the morning, and the ambulance only used the siren occasionally as it careered around corners and roared down streets. She felt strange inside the back of the emergency vehicle which bumped, turned and twisted on its' mercy mission. At the hospital the attendants wheeled her into the A & E Department which was crowded with people. There were white faced old men and women breathing through oxygen masks, young bloodstained men suffering from God knows what, and intoxicated people yelling loudly for attention.

The triage nurse checked her out initially, asking lots of questions. Then all her vital signs were checked, heart, blood pressure, temperature, blood taken for testing. Then she was passed on to a doctor and her hand was dressed. She was connected to a drip and given an injection for the pain. They found a trolley for her and she lay on the hard mattress uncomfortably, the thin cover barely giving enough heat, her feet and lower limbs quite cold. But she said nothing as the staff were very busy, and suffered on until sleep overcame.

When she opened her eyes again she saw both Nuala and the young man who had been at the restaurant looking down at her.

'Hi,' she smiled, feeling sluggish.

'How are you, my love? Are you in much pain?' Nuala asked, pushing back her hair from her damp forehand.

'I have to see the doctor - a consultant.'

'When?' the young man asked.

'I don't know.' She felt herself drifting. 'It's cold, I'm really cold,' she whispered.

'I'll get you an extra blanket,' he said and disappeared.

‘You’re going to be fine, love,’ Nuala said, ‘and we’ll have you home before you know it.’

The man returned and covered her with two extra blue covers. She smiled at him. For the first time she registered his dark features. The wide smile. Dark brown eyes. Light brown hair, cut tight. Vaguely she wondered what his name was but her eyes closed slowly again and she remembered nothing more.

The consultant arrived the following morning and reassured her that the burns would heal with treatment, and hopefully there would be no need for a skin-graft. But they decided to keep her in hospital under observation for a day or two. She was transferred to a ward later that day and felt better lying in a comfortable bed. The pain of her hand increased and decreased in intensity, but they kept her drugged and she slept most of the time.

Nuala came in for a couple of hours, and later, the young man. She was properly awake then. He put a bunch of flowers beside her on the bed. They were red and yellow chrysanthemums. She smiled at him.

‘I’m Steve Lewis, and I know you’re Amy Parker.’ He sat down in the chair by the bed.

‘Thanks for coming in.’

‘You’re looking much better. I’ve had a chat with the nurse outside and she said you’re going to be fine, they think I’m related to you, so don’t blow my cover,’ he said, grinning.

‘Could you phone Antonio for me, explain how things are?’

‘Yea sure, have you the number in your head?’ He pulled a notebook from the inside pocket of the black leather jacket he wore and made a note of the number. ‘I’ll find a phone,’ he smiled at her and disappeared.

She watched the door waiting for his return.

‘Antonio was very relieved to hear you’re going to be OK, he’ll be in to see you.’ He sat down again, and stayed for a while. Telling her about himself and his family. His business and his friends. All those little things that take a person from the status of a customer in a restaurant to a friend.

'I'm sorry I was the one who landed you in here,' he said. 'But I'll make it up to you.'

'Thanks for the flowers.'

'How will you manage to eat?'

'I still have my left hand,' she laughed.

'I must get a vase for the flowers.' He went outside and reappeared a few minutes later carrying a glass jar of water.

'They're not much, but they'll brighten up the place.'

'Thank you.'

'I'll let you rest. See you tomorrow. Take care.' He moved towards the door. And stopped to smile again at her before he left.

'Your boyfriend is very nice,' the woman in the next bed said.

'He's not my boyfriend,' Amy said.

'Well, if I were you, I'd grab him before somebody else does,' she laughed.

Antonio turned up, all concern and apologies. 'Cara.' He kissed her.

'Don't worry about me, I'm more worried about the restaurant, you're one person down now and it's so busy.'

'Can't I serve a few tables myself. Didn't I begin like that in Roma when I was a boy?'

'But I don't know when I'll be back, it could be weeks,' she said, genuinely worried.

'You get better, Amy, as quick as you can, and as for coming back, we will see.'

Amy's heart somersaulted inside. He didn't want her back, was that it?

'Now, you are not to worry. I will arrange for your money to be put into the bank for you so there is no reason to be coming back too soon. You understand me.' He pushed his heavy bulk out of the chair. 'I must get back now, but I want you to concentrate on getting well, that is all that matters.'

'Thank you so much, Antonio, for paying me, I'll work extra hours when I come back, to make up.'

'Amy, there will be no need.'

'It's so good of you.'

He kissed her on the forehead and backed out in the direction of the door where he stood and waved.

She only spent three days in hospital, but they were long boring days. It was very strange to be suddenly snatched from her familiar world and landed here. There were eight beds in the ward. Eight temporary holding pens. Separated by limp washed out curtains. She stared at the pink floral design. Daisies she thought. Or other shapes she hadn't noticed before. Animals skulking in the jungle. City scapes. Sea scapes.

The outside world had receded. When she looked out the window, there were only buildings to be seen. Unfamiliar grey box-like structures. Between them cars swept to and fro. Their occupants hidden. On secret missions to places she couldn't go.

Nuala came to visit and Steve too. Now she was up most of the time, sitting by the bed. Her long dark hair was tied up into a pony tail, and she had applied pink lipstick and dabbed perfume. She wanted to look good. She was more relaxed with him now and could fit him into a category. An ordinary guy from an ordinary family.

Steve's brown eyes were warm and crinkled at the corners. He sat in a chair beside her, leaning towards her, and she noticed his strong square tipped fingers describe things as he spoke, his fingernails cut straight across, white-edged. Not bitten down which was something she hated. Tiny personal details which only a woman who had a particular feeling for a man would notice.

Chapter Thirty-eight

'Isn't this cool, I can drive myself. No more chauffeurs.' Doug settled into the seat of the luxurious Mercedes.

'You should have arranged for a chauffeur, do you know the way?' John enquired doubtfully.

'It's not a big country, and there will be signs,' Doug said, grinning.

'There's a sign for Galway, look,' Harry said from behind.

'I think you should keep your mouth shut and stay quiet.' John turned around and glared at him.

'I'll be navigator. Dad, I must sit in the front.' Harry's head appeared between the two of them. 'Let me in.'

'Get back there and put your belt on. You're not sitting up front. And stop interrupting. Doug needs to concentrate,' John growled.

The boy did as he was told but immediately his high-pitched voice echoed. 'There, go around the circle and take a right.'

John reached back and took a swing at him but the distance between the seats was wide and his arm missed its target.

'John, let him keep an eye out,' Doug said.

The boy straightened up, a wide grin on his face.

'You keep out of this.' John stretched back further this time and grabbed hold of Harry's tee-shirt. 'I don't want to hear another squeak from you.'

John was irritated. He had not been in Galway since he had taken Maxine's ashes back and spread them in the garden of the house at Clifden. He had taken her suitcases, already packed by herself, up to the attic and left them there.

He hadn't thought returning here would affect him quite so much. He hadn't thought about it at all. Now as the miles took him closer, he couldn't get Maxine out of his head. It was like nothing had happened in the intervening years.

'Hey, leave the kid alone, John, he's only trying to help.'

'Turn left on to the next circle and take the first left,' Harry yelled.

Doug took the turn which directed him to Galway. 'We're on our way.'

'Galway here we come.' Harry bounced up and down. 'Galway here we come,' he chanted.

John raised his eyebrows, and grimaced. 'What did I say to you? Do they teach you anything at that school? No manners anyway. I might have to change you to a much stricter one.'

'No, CSA is the best school for sport.'

'You should study more and play less football.'

'Another sign for Galway.' Harry pointed.

'Where?' Doug was confused.

'Look, there, see, Galway - turn left.'

'Oh yea.' He put his foot on the brake, slowed, and took the sharp left, which caused the motorist travelling behind to blast his horn.

'Be careful, Doug,' John warned.

'We're OK, this is Ireland, the drivers are much more easy-going. No one's going to jump out of a car and pull a forty-five on you,' he laughed and increased speed.

'If you keep driving like this, I guess you couldn't be sure what might happen.'

Harry giggled.

'Should have left you at home,' John grunted.

No more was said. John stared out the window at the landscape whizzing by. Memories of their time spent here surfaced since he had landed at Shannon. It had been the beginning and end of a life full of promise. His hopes and dreams had come crashing down then and the promises had never been realised. Any films he produced after that had never won an Oscar, or even received a nomination. Harry was not remotely interested in acting, sport his only love. Amy didn't share her father's obsession to walk up that red carpet and follow in her mother's footsteps. She didn't understand what it meant to him.

That part of his life had sparkled. He and Maxine had been a very successful duo. They had topped the star lists, and were invited to every function. An invitation to one of their parties was to die for. Their photographs appeared in glossy magazines regularly, and articles were written about them. Every time they appeared in public they had been surrounded by paparazzi, with reporters shouting questions at them. It was something John enjoyed, something Maxine hated, and something Deborah would have given anything to experience although she just wasn't in the same league.

'Is Ame going to be here?' Harry asked.

'No.'

'Where is she?'

'In Dublin.'

'Can we go visit?'

'I don't know, maybe.'

'Will she come to see us?' Harry was persistent.

'I'll phone and tell her we're here.'

'Can I talk to her?'

'Yea, course you can,' John seemed disinterested.

'Oh look, cows, see, and calves, and there's some horses as well. Can I go riding when we get to Clifden?'

'Maybe.'

John sighed. The stream of chatter from Harry was tiring. He was glad his son was normally in boarding school.

'This is Galway ahead,' Doug said.

'It's only a small place,' Harry said.

'Everything in Ireland is small, that's the best thing about it.'

'Bet the horses aren't,' Harry said, grinning.

'That's smart.'

'We have to look for a sign that says Clifden.'

'Yea, right, keep your eyes peeled.'

'We'll take this turn here and I know we head out towards the coast. I remember that bit at least. It's all becoming more familiar.' Doug swung the wheel.

'There's the sea. It's just like home,' he yelled. 'I didn't think there was any sea here.'

'You've never been before.'

'The houses are very small. Are there no high rise here?'

'No, Harry, it's all low rise here thanks be to God,' Doug smiled as they approached Clifden.

Harry stared out through the window.

They drove through the town slowly, and taking the Connemara Loop, they drove along the coast road until they arrived at the house.

'Is this it?' Harry asked.

'Yea.' John was glad the journey was over.

The car tyres screeched to a halt on the gravel frontage. Brid appeared at the front door, followed by Sean who had walked around from the back.

'You're welcome, sir.' Brid shook John's hand, as did Sean.

'It's great to be back, and thanks for looking after the house for me. You remember Doug?'

They shook hands also.

'And this is Harry.' He looked for him but he had disappeared.

'He's exploring already, I'll keep an eye on him.' Doug followed him around the side of the house.

'The place is looking wonderful, I had forgotten how beautiful it is,' John said softly.

'Would you like to go to your rooms and relax? Or have something to eat first?' Brid asked. They walked into the large kitchen. The pine table and chairs were still in the centre of the room, an old fashioned dresser with the dinner service on the shelves, brass pots hanging from hooks. The windows were open, giving a wonderful view of the sea. A large pot of soup simmered on the Aga.

'Do you want to eat here or in the dining room?' she asked.

'We'll sit here, Brid, it's so good to be back.' He was shocked to see that the place was the same as it had ever been.

The back door burst open.

'Dad, there's a horse in the next field, can I ride him?'

'I don't know who owns him.'

'It's my daughter's pony, Harry can ride him whenever he likes,' Sean said.

'Cool, can I go now?' He was already half way out the door.

'Have something to eat first and then maybe later.'

'There you are, I thought you'd got yourself lost already,' Doug appeared.

'I was looking at the horse.'

Brid poured bowls of soup and placed them on the table with a platter of brown bread and butter.

'That looks good,' Doug sat down.

'We'll bring the bags in later,' John said and joined them at the table.

As he sat there, he expected Maxine to come into the kitchen any moment. A sense of unease swept through him. That last day they had had their meal at this very table. It was Amy's birthday. There was a row. He was angry. Oh yea, Maxine always made him angry. He shook the intruding memories away.

'Can we ring Ame?' Harry asked his father.

'OK.'

The boy grinned.

Chapter Thirty-nine

The space in the small white BMW sports car was tight and Amy became conscious of Steve's closeness as they sat in the low slung seats.

'I'll miss going into the hospital to see you, but I'm glad you're out of there and getting better,' he said with a smile. 'And that you didn't need the skin graft.'

'Thanks for picking me up.' She glanced at him but his eyes were fixed on the road ahead.

'Amy,' he began to say something and then suddenly slowed down and pulled into a side street just ahead.

'Why have you stopped?' she asked, looking around for a reason.

'I want to talk to you,' he said and turned off the engine.

'You were talking,' she laughed.

'Need to look in your eyes, explain, face to face,' he hesitated and seemed ill at ease. This transmitted itself to Amy instantly, and she immediately thought whatever he was going to say to her had to be negative. It was nice knowing you. I'm going back to my old girlfriend. I'd like to be friends. But Steve said nothing, just moved very close until his lips softly touched hers. At first gentle, searching, then more urgent. A wild surge of excitement and wonder made her almost breathless and she could feel his heart hammering against her breast as she kissed him back.

In a few weeks, Amy's hand had healed, and she had grown much closer to Steve. When Harry phoned, she immediately decided to go to Clifden. Steve borrowed his father's car which was bigger and more comfortable than his own. With Nuala, they drove to the west the following weekend. As the miles passed, Amy grew more emotional. Snapshots flashed in and out of her mind, and she was taken back in time to when she had last been here.

After stopping to have lunch in Galway, they continued to Clifden, and along the coast. As they approached the Victorian house, the sun came out through the dark overcast sky above, and the foliage caught the light and glimmered.

'This is beautiful,' Nuala gasped.

They drove slowly up the wide tree-lined avenue and pulled up near the side of the house. There was the sound of footsteps on the gravel and a tall figure wearing wellington boots appeared.

'There's Sean.' Amy climbed out of the car and walked towards him. 'Bet you don't remember me?'

'Of course I do, Amy, you haven't changed that much. I'd know you anywhere.'

She kissed his cheek, and then introduced the others.

'Where are my Dad and Harry?'

'The men are fishing, and Harry is down in the lower field with Brid. They're having a look at the cattle. We can't keep him away from the animals - a bit like yourself.'

'Ame?' A shout heralded the arrival of a tall fair-haired boy who rushed around the house and threw himself without any hesitation on her. She hugged and kissed him.

'I want you to meet Nuala.'

'Hello Harry.' Nuala put out her hand and he took it.

'And this is Steve.'

He stared suspiciously at him.

'He's a very good friend of mine.'

'Let's go over to the farm,' Harry said.

'Can I come too?' Steve asked.

He nodded.

So Harry took them over to the farm and they were all firm buddies by the time they returned and made their way down to the beach. Steve was immediately persuaded to climb up on the rocks and search for crabs and other weird aquatic things in the pools. Nuala and Amy kept to the sand. It was a pleasant day and the breeze was light. There were a few people walking, taking advantage of the sunshine.

'It's a beautiful place. I can understand why your mother loved it so much,' Nuala murmured and pushed her arm through Amy's. 'You should spend more time here.'

'I'd love to, but I'll be starting back to work soon.'

'I'm sure there will be a chance before your Dad and Harry go back.'

John seemed really pleased to see Amy, and welcomed Nuala and Steve warmly. So long since Amy had seen her Dad and Harry, it was very emotional for her, but that was covered up by all the excitement of introductions and welcoming. Doug and Steve hit it off straight away.

Dinner was long and leisurely, and a couple of bottles of wine were consumed. To Amy's relief, there wasn't any talk of bankruptcy or divorce, particularly as Harry was listening. It was the general chat of Hollywood and the stars, and the great heights achieved in the past. For Amy it was hard. She had heard all of the anecdotes before. But for Nuala and Steve it was fascinating.

On the following day John and Amy fell behind the others as they walked in the countryside and that was when she heard the full truth. How Doug had bought a share in the house which went to pay off Deborah. Amy was shocked also to hear that she seemed to have very little interest in seeing Harry. But the divorce case would come up in court in the Fall so it remained to be seen what would happen then.

'Maria packed up your things and put them in your new room at Doug's. He's had it refurbished so it looks good. I'm very grateful to him for what he's done. And now, tell me, what is the situation with Nuala? How come she can cover your costs at Trinity?'

'I told you, Bridget and Nuala saved their money.' Amy felt under pressure.

'But she's only your grand aunt, and is amazingly generous.'

'Nuala's actually my grandmother.'

'What?' He stopped walking and turned to her.

'Mom's mother.'

'Why the hell wasn't I told of this?'

'I don't know, I only heard recently.'

'And why did you not tell me immediately?'

'I wanted to talk to you face to face.' She felt intimidated by him.

They walked in silence for a time.

'I'm sorry for losing my cool, but it's just ... ,' he said softly.

'It's OK.'

'Now about this guy Steve?' He gave her a look which seemed to demand an immediate answer. 'What about him?'

'He's a very good friend.' She tried to create an impression that it was very casual.

He frowned.

'What does he do?'

'He's an architect.'

He nodded. 'And how is Trinity, is it really going well for you?'

'Wonderful, we're all waiting for our results, I hope I get through.'

'You know Doug has offered to finance you.'

'No, that won't be necessary.' She shivered. 'Tell him thanks.'

'You tell him yourself. He's quite extraordinarily generous, supporting all of us.'

She found it difficult to approach Doug that day. It was only as they were saying goodbye on the Sunday that she murmured a few words of thanks, but it seemed to go against the grain with her. More conscious of her Mom at this time, she remembered how Maxine had warned her against Doug. She couldn't remember her exact words or when exactly it had happened. What was it about Doug?

Quickly she turned from him and hugged Harry again, and her Dad.

'Will you come up to see us before you leave?' she asked him.

'I don't think I want to chance Doug's driving in Dublin, it was bad enough coming up here,' John grinned wryly. 'We're all too used to being chauffeur-driven. Although back at home he's got enough classic cars to drive a different one every day.'

'But I can be the navigator,' Harry said, 'I got us up here, I can get us to where you are, Ame.'

'I'm a good driver,' Doug protested. 'Haven't I driven in and out of Clifden without a hitch?'

'Which is a small town, not a city,' John replied.

'I think we'll come down, it would be better,' Steve suggested. 'When do you go back to the States?'

'We've four more weeks.'

'There's plenty of time.'

They came back to Clifden every weekend until John, Harry and Doug left for LA. But Amy's last chat with her father wasn't altogether a positive one.

'You're enjoying Dublin, I can see that.'

'Yes, I love it.' Amy was enthusiastic.

'I've been looking at a really interesting film script for your debut. We will have the money in place before we start. But it all depends on you, Amy, our future is in your hands. Amy Parker - daughter of Oscar winner Maxine Howard - it's got a good ring to it.'

‘I’m not sure I want to go into the movies. You know I prefer to work in the theatre.’ She had told her father that many times but it never seemed to register with him.

‘You’ll have had your fill of it by the time you get your degree and then you’ll be ready to come back to the real world. You’ve a much better chance of making it than any of your friends. I guess they’ll probably end up teaching or something minor like that. They’re never going to achieve the heights you will. Work as hard as you can and I’ll do the rest. Honey, we’re going to make a great team. It’s very important to me, vital.’ His fingers dug into her shoulder as he spoke. ‘Promise me you’ll just do that one film. That’s all I want. Promise?’ He swung her around to face him. His eyes bored into hers.

She could feel herself being forced to do his will, and tried to resist.

‘Please, for me? For your Mom?’

She knew what he meant, and slowly nodded. ‘OK, just one.’

Amy never got an opportunity to talk with Harry alone and had to say goodbye to him on the last day without mentioning her misgivings about Doug. He ran along beside the car as they drove down the avenue, until it turned on to the main road.

‘That young fellow must be quite lonely,’ Steve commented.

‘He’s full of beans, a wonderful boy,’ Nuala added.

Amy stared out of the window, the light dulling now, her eyes flooded with tears.

Chapter Forty

Amy did well in the first year exams as did her friends, and all of them got through to second year. She continued to live with Nuala. Although she usually stayed over with the girls at Trinity Hall at the weekends.

She was back at work now and felt guilty that Antonio had paid her for every week she was out and wanted to make it up to him.

'I am so happy to see you, cara.' He kissed her in his usual fashion. 'Let me see the hand.'

She held it out and smiled. 'Completely better.'

He kissed it gently.

'Such a thing to have happened. Come, let us have a drink, I want to talk with you.'

They sat down and he poured two glasses of red wine. 'Now, I have a new job for you, that is if you want?' He sipped.

'What is it exactly, Antonio? I wouldn't be any good in the kitchen.'

'We need an extra person in reception. Taking the bookings. Doing the bills, you know. It is a nicer job, more responsibility for you and not so tiring on the feet. What do you think?'

'I'd love it, Antonio,' she was astonished.

'It is for you when you want.'

'I'll start right now if you like.'

'There is something else I must ask you cara, our head office in Roma, you understand, have asked me to discuss with you.'

He seemed suddenly ill at ease and gulped back his wine uncharacteristically.

'What is it?' she sensed his discomfort.

'I should not ask you this, but I think I know you well enough and that you will not think it improper.'

'What, Antonio?' she laughed.

'Do you intend to take a case against the company?' His words came out in a rush, his large brown eyes serious.

'A case?' She was puzzled.

'Yes, a legal case, for compensation.'

'No I'm not, I hadn't even thought about it. It was an accident and not your fault. If anything it was my own fault and Steve's, it had nothing to do with you.'

'It is your right.'

'I wouldn't dream of doing that. You've been so good to me. Don't look so worried,' she smiled at him.

'I want to tell you that you have some years before you have to do this. And if you should decide, it is between your lawyers and our lawyers and the insurance company. It has nothing to do with us.'

'I'm not going to do it now or in the future. My hand is fine.'

'Once you understand that you can take a case, I am happy,' he beamed.

'Thanks a million, Antonio.' She leaned over and kissed him on the cheek. 'Now, please show me what I have to do, I'm anxious to start my new job immediately.'

Now she was even happier working at Antonio's, but to her surprise, at the end of that week there were two cheques in her pay packet. Mystified, she immediately went looking for Antonio.

'It is for you, cara, just a gift for all the pain you have suffered.'

'But I couldn't accept this, it's too much,' she spluttered.

'You will not put a claim in to the company so you must be compensated, so this is our way. But if you change your mind, you can still claim, so go and enjoy it.'

'Thanks Antonio, and thank everyone in the company, it's so good of them, it's incredible.' She stared at the cheque made out in her name for five thousand punts.

Chapter Forty-one

Steve absorbed Amy into his world and she let it happen. When he woke up and went to sleep, she was the first person he thought about. Gradually, happiness seemed like it could be grasped and held like those dry dandelion seeds flying by on the breeze. Catch one and make a wish.

He wanted to live with her. To have her with him all the time. To touch her when he wanted. To trail his fingers on her soft skin and draw her to him. To smell her own particular aroma. To open up her lips with his tongue and explore her warmth, knowing how much he loved her, but afraid to say the words, so unsure of her response. She wasn't someone who could be rushed, he knew that. There was a reticence in her nature. A shyness. A hand held up against him keeping him at bay. He would have to wait until he judged the time to be right. When she came to him of her own volition.

So he gave it time. Always there for her. Until one night, she acquiesced. It wasn't the most comfortable place in the world, in fact it was decidedly uncomfortable. There was very little space in the small sports car, but the difficulty added to the excitement as they opened zips and buttons.

'My love, I've imagined this so many times,' he whispered into her dark hair which was delicately scented. 'You are so beautiful.' He drew a deep breath. Their rhythm built up and with much laughter they tried to find their way around the hand brake, and gear lever. She whispered incomprehensible words to him and moved closer along the seat, tantalising. Now he was in that place which was so special. That was Amy. The very depths of her. Her softness so unbelievably enticing, letting him know that she loved him too. He didn't know this Amy. This was the first time they had been so close.

'Amy, Amy,' he whispered.

It was a turning point that night. They loved each other. It was true. They had confirmed it.

PART FOUR

2000

Chapter Forty-two

Ballsbridge, Dublin, late morning –

'You will marry me, Amy, won't you?' Steve's eyes were intense.

'Yes, yes, I will,' she whispered.

Their lips met and they were silent after that, only loving murmuring passing between them as they made love. They tossed in the bed, the duvet slipped off, their naked bodies were slick with perspiration, and they finally ended up on the floor.

'I love you more each day, do you know that?' Steve said, kissing her.

'And I'll always love you,' she responded.

'I'll keep you to that, no matter how far away you go. You're not going to get rid of me.' His finger traced the shape of her face gently. 'You're mine and don't forget it.'

Amy had finished her degree course, four wonderful years spent in Dublin and part of the third spent in Paris studying mime. She had become very close to Nuala and she loved her dearly. But the most important person in her world was Steve – her first real love.

But the promise to her father must be kept, and now she had to return to the US.

'Doing this film is going to be such a bore. I'll miss you so much, and Nuala and the girls.' She was morose.

'The girls would probably give their right arms to be in your shoes.' Steve wound his arms around her. 'I know I would.'

'We might get a part for you, what about that?' she smiled at him, suddenly excited.

'I can't act for toffee,' he laughed out loud.

'We could get you some coaching, you never know how good you might be,' she persuaded.

'And what about my job? I've studied to be an architect and it's all I want to do, you know that.'

They had had this conversation more than once in the last couple of months as the date for her departure grew closer, and it always came around to the same conclusion.

'Come back when the film has finished shooting and we'll make it official. Engagement ring, wedding ring,' he gazed at her seriously.

It was the morning after a great going-away party for Amy. She was due to fly to LA the following day, and while she would have loved to spend every minute with Steve, she wanted to be with Nuala too. So together they went over to Ringsend and picked her up. They had lunch at a small hotel in Wicklow and then drove to the coast to walk on the beach at Brittas Bay.

'This is lovely,' Amy pushed her arm through Nuala's and they walked closely against the wind, Steve following.

'I'm going to miss you,' Nuala said, smiling, brushing her hair out of her eyes.

'And I'll miss you. Only for this film I wouldn't go home at all. But Dad is so insistent. He's been planning this for years and everything is just coming together now, they're already on location.'

'Where are you filming again, I've forgotten.'

'It's a small place on the edge of the desert in Mexico. Originally Dad wanted to set it in Italy and that would have been great, because it's so much closer, but as the script was developed the story changed and he chose Mexico.'

'What do you think of it?'

'It's good, I like it.'

'And you're playing the lead, I think that's great. It will be your first chance to make a name for yourself, your Mom was already out in Hollywood at your age.'

'I don't know if I'll be as successful, she was much more talented than I.'

'You will be too.' Nuala squeezed Amy's arm affectionately. 'You're a budding film star.'

'Listen to Nuala, Steve,' she called out to him but he was staring out to sea, his face set grimly. 'Hey there?' She turned back and stretched out her hand.

'Yes love?' He took it, and moved closer to them. The rather serious look on his face chased away.

'Keep up with us.'

He smiled.

It was a lovely day. That last day. Happy yet sad. And the next morning Steve drove her to the airport with Nuala. That was tough. To say goodbye to them both and not know when she would be back.

'Safe journey, my love, and phone me as soon as you arrive.' Steve hugged her.

She couldn't speak. Tears welled up in her eyes.

'Take care, Amy, and come back soon.' Nuala held her for a long time.

She nodded and tried to gather her strength to actually join the queue going through into the airport security.

'Have you got everything? 'Nuala asked.

Amy nodded and began to move closer to the end of the queue.

Take care.' Steve held her close.

'Mind yourself.' One more hug from Nuala.

'I love you, just don't forget that.' Steve kissed her again.

She dragged herself away from them. Forced to move along with the people and lose sight of them. She turned back for a few seconds and waved again, only barely able to see them through the mist of tears. They stayed there waiting while she moved with the queue towards the door, gave one final wave, showed her boarding pass and passport to security and went through.

Chapter Forty-three

It was straight into shooting as soon as she got back into that celluloid world of film on location in Mexico. She had studied the script of *Veil of Sand* and was glad to throw herself into the role which took her mind off Steve and Nuala, for a short time at least. But she found it hard, missing them both so very much. Especially Steve.

She had to be on set very early, and was picked up by the driver at five thirty in the morning. She wasn't used to that, or going to bed early either. The time difference meant that she couldn't always talk to Steve or Nuala as their schedules clashed and that was frustrating.

The only good thing about being here was that her part required her to ride. She hadn't had the opportunity to ride since she had come to Ireland, and when her father had become bankrupt, she couldn't have afforded it anyway. Now she enjoyed every minute she spent with the horses. She had a double for the more dangerous scenes, but really she would have preferred to do all of it herself, but the insurance wouldn't allow.

Other aspects of filming bored her to tears. Each morning, as soon as she had arrived she would have to check in with make-up. To stare at herself in the mirror as she was transformed. Her hair was straightened and drawn back off her face with clips. Foundation pasted on, giving her a golden suntan which never looked natural except on the screen. Then eyes, contours, lips, and finally the wig was fixed on her head. She was now a blonde. She hated the look. So unnatural. But had to endure it.

She would wait in her trailer until she was called. That gave her a chance to phone Steve, and the girls, or write letters to Nuala. But still the time hung heavily, and made this enforced separation from them all the more painful.

Harry flew down one weekend.

'I thought I'd see more of you. I was sure Dad had a part for you in this movie and that he was going to offer you so much money you couldn't refuse.' She hugged him.

'He wanted me to play the part of some kid, and so did Mom, but I never read the script, couldn't be bothered.'

'Where is your Mom living now?'

'South of France.'

'Is she doing a movie?'

'No, the Count has plenty of money so she doesn't bother.'

'Do you think you'll ever act?'

'Naw, Ame, what do you take me for? It's not for me. I want to play professional football, you know that.'

'Do you think you'll get a place in college?'

'Of course I will. Don't you know I'm good at sports, especially football?' he said, grinning. Harry never lacked confidence and even though he was only thirteen, he could have been much older in many ways.

'I wish we had some time to hang out together.'

He looked awkward. Hands pushed into pockets, filling the space with his fists.

'If you ever need anything, or want to talk, Harry, you would phone me, wouldn't you?'

'What do you mean?'

'Nothing in particular. I was thinking if there was something, you'd remember I was there for you.' Her voice petered out and she said no more.

'Yea sure.' He didn't seem to grasp exactly what she meant.

'I love you, Harry,' she said softly, after a moment.

He stared out the window, his shoulders sloped.

He was just a teenager and at that awkward age, and very likely embarrassed. She put her hand on his arm and squeezed.

He turned and smiled.

Lights - camera - action – those words echoed in her head over and over. Her father strutting about. Always on set. Watching everything like a hawk. Doug sitting in the Director's Chair controlling every move. She still didn't like him but had to put up with his familiarity. Sometimes she wondered whether he fancied her? Now that she was a grown woman she could observe depths in him which she had never been able to do before. When younger she had never really analysed Maxine's attitude towards him, but her apparent dislike had stuck with her.

John and Doug were very happy with this film. There were no problems at all and they kept to schedule and were under budget.

'You're wonderful, Amy, so professional.' Doug put his arm around her at the end of shooting one of the days.

She felt awkward, and stared fixedly across the studio as if something had taken her attention.

'You are so tense. Let me massage your shoulders.' He immediately moved behind her and began to manipulate her neck.

'No, it's all right, I'm fine.' She moved away from him.

'Maybe we should employ a masseur for you, it isn't good to be that tense, the way you are feeling will be picked up by the camera.' He was concerned.

'No.'

'I'll talk to your Dad.'

'I'd rather you didn't.' She had to force herself to be pleasant.

But any time Doug came too close that was exactly what happened. She did tense up.

Her life in Ireland had become increasingly distant. Steve and Nuala seemed to be drifting further and further away from her. Their images blurring so that sometimes she had to take their photographs out of her wallet to remind herself of their features. She wondered sometimes would she ever get back. Would her life take a completely different turn caught here in this make-believe world?

Chapter Forty-four

'I'm going back to Dublin,' Amy announced to her father as soon as they had finished shooting and returned to LA. They had the house to themselves. Doug was in New York beginning the post-production process, and Harry had gone to stay with his mother in the south of France, which he did occasionally.

Her father jerked his head in her direction. Eyes stared fixedly under a frown.

'For a visit?'

'I hope to get work in the theatre.'

'I've another script for you. We have to do a second film. Keep up the momentum.'

'I don't know whether I want to do another.' She felt guilty.

Over the past few weeks of shooting which she thought would never end, the dread of trying to explain to her father what she wanted to do with her life loomed ever more terrifying.

'But don't you want a career in film? I thought after this one you would be full of enthusiasm to do another. That you would see what a wonderful life it is. What could be better?'

'It's not the career I want.'

'But it's your life. The blood that runs in your veins. Can't you feel that? I want you to walk that red carpet and accept an Oscar like your mother. Don't you want to follow in her footsteps?'

'Of course I do. Mom was a wonderful actress and I'd love to be as good as she was, but it's the theatre for me, not film, you know that.'

'There's no future in theatre, and certainly no money,' he said

'I'm not interested in money.' She shrugged. 'And there's something else ...' she hesitated for a few seconds.

'What's that?'

'I'm getting engaged.'

'To whom?'

'Who do you think?' she laughed.

'Not that guy you've been hanging around with? I thought he was just a friend.'

'Dad, we've known each other for years.'

'You can't get married,' he said bluntly, lighting a cigarette.

'Why not?'

'If you're starring in my films, you can't be married.'

'I haven't agreed to do another. While I was here I felt part of my life was stolen. My real life. I can't wait to get back.'

'I'm depending on you, Amy. You're the one who will turn our fortunes around. This film is good. It will be a big success. I feel it in my bones. You'll be nominated for an Oscar for sure. So we'll have to follow on with another film which will be even better.'

'My life is in Ireland, it's where my heart is.' She tried to explain to him.

'Don't you understand that if we make it then we can set ourselves up again, buy our own house. I want my own place, my own independence, we've been living off Doug for long enough. I sound like a teenager I know, that's like something Harry might say, but you're our ticket out of here. I can't believe that you would let me down?'

'It's not what I want. I'm sorry, Dad.' She felt the old pressure emanate from him. Like she was held down helplessly by his sheer will.

'But you've so much time - years and years - I haven't.' He put out the cigarette in an ashtray, viciously squeezing the white tip into the squish of orange tobacco edged with black.

'I've promised Steve, I can't go back on that.'

'You're only kids, why would you tie yourself down, it's heading for disaster.'

'I'll take my chances.'

'When I was young, before your mother, I did the same thing, settled down, had a couple of kids. But do I ever hear from that bitch I married or the kids? They took me to the cleaners and that was it. Take a leaf out of my book and forget it. There'll be plenty of men down the line for you. They'll be queuing up, gal, believe me. Seriously wealthy guys who would give their eye teeth for someone like you.' He shook another cigarette from his silver case, and placed it carefully between his lips. Then he lit it with the lighter which had been a present from one of his more recent women. 'Don't be stupid Amy,' he said slowly through a haze of blue smoke.

'I'm not stupid. I know what I want.'

'You're too young to know that.'

'Don't keep telling me I'm too young, I'm twenty-three.'

'What does this guy earn a year?'

'He's doing very well.'

'But he can't give you anything like you could have over here. See the way we live. Ireland is a backward third world country.'

'It is not, Dad,' she was shocked.

'If I tell you it is, then it is.'

'Well, I'm happy living in a backward country.'

His phone rang but he ignored it, and the incessant ring continued for a few seconds and then stopped. That brief interval seemed to give them some breathing space.

'So my plans for you are worth nothing, is that what you're saying?' He continued in a belligerent tone.

'I want something else.'

He glared at her.

The tears came when Maria put her arms around her and held her close. 'Chica, don't you worry, your father will understand.'

'But I love Steve. And even if I did agree to take part in Dad's movies it would be impossible to live between Ireland and here, and I can't ask Steve to give up his work, he's doing what he loves most.'

'It is difficult for you.' She handed her a tissue. 'Don't cry, something will be done.'

'But what, Maria?'

'Now that you have come back to us your father he doesn't want to let you go again. For so many years you have been gone, and even myself I am very sorry that you go again. We love you.' Tears filled Maria's eyes.

'I know you do, and I love you too,' Amy kissed Maria. 'You are like my second mother, my only mother since Mom died.'

Maria snuffled. 'So it is the same for your father.'

'I hadn't thought of it like that. I love him but he doesn't really show how he feels. I don't think he's ever told me he loves me.' Suddenly, she felt lost and longed for Steve.

'He does love you chica, I know.'

'But I love Steve so much, why can't he just be happy for me?'

'It is sometimes that way, fathers don't want other men taking their daughters.'

'That's so old fashioned, Maria,' Amy had to smile through the tears. 'But I can't go back on my word, I've promised to marry Steve.'

'Then you must go with your heart, to Ireland. All I want is for you to be happy.' Maria held her close again.

She left for Ireland a couple of weeks later, and by then her father had already joined Doug in New York so there was no opportunity for fond goodbyes. They hadn't had any further discussion about her going, except a couple of brief telephone conversations. John seemed to have accepted her decision.

Chapter Forty-five

'Amy, you've been nominated for Best Actress, Doug's got Best Director, and Jack has Best Screenplay,' John shouted down the phone line. 'Can you believe it, honey?'

She was astonished and couldn't say anything at first as excitement spiralled through her.

'That's fantastic, Dad.'

'The film hasn't done well at box office, but this should make a difference.'

She could hear voices laughing and talking, and the sound of music in the background.

'We're celebrating. Listen.'

The noise of the crowd grew louder.

'You'll have to get over here for the big night. I want us to walk up the red carpet together, father and daughter, successful partnership, on the cusp of a wonderful career. I've been here before with your mother when we were nominated and she won. I'm telling you it's all going to happen again.'

She didn't know what to say. So happy to be back with Steve, she had forgotten about the Oscars in the excitement of making their wedding arrangements, and having been successful in getting a part in her first professional production.

'Come over immediately, we'll have to talk, make plans. It's going to be so big.'

'I can't come over just at the moment, I'm in rehearsal for a play, remember I told you, it's at the Project Arts Theatre and we're opening next week.'

'What?'

'And I'm getting married around the time of the Awards so that could be difficult too. What date is it?'

'Twenty-fourth March.'

'My wedding is on the twenty-third.'

'You'll have to be here on the night.'

She could hear his anger rising.

'I'd forgotten about the Oscars, I'm sorry.'

'Listen, just come for the ceremony, accept your Oscar. And you must wear something really fantastic, one of those designer creations,' he persuaded.

'But I want you to give me away at my wedding, so you'll have to be here, and Harry and Maria too. I've just sent out the invitations. It was to be a surprise.'

She hadn't mentioned it before now. Knowing she would be harangued from a distance and thought the surprise announcement might alter her father's thinking.

'Can't you change the date, put it back, Oscars don't happen every day, you can get married any time.'

'But it's all been arranged. The church, the hotel. It's not possible to cancel now.'

'And you're putting him before your own flesh and blood?'

'I love him, Dad,' she said softly. 'Can't you understand that?'

The line cut.

'He's furious, Steve, it seems the Academy Awards are the only thing that matters to him. I can't believe it.' She was in tears.

'Don't worry, love, he'll come around. The whole Oscar thing is just so important to him he can't see anything else, it's understandable.' He hugged her. 'Do you want to consider changing the date, we could check with the church and the hotel, see what the possibilities are?'

'You'd do that, for me?'

'Of course, my love, anything, you know that.'

'Thank you.' She kissed him softly.

'Do you want to get on to it then?'

'But what about the guests, some of them are coming quite a distance, Cindy from the States, Babs from Paris, and other people have made special arrangements at work, it's too much to expect everyone to change their bookings at this late stage.'

'I suppose it is a bit much,' Steve admitted. 'But nothing's impossible.'

'And anyway, why should we change, he's not prepared to even consider it, and he put down the phone on me, he didn't want to hear what I had to say.'

'He'll ring soon, just give him a bit of time.'

'I think you're on his side,' she said, shocked.

'You're the only one that matters to me, I want you to be happy, that's all.'

She phoned her Dad some time later that day, hoping that his anger would have dissipated, but all she got was the answering service. Then she tried the other line but that was busy. She was disappointed.

Within a few hours, the excitement of Oscar nomination hit the headlines, and the phone in the Lewis household began to ring.

'This is great for you. Such publicity for the opening of *Moonlight* next week, the company must be thrilled.' Steve was over the moon for Amy.

'I've been asked to go on the Late Late Show on Friday, and TV3, and various radio shows, it's amazing.' Amy was flustered.

'So there is a lot to be gained by Oscar recognition, it endorses your undoubted talent, my love, let's open the champagne.'

'Better talk to Dad and let him know what's happening over here.' Amy lifted the phone and pressed the key, praying that he would pick up. But as before, it went on to the answering service. She stared at Steve. 'Do you think he's doing that deliberately?'

'Hardly. There's probably a lot going on over there with the press as well as here.'

'I'll leave another message.'

But there was no response from her father. After a couple of days she phoned Doug. She hated doing that but had become worried by her father's silence. Maybe there was something wrong?

'I've been trying to contact Dad, but I can't, is he all right?'

'Yea, he's fine, don't worry.'

'But I can't get through to him.'

'It's hectic, the paparazzi are at the gate permanently, we can't get in or out. There's a great buzz.'

'It's the same here, I wanted to tell him about it, I'll be on television on Friday night, and on Saturday as well, and on radio too. It's amazing how the press have responded to the nomination, my play opens on Tuesday so it's going to be great publicity.'

'I'm really glad for you, but I'm sorry you can't make it for the ceremony.'

'So am I, but the date of my wedding is so close it would be just impossible, and everyone's staying at the hotel for the weekend so I just can't up and leave. Then on Monday we fly to Paris for our honeymoon.'

'I understand, Amy, it's a difficult one.'

'When I explained to Dad, he wasn't happy about it, but I guess I was hoping he'd have calmed down by now. Has he?'

'Sad to say no, he's taken it very badly.'

She said nothing for a moment, her heart thumping.

'Would you talk to him for me?' To ask Doug to intercede for her was something she could never have imagined herself doing, but he was the closest person to him so maybe there was a chance.

Over the next few days, in between rehearsals, she spent some time shopping for clothes, particularly for the Late Late. Finally, after walking the streets of Dublin with Rachel she decided on a simple black dress, and high-heeled black suede shoes. And for Saturday, a more casual outfit in blue.

'You look a million dollars,' Rachel admired the complete outfits when they arrived home. 'Now with the hair done, and the make-up, you'll look every bit the Oscar winner.'

'I can't believe this.' Amy stared at herself in the mirror.

'You should wear more gear like that, throw your jeans into the bin,' Rachel urged.

Rachel came to RTE with her while Steve hosted a party at home with family, friends and the cast of *Moonlight.*

'This is worse than being on stage,' Amy confided as they were waiting to be brought through by the production people.

'You'll be fine, don't worry, this is your big moment, make the most of it,' Rachel said, grinning widely. 'Wish I had a chance like this.'

'That big part is just waiting for you.'

'There's a few auditions coming up, so I'm praying.'

'You'll make it, don't worry.'

The researcher reappeared and took Amy to make-up, and then she rejoined Rachel in the Green Room.

'This is very nice,' Rachel raised her gin and tonic.

'How do I look?' whispered Amy.

'Do you want me to be truthful?' she giggled. 'You look gorgeous.'

The time crawled by. Amy was going on somewhere in the middle of the show, and although they were chatting with some of the other people who would also be on - an author, a politician, a singer - it seemed it would never be Amy's turn. But eventually, it came around and she was ushered through, and on to the set in a blaze of lights and a loud round of applause from the audience.

Pat Kenny came forward to meet her, his hand outstretched, and he kissed her on both cheeks before sitting her down. He was friendly, asking her about her life in LA, the films she had made when she was a child, and her Mom, Maxine, the Irish connection, and of course, her Dad. Then he brought the conversation around to the present and *Veil of Sand,* showing a clip of the film, and a link with Doug who spoke about receiving the nomination for Best Director. It was very emotional for Amy to see her Mom on the screen, and she had to try hard not to show her feelings.

'We tried to get your Dad to talk to us, but unfortunately he was unavailable. So, you're living permanently in Dublin to work in theatre?'

'Yea, it's what I love, so I'm hoping to make my career on the Irish scene.'

'And you're opening in *Moonlight* on Tuesday at the Project Arts Theatre?'

'Yes. It's a great play, and I'm really loving the part.'

'By an Irish playwright as well I believe.'

'And set in the States,' she added.

'I'll bet the tickets will be sold out for the run, but just in case that happens we have a few extra here. In fact, there's two tickets for everyone in the audience to *Moonlight.*' There was a loud cheer and burst of applause. 'So Amy, we all wish you every success in the play and also at the Academy Awards. Hope V*eil of Sand* wins all three of those Oscars, you deserve it.' They stood up and he kissed her again, amid another loud round of applause from the audience.

'You were great, I could see you on the monitor.' Rachel hugged her when she returned to the Green Room.

'Have a drink, Amy, and you too Rachel,' the researcher brought them over to the bar.

'I need it now, wow, that was some experience.' Amy accepted a gin and tonic, as did Rachel.

They stayed on until the end of the show, chatting with the rest of the people there. Amy was much more relaxed now, and eventually, a taxi whisked them home where they were greeted with wild enthusiasm by the crowd who were all pretty high at this stage.

'My love, you were wonderful.' Steve kissed her.

Everyone crowded around, more bottles of champagne were opened, corks popped, and the night went on until the early hours of the morning.

Moonlight opened on Tuesday to a great reception, and the reviewers really loved the production. The run was booked out, and Amy had already received approaches from directors who wanted her to audition for parts in other plays.

However, there was still a dark side to her life. She still hadn't managed to talk to her father. Sometimes, he answered the phone but put it down when he heard her voice. Sometimes Doug answered.

'Do you know if my Dad is coming to my wedding?' She came straight out with it one day.

'I don't think so, Amy, I'm sorry.'

She barely managed to continue to speak. Doug sounded so certain that he wouldn't be there.

'Did the invitations arrive?' she whispered after a moment.

'Yea, and thank you, I didn't reply yet as I wasn't sure if there was going to be a change of plan nearer the date.'

'Do you think there will be a change?'

'I don't know.'

She asked Maria the same thing.

'Can you come to my wedding?'

'No, I'm sorry, as Señor Parker is not going, then we cannot go, he has told us.'

'And Harry?'

'No, chica. Your father he is not happy these days.'

It seemed her Dad had cut her out of his life completely.

Chapter Forty-six

'And the Oscar goes - to Amy Parker!' Rachel handed Amy an imitation gold figurine.

'Champers,' Babs poured the fizzy liquid. 'To our Amy, congratulations,' they clinked glasses and danced around her.

'I haven't won it yet, girls,' she laughed.

'It's so cool,' Cindy squealed.

She smiled.

'It's the icing on the cake. What amazing timing. We'll have a fantastic celebration, Oscars and wedding days,' Babs was over the moon.

Rachel made last minute adjustments to Amy's white taffeta silk dress, repositioned the flowers in her hair, checked eye shadow and lipstick in a flurry of excitement.

Amy had persuaded herself she didn't mind that her Dad, Harry and Maria were not there. She had tried. Hard. Her father had chosen to be at the Oscars instead of being here with her. Suddenly, an intense sense of loss attacked and found a tiny chink in her armour.

'Hey, what's wrong?' Babs asked. 'You're looking worried all of a sudden.'

She shook her head.

'Nerves,' Rachel said.

'We're going to be late,' Cindy reminded.

'And who decided she was going to be early for once in her life?' Rachel put an arm around her.

‘What’s with the tears?’ Babs handed her a tissue. ‘You’re going to ruin your make-up and I’ve spent half the morning making you beautiful.’

‘You’re not going to change your mind at this stage, are you?’ Cindy demanded.

‘And we all dolled up to the nines,’ Rachel squeaked, repositioning the fall of her magenta silk.

They fussed around her.

‘Amy, this is the biggest day in your life, and the most gorgeous guy is waiting in the church for you at this very moment, surely you’re not going to disappoint him? If you don’t appear I’d say it’s very likely that he’ll come straight up here and refuse to take no for an answer. He’s a very determined man. Do you want that to happen?’ Babs said, grinning as she repositioned a strand of Amy’s dark hair. ‘Now you look perfect,’ she pronounced.

Amy managed a crooked smile.

‘Let’s go downstairs. Just give us five minutes to reach the church and then you and Nuala get into that car. We’ll be waiting for you. There are a couple of the neighbours across the road loving every minute of this. Have your last minute regrets after the ceremony, will you?’ Babs kissed her, and the three walked down the path to where the limousine waited, receiving a round of applause from the neighbours who had gathered outside.

‘You all right?’ Nuala asked gently, as she adjusted Amy’s veil. She smiled and kissed her. ‘This is the best day of your life and mine too, and thank you for it, and for asking me to give you away. It means so much to me.’

Nuala and Amy stood together at the back of the church, arm in arm. In those last heart-stopping moments Amy waited for the music to peal out and signal their walk to where Steve waited at the altar. As the first notes of Pachelbel’s Canon echoed through the church, she took a quick glance around but there was no-one else standing there.

She turned back and they began to walk up the aisle. Heads turned and there was a murmur of anticipation as they approached the altar rails of the church where Nuala moved to one side and Amy gave her hand to Steve.

In trust for life.

In sickness and in health.

Till death us do part.

She stood beside him. That tremor which had rocked her steadied and she stood on terra firma again, secure in his love. He took her hand and slid the gold band on to her finger. As she did the same, he smiled and kissed her. Now she knew that this was the happiest day of her life.

They were identified now.

A couple.

Partners.

Long after, it was the small individual things she remembered.

The heavy aroma of the white lilies on the altar.

The rainbow colours of a sunbeam which shone through the stained glass window.

The pinch of the new shoes.

The cry of a small child from the back of the church.

The smoothness of the gold ring on her finger.

They signed the register. The photographer's camera flashed. A friend of Steve's recorded those special moments. Then the triumphant march down the aisle. Steve handsome in his dark suit, Amy dreamy in her white silk. The guests all smiles and tears.

Outside they were surrounded, kissed and hugged.

'Congratulations.'

'Hope you'll be very happy.'

'Good luck.'

Carmel, Steve's mother, dressed in pale green with a wide-brimmed hat, threw her arms around Amy and held her close. Tears stood on her cheeks and trickled off the powdered double chin. His Dad was more reserved. A small slight man not given to outpourings of emotion. But tears filled Amy's eyes when she heard his gentle whisper as he kissed her on the cheek.

'You're our daughter now, part of our family.'

And she was. They closed around her protectively and took her to their hearts. Most important of all were Nuala, Cindy and the friends they had made that first year at college - Babs and Rachel - who had shared that small apartment at Trinity Hall. Their money. Their food. Their knickers if necessary. Whatever.

She didn't change her name. Just added Lewis to Parker.

She didn't win the Oscar for Best Actress.

Chapter Forty-seven

Amy and Steve set up home in their new house in Sandyford which had been designed by Steve on a beautiful site at the foot of the Dublin Mountains. Amy had used the money she received from the film to pay for a considerable amount of the cost, a mortgage covered the balance of over a million euro. Steve's business was doing really well, and they were comfortably off these days.

Amy's acting career continued to be successful. One role followed another in various theatres around the country. She didn't always play the lead, but she was working, and that was everything to Amy. *The Glass Menagerie* by Tennessee Williams was her favourite play and she toured with that on Broadway, very much regretting the fact that she couldn't go home while in the States. But her father had never made any contact with her, and although she phoned regularly and left messages for him on his voicemail, and with Doug, she heard nothing from him. When she became pregnant a year later, she hoped that he would relent, after all, she was carrying his first grandchild, but there was nothing from him.

But she managed to put the loss of her family to the back of her mind, loving every minute of her life with Steve. When the nurse placed the soft wet seven and a half pound bundle into her arms, a burst of emotion flared inside as she looked down at her daughter, and she was the happiest she had ever been.

'She's gorgeous,' Steve whispered, and kissed her.

Amy gently touched the scrunched up face of the tiny baby.

Steve wiped his eyes with the back of his hand.

'We'll take her now and tidy her up.' The nurse reached out, but Amy didn't want to let the baby go. Wanted to hold on, keep her close, loving her intensely. Both Steve and herself in a glow of wonder and delight that they had produced this beautiful child. After hours of holding back, pushing, holding back, pushing. Of trying not to cry out loud with pain so Steve wouldn't be too upset. He wasn't the best where pain was concerned. His face white with worry. Hands sweaty, gripping hers with almost too much ferocity. He wanted to help, but could do nothing. Only watch as the greatest event in their lives came slowly and painfully to conclusion.

Amy came home with her new daughter after a few days, feeling surprisingly well, despite the soreness of the stitches. The baby no longer a vague "it" inside her womb, but now a person in her own right formally registered Emma Maxine Parker Lewis, occupying her own individual position in the world. Their family cocoon stretched outward to include this new member and reformed into a new shape.

The arrival of Emma was the most wonderful event in their lives, but most especially for Nuala, her great grandmother. Photographs were sent across the Atlantic. Amy talked to Maria and Harry. Even Doug seemed delighted to know that Amy's first child had arrived. Cards and presents were delivered from them all, but nothing from her father.

'I've told John,' Doug mentioned.

'Is he there now?' Amy enquired, hoping, praying.

'No, at a pre-production meeting with the screenwriters.'

'Have you got a good script.'

'Yea, it's good, but we're looking for backers.'

'Shouldn't be difficult to get.'

'I don't know, money has become tight.'

'Have you been over to Clifden recently?'

'We're going in a couple of weeks.'

'Maybe you might call me when you arrive?' It was a hopeful cry.

'Yea, sure.'

'You've seen the photographs of Emma?'

'She's beautiful.'

'Make sure my Dad sees them, will you?' as she said the words, she realised the position in which she had put herself. To be asking Doug, begging almost, was something she didn't want to do. But surely her Dad would want to see his granddaughter. He would love her immediately she was certain of that. But it seemed he had no interest in meeting Emma. Deeply hurt, that was when Amy decided she would never make an attempt to talk to her father again. He would have to come to her.

Amy and Steve were like children themselves. Playing house. Unbelievably happy with baby Emma, their pride and joy. Amy wasn't working, having taken some time off to look after Emma and enjoy the growing of her child.

Now she was drawn to the garden. It needed a lot of work to keep it up but was so much better than the tiny patch of grass outside their first home - the ground floor apartment where they lived before they were married.

She loved gardening. Never aware that it was something in her genes. That it had been handed down to her. She just knew that she was happiest when she was pottering there, regardless of the weather.

Steve padded across the grass silently and put his arms around her. She screamed with fright.

'I love you.'

'Didn't expect you to be home so early.' She pulled off the gardening gloves she wore.

'I made a point of getting away, couldn't stop thinking about you.' He kissed her ear.

‘Hope you didn’t imagine me in this gear.’ She turned in his arms, brushing earth off her old red tee shirt and jeans.

‘No, imagined you without anything on at all,’ he laughed. ‘You and me, now, come inside.’ Softly, he pressed his lips on hers.

‘You’re mad.’

‘Emma’s sleeping.’ He glanced down at the baby who lay in her buggy in a shady spot.

‘She might wake up,’ she giggled.

‘We’ll bring her in.’ He pushed the buggy into the conservatory. Then he drew the blinds and put his arms around her again. Quickly pulled off her top and jeans, and stripped himself.

They lay together, bodies warm. The air in the conservatory was humid. He kissed her deeply. Slowly. There was no hurry now. No rush. Just that thrill which accompanied the slight risk of discovery when they made love like this. At unexpected moments. Downstairs. Upstairs.

‘What if someone comes around the side?’ Amy whispered.

‘The door is locked.’

The rhythm of their movements increased.

‘What if your parents arrive unexpectedly?’ The insidious thought swept through her. But Steve’s kisses brought her back to him, and there were no more what if’s and she was overtaken by his ability to bring her to the utmost heights of pleasure. The only sound their combined breathing. Little moans and cries, whispers, the slight creak of the couch. In the end it was quick. Urgent. Their bodies had taken over and demanded fulfilment.

‘I love you, Amy, love you.’ Steve kissed her again and again.

‘Love you too,’ she murmured from some drifting dreamlike place.

Then from the buggy came a gurgle, a tiny cry, and they both laughed.

‘Just in time,’ Steve said.

‘Back to work,’ she smiled at the baby’s face which was crinkled up on the brink of a loud demand for food.

‘I’ll feed her,’ Steve murmured, his head resting on her shoulder, eyes closed.

‘I’ll feed her,’ she whispered.

But neither moved. Reluctant to break apart and begin to operate again as two separate people.

‘We’ll go to bed early.’ He opened his eyes and smiled.

She tightened her arms around him.

‘Promise you’ll always love me?’ he asked, and kissed her softly.

‘Promise.’

PART FIVE

2010

Chapter Forty-eight

Sandyford, Dublin – evening.

'I'm sorry, Harry, but we can't make it,' Amy said. She talked to him regularly and was disappointed that she wouldn't see her brother this year. They had travelled to California for a couple of weeks each year with the express purpose of seeing Harry and Maria. He studied at the University of California and they had to work around his own activities. It was the only chance Amy had. Once a year. And while in the US she managed to see Maria as well, but could only meet on her one day off away from the house. There had been no contact with her father since before she had married Steve, and as far as he was concerned she was cut off from both Harry and Maria as well.

'What's happened?' Harry asked.

'The business isn't doing well, you know the property market has collapsed over here. Steve has had to let staff go.'

'How are you guys managing?'

'We'll be all right, it's just the extras that suffer. But if things improve you can be sure we'll take a trip over to see you.'

'How are Steve and Emma? I'll miss seeing all of you. Have you done any auditions?'

'I've a play coming up in a couple of weeks, but after that I don't know.'

'Maybe it'll run,' he suggested.

'I'm hoping.'

Harry had grown into a tall broad shouldered young man, a great footballer, who was going to join the Boston Red Sox the following year, and begin his career in professional football.

Amy's sadness that she hadn't seen her brother this year added to the bleakness of life in Ireland as they came to the end of 2010. In deep recession and indebted to the EU and IMF, the country was almost insolvent and everyone was affected. It seemed to make the loss of her family even more poignant. Steve's father had passed away in 2005, and in October 2009 Nuala had died. Amy still missed them both, but most especially Nuala.

She had gone without saying goodbye. That was the worst aspect of it for Amy. Not to be able to tell her that she loved her. To be with her during those last moments of her life. Was she in pain? Was she crying out for help and nobody came? How awful that must have been. Amy couldn't bear the thought of it.

When she didn't get a reply to her regular morning phone call to her grandmother, Amy asked a neighbour to check on her. But by the time she arrived, the ambulance men were already putting her on a stretcher. As calm and peaceful as she had ever seen her. With closed eyes and a slight smile on her lips.

The first time Amy went to Ringsend after Nuala died she expected to see her come through the door to meet them. But the hall remained empty, the door into the sitting room half open. Inviting. Steve held her hand as they walked through. Rays of late afternoon sunshine drifted across the room and particles of dust whirled within the brightness. Coloured book covers came to life as it touched them. Amy picked one up. It was a random choice. *Emma* by Jane Austen. She smiled and held it close to her cheek.

'Nuala's here, I can feel her.' She moved around the room, through the rays of sunshine, feeling the warmth on her body. Finally she sat in her grandmother's own special chair, sinking into the pile of cushions. She closed her eyes. It was as if Nuala's arms curled around her and held her close.

Images drifted through her mind. Snippets of the past. Scenes of days spent together. Glimmers of evenings by the fire. The flames leaping up the chimney. The heat. The glow. Chatting. Laughing. Just being together.

Nuala had left Amy everything she possessed. It was as if she knew it would help them by her going. Steve's business was in bad shape and they had invested their savings in bank shares, thinking they were safe, but now they were worth almost nothing as the banking crash had deepened.

'I don't want to sell Nuala's house,' Amy had said from the outset.

'Couldn't sell it now,' Steve had commented laconically.

'Maybe we could rent it.'

'We'd have to clear it out, give it a lick of paint.'

'It's not that bad,' she looked around.

'No, but when all the stuff is gone then we'll see how much of a face lift it needs. What will we do with all the books?'

She didn't reply. Just ran her hand over the neatly positioned spines. Titles in alphabetic order. Images of plots flashed through her mind. Heroines. Heroes. Love. Kisses. Happy endings.

'I don't know.' She didn't want to do anything with them. She wanted to leave them here. They were part of this place.

'Maybe we should give them to a hospital or somewhere like that. They would be appreciated,' Steve suggested.

'I feel guilty doing that.' She flicked through the pages of the Jane Austen book which she still held in her hand.

'We can't let the house with all the books still here. There's no room for a tenant.'

She nodded in agreement.

'We'll find somewhere.'

‘Maybe the place where she read her books. It would be nice to do that in her memory.’

The Day Centre was delighted to receive so many books, and had the space to store them also. On the morning they sent the bus around to take them, Amy felt as lonely as she had been when Nuala had first died. They were so important to both Nuala and her sister Bridget that the house looked bereft without them. But she knew that Nuala would have wanted them to go to the day centre, and that she was carrying out her wishes.

The diaries were a different matter. These she hugged to herself, and packed them up in boxes, each decade to its’ own, Nuala’s and Bridget’s. They made space in the attic and put most of them there. But Amy kept the diaries covering her own life close to her hand, and began to read through them slowly.

It helped her get over the shock of Nuala’s death. Some days she felt in control of her loss and could manage to cope. Other days while doing the most mundane things she would suddenly remember her and the loneliness would savagely tear through her and leave her quivering. It took her back to when she lost her mother. It must have been the same - a terrible loss for a small child. But that time was clouded. She felt she should have been able to remember more. Of visiting her Mom in hospital. Sitting by her bedside. Holding her hand. Bringing flowers. But after that wonderful day of her birthday, her Mom just wasn’t there any longer. She had disappeared out of her life.

Chapter Forty-nine

Amy stood in the wings of the darkened theatre. Breathed in that particular scent of grease paint and dust. Her heart thumped. It was always the same. Night after night as she waited for her entrance. The play was a contemporary American piece by a new author about drug users and dealers, a harsh look at life.

'Best of luck.' The director patted her on the shoulder.

She smiled but didn't turn her head. Counting down, five - four - three - two - one - and she was standing there in front of the audience, her eyes momentarily dazzled by the spotlights which illuminated the stage. The other actors responded. Their lines bringing her into their milieu. She was someone else now. Playing the part. It took her over. For ninety minutes she was a woman high on cocaine. As the climax unfolded, she played it for all she had. And when the lights went down after she said those last lines, and the audience burst into applause, she stood in line with her fellow actors and bowed. They ran off stage but the clapping continued and they took numerous curtain calls until finally the people rose in appreciation. They had a full house on Fridays and Saturdays but the rest of the week it was only half full, although whoever was there really enjoyed the show. It was not a financial success.

'We're going over to the Troc, are you coming?' The main lead actor asked, coming out of his dressing room carrying a holdall.

'Sorry, I can't make it, Steve's away, and my sitter only stays until twelve.'

'Come over for a while, have a quick drink?' someone else suggested.

'Hey, it's the last night, you should have organised things better.'

'She wouldn't stay later, unfortunately.'

'Not even a quick one?'

'Sorry.'

'It was great tonight.' Her opposite number hugged her.

'What's next for you?' she asked.

The shrug of the shoulders told her everything. It was the business. So uncertain. Your agent told you about a part. You auditioned. You didn't get the part. So you went on to other auditions in the hope that this time it would be different. Or you got the part. Over the moon if it was something you really wanted to do. You rearranged your life for six weeks or so, and hoped that the play might travel, or be brought back if it did well.

It was the career she loved. She wished that the run had continued for a little longer. It was a demanding part. It had taken her to another place, and now she felt lonely for that woman. Who was she? Amy wondered. Living on the edge. In the grip of a drug dealer. Forced to do his bidding. She thought about her. Tried to imagine how she managed to live such a life. And compared that life to her own. There were real people out there who lived like her. But Amy knew nothing of such things.

The recession deepened.

'We'll have to watch our budget,' Steve warned gently.

'How bad are things in the company?' Amy asked.

'The remaining staff have to take a thirty per cent cut just to keep them on board. I've explained how it is, and suggested they might look elsewhere for jobs.'

'How many contracts have you in the pipeline?'

'Just a couple, we've tendered for a few more but I've had no response as yet. There's very little out there, and I think some of the tenders will be on jobs which will never happen.'

'What about that one in Galway?'

'Nothing.' He shook his head.

'Does anyone owe you any money?'

'There's quite a bit outstanding, if we could get that in it would make a big difference but I don't hold out much hope.'

'Get on to them, insist that you must have something, even a partial payment,' she urged vehemently. 'Get post-dated cheques.'

'Most of them are in trouble, some are gone bust already. I'll have to write off a lot of the debt.'

She stared at him, horrified. Then put her arms around him and kissed him. 'Don't worry, honey. I'll call my agent and see if there's anything coming up. If I could go to a few auditions I'm sure to get a part in a production or maybe some voice-overs.'

'There's something else,' he said hesitantly as a shadow crossed his face.

'Don't look like that, there's nothing we can't fix,' she smiled. Refusing to let him see how worried she was herself.

'I haven't taken a salary for a few months, and the balance in the bank account has run very low. I just hope we can cover the mortgage. Only we have the rental from Nuala's house, we'd be bunched altogether.'

'Why didn't you tell me?'

'I didn't want to worry you.'

'But we're in this together, we share everything, you can't be shouldering all the burden. Promise me that you won't ever do that again.' She kissed him. 'I have some of the money I earned with the play, that will keep us going for a week or two.'

'I don't want to take your money, that's for yourself.'

'It's our money, and will be used for whatever we need. Let's sit down this evening and go through the household budget, see where we can tighten up. There's bound to be savings, bet you.'

Chapter Fifty

Amy's mood fluctuated. She had no control over it. Desperately concerned about their financial position she waited daily for a phone call from her agent. Prompted to contact him every couple of weeks just in case. But he assured her that if he heard of anything that would suit her he would immediately get in touch, but he didn't hold out much hope.

She sat up abruptly. Stared into the darkness. The end of a scream in her throat.

'What's wrong, love?' Steve put his arm around her.

'I don't know.' She pulled the duvet around herself, and lay down again.

'Was it a bad dream?' He cuddled her close.

'Must have been.'

'Can I get you anything, a drink maybe?'

She shook her head. She was still in the dream. But couldn't explain it to him. Often, they would laugh at their dreams in the morning. But this time it wasn't a dream in the usual sense. It seemed as if she existed in a parallel universe. Out there watching herself go through the motions. She was scared, and couldn't understand why.

Now there was no script to read and know instantly that she loved it. To focus and understand the plot. To delve deeper into the other characters in the cast and familiarize herself with their idiosyncrasies. To learn the lines. So that she could become the character she would play. Eventually able to throw away the script and take on the personality and let it take her over when she stepped on to the stage.

So she slept a lot. Sometimes even going back to bed during the day when Emma was at school. Some days she lost sight of her surroundings. Outside the house became a shadowy place of vague grey lines and spaces. Other days, those neutrals turned to colour. Pale blue green to strong aquamarine. Pink to rusty red. Lemon to orange.

Steve was her rock. She was unable to understand how he could deal with the problems of everyday living with such strength. When he left in the morning and she faced the day alone she thought he would never come home to her. The waiting was endless. It could be nine or ten o'clock at night before he left the office to drive home. She would embrace him as he came in the door, his exhaustion apparent as he put down the briefcase and lap top and wrapped his arms around her.

Sunday was the only day he stayed home, although he often had work to do. In the morning he would curl his body around hers. It felt right. The way it should be. Her limbs eased out, muscles soft. Their breathing evenly matched.

'Mummy?'

She sat up. Emma rushed in and scrambled awkwardly on top of them. Cuddled down. Amy wrapped her arms around her. Aware that she needed to keep her safe. Vaguely, she questioned the word. A fleeting memory of someone else saying that to her. A long time ago. And fear around it. What did it mean? Her head snapped up. She was terrified. The room whirled around her. There were tears in her eyes and she couldn't see clearly. For a few seconds she was still in that place, then such relief when she realised that it was only a dream. Her arms tightened around Emma. She tried to remember exactly what happened in the dream, but it eluded her. She put it out of her head. It was meaningless. She cuddled up to Steve and closed her eyes, hoping for another hour of sleep. But Emma kept moving about, and eventually she had to get up with her.

‘Why did you leave me in bed so long?’ Steve laughed when he appeared in the kitchen at about twelve o’clock.

‘Looked like you needed the rest.’ She flicked on the kettle. ‘Fancy a coffee?’

‘No, thanks, we’ve had our breakfast.’

He made himself a cup, and glanced through Saturday’s Irish Times.

‘Can I take Joey for a walk down to Lucy?’ Emma appeared with the dog in tow.

‘No,’ Amy spoke sharply, unintentionally.

‘Why?’ Emma’s face was crestfallen.

‘I’ll go with you later.’

‘But I want to go now,’ she appealed to Steve. ‘Dad, can I?’

‘Yea, sure, why not, it’s just up the road. But don’t be too long.’

‘I said no.’ Amy’s voice was hard.

Emma began to cry. She stroked Joey’s fur.

‘She’ll be all right, Amy, she’s just going down to her friend,’ Steve argued.

‘No, walk him in the garden.’

‘Mum?’ she wailed.

‘I’m getting lunch, I’ve no time for this.’

‘But I told Lucy I’d come.’

‘Later.’ Amy didn’t know what made her speak the way she did. But a sudden fear had thrown a shadow across her heart when Emma asked to go for a walk. And the word “safe” still echoed in her head.

‘What’s with you, Amy?’ Steve asked quietly when Emma had gone out into the garden with the dog. ‘Why so sharp?’

‘I don’t want her going out alone.’

‘You can’t keep her locked up. There will be lots of occasions when she has to go out on her own, anyway, she needs independence.’

She compressed her lips and began to prepare the vegetables for the lunch. A sense of vehemence in her movements. She didn't say any more to Steve, but after a few minutes, she ran out into the garden where Emma sat on the swing chair pushing herself slowly back and forward.

'I'm sorry, my love, are you still upset?' Amy sat down beside her.

She shook her head.

'Good, now I promise I'll take you out later, just the two of us. Sweetheart, have you a kiss for me?' she asked, smiling.

Emma kissed her.

'We're letting this thing get to us,' Steve said later that night.

'What thing?' Amy's query was abrupt.

'Money.'

'We're not the only people with problems,' she snapped. Aware that she didn't even want to talk about it. Money didn't matter, not when she had lost Nuala, and that on top of her Dad and Harry too. In all the years there was still no contact from John. She wouldn't be able to see Harry this year and he was a grown man now, at twenty-four. She longed to put her arms around them both and hug them close.

'But we're not coping. You're not in good form. Today particularly. And I don't want that. The only thing I want is to be able to provide for you and Emma, and make you happy - I can't even do that.' He was downcast.

'It's not all about the money.'

'I know that, but it's a very important part of life, and we can't do the things we want without it.'

'For me, there's more going on.'

'I know, you're still missing Nuala, and this situation only makes it all the more difficult for you. Would you like to take a trip back home, see Maria and Harry? We could stretch that far.'

'We can't afford it.'

'Maybe if you turned up unexpectedly your father might react differently, it's been a long time.' He moved closer to her on the couch.

She shook her head. 'He has made absolutely no effort to see us over all these years. Did he even lift the phone when Emma was born? Or send a card? No he didn't. And you know how many messages I've left for him, I never gave up.' There were tears in her eyes.

'I'm always with you, remember that, my love.' He hugged her.

'Maybe I should give in but I know I'm stubborn, as stubborn as he is,' she admitted.

'Don't I know it, there's a pair of you in it,' he said, laughing. 'But if you change your mind we'll manage it somehow, I promise.'

'You've enough on your plate.'

'It doesn't matter. What's going on with you is more important. I can't have my darling girl all upset. Just remember that I love you most of all in the world, and Emma too, so always tell me what's going on in your head, will you?'

Chapter Fifty-one

Now in their early seventies, John and Doug had become more irascible. The film John hoped to produce never became a reality. No-one was prepared to back their projects financially, although they still received scripts from hopeful writers. They continued to live together mostly in Malibu, two bachelors, and the beautiful girls lost interest. Still invited to various functions, cocktail parties and the like, now they were usually to be found at the bar with other old soldiers like themselves, reminiscing on the glories of the great Hollywood they had helped create. John had repaid Doug the money he owed him from the profits of *Veil of Sand*, and now had enough to live a comfortable life, but he and Harry continued to share a home with Doug. Neither of the men wanted to live alone at this stage of their lives. They played some golf, fished, and practised yoga which kept them extremely fit, and they still spent their summers in Clifden.

John sat and stared out the window at the sea which crashed up on the rocks. Today, he was thinking about the script which he had just finished reading. It was good. A dramatic thriller. And he could see Amy in the female lead role. He jotted some notes in the margin. Develop this scene. Delete this character. Spice up the dialogue.

Doug came into the room. 'Fancy a game of golf?'

'No, I'm going through this script. It's perfect for Amy. A girl of twenty. Innocent. Caught up in a web of intrigue. Want to read it?'

'John, you're wasting your time.' He sat down tiredly.

'What do you mean?'

'She's never going to play such a part, and anyway she's no longer twenty.'

'Maybe twenty-one, makes no difference. She has that look. The ingenue. She was wonderful in *Veil of Sand*. I'll have another look at it later. It's got everything.'

'John, you've looked at that film too many times. Just let it go. You're never going to produce anything again. There's no money out there. I've lost millions in my investments. OK, we've enough to live on. But going through all those scripts is a waste of time.'

'But writers send them to me.'

'They're just crap, they'll never go anywhere.'

'You don't realise how much people look up to me. I'm a successful producer. My films have received Oscars, the highest accolade. I'm going to do it again. And Amy will be my star.'

'For God's sakes, you're living in a dream world. That girl has her own life. And she's happy. She's never going back to the film business. I know. I've talked to her.'

'When?' John barked.

'Just last week.'

'What did she say about me?'

'She asked for you, and said to give you her love. I've told you that time after time. But you just want to have her on your terms only. One of these days you'll realise what you've lost. Not a film icon, but a daughter. Your family.'

'How can you say that? What do you know?' He turned on his friend furiously.

'It's the truth of it.'

'It isn't. She let me down. She promised, but went back on her word.'

'She agreed to do one film and that's what she did. She's a really good person, your daughter. You don't deserve her. And you didn't deserve her mother either.'

'How dare you?' John roared.

'I dare because I've been waiting a long time to say it to you.' Doug stood up and walked towards the door.

John fumed, his face contorted.

Just before Doug opened the door, he turned back. 'I saw how you treated Maxine. I know there were a lot of bruises that no-one could see. I've often wondered exactly how she died, and how much you had to do with that.'

John picked up a heavy paperweight from the table and flung it at him. It hit the wall and tumbled down on a mahogany side table, knocking over a small china figurine of a child which splintered into pieces.

Doug had already left the room.

John went upstairs. He was still angry. He stood outside Doug's door. He wanted to kill him for saying such a thing. But then he wondered how much he really knew? He decided to wait until he came down and tackle him then. He poured a whiskey and sipped it. Then inserted the DVD of *Veil of Sand* into the player. He had looked at it so many times he knew every line off by heart. Every move. Every shot. Every cut.

He heard footsteps on the stairs, stood up, and turned down the volume of the television. He went into the hall, and saw Doug standing at the door, his suitcase outside.

'I'm going a day early, I think we need a bit of breathing space. I'll be back in a few weeks,' Doug laughed wryly.

'Before you go, I want an explanation for those inferences you made,' John demanded.

'It's what I think, John, but don't worry I'm not going to broadcast my suspicions to the world. There's my taxi.'

He went out. The driver climbed out and put the suitcases in the car.

'See you,' Doug said, and sat into the car.

John turned back into the hall. The heavy door closed behind him. But whatever way he stepped, he lost his balance and fell.

He tried to get up but couldn't put any weight on his leg which was twisted underneath him.

'Doug,' he called out weakly. 'Help me?'

Chapter Fifty-two

The call came through a few days later. It was Brid.

'Amy, I thought I'd better let you know that your father has broken his leg.'

'Oh my God, how is he?' Amy was immediately concerned.

'He has had a plaster fitted, but he isn't feeling well.'

'Is Doug there?'

'No, he's gone back to the States. Your father is all alone except for when myself or Sean call over. I know you haven't been here in a long time, but maybe you might call down to see him, that would do him good.

'Yea, sure, I will. I'll phone him. Although you know he has never returned any of my calls over the years.'

'I understand. Maybe this is an opportunity for you and he to make up. We're doing as much as we can, but you know how busy we are here on our own farm.'

'Thanks for that, Brid, I really appreciate it.'

Amy held the phone tight in her hand. She punched in her father's number immediately. Not sure at all what his response would be. The phone was picked up. She could hear rough breathing at the other end of the line. 'Dad?'

There was a grunt.

'Is that you, Dad?'

'Yea.'

'How are you? Brid told me that you've broken your leg. Are you in much pain?' she asked. All the time afraid that he would put down the phone as he usually did. And at the same time amazed that he didn't.

'Hellish.'

'I'm sorry, how did it happen?' She asked gently.

'I slipped.'

'That's terrible.'

'Tell me about it.'

'Is Doug coming back soon?'

'Don't know, don't care.'

She was silent then, wondering what had happened.

'We might come to see you at the weekend?'

'Yea, if you want.'

'Great, I look forward to that.'

Another grunt.

'I'll let you know the time later in the week.'

'Don't worry, I'm not going anywhere.'

They drove down on the following Saturday, all three of them. Amy was nervous. It was over ten years since she had seen her father and she didn't know how he would react to meeting her again. She had changed, that was obvious. She was thirty-four now, but still the same weight. She wore her hair differently, a straight pageboy style to her shoulders and wondered how changed he would find her.

'Looking forward to seeing your Dad?' Steve grinned at her.

She nodded.

'It's about time, we should never have let it happen, and he's missed all those years with Emma.'

Going back to Clifden was emotional. It had always been that way for Amy, and driving up the wide avenue which led to the house was something which she had imagined many times. Now she was unable to believe that she was going to see her father again after all this time.

Steve drew up outside the front door, and they climbed out.

'Brid said she'd leave the back door open.' They walked around, and knocked. There was no response.

'Go on in, your Dad probably can't hear.'

They went through into the kitchen. From there into the back hall which led to the living room. He was sitting in the window, and looked around when he heard them.

'Hi Dad.' She went across the room and kissed his cheek. 'How are you feeling?' She wanted to throw her arms around him but held herself back, unsure how he would react.

'Pretty awful.'

'Mr. Parker.' Steve shook his hand. 'Good to see you. This is Emma, your granddaughter.' He brought her forward by the hand but she was shy and hung back.

'Emma?' He peered at her from under bushy brows, totally white now, as was his hair, what he had left of it.

'Say hello to your granddad,' Amy encouraged.

She smiled shyly.

'How old are you?' he asked gruffly

'Seven,' she whispered.

'Do you like candy?'

She nodded.

'There's a box over there, I asked Brid to buy them.'

Emma picked up the box of sweets.

'Would you like one?' John asked.

She nodded.

'Open it then.'

Emma looked at Amy and then quickly opened the box. She handed it to John who refused, and then to Amy and Steve.

Amy was shocked by the appearance of her father. He had aged greatly, and she was very worried about his condition. She had brought food, although Brid had left some cold meats and salad in the fridge, but Amy felt the lasagne she had made was much more nourishing for her father. After they had finished lunch, her father took a nap and they went down to the beach.

‘I’m very worried about him. Brid is not there all the time, and anything could happen to him.’

‘Why don’t we bring him back up with us, then you could look after him yourself,’ Steve suggested.

‘Would you mind?’

‘Of course not, if it makes you happy then I’m happy. Why not ask him when we go back in.’

‘But he would be an extra burden on the budget, and I don’t want him to know about our financial situation.’

‘One person won’t make any difference, we still have the same basic costs. Don’t you worry, my love.’

Chapter Fifty-three

Steve came in the back door, threw his briefcase down, and sat in the conservatory. He lay his head back on the cushions and closed his eyes. The house was quiet. He didn't know where anyone was, and didn't want to know. Not just yet. He needed some time to himself. After a short while he got up and went into the dining room, took a bottle of whiskey from the sideboard and poured a good measure into a glass. He swallowed. The liquid burned but it felt good. He needed that. He didn't drink much whiskey, one was usually enough, but then he reconsidered and poured another.

John had been with them a couple of weeks now. Steve knew that Amy was happier now than she had been in a long time, and having her father around meant everything to her. While they didn't talk about the business by choice, for Steve that had become difficult. He needed to talk to Amy, but was reluctant to reintroduce the negativity of the future as she seemed so well. There was very little opportunity to talk as John was always there, and as the time passed Steve became more and more irritated with the situation.

Amy and Emma arrived back in a flurry.

'We had to take Joey to the vet, his limp became even more pronounced today so he gave him an injection, and he may have to have another,' Amy explained as she put the shopping bags on the counter. They shopped every day now instead of doing a large shop once a week. It seemed to stretch out the money.

'Dinner won't be long, honey. Did you have a look in on Dad?' She kissed him. 'It's great to see you home so early.'

'He's probably asleep,' Steve said. 'I'll go into the study, I have some work to do,' he said, knowing that once John had had his rest he would have to listen to him go on and on about the film business. It was all he talked about. His plans for the future. The films he was hoping to produce. The wonderful scripts he had received, one in particular he was sure would be an Oscar winner.

Steve's patience was just strained too far these days.

He had had a meeting with his accountant today and according to him, the company was insolvent.

'It's not good. I can't see any way out. It's better to cut your losses at this point. This business has no value and no-one is going to be interested in taking it over. On a day to day basis, it's not profitable, and the bank won't increase the overdraft,' Larry explained.

Steve stared at the figures in front of him. He wanted to argue with Larry. This business has value. I created it. I've put my heart and my soul into it. Don't tell me it has no value. He swallowed the angry tirade.

'I feel bad about the staff, they've been marvellous, supporting me, I think they'd work for nothing if they thought it would get us through,' he said slowly.

'There's no point in that. They will have to be made redundant, and at least they'll get the statutory in due course. Mind you, it is taking a long time, at least six months or even more, but they will probably get the dole in the meantime to keep them going.'

'What if we used the house as collateral for a loan?' Steve asked.

'Are you crazy, Steve? You have a substantial mortgage, and with the reduction in value you're probably in negative equity, no bank is going to give you money at the moment.'

'Just grabbing at straws.'

'This isn't the time for that. We'll have to call a creditors meeting and the liquidator will come on board. Make the decision today. I can't allow you to continue anyway.'

'I'll have to get a job,' Steve smiled ruefully.

'What other talents have you besides being a good architect?' Larry laughed.

'None.'

'If you try hard you'll find something, or you might go into another field. Or operate as a sole trader. Employ people as you need them. With your background there have to be many of your old clients out there who will want to deal with you again. Maybe even use some of your staff.'

'Yea, I could do that.' He suddenly felt a little brighter.

'But I advise you to tell the staff as soon as possible. You have to give some of them quite a bit of notice so they will have to be paid. When do you expect payment on the last couple of jobs?'

'I've been promised this week, but I'll call again, try and push them. I don't want them to get the idea that they can rescind because of the situation.'

'Call a meeting of the staff tomorrow. Do it,' Larry advised.

Chapter fifty-four

To Amy's surprise, Doug flew into Dublin unexpectedly, arriving at their door within an hour of his phone call.

'Sorry, I haven't been able to get here sooner, how is he?' he smiled, with that old friendly grin.

She didn't know what to say. It was a long time since she had seen him, although they had talked on the phone. But in close proximity, in her own home, her sanctuary, she still felt exposed. Dark shadows danced around her. That old discomfort rushed back and she wanted him to leave. To turn around and go back the way he had come.

But she welcomed him in and then ushered him through the hall. 'Dad's feeling much better, and the cast should be off next week.'

'I'm glad to hear it, we had a few words before I left and I felt guilty I wasn't there when the accident happened.' He put down his bag.

'Don't worry, I guess he's forgotten about it by now.'

She wasn't sure what he was talking about, her father had said nothing.

He shook his head. 'It's not often we have a row.'

'Dad, Doug's here,' she brought him into the conservatory where her father sat in a comfortable chair, his leg resting on a stool.

'Sorry you're in such a state, John,' Doug sat beside him.

'Sure you are.' There was heavy sarcasm in his voice. But he grinned as Doug shook his hand.

'I lost the head that last time, don't know what got into me, sorry about that,' Doug apologised.

'It's happened before, and we've got over it, guess I shouldn't have flung that lump of glass at you, could have done you an injury,' John laughed. 'Let's have a drink. Get the bottle of whiskey out, Amy.'

'Yea, sure,' she went into the kitchen and checked how much whiskey was in the bottle, glad she had still got enough. She took the glasses from the press and went back inside.

'That script I received recently is very good and would suit you, Amy. Maybe you might consider doing another film with us?' her father asked. 'We've been looking for something to get our teeth into, haven't we, Doug?' John looked at her expectantly.

'You know I'm not interested in film,' she said, trying hard not to sound ungrateful. But she had to stop this now. Once she gave her father the impression that she might consider his offer, she knew there would be no going back. She poured the whiskey, and handed each of them a glass. She took nothing herself.

'No, but you should think about it, you're not exactly busy at the moment.' His eyes met hers. 'The phone hasn't been ringing.'

'No, I guess there isn't much happening at the moment, a lot of actors are out of work.' She felt under pressure.

'Well, this is the ideal opportunity for you, don't you agree, Doug?'

'It could be,' Doug agreed.

'Will you have a look at the script?'

'Yea, sure,' he was hesitant.

'I have it on my computer.'

'Email it to me.'

'Now, the first step is to find backers. Approach a few people. What are your plans?' John asked.

‘I’ll have to get back to LA later this week, haven’t finished up with my legal people yet.’

‘Get on to it then. I’ve been thinking if we use Arriflex SR 416’s and Canon 7d cameras like they used on *Black Swan* then we can reduce the production costs by a huge amount and that will make it easier to pull in the backers,’ John said.

‘I’ll do some research into that,’ Doug said.

‘Is there any point if I’m not going to be involved?’ Amy asked.

‘This is going to be the most successful movie we’ve ever produced,’ John said, grinning.

Chapter Fifty-five

Emma cuddled close to her grandfather and listened wide-eyed to the re-telling of that old story - *Goldilocks and the Three Bears*. She was completely obsessed with him now. Once he had come home with them to Sandyford, she had warmed immediately. Holding his hand. Sitting close to him. Her first words in the morning and her last words at night were about her Grandad.

'Maybe Grandad's tired, Emma?' Amy suggested. 'And it is getting late.'

'No, Grandad promised to tell me the one about the green dragon.'

'Is that OK with you, Dad?' Amy asked.

'Yea, sure thing.' John opened the book again.

Amy was trying hard to make her Dad's visit enjoyable. They were getting on well these days, and there was no mention of why they had become estranged for so many years. He didn't apologise although she did feel that he could have at least made some expression of regret. But she said nothing, deciding to put the past behind her, and make the most of their life now. And he made no further mention of her starring in the film he wanted to produce.

Amy and Steve's financial problems were still there, but they didn't talk about money any longer. Small things had to go. Amy didn't get her hair done any longer. Her regular beauty treatments didn't happen either. Her nights out with Babs and Rachel became quick chats over a cup of coffee. At home they no longer drank wine with their meal. The drinks cupboard wasn't replenished except for a bottle of whiskey for John, who liked a couple of glasses each evening. They planned no holidays. Those occasional weekends in a hotel down the country which they had enjoyed was a luxury they couldn't afford now. The three weeks, or even a month, spent in the south of France was out of the question, as was their skiing trip in Austria each New Year. Amy spent time reading through cookery books looking for tasty dishes which could be made with cheaper cuts of meat. They were managing.

She grew closer to her father. Getting to know the man again in her own home was like meeting him for the first time. She cherished those quiet moments when they were alone during the day or evening. To talk. To look him in the eyes. To put her arm round his shoulders. To show him that she loved him - no matter what. She longed to work her way back through the years with him. To put a shape on her life with him. Slot events into their natural perspective. But the swings and roundabouts of conversation revealed nothing beyond today.

But John was a man of many facets. Warm and communicative at one moment, closed and cold the next, like an animal in the forest used camouflage. Now that he was well again, each night, after the house had settled, he would slip out of bed. Sitting on the floor he would complete a series of yoga exercises. Sitting in the lotus position. Deep breathing. His muscles flexed without an ounce of excess fat. Sometimes, it was two or three in the morning when he finally lay on his bed to sleep. He didn't need very much. When he awoke again at about five-thirty, he began the exercises all over again.

He played a tight game.

Amy didn't even suspect the depth of the man.

'What happened to Mom? How did she die?' she asked him one morning when they were alone. The words which had been hovering so close just burst out without any warning. Like they had lost patience with her reticence.

'She had an accident. You were too young to know what was going on,' John said, unemotionally. Like a newsreader announcing the factual details of the events of the day.

'I can't really remember that.' She continued to press Steve's white shirt on the ironing board. The point of the iron smoothing out the creases on the shoulder meticulously.

'It was a long time ago.'

'I was eight,' she whispered.

'About that.'

'Twenty-seventh of May, my birthday.' She smoothed the cuffs. 'Mom baked my birthday cake. Where is she buried?'

'Why do you have to dwell so much on the past?' The sharp query was accompanied by an irritable frown, the ridges on his forehead deepening.

She stared down at her hand which gripped the iron, knuckles white through translucent skin. It was as if she looked at someone else's hand. Suddenly, she didn't know what she was doing, or saying, confused.

'I've been trying to get away from it but it has always bitten at my heels, all the time, never lets me alone.' John's face flushed red as he spat out the words. 'Even Doug quizzed me, can you imagine?' Almost tasting his vehemence, she could feel her insides melt as courage deserted her. Maybe she was hurting him by insisting on knowing. But his power to demolish her confidence still held strong. He could reduce her to a quivering mass by one look. And what did he mean about Doug?

'What's that?' he asked, wrinkling his nose.

She looked down again. Raised the iron to reveal a dark brown imprint on the cuff, and breathed in the unpleasant acrid smell of burnt fabric.

Chapter Fifty-six

'Steve, have you already had a drink?' Amy asked, laughing, after she had kissed him.

'Just a quick one on the way home,' he smiled.

'Now, come on, no need to hit the bottle, things aren't that bad.'

'They are.'

She stared at him.

'I'll tell you later.'

'Tell me now.'

'When we're alone.'

'Sounds serious.'

He put his arm around her waist. Leaned into her and kissed her hair. 'Mmm, you smell so good.'

'Shampoo.'

'It's more than that, it's you.' He closed his eyes. 'Let's go to bed early.'

She smiled.

'I'm sorry, but we've come to the end. The company is finished.' Steve's eyes were tired.

'We'll manage, don't worry.' She kissed him, and he held on to her for a moment.

'I don't know how. We've almost run out of money, and there's the mortgage to be covered this month.'

'We will manage. I'll look for a job. Any job,' she said fiercely.

'Thanks, love. But I'll be the one looking for a job. Every day. I'll tramp those streets.'

'What will we live on?' she whispered the words in both their minds.

'My mother has said she'll lend us some money.'

'I could ask my father?'

'No.'

She looked at him. Puzzled at his attitude.

'I couldn't bear to tell him.'

'But he'll guess.'

'He'll be going home soon, he doesn't have to know.'

She was silenced.

'We missed our weekend away last year, let's plan something soon,' Rachel suggested when they met for coffee the following week.

'I'm game, where will we go,' Babs asked. Working her way through a large double decker sandwich.

'How about pampering ourselves. We'll go to one of those health farms, not a really harsh regime, but one of the more luxurious. What do you think?'

'Great idea, might even shed a few pounds,' Babs grinned, pointing at her stomach.

'I'll do a bit of research, a couple of girls in work have been to a place in Carlow, I'll find out,' Rachel promised.

'It'll do us the power of good to get away, we won't know ourselves,' Babs grinned.

'We'll be new women,' Rachel laughed, enthusiastic.

'Hey, what do you think, Amy, not a squeak out of you.'

'I don't know whether I can make it or not.'

'Why? Is Steve tied up, or is it your father?'

'My Dad needs me to be there.' She chose that excuse.

'But you can't shut down your life, which is the way it is at the moment,' Babs was always the most outspoken of the two.

'I haven't seen my Dad for such a long time, I want to spend as much time with him as I can.'

'But it's only a couple of days, one night,' Rachel exclaimed.

'There is something else - our business is gone, we're broke. I can't afford to go.'

They stared at her, eyes wide, shocked.

'You should have told us,' Babs said.

'It only happened a couple of weeks ago, and Steve's mother is helping. But we have to watch the budget. Can't splash out on weekends.'

They were both astounded.

'What can we do?' Rachel spoke after a moment.

'Girls, we're going to be fine. We have to find work, and as there are so few auditions at the moment, that might mean a part-time job at the supermarket for me,' she smiled ruefully.

'Let us help,' Rachel offered. 'Just a temporary loan, you can pay it back whenever.'

'There's no need, but thanks a bunch, it's so good of you.'

'Let's have a drink, something to keep us going,' Babs suggested, grinning. 'We won't let this beat us, we're all in it together.'

'And we're heading down to Carlow for that weekend. It's on us.'

'No, I couldn't, it's too much. I can't go,' she protested. 'To leave Steve on his own would be too tough on him, but thanks girls, I really appreciate your generosity.'

Meeting the girls cheered Amy up. They gave her courage, and she tried to pass it on to Steve.

'I wish we could get away for a weekend ourselves, I'd give anything to have you to myself for a couple of days, or even a day, or a few hours even, let's do it, Amy, we'll splurge on our last few bob,' his brown eyes smiled into hers.

'What last few bob? There isn't enough money.'

‘God, when are things going to get back to normal? Where has our life gone? I spend my days at the office reading papers and signing forms. And next week the place goes back to the landlord and then I’ll have nowhere to go.’ He leaned his head on his arms.

She ran her hand through his hair. ‘Honey, don’t worry so, things will get better. And remember we have each other and Emma, and we’re all well. We have to be positive.’

‘But that’s the problem, everything’s so crowded around here I can’t get you to myself.’ He wound his arms around her.

‘Don’t love, Dad might come in.’ She glanced towards the half-open door which led into the living room.

‘Come to bed.’ He stood up and pulled her close.

‘I can’t yet, not until Dad has had his supper.’ She wriggled out of his grasp.

‘God, this feels like I’m a teenager trying to snog on the couch with my parents in the next room,’ he groaned. He went into the kitchen where the bottle of whiskey stood. ‘If he can have it, then so can I.’

‘Don’t love, you’ll have to leave some,’ she warned.

‘Why?’

‘You know Dad enjoys his drink at night.’

‘So do I, and I’m paying for it. Or my mother is.’

‘Steve, please don’t.’

‘Don’t?’ He lifted the bottle, and took a swallow.

She tried to take it from him, but he was able to avoid her hands, and held the bottle higher than she could reach.

‘I’m going to bed, are you coming?’ he took another gulp and went into the hall.

She put on the kettle. Buttered slices of bread, and placed home cooked ham, topped by mayonnaise, between them. She made a mug of coffee, added a spoonful of sugar, and took it in to her father.

'Thank you, Amy, that looks tasty.' He tried the sandwich, and nodded. 'Are you having something?'

'No, I've just had a quick cup of tea, I'll be heading to bed soon.' She left him there, wondering would he insist on his nightcap. She tidied up the kitchen, and went back in after a while. 'Ready for bed?'

'Just waiting for my usual,' he said.

She stood looking at him. Knowing exactly what he was getting at, but trying to be deliberately vague.

He grinned. 'My mouth's dry.'

She nodded, and went to check the sideboard. 'I'm sorry, there's no whiskey left. I think I threw out the bottle.'

'What? It was at least half full last night.'

She waved her hands in the air helplessly. 'Maybe I didn't realise there was some in it.'

'Surely you have another bottle?'

'Don't think so.'

'Have a look around.'

'Steve had a friend in earlier, they may have finished it.'

'Didn't see any friend. Anyway, Steve should have remembered I like my whiskey.'

'It's a bit awkward if the friend likes a drink as well,' she smiled at him. 'I'll buy another tomorrow.'

'Why can't you pick up a case at a time, this business of shopping for one at a time is such a pain.'

'We don't like to buy too much.'

'I want a case bought tomorrow so that I can keep an eye on it. And I'll store it in my room. I'm not used to living like this. And I never want this to happen again,' he pushed himself up, and went to his room, grumbling all the time.

'Thanks for that,' she said to Steve, who lay on the bed in their room, half undressed.

'What?' Steve pushed himself up.

'Taking the whiskey.'

'It's mine.' He kept the bottle close to him. It had very little left in it.

'You put me in a very awkward position with Dad.'

He didn't answer, just took another gulp and lay back on the pillows. 'Come to bed.'

She went into the en suite and showered. She was angry with him, and it was a long time before she turned off the light and returned to the bedroom. But by then Steve was fast asleep. The bottle on its side, the last of the liquid dribbling out of it on to the white duvet. The room stank. She pulled the sheets and duvet off the bed, sliding Steve on to the floor, something he didn't even seem to notice. She changed the bed. Threw a spare duvet on top of him and climbed into bed herself.

Steve snored loudly, and after a while, really frustrated, she grabbed his arm and tried to wake him. She succeeded after a few minutes and in a semi stupor he clambered back into bed, to immediately collapse into a deep sleep again. She lay back but her mind refused to be calm. Caught between Steve and her Dad, an unenviable place.

Chapter Fifty-seven

'Steve's late again,' John said in a flat accusing voice.

'He's busy,' Amy flew to his defence immediately.

'He expects you to keep his dinner, never knowing when he's going to turn up.'

'It's only a casserole.'

'How do you know what he's doing?' He sniffed. The question hung between them. Unanswered for a few seconds while she hunted for a reply which would satisfy him.

'He works hard,' she said. John hadn't yet been told of the liquidation of the company.

'How many nights a week?'

'A couple, I suppose.'

'Two last week, three the previous,' he announced with obvious pleasure.

'It's the time of year.'

She went into the kitchen and said no more. A mixture of emotions inside her. Annoyance with her father for suggesting that Steve was doing something he shouldn't, and worry that maybe there was some truth in what he said.

'Amy?' Her father called.

She went back to him.

'Come here.' He put out his hand. Open-palmed. And took hers. His soft skin warm to touch. 'I'm sorry for griping about Steve, I shouldn't have, it's none of my business,' he smiled.

'It's OK.' She sat down on the broad arm of his chair.

'It's just I hate to see you so much alone. It's not good. Steve should be here with you every evening and at the weekends, you need him.'

'It's a bit tough, but I have to put up with it, this is a recession you know.'

'That's not enough. I want my girl to have the very best in life. I can give you so much more than you have here. More than Steve could ever give you in a month of Sundays. The way you grew up is very different to the way you live now. Remember home in Beverly Hills. There's no comparison.'

'I love my life here. It's mine.' She didn't want him to denigrate Steve and what they had. Maybe he couldn't understand such love between a man and a woman. Or their love for an only daughter who was the light of their lives.

'You won't always feel like that, one of these days you'll see through it.'

Amy went upstairs, and looked in on Emma who slept soundly. She undressed in the bedroom and pulled back the curtain to look outside. No sign of Steve yet. She searched for headlights turning into the drive, but the road was dark except for the faint pools of light splaying down from the two street lamps in the short cul de sac. She glanced at the bedside clock. The green glow of the digital read-out told her it was just before ten. She tried to be understanding, aware that there was still a lot of files and equipment to be cleared out of Steve's office before the deadline to give back the keys. She decided to phone, and punched in the numbers of his mobile. He answered and she relaxed.

'Just want to finish off some paperwork, I'll be home soon. I did tell you I'd be late, didn't I?' He sounded tired.

'This morning we weren't exactly on the same wavelength - you were under the weather.'

'I'm sorry love, I can't recall much of last night.'

'Come back as soon as you can,' she urged. All she wanted was him home.

She sprinkled drops of lavender essence into the bath water and slipped in. It was almost too hot, but bearable, and she needed the heat to penetrate through her body, to soften the muscles and sinews, and ease the tension away. She breathed in the scented steam. Lay back on the cushion and closed her eyes, swirling the water with her hands. The languid movement of the mini waves caressed her body, and she drifted into a gentle almost doze. But she still listened for sounds which would tell her Steve was home. As time passed and the water cooled, her stomach tightened up. Uncertainty attacked her delicately reconstructed confidence.

She massaged her body with the soap, aware that she was still thinner than she liked to be, her bones too noticeable. Shoulder. Ribcage. Hips. She climbed out of the bath, and dried herself. Then she slipped into a robe and went into the bedroom.

'Where are you, Steve?' she asked out loud. Are you still working, Steve? Head bent over a report. Running down the lines of text with a pencil. Making notes in the margin. Underlining the more important sections for detailed perusal later. Sitting at the computer. Tapping in information. Tie loosened. Shirt sleeves rolled up. Eyes tired from concentration.

Or are you enjoying yourself somewhere?

She stopped as she pulled back the duvet.

Was his reassuring explanation for being late too pat?

Could she trust him?

What horrible thoughts had her father put into her head?

Chapter Fifty-eight

Amy peeled potatoes. Complete rounds of dusty brown peel falling on to the sheet of newspaper spread over the black marble counter top. Don't let the peel break. Keep it going. Some old wives tale about it forming the initial of the man a girl would marry. She had never done that before she met Steve, and now it didn't matter. But she still tried to achieve the complete round for some obscure reason. She was going to make one of Steve's favourites - roast lamb. She had saved on the rest of the week's menus to be able to afford it. She glanced at the clock. Maybe he would be home a little earlier tonight. She hadn't wanted to quiz him this morning. As usual, he was in a hurry to avoid the traffic.

It was almost nine when he arrived and she ran to meet him as soon as she heard the front door close. She kissed him. He put a pile of files and his briefcase on the hall table.

'I'll put out your dinner, it's warming.'

'I'll have a look in on Emma first.' He went upstairs.

She had set the table for two in the kitchen, although she only intended to have some cheese herself. But she wanted to sit down with him and talk. She would have loved to open a bottle of red wine, and share it with Steve over a leisurely evening but that was something which couldn't be afforded any longer. Amy checked she had everything on the table, but for some reason she was unusually nervous. Like there was someone really important coming for dinner.

Her father sat in the living room watching television and she pulled over the door a little, hoping to have a bit of privacy with Steve. She went into the hall and called him.

There was no response. After a moment, she went upstairs to Emma's room, but he wasn't there. Then she went into their own bedroom, and to her surprise, found him lying on the bed, fully dressed, eyes closed.

'Steve?' she called softly.

He didn't stir.

She sat on the edge of the bed and watched him. Hair tousled. A shadow of stubble on his face. Dark circles under his eyes. She had a sudden impulse to gather him up in her arms and hold him close.

They were invited to Babs and Jimmy's on Saturday night. Emma was in bed asleep when they left, and John was there to keep an eye on her. They felt awkward about being unable to return the invite on another occasion, but stretched to a bottle of decent wine as a gift. It was so good to be out socially. They relaxed. Enjoying the chat with their friends. The delicious meal.

'Steve is exhausted by the time he arrives home in the evening,' Amy confided to the girls.

'It's not good for him, don't forget that was why my Jimmy had a heart attack,' Babs said.

'I'm afraid to talk to him, much less warn him of the possibility of a health scare.'

'You two were never like that. I thought you discussed every little detail. Did everything together. So romantic. I used to be jealous.' Babs picked up the coffee percolator.

'It's the business, he's very cut up about it.'

'He's chatting away ten to the dozen with the lads.'

'Why not organise a weekend away, just the two of you?' Rachel suggested.

'He wanted to do that a while back, but really, when we thought about it, we couldn't afford it.'

'Amy, would you take the dessert out of the oven and bring it in,' asked Babs. 'Rachel can carry the cream and I've got the coffee.' They did as she asked. Although Amy would have loved to continue the conversation to get the girls' view on everything.

Babs had served up bread and butter pudding. It completed the delicious meal that evening, but they lingered long afterwards sipping port and brandy, talking and laughing.

'Don't know what you're saying about Steve, he seems in great form,' Babs whispered.

'He's different at home.'

'Street angel, house devil?' Rachel giggled.

'Something like that.'

'Are we all heading down to Rosslare this year?' Jimmy asked.

'Let's all go,' Rachel grinned. 'Couldn't miss it.'

'No choice, kids won't have it any other way.'

'Remember last year.'

Amy had an image of the cosiness of the hotel. The delicious food. The relaxed evenings.

'It's decided then.'

'Don't know whether we can go or not this time, my Dad may still be with us, and there is the matter of money,' Amy murmured hesitantly.

'When is he going home, that's the question?' Steve asked.

She stared at him, shocked.

'I've got my father in law staying permanently.' Steve gulped the wine in his glass.

No one said anything for a moment.

'Take a break, get rid of the stress, do you good,' Jimmy said, laughing.

'Wouldn't make any difference,' Steve snapped. 'No-one understands what's it's like to have someone watching your every move. And then the smart cracks drive me around the twist, I only have to come in the door and ...' he muttered, his face grim.

‘Sounds a bit much. Ever thought you might be imagining it?’ Tom argued.

‘No, I don’t bloody imagine it.’ Steve topped up his glass of port, filling it to the brim and overflowing.

‘Hey Steve, that’s my best table cloth,’ Babs shouted.

‘Sorry.’ He lifted the glass and gulped the liquid.

Amy mouthed an apology to Babs, but said no more. She could see that Steve was heading towards boiling point and didn’t want to add to the pressure.

Suddenly, the mood of the party had collapsed. Amy listened astounded. Why hadn’t he told her exactly how he felt?

‘Not surprised you have that persecuted feeling. The bank, the revenue, the creditors, all pushing you. Sorry, man.’ Jimmy was sympathetic.

‘Look what happened to Jimmy when he pushed himself too hard,’ Tom said.

‘Maybe you should have a check-up, blood pressure, heart, all that stuff,’ Rachel added.

‘I do it regularly now. Take no chances, Steve. We’re only young once,’ Jimmy said. ‘And I’ve cut down on the drink, just a couple of glasses of wine a week.’

‘Look at me, I’m drinking water.’ Rachel raised her glass.

‘Nothing’s going to happen to me, I’m as fit as I ever was,’ Steve retorted and took a gulp of the sweet drink. ‘For years life was great and now - it’s shit.’

‘You’re getting a bit het up even talking about it,’ Tom observed.

‘No, I’m not,’ he growled.

‘Let’s lighten up. Take a consensus on this. Is our number one suspect stressed out?’ Tom grinned. ‘Hands up yes - one, two three, four - hands up no? There you are, vote yes carried unanimously.’ They roared with laughter. Amy half smiled. Steve glowered.

‘Hey, I don’t think we appreciate what our Steve is going through,’ Rachel said.

Steve stood up abruptly and left the room.

'Where the hell is his sense of humour? I don't think I ever saw him lose his cool like that before. Stevie boy was so laid back, you could never rise him. What's with him, Amy?' Jimmy asked.

'It's the business.'

'Can we do anything to help?' Babs asked.

Amy shook her head.

Steve reappeared, carrying Amy's black rain coat over his arm. 'We're going, Amy,' he announced curtly.

'Come on Steve, don't break up the party,' they chorused. 'Sit down and have a coffee, here, I'll pour it for you.' Babs lifted the percolator and did so.

'It's late,' he said, holding out the coat to Amy. She rose silently and put it on. Knowing there was no point in trying to persuade him to stay. She had never seen Steve in such a mood and really didn't know how to handle him.

'I'll ring for a taxi,' Babs lifted the phone.

'We'll hail one on the road.' Steve strode down the hall.

'Are you mad? You could be waiting for ages, and it's not exactly warm tonight,' someone said.

'I'll drop you home,' Tom suggested.

'You've had far too much to drink,' Steve snapped.

'I'm not going to see you wandering the roads this hour of the night.'

'Wish to God we had brought the car.' Steve opened the front door.

'We all decided that no-one was going to drive tonight,' Rachel said, 'so that we could relax and not be worrying about being breathalysed on the way home.'

'Yea, I was done recently, got a fine. Amy, let's go.'

'Hey, why didn't you tell me that?' Amy asked. But he ignored her.

'The taxi should be here soon,' Babs said. 'Hang on.'

'Can't you wait for a few minutes?' Rachel begged.

'Do you have to drag your poor wife out into the night to hang about for God knows how long?' Tom asked.

'No, I don't. She can stay here if she likes.' He stepped outside and banged the door behind him.

'Fucking idiot,' Jimmy exploded.

The others looked puzzled.

'I'd better catch up.' Amy followed.

'He'll probably come back with his tail between his legs after waiting outside for ages,' Rachel peered through the hall window.

Amy said goodnight, ran down the drive and out on to the road, looking left and right for Steve. But the house was positioned on a bend and it was difficult to see very far in either direction.

Which way did he go? Amy wondered, deciding to head towards the main junction at the end of the road. It would be the best place to catch a taxi. He'll probably have done the same, she thought. But it was dark and deserted, and she felt increasingly nervous. Aware that it was crazy to walk the streets all alone at three in the morning. She almost turned back, but that was as scary as going forward so she continued on, aware of the loud click of her high heels on the concrete path. And hoping no one else did. She glanced behind, wondering whether she heard the pad of soft shoes behind her. Her heart thumped. Was that a figure hiding in the shadows? She increased her pace. The traffic junction was close now and she was relieved to see a man standing on the far side.

'Steve?' she called out. But at that moment, a taxi swung around the corner and stopped to pick him up. She began to run, hoping that he might see her and stop the car. But just as she approached the lights she caught her heel in a crack in the pavement and fell forward heavily. Hands stretched out to save herself, she flopped on the ground, the breath knocked out of her. She was shocked and lay there for a couple of minutes before she tried to push herself up.

Suddenly, there was a screech of brakes. A car pulled up, a door opened, and someone came over.

'Amy, are you all right?' Jimmy knelt beside her

'Yes, I feel so stupid.' She tried to get up.

'Jesus, are you hurt?' He was very concerned.

'No, just a bit shook.' She bit her lip and held on to him. 'Thanks Jimmy, I'm so glad it's you.'

'Let's get you back to the house.' He helped her into the car.

'Oh my God, look at my tights.' Tears filled her eyes and she burst out crying. The pain of grazed knees and hands only beginning to make itself felt now.

'Your legs don't look too good either.' Jimmy pulled a handkerchief from his pocket. 'Here, mop up.'

When they arrived back at the house, the others were horrified to see the condition she was in. Babs made her lie on the couch and cleaned the cuts with disinfectant, which was a painful process. 'Stop whimpering, you're like one of the kids.'

'Sorry.'

'Drink this, Amy, you'll feel better.' Rachel handed her a cup of hot coffee.

'I'll give you a lollipop as a reward when it's all over. That's what we do here.' Babs placed a plaster strategically on each knee.

'No sign of Steve?' Jimmy asked.

'He got a taxi at the lights, I was running after him but he mustn't have seen me, that's when I fell.'

'Bloody glad I followed you.'

'You shouldn't have been driving,' she managed a smile. 'But thanks for rescuing me.'

'Don't worry, I didn't gulp down as much as you lot did.'

Amy took the taxi when it finally arrived. At home, she walked painfully up the stairs wondering what reception she would get from Steve. But the bedroom was empty. She checked Emma, but she slept soundly. It mustn't have been him who got into the taxi after all, she decided. He was still waiting somewhere. She rang his mobile but it was powered off, so left a message on the voice mail. Then she crept between the sheets stiffly and tried to sleep, but with the pain and worrying about Steve, she lay awake until dawn filled the room with light.

A small figure in pink pyjamas came into the bedroom. 'Mummy, why is Dad sleeping on the couch?'

Chapter Fifty-nine

Steve's practice was wound up. The staff were made redundant. Those people he had got to know over the years, many of whom were close friends were suddenly gone. He missed them, the loss of their different personalities left a gap in his life.

The office closed. Steve had nothing to do now. He spent the time reading the job sections in the papers, and registering with various on line websites. But there was nothing out there. He sent his CV off to so many companies without receiving one reply, it was depressing. While he wasn't hopeful of getting a job in the architectural field, he applied for any job which needed management or marketing ability. He didn't care what type of job it was, and would have accepted anything. They were now trying to stretch out the money his mother had loaned them, and the income from the rental of Nuala's house helped to pay the mortgage and bills. As far as Emma and John were concerned he was taking a few days holiday. But he found it difficult to fill the time. Without his usual routine he felt lost. Without purpose. Useless.

But when he pushed open the door and the warmth of the house extended its' arms around him, he knew that this was where he wanted to be. An aroma drifted out from the kitchen and he stood for a second and tried to identify it. Amy had been baking. He smiled to himself. He crept up behind her as she stirred something in a pot on the cooker. He put his arms around her and squeezed.

'Hey,' she turned to him with a broad smile on her face.

'Love you,' he murmured and kissed her. Not lightly. Not passionately. But intimately. A secret message transmitted between two people.

'Where's Emma?'

'Playing one of her games on the computer in our room. We couldn't get the computer in the living room to open up.'

Steve opened the door of the bedroom quietly, thinking he would surprise her, but to his astonishment he saw John sitting on the bed also, and the two watching the screen. His mind computed this unexpected sight. Like in a nightmare, he wanted to say something, but for a split second incoherence twisted the words, and his lips felt numb as if he had just had a tooth extracted.

'Dad?' Emma turned, caught sight of him, and smiled.

'How's my girl?'

'Watch this with us, it's really funny.'

'Dinner's almost ready.' He nodded to John.

'Can you help me downstairs?' John asked.

'How'd you get up?' the question snapped out like the snarl of a dog.

'Emma helped me.'

'You let a little girl help you up? What if you had fallen on her?' Steve tried to curb his rising temper, took Emma's hand and went out on to the landing.

'Wait for Grandad,' Emma said in a peremptory not to be disobeyed tone.

He forced himself to stop and moved back into the doorway. John tried to push himself up from the bed, but seemed to be having some difficulty. Steve didn't move and it was only when he felt Emma pull forward that he reached to help him into standing position.

Steve's supposed holiday ended, so each day he rose at seven in the morning with Amy and Emma. Showered. Dressed. Ate breakfast. And left the house to drive towards the city. He couldn't break the habit of years. To turn into the laneway at the back of the building and drive into the parking area. Enter the house by the back door and walk through to his office. But he didn't have a key now. It had been returned to the landlord. The "To Let" sign on the Georgian building screamed his failure to the world. He hated to see it. And when he removed the brass plate on which the company name was engraved from the front door, he was at his lowest ebb.

No longer having anything to do, at first he had called to see friends in their offices, hoping that there might be something they needed him to do, but realised soon that it was waste of time. They had all cut back too, and were barely surviving.

Today he pulled into a side road and sat there. Staring vaguely at the houses on either side of the road. There was no-one around. Children all gone to school, their parents at work if they were lucky. He leaned his head back and closed his eyes. He hadn't slept well and now it caught up with him and he dozed off. It was a knock on the passenger window which woke him up. Startled he stared at the woman who stood there.

'Are you OK?'

'Yes, thanks, I'm fine. Too early for an appointment,' he lied, hoping that it sounded plausible. He glanced at his watch and could see that it was after eleven.

'Bye then.' She moved away, pulling her small white Jack Russell after her on a lead.

He felt self-conscious, and glanced at himself in the mirror. He didn't look very fresh, the lines on his face had deepened lately, and he felt older than his thirty-five years. He had to move on then. Smiling at the woman as he passed her, then turning to swing back out on to the main road. At a nearby shop, he bought a paper. He could justify that. He drove further into town, and pulled in again. Opened the paper and turned immediately to the jobs page. But there was nothing there to suit him.

After reading the paper from front page to back he decided to go home. Part of his reluctance being that he didn't want John to know the business was gone, but he realised that he couldn't go out and sit in the car all day every day. It would drive him crazy.

He told John the situation later that day.

'I know what that's all about. I was a bankrupt. Lost everything,' he laughed. 'But I got back up on my feet, you just have to believe in yourself.'

His advice didn't really help Steve. If anything, it made him feel worse. And being home every day accentuated Steve's irritation with the man. His lack of opportunity to have any private time with Amy in their own home was now accentuated even more. He couldn't even talk to her without feeling that John was around every corner, that his piercing eyes slid into their lives, and noted every move. He wondered for the thousandth time when John would return home.

He wanted to shout out loud. How long before I can wave goodbye to that crabby geezer who sits in my chair, looks at my television, fingers my books and possesses the minds of my wife and daughter. But he didn't say it. Swallowed up the furious shout and kept it inside him like an angry wasp trapped in a jar.

Chapter Sixty

The following Sunday, Steve suggested they take a trip to Brittas Bay. He would make it up to Amy and Emma. He had been so awful to them lately and wanted to make it up, and take them somewhere out of Dublin to enjoy themselves. Emma was delighted at the prospect, as was Amy. But John's grimace was unenthusiastic.

'Might be too much for me.'

'You won't mind then if we go on, we won't be that late,' Steve said, trying not to sound too impatient.

John didn't look happy.

'Perhaps I might stay, I don't want you to be here all alone,' Amy said.

'We're only going out for a few hours, and we haven't been anywhere for months now, it's like we're imprisoned,' Steve burst out.

'Dad's not fully recovered yet,' she argued with him.

'All I can see is that you prefer his company to ours.' Disappointment began to boil up into something much worse in his mind.

'You're crazy, we'd both love to go but Dad just isn't fit.'

'You're neglecting Emma,' he accused.

'I don't neglect her, how can you say such a thing?' Her anger matched his now.

'Because I'm fed up to the teeth with you spending all of your time with your father to the exclusion of everyone else. You're glued to him like the pair of you are one bloody person.'

'You're crazy.'

'Mummy, I can't find my swimsuit.' Emma appeared in the doorway.

'I'll get it for you.'

'Look, just go on, don't worry about me,' John intervened.

'Are you ready, Grandad?' Emma looked at him. 'We have to go soon.'

'I'm not going.'

'I want you to come,' she pouted.

'I'm sorry, honey, but not today, maybe another time.'

'I don't want to go then,' she seemed close to tears.

Steve stood in the doorway, aghast. Then he turned and stomped down the hall, banging the front door behind him.

He headed up into the Dublin Mountains, driving far too fast as he followed the narrow roads until finally he parked at the pine forest. He walked uphill through the forest, out of breath from the steepness of the incline. He wanted to push himself. Get rid of the anger. But that wasn't easy. He felt so isolated. The burden of losing the business cut deep. As if it was his child. Nurtured for years and now taken away from him by faceless bureaucrats. There was guilt too when he thought of the staff who had been with him. So willing to support him no matter what, and who were now facing the same problems as he was himself.

He kept on climbing. Occasionally catching a glimpse of the hills and valleys in the distance through the trees. The sun beamed down, the vista was magnificent. He remembered suddenly his boy scout days, and hiking to Larch Hill which was only a few miles from here. Carrying their gear and food in haversacks, billy cans, enamel pans and mugs, beans, rashers, sausages. At the place chosen for camp, usually by the river, they would cut a square sod out of the grass and forage for dead wood to light a fire. Their food usually ended up burned black on one side and raw pink on the other, but that didn't matter. After everyone had eaten their grub, they would explore the upper reaches of the river. Slipping, sliding, falling in. Having a great time.

Occasionally, there would be tests for merit badges. First aid. Night trekking. Paper trails. Pitching tents. He sat and stared out over the hillside remembering the fun of those days. And coming down the hills in dark damp evenings, singing the scouting song - "ging gang gooly gooly wash wash". Names and faces of guys he used to know flashed through his mind and he wondered where they were now.

He walked on. The evening was closing in and he made his way through pockets of dense woodland. He wasn't sure of the direction assuming he would finally come back to the car park. But it took longer than he expected. The anger which had churned through him earlier had diminished somewhat but he still felt that he was being ousted from his own family by John. He hated the man. He searched in his pockets for the phone but couldn't find it, only then realising that he must have left it behind. He increased his pace, trying to keep his footing on the rough track and it was dark when he arrived back to the car.

Chapter Sixty-one

'Amy, come back to LA with me. There are some people interested in getting together on this film. It's a really good script and a hell of a part. You know we're talking millions.'

She couldn't imagine what it might mean. It was mind-blowing. She had heard figures like that bandied about when she was young, but it meant nothing to her then either.

'You'll have to think about my suggestion, honey. Look at you, like a skivvy, cleaning the house, washing dishes and clothes as well, it's crazy.'

'I don't know if I want to, you know film is not my thing.' She wanted to be true to herself, hating to leave her hopes for a career in the theatre behind.

'It will change your life. You can't live like this.'

'We'd have to go to LA, and Steve won't want that.'

'He might get a business opportunity there, there's nothing here.'

'He doesn't want to move away.'

'Sometimes there's no choice, and you have to think of Emma. What about her future?'

She nodded.

'Amy, be sensible. This film will give you more than you ever imagined. I know that. And you'll be the star, with all the publicity that goes with that. All the razzle dazzle of Hollywood.'

'Daddy, we're going to LA,' Emma said excitedly.

'No, we're not,' Steve replied bluntly.

'I heard Grandad say we are. Come in and ask him.' She grabbed his hand and tried to pull him into the living room.

'No, Emma.'

Her expression was suddenly dejected.

'Leave me alone, Emma, I'm busy.' He went into the study and sat in front of the computer. He stared at the screen. Vaguely googling jobs, architects, building, anything associated with his profession. Drawn into other websites which had little to do with what he was searching for. One site leading to another. He logged on to Facebook. Twitter. Read other people's comments. He wondered how he might use the opportunity to get a job. He sent out a short job seeking plea. Responses came in but they were mostly from people in the same position as himself. They swopped stories. Some were much worse. No-one to support them. The bank was going to repossess. It did little for his morale.

'Your Dad told Emma that she was going to America.' He spoke quietly as was his habit these days, but there was always that undercurrent of anger he couldn't control. He was so conscious of being overheard by John, even here in the garden.

'She must have overheard Dad talking. You know how keen he is to do another film.' Amy twisted her lip. A frown on her face as she pulled weeds from among the flowering plants.

'He shouldn't have been talking about it. There's no point getting her all excited about something which isn't going to happen.'

She didn't reply.

'Is he trying to persuade you to do a film?' he demanded.

'Yea.' She felt guilty.

'And?'

'I don't know.'

'What does that mean?'

'It means exactly that.' She broke up the dark earth with a trowel.

'But you might?' he insisted in taking the conversation further. Wanting an outright denial.

'Don't keep pushing me.' She didn't meet his gaze.

'He's got you in his grip. Controlling you like a puppet. I know. I can see it. The bastard.'

'Don't call him that.'

'I will if I want.' He was too far gone now to even realise what he was saying. She was moving away from him and he didn't know how to get her back.

He went inside. Determined to repossess his own space which was now occupied by his father in law. In the living room, John was on the phone. Papers were strewn across the coffee table.

'Yea, I'll email the script. It's good. About an army family. Some of whom are serving in Iraq. Topical. It deals with post traumatic stress and the effect it has on the main characters. You'll like it. Get back to me as soon as you've had a look at it, there's a lot of people interested.' He cut off the phone, and looked up at Steve.

'Why are you filling my wife's head with this film nonsense? And my daughter's too?' Steve demanded.

'If you could use your brain, you'd see what a marvellous opportunity it is for you, for Amy and Emma too.'

'I'm well able to use my brain, and I don't see it like you do,' Steve snarled.

'You're foolish, Steve. You're financial situation is crap and you're refusing this chance for your wife and daughter. What are you going to live on, may I ask?'

'I'll provide for my family. I've always done that.'

'But in the meantime, you expect them to live like paupers. I didn't bring up my daughter to live like that. She had the best of everything. You haven't even got the remotest idea of what it was like to live in Beverly Hills. We never had to think of money. It was always possible to have whatever she wanted. She just had to raise a finger and it was there.'

Steve ran out of words and went back into the study. He poured himself a drink. From his own bottle of whiskey which he kept in a drawer of the desk. The liquid burned, but the kick was missing.

Chapter Sixty-two

'Mummy, I'll need ten euro to go on the school trip to the zoo,' Emma announced as soon as she arrived home.

'Yes, honey,' Amy said absently. 'Go and change out of your uniform.'

'Where's Grandad?'

'He's on the phone.'

'He's always on the phone, I can't talk to him at all now,' she complained.

'He's busy.'

'But what's he doing? He never reads stories to me any more. Why is that do you know?' She leaned up against Amy.

'He's working.'

'At what?'

'Go and change, Emma. Please?'

She grimaced and went out of the room.

Amy wondered how she was going to find the money for the school trip. Ten euro was a very small amount. It would have been a miniscule amount just a couple of years ago, something to be given to a homeless person begging on the street. Now the money she had in her purse would just about cover them for the rest of the week. Eked out carefully each day. If Amy didn't have enough then she certainly couldn't approach Steve about it now. He was in vile humour. Closeted in the study most of the time. And drinking too.

So concerned with trying to make ends meet, she had tried to get a part-time job of some sort. Watching the notice boards of the supermarkets. Scanning the local free papers which she picked up. There was no point in going further afield because she would have to travel and couldn't afford to use the car now. But there were no opportunities.

Now this problem with Emma suddenly assumed enormous proportions. It added to the teetering pile of other problems in her life and the whole thing threatened to collapse around her. She gave Emma and her father something to eat, but really couldn't have touched food herself. She went into the downstairs loo, and locked the door. Stared at herself in the mirror, the image blurred by her tears. What was she going to do? She couldn't have shared their problems with her friends, she would feel disloyal. And there was no-one else to talk to.

Later Steve came out of the study. Unshaven. Wearing a tee shirt and jeans. He stood at the kitchen door and stared into the conservatory, hands pushed into his pockets.

'There's soup there, would you like a bowl?' She decided to make the first move. They hadn't talked in days.

He didn't answer, but took a bowl from the press and poured some into it.

'Do you not want to heat it up?'

He shook his head.

'How about bread?'

He opened the bread bin and cut a couple of slices.

'Steve, I want to talk to you.'

'What about?'

'We need to discuss things.'

'There's nothing I want to say.' His voice was rough.

'Steve, we can't go on like this.'

He stared at her, his eyes sunk back into his head, and then went back into the study.

She went after him.

'I'm not going to put up with this any longer. I can't. Do you understand what I mean?' She spoke gently to temper the meaning of her words.

He ate his soup.

'Not having any money is just proving too hard. Not for myself but for Emma. I can't do it to her.'

He broke up the bread.

'I've decided I'm going to make the film.' She gripped her hands together, flustered, nervous.

There was tense silence between them.

'It's for Emma,' she explained. So anxious for him to grasp why she was considering it at all.

'I don't want you to do it, Amy. I promise I'll get a job. Soon. I've talked to some people.' He clicked on the mouse. 'There are jobs out there.'

'It will take a while to get the film set up, but in the meantime Dad will give us an advance. That will make such a difference.'

'I don't want it.'

'You mightn't but I do.'

'I'm telling you not to do this, you're my wife.'

She was astonished. What was this possessive thing? 'Am I supposed to obey you?' she asked.

'You know how I feel.'

'How do you think Emma feels when she wonders whether we can give her the money for the school trip? Tell me that?'

'She doesn't understand what's going on.'

'She knows exactly. Do you think she's stupid? Kids pick up on everything, particularly the fact that you're a drunk.'

He didn't look at her, but she was aware that the slope of his shoulders had deepened.

'It's no way for a child to live. And I don't want to live like this either.'

He opened the drawer and took the whiskey bottle out. Shakily he poured some into the glass.

'And what about all the money you've wasted on whiskey? Disgusting. When your only daughter can't have what every other child in school has.'

He gulped the drink.

'You're pathetic. We're going to Clifden, I can't bear living here any longer.' She left the room.

Chapter Sixty-three

'Amy, Amy?' a soft voice called. She was instantly awake. She had been dreaming. A gentle untroubled dream. She closed her eyes. Longing to drift back to that place. She had been happy there. Loved. Protected. And she wished so hard that she could find that again.

In the bright colour of every day, she found herself standing back on the margins, watching as Emma slid into her place in this house like she had always been here. Her daughter was going to a new school now, and loved it. Delighted with all her little friends. But she missed her Dad. His absence excused by a business trip. But she constantly asked for him, never satisfied with Amy's explanations.

Amy was broken-hearted without Steve. But she couldn't have stayed with him, and hoped that this space between them would help him get things into perspective. Her father had given her money, and she had lodged part of that into their account, guessing that in his present frame of mind he would probably never notice.

Amy, her father and Emma had been in Clifden for a few weeks and there had been no contact with Steve. Their lives were peaceful. Uneventful. Amy was glad, particularly for Emma's sake. She felt she could breathe again, that feeling of watching around corners, and waiting for some catastrophe to occur had diminished.

It was a Saturday. Quiet. Amy hung freshly washed curtains on the windows. White voile with a tiny embroidered flower motif.

'When's Daddy coming?' Emma asked from where she sat at the kitchen table, painting a picture on a sheet of paper.

Amy's heart dropped. This week so many questions about Steve. More and more each day. Suddenly she realised that putting Emma off had been strung out for as far as it could go.

She sat down beside her. Looking at the painting which depicted the house, Emma, herself, John, Steve and the dog, Joey. Straight stick-like drawings in bright blue standing in a line among yellow and red coloured flowers. 'That's very good,' she said.

'I miss him.' She put a circle around his figure. 'And I miss Joey.'

Amy put her arms around her. Might as well tell her, she decided. This was it. The dreaded moment of truth. She should have told her before, not let her worry like this. 'Daddy won't be living with us any more, we're going to stay here,' she dived in and simply told it as it was.

'When will I see him?' Emma swished the brush in the jar of water which clouded reddish at first and then back to dirty green. Now she dipped it in the yellow paint.

Amy hesitated. Her heart pounded within her. 'I don't know, love.'

'I'll phone him.' Emma picked up Amy's phone, and opened it up. 'I just have to go into phone book and Dad's the first. Then it calls him.' She went to press the key.

'No, some other time.' Amy took it out of her hand. Feeling a little guilty at her abrupt move she stroked her hair. 'Sorry, love.'

'When?'

John passed through the kitchen.

'Look Grandad, it's a picture of all of us, I'm going to send it to my friends at home.' Emma waved it at him.

'Don't know why you need to be sending pictures to people you won't be seeing any more.'

She looked at him, her face puzzled.

Amy stopped putting dishes into the washer.

Emma looked down at the bright mass of colours disappointedly.

'But it's of you, Grandad,' she said, smiling. 'Look.'

'I don't want to be in a picture, how about a coffee, Amy? And I wouldn't mind a sandwich while you're about it.'

'Mummy?' Emma looked up at her, tears in her eyes.

'You finish your picture, Grandad doesn't mean it,' Amy dropped a kiss on her forehead.

'But he said he doesn't want to be in it, and I wanted everyone in my old class to see what my Grandad looked like so when they come to visit they'll know him.'

'He will like it when it's finished, bet you, so you keep going, it's a lovely picture.'

'No, I don't like it.' She swept the brush across the paper, heavily laden with yellow paint, and obliterated the scene into one mass of colour.

'That's such a pity.'

Emma climbed down from the table. 'I don't want to paint any more.' She wandered over to the kitchen door and stood looking out into the garden. Then she sat down on the step, a forlorn figure.

Amy sat beside her, both looking out into the garden, and beyond that the blue green of the sea. She put her arm around her shoulders. aware of a curious peace. As if another person was there beside them.

'Let's put on our jackets and go for a walk.' She took Emma's hand and they went back inside.

Just then there was a ring on the doorbell.

Chapter Sixty-four

Steve stood on the steps. At first thinking he was too near the door, and stepping back. He was nervous. In the last few weeks he had tried hard to reduce his drinking. He would never get Amy back unless he did that. He was still without a job but he tried to be positive. His heart thumped erratically. He had rehearsed what he would say to Amy but when she appeared in front of him he was unable to remember one word, and stood like an awkward boy. She didn't say anything either. He had made a special effort with his clothes. Dressed in his navy suit, and white shirt. He was clean shaven. And hoped that he looked more like the person she used to love.

He handed her a bouquet of red roses. She took them but didn't smile or say anything at all.

'Daddy?' From behind Amy, came a rushing bundle. She crashed into him. Arms wrapped around. Hugging tight. 'I knew you'd come.'

'Emma.' He held her close and then swung her around. She screamed with excitement. He was overcome with emotion and tears rushed into his eyes.

'Where have you been, Daddy?'

'I'm sorry but I've been very busy. But I came to say Happy Birthday.' He dashed the tears away, and handed her a large brightly coloured bag. He had come at the weekend before her birthday hoping to find them in. If he left it until the day itself, Emma would have been at school, and there may have been a party, so his chance of seeing them alone would be reduced.

‘Emma.’ Amy’s voice was sharp. ‘Go inside.’

‘But Mummy, it’s Daddy, he gave me a present for my birthday. Can we go home now?’ She waved the bag at Amy.

‘Yes we can, Emma, right now.’ He hugged her again and dropped a kiss on her head.

‘Emma, I told you to go in,’ Amy said sharply.

Emma didn’t move away from Steve.

‘Now,’ Amy said again.

Steve kept hold of Emma’s hand. ‘Don’t cry, pet.’ He dabbed at the tears with his handkerchief, and then looked up at Amy. ‘How are you, love? I’ve missed you both terribly.’ For the first time he spoke to her.

‘Daddy, I want to show you my Game Boy and all of my new dolls.’ She tried to drag him over the threshold.

Amy took her other hand and stepped back into the hall.

‘I want Daddy to come in.’

Neither let go.

‘Emma, if you don’t do what I tell you, I’ll be very cross.’ she warned.

The child’s eyes were full of tears.

‘Do what Mummy says, Emma,’ Steve said gently. He felt guilty. Poor child. Dragged between warring parents. God knows what it would do to her.

She nodded and peered into the bag. ‘Oh it’s Barbie Princess, I love her, Daddy.’ She lifted the box and held it out to Amy. ‘Look Mummy, isn’t she beautiful?’

‘She is, pet,’ Amy smiled for the first time.

‘Could we talk alone?’ Steve asked. Suddenly hopeful.

‘No.’

‘But there’s so much I want to say to you.’

‘I haven’t anything to say.’

John appeared behind Amy. ‘What’s going on?’

‘I’m talking to my wife.’ His hackles rose the moment he saw him.

‘Trying to persuade her to go back to you and not to make the film?’

‘Yes.’

‘You won’t succeed.’

‘How do you know?’

‘Because Amy knows that the best thing for her and Emma is to star in my film. Establish herself again. She was nominated for an Oscar in her last movie. She can easily do that again. She’s very talented. How can you stand in her way and condemn her and Emma to a life of penury?’

Steve’s face paled. He stood there looking at Amy. Her shining hair softly curved around her face. Her dark eyes sparkled with tears. He wanted to say he was sorry. So sorry. Persuade her that he would be there for her. Provide for her and Emma. And most of all that he loved them both so very much. He would always love them. He longed to reach out and pull Amy close to him. Kiss her full on the lips. But had a terrible premonition that he was seeing her for the last time. He opened his mouth, but no words came out. It was too late.

Chapter Sixty-five

Amy looked out the window over Emma's head. The fair hair soft against her cheek. Emma had wanted to go with Steve today. To leave her. That hit home. She wished things were different. That their perfect life hadn't crumbled into this chaos. She still loved him. She still loved the Steve she had married. But he had changed and she couldn't find that man she knew. Now she was forced into something she really didn't want to do. But she had to do it for Emma. To give her everything she wanted. There was no turning back, she'd committed to it.

She lay beside Emma until the little girl went to sleep. A deep lethargy made her body heavy and slow, and she wanted to drift into that innocent sleep of childhood as well. So that when she woke up, her mind would be fresh. Washed with spring water. Clear of stress. But too many things jockeyed for position in her head. Demanding that she listen.

She twisted her rings around her finger. The single diamond curved into the slight indent in the gold band. It meant a hugging close. For always. She tried to take them off. But it was difficult. Her finger must have swollen. Against her will, emotion seeped slowly around her heart. Just a little. Enough to make her uncomfortable. She had loved Steve so much. Once.

She had talked to Rachel and Babs on the phone a couple of times, sent emails and texts, but somehow it only seemed like meaningless superficial drivel.

'But how are you really?' Babs had insisted that last time.

'I'm fine.'

'But what about you and Steve? Are you talking?'

'No.'

'But surely you should?'

'No Babs.'

'You seem very hard these days, I can't understand you.'

'It's difficult to explain.'

Rachel took the phone from Babs. 'When are we going to see you?'

'I'm not sure.'

'We could call to see you some weekend, what do you think?'

'It's a bit of a distance.' Amy couldn't understand herself. Why didn't she want to see her friends?

'We're worried about you, do you realise that?'

'Of course I do, but I don't want you to be concerned, we're getting on fine.'

'How can that be? You and Steve were so together, you can't just suddenly separate and not give a damn about him anymore.'

'Look Rachel, things have been bad for a while. It's better this way.'

She was silent.

'I'm sorry. We'll get together some time when I'm in Dublin.'

'Make it soon, girl.'

'Can I have a party for my birthday?' Emma asked. 'And bring all my friends from Dublin?'

'It's much too far for them to come.' Amy stiffened.

'But Daddy could come.' The piping voice had a pleading note in it.

'No love, he's gone away.'

'Where?'

'To work. But we'll have your new friends over. Because this is the first time you've been in Clifden for your birthday.'

'What'll we do?' She jumped up and down.

'It'll be a surprise.'

Amy plopped a row of pink iced stars around the edge of the cake. She refilled the syringe with more icing and changed the shape. Then steadied her hand and began. But her attempt to write "Happy Birthday" was disastrous. The uneven lettering looked so unprofessional that she scraped the excess icing off, deciding to try a figure eight instead. After all, it was only two circles stuck together. But that wasn't much better, and in the end she angrily scraped that off as well and smoothed the top of the cake again."

'Amy, Amy?'

Someone called. She turned sharply. Her eyes swivelled around the kitchen. A voice curled around her like smoke. Clinging softly. So familiar. It was happening more often. There was a sharp awareness of her mother. She waited around every corner. Behind every door. Amy closed her eyes and opened them again, expecting to find herself waking up out of a dream. But she was still in the kitchen, trying to decide what to do about the cake. In the end, she put some silver stars on the top, and the eight pink candles.

Amy almost missed her daughter's eighth birthday. That special day. The party. The friends. The presents. The bouncing castle. Brid came around to help with the food and Amy felt that she couldn't have managed without her. Her father hadn't been keen to have such a crowd of children in the house, but had finally been persuaded by Emma to let her have the party.

Amy was there, but yet not there. Forcing herself to hide the bleakness of her mood. But children don't notice things like that. The air filled with screams of excitement as they played on the bouncing castle.

'Mum, come on, it's great.'

'I don't think I can, sorry,' she protested, but Emma took her hand.

'Go on, have a bounce,' Brid said, as she watched them. 'Wish I had the courage myself.'

'I'll fall, I know it.' Amy was certain.

'Come on, scaredy cat,' Emma screamed with excitement and ran ahead.

'Not even one little bounce?' Brid grinned.

'Mummy, Mummy,' Emma called.

Amy stepped on to the uneven surface. Her body heaved unsteadily, and she almost lost her footing.

'Jump, Mum, jump.' Emma grabbed her hand.

She tried to get control over herself, bouncing this way and that. After a while she managed to get into a rhythm and once she had started she couldn't stop. The shouts, screams, and laughter echoed all around her. The bright colours of the castle - red, blue, green, yellow - swept up and around her. She was at the centre of that crazy kaleidoscope. Whirling. Whirling. Until she collapsed on the soft surface, and lay there for a moment, stars spinning in front of her eyes.

'Come on, have something cool to drink.' Brid helped her up. 'And maybe it's time to cut the cake,' she suggested.

They gathered around the table. Amy lit the eight candles. Emma stood in front of it, smiling, all excited. The glow of the candles shining on her face.

'Make a wish, Emma,' someone shouted.

She closed her eyes.

'Now blow!'

She pursed her lips, leaned forward and blew. Some of the candles were extinguished, but it took a couple of more tries before she succeeded in blowing them all out. The kids cheered and sang loudly.

'Happy Birthday to you, Happy Birthday to you.'

Amy stood beside her, suddenly drawn back to another eighth birthday. When she hadn't managed to blow out all the candles either. But the shouting then had been different. A dreadful momentum gathered as the explosion of emotion spread like an atom bomb. Its' poison floated out of the air to settle invisibly on the remains of the birthday cake. Into their lives the contamination swirled and took root like another entity.

When you're eight.
You can't escape.
You go around and around.
On an endless wheel of repetition.

Amy didn't remember much of the rest of the day. It seemed to pass beyond her and she ran after it. And ran. And ran. But never caught up.

Chapter Sixty-six

To Amy's utter delight, in August Harry arrived with Doug. It was such a surprise that when she first saw him she clung to him, overcome with emotion. Her welcome for Doug cooler, more matter of fact.

'It seems so long,' Amy stared at Harry. 'A year is like a lifetime.'

'We've missed out on too much,' he said.

'Yea.'

'What did you miss?' Emma enquired.

'We missed each other.'

'Why was that?'

'Misunderstandings.' Amy's face was suddenly sad.

'What does that mean?'

They looked at each other, but said nothing.

'Don't ask so many questions, Emma,' John muttered.

'We all have misunderstandings, but we apologise and it's all forgotten,' Doug added.

'I ask the most questions in school,' Emma grinned.

'She does,' Amy laughed.

'Beer, Doug? Harry?' John asked.

'Thanks,' Doug grinned.

Harry shook his head. 'Coke is fine.'

'My teacher answers every one of them. She says I should be able to answer them myself. I will too.' Emma swung out of Harry.

'Little girls who ask too many questions are just a nuisance.' John wagged his finger.

'I'm not a nuisance,' Emma retorted.

'I think Emma is very clever, and I hope that someone can answer all her questions,' Harry laughed.

'Yes, I am clever, aren't I, Mum? And Daddy says I am. He can play football with you Harry, we always play in our garden.'

'That sounds cool.'

'We used to have all sorts of games,' Emma said, and slowly her voice trailed off.

'Let's go for a run on the beach tomorrow,' Harry suggested. 'We can kick a ball around. I'm supposed to be training.'

'Boston Red Sox,' Amy said, laughing. 'It's wonderful, you're going to be a great footballer.'

'It's what I've always wanted. Just lucky, I guess.'

'It's a short season, just a few years at the top level. What will you do after that?' John asked.

'Coach hopefully, that's where the big money is. Three or four million dollars a year at least.'

'That's chickenfeed,' John was dismissive. 'You could earn ten million dollars for one film.'

'I'd be no good, Dad, you know that. It's not in me. Never was.'

'I don't know how that could be.' He shook his head.

'Sport is in Harry's blood, you can't deny it,' Doug spoke for the first time in a while.

'My only son deserted me,' John muttered. 'And my daughter too for a long while.'

'I never wanted that, Dad,' Harry said.

'Why did both my children turn their backs on me. What did I do to deserve that?'

'John, they had to follow their own hearts,' Doug said. 'Anyhow, Amy's doing this film with us now, and it's going to be a great success, I feel it in my bones.'

'She's not doing it for me.' John's expression was cold.

There was an awkward silence.

'We'll all go?' Emma interrupted.

They looked at her.

'Where?'

'To play football on the beach tomorrow.'

'Doug and I will be busy, we won't have time,' John said.

'You and I will go and maybe your Mom,' Harry agreed.

'What time?'

'In the morning.' He looked at Amy, his eyes smiling.

Harry stayed for almost two weeks and it was the happiest Amy had been in a long time. They spent the days walking the beach. Driving around the area. Visiting Roundstone, Leenane, Maam Cross and other beautiful areas of Connemara.

'It's great to be back, I love it here,' Harry said.

Amy nodded. 'I feel the same.'

'Tough on you knowing we were so close to Dublin and yet Dad didn't want to see you.'

'You know Dad, stubborn as a mule,' Amy muttered.

'Has to have his own way. I don't know how I escaped to do what I wanted.'

'You started early. There was never anything else for you but football from the time you were just a small child.'

'Harry,' Emma yelled and threw the ball.

He caught it and lobbed it back. She missed it and had to run further to pick it up.

'How is Deborah?'

'I haven't seen her in a while.' He kicked a stone.

'Where is she living now?'

'Still in Cannes.'

'And the Count?' she asked hesitantly, reluctant to pry.

'Gone. There's someone else now.'

'You could take a quick flight down to see her, it's not very far from here, couple of hours.'

'No, I've got to get back. She isn't interested, anyway. You know we were never very close.' He stared out to sea. A shadow in his eyes.

The ball whirled in their direction. Emma ran up to them, out of breath.

'Can you catch it?' Harry held the ball high out of her reach.

'Yes I can,' She jumped up and down until eventually he threw it and she was off again.

'She's a super kid,' he said.

'Yea, I know,' Amy smiled, looking after her.

'I'm really sorry you've split with Steve, you always seemed like a really happy family.'

'I can't believe it's happened, it's like a bad dream,' Amy admitted.

'Maybe things will change, sometimes you just need to get away for a bit.'

'Don't know.'

'There's Doug.' Emma ran towards him.

A flare up of irritation swept through Amy. Doug was the last person she wanted to see. He was taking from her time with Harry. Precious time.

'I took a break, and I've been hoping to get you two together,' he said, throwing the ball back and forwards to Emma. 'Amy, there's something I've wanted to say to you for a long time, but I never had the chance.'

Amy said nothing.

Harry looked at him, an enquiring smile on his face. 'Do you want me to head off?'

'No, no. I want you to know this as well. If you ever need anything, money, help in any way, always remember you can come to me. I don't have any children of my own so you two have always been my family, particularly as I was so fond of your mother, Amy.'

Amy felt a sudden regret for her initial irritation.

‘Thanks, Doug, that’s much appreciated.’ Harry was first to speak. ‘But I hope we won’t have to put you on the spot.’

‘Amy, John mentioned that you and Steve have been under financial pressure for some time and that is the reason for your split, so I want to offer you some money, just to get you over this difficult patch, and there’s no need to repay it, it’s a gift. Just let me know how much you want.’

‘Thank you,’ Amy couldn’t say much more.

‘I loved your mother, Amy, very much, so I always thought of you as my daughter, my imaginary family. We were all very close in the old days. I have to admit that for a long time I hoped that Maxine and I might be together. Crazily hoped she would leave your Dad. Of course it was madness on my part, but when you love someone like I loved Max, you imagine anything is possible.’

‘Did you and she ever ...?’ Amy asked softly.

‘Sadly no,’ he smiled. ‘Not that I didn’t dream about it every night of my life. But no. Maxine didn’t feel the same way. It was always John for her.’

‘Hey dude, that’s tough.’ Harry whistled.

‘I thought so at the time. I was devastated when she died.’

Amy couldn’t believe what she was hearing.

‘So you’ll understand how I feel about you two, and why I want to help.’

‘That’s cool,’ Harry said.

‘I didn’t realise,’ Amy managed to speak at last.

‘It wasn’t something I was shouting from the rooftops. Had to keep a low profile, and hope. I often used to wonder whether she even realised the strength of my feelings.’

‘You never said anything?’

‘No, it’s not something you can just blurt out. I tried to be as close as possible to her, and you too Amy, to make myself indispensible. To always be around so that maybe she’d see me differently, but to be honest I don’t think she even liked me in the last couple of years. I got that distinct vibe, but couldn't understand why.'

Amy stared at him. It was true. Maxine had disliked him intensely. She remembered that time when she had warned her to be careful.

'Amy, don't talk to him, or go anywhere with him. When you are alone don't let him touch you, or do anything else. If that happens you must always tell me, remember that,' her Mom's voice was very clear. She looked around almost expecting to see her standing beside them at that moment.

Amy suddenly questioned her opinion of Doug. Her Mom's attitude towards him had been transferred to herself. She had never given him a chance, always suspicious of him, even where Harry was concerned.

Perhaps she had done the man a disservice. There had been no evidence that he had ever done anything wrong. And it was obvious Harry was extremely comfortable in his presence.

Maybe she had got it wrong?

Maybe Maxine had got it wrong?

Chapter sixty-seven

Steve let himself in the front door. Grimly aware of the emptiness of the house. The lack of warmth. The absence of love without Amy and Emma. He had been with his mother for dinner. She was insisting on cooking for him, obviously not trusting him to do that himself. But he had to feed the dog, Joey, who was looking hopefully at him through the conservatory door. He let him in. The dog jumped up on him enthusiastically, and he played with him for a moment. Then he put out his food, and water, reached for the whiskey, poured himself a glass, and slumped in front of the television.

He had met a friend of his for lunch. Ken was someone he knew at college and whom he had bumped into unexpectedly. The guy owned a number of bars and restaurants and Steve had asked him if there was a job in his organisation for him.

'Maybe, although we're affected badly by the recession, but we're always looking for good people so you never know. Let's meet for a bite of lunch and chat it over.' He was a smooth talking guy and Steve didn't particularly like him, but he wasn't going to be fussy if there was a job at stake.

They met at one of the restaurants, an Italian place in Temple Bar.

'What do you think?' Ken grinned.

'Nice. Going well for you?' Steve was impressed.

'We're just about managing to keep the head above water.'

The waitress handed them the menu cards. He scanned the list, and quickly chose a simple pasta. Ken poured wine, but Steve only sipped a little from his glass. He needed to be sober on this occasion. They chatted about old times. Only coming around to the possibility of a job as they finished off the meal with coffee.

'Have you any experience of the bar and restaurant trade?'

'Not very much,' he grinned. 'I did some summer work in New York years ago.'

'Pity about that.'

'Is there a chance of something? I'll do anything. Anything. Just to get myself back into the work force.'

'We pay the minimum wage.'

Steve was shocked. It showed in his expression.

'I know, it's a hell of a jump from what you've been earning, but it's all I can offer.' He cut a square of cheese with his knife, and popped it into his mouth. Poured another glass of wine.

'Is there a job at the moment?' Steve took a deep breath.

'I'll check with my personnel man.'

'Then it could take some time?'

'There's a lot of people looking for jobs.'

'I understand.' He stared down at the table. At the remains of their meal. Some cheese. Water biscuits. The small knife with a sliver of butter on the shining blade. His coffee cup, the dark dregs at the bottom. It was all so normal. Or so abnormal. He couldn't afford to eat in a place like this now, and wondered would that ever happen again.

Steve poured another whiskey, but was still quite clear headed. As every other night, he longed for oblivion so that eventually he could sleep, but now he stared at the liquid in the glass. Then abruptly he stood up, went into the kitchen and threw it into the sink, turned on the tap and flushed it away. No more whiskey. If he was lucky enough to get a job then he had to be sober to hold that down. Had to be sober if he expected Amy and Emma to return to him.

The following morning he went out and tackled the garden.

Chapter Sixty-eight

Doug and John spent days discussing film production procedures. Their spat of some months before had been forgotten. They talked over the internet with the script writer they had chosen. Already, some financial backers had come on board, so now they had to choose locations, cast, crew, and contract all the other people who would be involved. The script was sent back to the scriptwriter by email. Adjustments were made. And it came back again to John and Doug. Over and over.

'What do you think of the changes to this scene?' John asked.

'It's not giving me exactly what I want.' Doug read over the text.

'What about asking Amy? She will be playing the part.'

'I'll get her, she's outside somewhere.'

Gradually it became a reality for Amy. She was going to play Lea, the wife of the soldier. She read the script again and again, and slowly began to get into the mind of the woman. Now she had a purpose. It gave her reason to get up out of bed in the morning.

There had been no contact from Steve and she was glad of that. Something would have to be arranged, she knew that. But she pushed it away from her. Only able to deal with her life on a day to day basis. She would do this film. They would be financially secure. Even thinking about Steve's attitude to her decision made her angry. That was the worst part of it. He wanted to dominate her. To turn her against her father. She couldn't understand that, particularly when she had only reconciled with her Dad so recently.

Harry and Doug left for the US a couple of weeks later, and it was just the three of them again. Her father, Emma and herself. She cleaned. She cooked. She baked. She spent all her time with Emma after school, but once she had gone to bed the hours hung heavily.

Storing away some things in the attic, she saw the box which contained the diaries. She had put it in the back of the car when she left Sandyford. A spur of the moment decision. There was so much of Nuala between those pages she couldn't have left the diaries behind. Now she went through them. Put them in order. She had already flicked through some of them, and now she came to 1985.

The year she was eight. The year her mother had died.

She turned the pages until she came to the month of May. Her heart began to thump. All that week the entries were normal. Short lines in Nuala's neat handwriting about her daily activities. Then Saturday. A much longer entry. She flicked forward. The writing covered the days. One long entry for at least two weeks. Her eyes moved across the lines. They varied in clarity. It was all about Maxine. All about her mother. She went back to that first day.

May 29, 1985.
"John phones. He tells me that Maxine has had an accident and that she is in St. Vincent's Hospital. I ask him questions but he won't give me answers. Just says she is in a coma and would I go to see her? He is returning to LA.

My darling lies in a sterile hospital bed. Wearing one of those horrible gowns so different to what she usually wears - all silks and satins. She is still bruised from the accident. A purple weal across her forehead, black and blue shadows everywhere else on her body. The nurses say the internal injuries will heal in time. But she is somewhere I can't reach. I hold her hand. I kiss her. I talk to her. But she doesn't answer. She lies there, her eyes closed, tubes attached. I listen to the constant sound of the machines breathing for her. The lights flickering. Soft voices of the nurses dealing with other patients. Footsteps. Rustling. The clink of dishes. I try to breathe for her. To communicate. Wake up, Max, wake up. I whisper. I sit at her bed. The nurses give me a blanket and a pillow. I sleep there. A few minutes at a time. They check her constantly."

Amy couldn't believe what she was reading. And how could her father return to the States when Maxine was so ill? Why wasn't he on the other side of the bed holding her hand? She had an immediate urge to rush downstairs and demand that he explain that fact to her. She read more quickly now. Understanding how the events had unfolded with an increasing sense of horror. The arguments between Nuala and John about the decision to turn off the life support. His acceptance of the doctors' opinion that there was no activity in Maxine's brain. Nuala's disagreement with that. Fighting their medical expertise.

"I beg John. I cry. I tell him what Maxine was like when she was little. And how beautiful she was. And talented. And how her life was all ahead of her. And that now she must be there for Amy. A child needs her mother. There were people living full lives now who had come out of coma after a few weeks. Or maybe even a few months. Or years. I tell him I'll wait here by her bedside. Every day. Every night. For however long it takes."

Tears moistened Amy's eyes. She dashed them away.

"John stands by the bed and stares down at my Maxine. For someone who supposedly loves her, he doesn't show it. His eyes cold. I can't understand him. How anyone could be like that. He talks with the doctors. They ignore me. I feel so helpless all of the time. If only there was something I could do. I pray. Rosaries. Unending rosaries. Begging God to bring her back to me."

Amy mopped the tears which fell freely now.

Guilt resurged. Was it her fault? Amy wondered. She couldn't blow out all the candles. Her father had been so angry. The air was filled with shouting. Screaming. Was that when the accident happened, and her mother was taken away from her?

Chapter Sixty-nine

She went into the dining room where her father had his scripts and papers strewn across the long dining table. He worked on his laptop. His back to her. She twisted her hands nervously.

'Dad?'

'Yea?' He didn't move, still concentrating on the screen.

'Can I talk to you?'

'Not now, I'm busy.' The sharp retort took her back.

'It's just a question, I have to know,' she insisted.

'Know what?'

'How did Mom die?'

His fingers stopped moving.

'I told you. There was an accident. How many more times do I have to repeat that?'

'Tell me exactly what happened?'

'What are you bringing that up for now?' he asked, his voice low.

'I want to know.'

'It's history. Don't want to talk about it,' he grunted. His fingers began to touch the keys again.

That annoyed her. She moved around the table to face him. 'She lived for two weeks after it happened.'

'She didn't.'

'She did,' Amy insisted.

'How do you know that?' He continued to look at the screen.

'From Nuala's diaries.'

'Bloody woman, always trouble,' he sighed.

'Don't say that about her.'

'Let it rest, Amy, there's no point in going on about it now. I have a lot to do. Contact people in LA, send emails, make calls. We're at a crucial stage.'

'I have to know whether it was my fault or not. I have to know.' She pushed the screen of the laptop and it fell on to his hands.

'What are you at?' He pulled his hands out. 'Trying to injure me?'

'I'm trying to get your attention. It was my birthday. I was eight. Or don't you remember that. And there was a row over the candles. And you shouted at Mom and she screamed, and the cake went everywhere.' Amy's voice died away. Her breathing was heavy. There were tears in her eyes.

'For God's sake. That was years ago. How could you remember what went on? You were just a child,' he growled.

'It's become clearer each day since I've been here. I can see her. Feel her. We were so happy here.'

'Rubbish, it's all in your imagination.'

'Tell me how the accident happened? Nuala didn't even know that.'

'She ran down the avenue out on to the road.'

'Why did she do that?'

'How do I know?' he shrugged.

Amy paced the room. A sudden memory. An image of hands held tight. 'Don't hurt my Mom.' She heard a childish voice cry out. It was so clear.

'Did she run from you?'

He stared at her.

'Was she afraid of you?'

'Don't be crazy.' He looked away. 'I loved her.'

'I want you to answer me.'

'I tell you I loved her.'

'I think you caused that accident,' she said emotionally. 'You hit her, you dragged her away from me.'

'Amy, it's not true.'

'Why did you agree to switch off the life support?'

'The doctors told me it was the only thing to be done. They didn't expect her to recover. And if she came out of the coma she would be in a vegetative state.'

'But you couldn't be sure about that. Nuala begged you. Mom might have woken up from the coma at any time. It wasn't as if you couldn't afford to pay for her care. You had plenty of money then and could have paid for years if necessary, until there had been advances in medicine which may have helped her. But you turned off the machine. And she died. How could you have done that?'

'I had to follow the medical opinion.' He stood up, went to the drinks cabinet and poured a glass of whiskey.

'It's so easy to blame them. But what about this scenario? Maybe you were afraid that if she did recover then everyone would find out exactly what happened. That she was afraid of you. Why else would she run down the avenue on to the road?'

'How dare you accuse me of such a thing.' His face flushed. He gulped the drink. Walked around the room. Past the ornate marble fireplace. He touched the backs of the row of dining chairs as he passed. Up to the window and back again. 'Another guy knocked her down. He was going too fast. It was his fault. Although all he got was a fine, and lost his licence for a couple of years.'

'I just want the truth. So I can go on. I need closure. For Mom. I don't even know where she's buried.' Her anger matched his now.

'She was cremated.'

'And her ashes?'

'Scattered.'

'Where?'

'Here.'

Amy rushed to the window and stared out into the garden. It was a windy night. The trees swayed. Shadows shifted. She turned back to him. 'Tell me the truth,' she screamed, crying hysterically.

'Calm down will you. This has to stop now.' He moved closer to her. 'Amy, do you hear me?'

'You killed her. It was you. And what were you doing in the back garden in the middle of the night? You were digging. What was that all about?'

'I was burying the bloody dog,' he roared.

She stared at him in silence for a moment, horrified. 'Was that when you buried Mom's ashes too?'

'For God's sake, Amy, you're losing it altogether.'

'You killed my mother.'

'I made Maxine Howard. Created her. And I created you. All the best parts of you are me. And we're going to walk up the red carpet and win Oscars with this next film.'

Their eyes bored into each other. So much anger and unhappiness in hers. So much anger and God knows what else in his. 'You can walk up the red carpet on your own. You're obsessed with that red carpet. I don't want any part of it.'

She rushed upstairs, and into Emma's bedroom. 'We're going, Emma, get up.' She pulled out a suitcase, dragged clothes off hangers, and began to bundle them into it.

'Mummy?' Emma sat up and stared at her.

'Come on, pet.'

'Where are we going? Home?'

'I don't know yet.'

'Will Daddy be there?'

'I don't know.'

'Amy?' her father roared.

She could hear his footsteps on the stairs. Heavy. Ominous.

'What's wrong with Grandad?' Emma turned towards the door.

Amy pushed the door closed. But it immediately burst open again and her father stood there. Breathing heavily.

'Get downstairs,' he growled.

She was helping Emma to dress. Her hands were shaking.

He grabbed her by the shoulder. His fingers dug into her. 'I want to talk to you - now.'

She pulled a fleece on Emma, and stood up. 'Put on your shoes, honey.'

His hand slipped down her arm and gripped tight. He began to pull her towards the door.

'Mummy,' Emma cried, and ran to her.

'Let go of me.' Amy was in tears again.

'Stay there, Emma,' John yelled, and pushed her back into the room. She fell awkwardly against the bed. Then he dragged Amy through the door and on to the landing. He held her arm painfully behind her back and forced her to walk ahead of him.

'Mummy?' Emma called.

'I'll be back in a minute, Emma.'

'Get down those stairs.' He hunted her down.

Her feet slipped on the carpeted stairs. 'You're hurting me.'

'That's what you deserve.' He forced her into the living room. 'Now, take back what you said. I never want you to repeat that again. No-one is to hear those lies.'

'I won't take it back. It's the truth.' She stood up to him.

He bent down and picked up something and then his arm swept towards her. She backed towards the door, watched him come towards her. In slow motion. As if it was happening to someone else. The blow struck hard. The pain was excruciating. She fell sideways. And crashed to the floor.

Chapter Seventy

John dropped the brass poker which thumped on the carpet and rolled slowly to a halt against the edge of the marble fireplace. He looked down at Amy. His face expressionless.

'Maxine,' he whispered, and bent on his knee to touch her face with his hand. 'Maxine? Wake up, please, wake up,' Tears filled his eyes. 'I'm so sorry for everything. I didn't love you enough. I've been obnoxious, it should have been me that night, not you.'

He rose slowly, and walked across the room towards the French doors. He opened them and went out on to the patio, his figure silhouetted in the light of the full moon in the sky above. He stood there for a time, and then walked into the shadows of the garden and disappeared.

Chapter Seventy-one

Emma covered her face with her hands and sobbed. Then she climbed back into bed suddenly afraid. What if Grandad came upstairs again? She burrowed down under the duvet and squeezed her eyes shut.

After a while the noise stopped. It was quiet downstairs now. She climbed out of bed and crept on to the landing. Her small hand rubbed the wooden knob of the banisters, its' warmth comforting. She put her foot on to the first step, and continued on down. At the bottom turn in the stairs, she peered over the edge and could just see into the living room. Tears filled her eyes when she saw her mother lying on the floor.

'Mom?'

There was a bang and a rush of icy cold air. And another bang. And another.

She turned and ran back upstairs again, very scared.

Chapter Seventy-two

Steve heard the phone ring. For a moment he was tempted to ignore it, but then he pushed himself up out of the chair and picked it up. He had made a great effort this last week to cut his alcohol intake, only taking a couple of drinks in the evening, usually wine instead of whiskey. So he was quite sober when he saw Amy's number on the read out.

'Daddy?'

'Emma, is that you, Emma?' he asked emotionally, so long since he had heard her voice.

'Daddy, Mummy's lying on the floor, and Grandad was shouting at her, and there's something banging, Daddy are you there?' She was crying.

'Yes, I am, Emma, my love, stop crying now.' He was shocked to hear his child so distressed, and at first he didn't know what to do, or how to help her. 'Now listen to me, pet, listen.'

'Yes, Daddy.' She snuffled.

'Where are you now?'

'In Mummy's room.'

'And where is Grandad?'

'I don't know. Come quick, Daddy.'

Slowly he became focussed.

'I'll be there as quick as I can, but I'm going to ring the Gardai and they'll be there in a minute. But you run somewhere and hide, like when we play hide and seek, you're great at finding places.'

'I'll go under Mummy's bed.'

'That's a good idea and when you hear a nice Garda looking for you, come out then. Now you click off the phone, you know the little red button. And when it rings, press the green one and it will be me. I love you, Emma.'

He rushed down the hall, only stopping to pick up his jacket and keys, but as he punched in the alarm code he realised that he couldn't drive. The two glasses of wine could possibly have put him over the limit as he hadn't had much to eat. He had a dreadful sense of helplessness as he stared at the car parked in the drive.

He took out his phone and rang the Gardai. Telling them what was happening and giving them directions to the house. He called Emma again relieved when she answered the phone. 'Are you all right, love?'

'Yes,' she answered.

'The Gardai are on their way. They'll look after you. I'm driving down now.'

He dialled the number of a taxi firm he knew. Furious when they said they hadn't anyone to take him that distance. He tried another firm, and another, but the answer was the same. Then he rang his friend, Jimmy. Feeling guilty that he hadn't been in touch in a while.

'I need to get to Clifden immediately, Jimmy, but I've had a couple of drinks and can't drive, any chance that you?' he hesitated. 'I know it's a lot to ask.'

'What? Galway?'

'There's something wrong with Amy and Emma.'

'Sorry Steve, but I've had a few drinks, I'm in the pub now, what about a taxi?'

'No luck.'

'I know Tom's away, but Babs, she's at home. She'll run you down, no prob.'

'Do you think? It's a very long way.' He now realised the enormity of what he was asking. But he called her and was so grateful when she agreed immediately.

He rang Emma. 'Have the Gardai come yet?'

'No Daddy.'

He rang them again. They said a car was on its' way. He rushed upstairs and grabbed a bag, running from the bedroom to the bathroom in an agitated state, putting things in that he didn't need and forgetting others. He continued to talk to Emma as he floundered around. She seemed less upset now. Telling him about school and her friends. And that it was cold under the bed.

'Pull the duvet down, that'll keep you warm.'

Babs' car pulled into the driveway and he rushed out. Joey bounded after him.

'Thanks a million, Babs, don't know what I'd have done if you couldn't - just give me a minute.' He grabbed Joey by his collar and managed to get him through the house and out into the back garden. He normally slept outside in his kennel, and now Steve left out water and food for him. Then he locked up, and climbed into the car. He threw the bag at his feet, surprised to see Rachel sitting in the back seat.

'Tell us what happened?' she said.

He rang Emma again.

'There's someone coming up the stairs, Daddy.' She sounded nervous.

'I'm sure it's the Gardai.' He prayed that it was.

'There's someone calling,' she whispered.

'What's he saying?'

'He said my name.'

'Don't move until he comes into the room.'

'The door is opening.' Emma's voice was high-pitched, so afraid.

'Don't worry.'

'He's got big black shoes.'

Steve listened intently. Trying to pick up the sounds made by the other person in the room.

'Emma, what did he say?'

'He said he's the Gardai.'

'Give him the phone and I'll talk to him.'

He could hear her crawl out, her breathing fast.

'Hello, Mr. Lewis?'

'How is my daughter?'

'She seems fine.'

'And my wife?'

'The ambulance crew have just arrived. They are looking after her.'

'Can you find out how she is, and let me know, please?' he insisted.

Suddenly the phone went dead.

'Battery must have gone,' he mouthed an obscenity under his breath.

'Phone the land line,' Rachel suggested.

He pulled the number up on his log and it dialled. The phone rang out until it went on to the answering machine, a pseudo American accent prompting him to leave a message.

'Can't imagine the Gardai having time to answer the phone under these circumstances anyway,' Babs said.

'Don't suppose so.' He cleared the line dispiritedly, and leaned his head back on the seat.

'They'll phone you back.'

'Yea.' He stared out the window.

Chapter Seventy-three

Amy had been flown by helicopter to Beaumont Hospital in Dublin and now lay in ICU, wired up to various machines which hummed and beeped keeping her alive. There was purple bruising along the side of her face which was stark against the pale pallor. A dressing covered the injury which had been operated on. But she hadn't woken up after the trauma and the medical opinion was that she was in coma. Steve sat by her bedside and held her hand.

'Amy?' he whispered her name. 'My love. Please wake up.' He had repeated the same words so many times, his throat was hoarse. 'I'm so sorry about everything that happened, I've treated you and Emma so badly, I've been despicable, but I've always loved you both, please believe me.'

Her eyes were closed, she was motionless.

'Just move your finger a tiny bit, then I'll know that you can hear me.'

A nurse came into the cubicle, and began to check Amy.

'How is she?' he asked nervously, almost afraid to hear what she had to say.

'She's stable at the moment, we'll be having a team meeting later and will talk to you then.' She was gentle, but not very reassuring.

'How soon do you think she'll come out of the coma?' He moved with her towards the door of ICU.

'We don't know, but we'll talk to you after the meeting.'

‘Thank you.’ Steve turned back to the cubicle where Amy lay. He sat by the bed again and kissed her. Shoulders hunched. Face gaunt. He sat there, his mind caught in a crazy maelstrom of regret and heartbreak. Emma was being looked after by his mother, and Doug and Harry were on their way over from the US. Now he wondered about John’s whereabouts. The Gardai had told him that he wasn’t at the house when they arrived.

The medical team meeting later that day was inconclusive. In one way the medics seemed to think that Amy’s own body had closed down in order to give her injury a chance to mend and for a few days this wouldn’t be any harm. But if that wasn’t the case then continuation of the coma beyond that length of time could prove to be dangerous and possibly fatal. Steve was distraught. Holding himself responsible for everything.

Babs, Rachel, Jimmy and Tom, came in later.

‘How is she?’ All were very anxious.

‘There’s no change.’ He was grim.

‘What’s the prognosis?’

‘They don’t know yet.’ He shook his head.

‘I’ve brought a player and some CD’s to play. It might remind Amy of old times,’ Babs said. ‘Do you think that would be allowed?’

‘I’m not sure.’

‘I’ll ask. You go home and get some rest, you haven’t slept in forty-eight hours,’ Babs suggested.

‘I don’t want to leave her. I want to be here when she wakes up.’

‘You can’t stay here night and day, that’s ridiculous,’ Rachel admonished. ‘Have some sense. We’ll phone you if there’s any change, and they won’t allow all of us in anyway, so go home and spend some time with Emma.’

‘You’re right.’ He gave in.

‘Of course we’re right.’

He drove home. The emptiness of the house was ominous but as he walked through he heard Joey bark from outside. He let him in and put out food and water for him.

Then his eyes spotted the wine bottle and the half full glass he had been using on the night he received the phone call from Emma. A sudden craving swept through him. God, he needed a drink. He began to shake. He held on to the table as the tremors moved from his hands to his arms and through his body. He bit his lip, and could feel blood ooze into his mouth. He sank into a chair and stayed there trying to control his addiction.

But he couldn't do it. After a time, he got up, and opened the presses, searching for a bottle of whiskey which he knew he had put there. Frustrated, he pushed the contents of the presses aside. Some of the bottles, jars and other kitchen utensils fell with a loud crash on top of him and on to the floor.

'Where the fuck is it?' he shouted. 'Fuck!' He swept his hand across the items on the counter. Mugs toppled and rolled. The toaster slid. The kettle fell with a clunk. Among the debris he spotted the bottle of wine still standing. Graceful. Like a woman. Tantalising. He grabbed it by the neck and raised it. He had to have it. Every nerve-ending craved. The liquid raced towards his mouth. Swilled inside. Bitter. He gagged. Coughed. And spat. Shakily he stared at the bottle. Then with a shout of derision, he threw it into the sink. What was left of the red liquid swilled around and around in diminishing circles until it disappeared down the plug hole.

He stood under the shower. The hot water spattered over him. He closed his eyes. The sharpness of the spray cut through him. He lost any sense of time. He didn't know where he was. He turned the setting and the water was suddenly freezing. He held his breath. A cry of shock caught in his throat. But he stayed there, becoming colder and colder.

Chapter Seventy-four

'Daddy?' Emma threw herself at him as soon as he arrived at his mother's house. 'Is Mummy all right, did you tell her I love her?'

He lifted her up and hugged her, suddenly overcome with emotion. It whipped through him and he felt weak and helpless.

'Steve?' His mother appeared from the kitchen, wiping her hands on her apron. 'How's Amy?'

He shook his head dispiritedly.

'Give it time, she's going to be fine. Why don't you have something to eat, I've a roast in the oven and it's just ready.'

'Daddy, can I go into the hospital to see Mummy?' Emma tightened her grip around him. Her eyes on the same level as his own. Amy's eyes. Dark brown. Velvet.

'I'll have to ask the doctors, but I'm sure we can bring you in soon.'

'Will I be going back to my old school?' she asked.

'I don't know.' He was caught. He didn't know what was going to happen and didn't want to tell a lie. 'Why don't you take a holiday, I'm sure your teachers won't mind.' That reminded him that he should contact the school in Clifden.

'I have to bring in a note.'

'I'll do that.'

'You won't forget?'

'No, pet.'

'Come on, you two, inside now, and sit down.' His mother busied herself at the cooker.

'Dad, I went shopping with Gran. She bought me new things. Do you like my lilac skirt and top?' She raised her hands wide and circled. 'And there's a little scarf that matches it. Look at me.'

'You're really pretty, love.'

Steve hugged his mother and whispered his thanks. He felt so grateful, aware that he had never really appreciated her until now.

'I'll set the table.' Emma took cutlery from the drawer.

He suddenly realised that he was starving.

'We've been praying to Baby Jesus for Mummy, haven't we Gran?' Emma tucked into her dinner.

'Indeed we have.'

'What about Mummy's clothes and mine too? We left them all in Clifden.'

'She doesn't need them yet.' He could feel the soreness of the cut inside his lip. It seemed to remind. He winced.

'Will we buy new things for her too?'

'Yea, we will.'

'Can I choose?'

'Of course you can.'

'I know what she likes.'

He smiled at Emma. Only noticing now that she had grown taller since that last time he had seen her. He regretted losing all of those months with her. His child was growing up and he had missed out.

'We've prayed for Mummy. We said a rosary in the morning and one in the evening, and asked God to look after her especially. Do you think he will?'

'Of course.'

'Where's Grandad?'

'He's still in Clifden.'

'Is he coming up to see Mummy in the hospital?'

'I don't know, pet.'

'He shouted at Mummy and she fell.'

'Did you see him hit Mummy?' he asked gently.

'He pulled her away from me. He'll have to say he's sorry. I was afraid.'

'You don't have to be afraid any more.' He kissed her on the forehead. But inside him, anger raged. If he could only get hold of that bastard he'd beat him to pulp.

'Will you be staying with us, Daddy?'

'Yes, my love,' he kissed her again.

'I don't want Grandad to be here ...' Her white teeth gripped her lower lip.

'Don't worry, if you don't want to see Grandad then that's OK.'

She put her arms around him and hugged close.

His mobile rang. It was the Gardai in Clifden. He went outside to take the call. They wanted to interview him.

The two plain clothes Gardai who came to the house the following morning were pleasant, but thorough. Their forensic team had been examining the house in Clifden, and had established a search for John. But so far they had not found him in the area. They asked Steve a long list of detailed questions which he struggled to answer accurately. Although, as they repeated a lot of them he wasn't sure whether he gave the exact same reply each time.

'Where were you at the time of the alleged attack?'

'I was driving from Dublin, being driven actually, I phoned you myself to go over to the house.'

The Garda made a note.

'And what time did you arrive?'

'I think it was about eleven.'

'Were you alone?'

'No, there were three of us.'

'We will need the names of the other two people.'

'I've already given them to you.'

'Do you have a key to the house?'

'No, I don't.'

'But your wife would have one?'

'Of course, she was living there.'

'With whom?'

'Her father and daughter.'

'What is the name of her daughter?'

'She's also my daughter, and her name is Emma, and you know that already,' he snapped.

'Did you speak with your wife?'

'No, I didn't, she had been taken to hospital in Galway by that stage.'

'Why did you come to Clifden on that night?'

'My daughter phoned me.'

'For what reason?'

'Because she had seen her mother lying on the floor.'

'Would it be possible to talk with your daughter?'

That question shocked him. He didn't know what to say. His immediate response was to say no. Emma was so young, he didn't know what it would do to her to be in the presence of the Gardai, who had already made him feel under pressure with all their questions.

'I don't know.'

'It would mean a lot to the case if we have her evidence, although she did explain to the Gardai who arrived on the night that there had been a row between her mother and grandfather.'

'Then surely that's enough.'

'Children don't always understand the way things happen. She may have been confused,' the man suggested slowly.

'Who do you think it was then? There was no-one else there.' Steve was puzzled. What was he getting at?

'It could have been anyone. An intruder perhaps.'

Steve stared at him, his mind trying to keep up with him.

'So you can see how important it is for us to talk to your daughter.'

‘At the moment, her mother is very ill and she is disturbed about that, I don’t want her worried.’

They nodded. ‘Have you any idea where John Parker might be?’

He shook his head.

‘Has he travelled much in Ireland?’

‘I don’t think so, he spends most of his time at the house outside Clifden when he isn’t in LA.’

They looked at their notes.

‘Do you get on well?’

‘Not particularly,’ he grimaced.

‘How long did it take you to drive from Dublin?’

‘The usual, I wasn’t looking at the clock, and I wasn’t driving.’

‘Would you ask the other two people to contact us, we’re anxious to see them.’

He agreed.

‘Let us know if you have any contact with Mr. Parker, or anyone else in the family.’

They shook hands.

‘Hope your wife makes a full recovery.’

Steve closed the door after them, trying not to bang it too hard. Talking about John allowed his anger to surface again and all he wanted was revenge for what he had done to Amy.

Chapter Seventy-five

Steve picked Doug and Harry up from the airport, and drove them straight to the hospital, where Amy was in the Richmond ICU, Neurosurgical.

'Has there been any improvement today?' Harry asked.

'Her head wound is healing, but she is still in a coma.' His voice was grim.

'Should we transfer her out of here, maybe to the States, she might get better treatment,' Doug suggested. 'I know people in the Mayo Clinic, the top doctors, it could make all the difference.'

'She's getting the best here, and we're hoping that as her injury heals she will come out of it,' Steve defended. 'And it might be dangerous to move her.'

'That's up to the medics here, but if they agree I can pay for it, whatever it costs,' Doug offered. 'There's no need to think about money. We can have a private medical jet here in a matter of hours, fully staffed, she'll get top class treatment.'

'I think it's more important to have her family and friends around her, they say that familiarity can often bring a patient around.' Steve felt he was being boxed into a corner. Most of all, he didn't want Doug's money, no more than he had ever wanted John's money. And he didn't want to lose Amy. He wanted to be there when she woke up. And she would. He knew that. She would come back to him.

'Well, I'll leave that up to you, but remember the offer's there,' Doug said.

‘Thank you, I appreciate your generosity,’ he said.

There was only one person allowed in at a time to see Amy and Steve gave Harry the chance to see his sister. The nurse who was personally looking after Amy today took him in and he sank on to the chair by her bedside. He was shocked and said nothing at first.

‘You can hold Amy’s hand if you like, but watch the i.v. line,’ the nurse suggested. She checked the various tubes which were attached to her, and repositioned the pillow and quilt.

‘Can she hear me?’ His tanned fingers covered hers. Small. Pale.

‘We don’t know.’

‘But it’s possible?’

‘Of course, and if she can she will be happy to hear your voice. Talk to her, it might bring her back to you.’ She left.

‘Ame, it’s me, hi,’ he whispered. ‘God I wish this hadn’t happened, I can’t believe you’re just lying here and you can’t talk to me. Wake up, please,’ he paused for a while, too upset to speak. Then began again after a few moments. ‘I’m having a great season with the Red Sox, and I do some horse riding at a stables near where we train. You’d love the horse I ride, I know you would, he’s a great jumper and really cool. As good as Dancer was, remember him, and how he used to leap over the five barred gate in the meadows and the two of us on his back. Can you hear me?’ He kissed her fingers. ‘We used to brush him so much, his coat was always gleaming, and he loved a lump of sugar or an apple.’ Tears filled his blue eyes. ‘Remember when I was little I called you Ame, and Maria used to make me try to say Amy but I couldn’t ... ’

The nurse came in, put her arm on Harry’s shoulder and stood by him. She gave him a few minutes then she helped him to his feet. The tall broad-shouldered man and the diminutive girl – an odd contrast.

He came out into the waiting room and sat down heavily. He said nothing.

Steve looked at him. 'Are you all right?'

Harry nodded.

'I'll get coffee.' Steve went to the dispenser and poured three cups.

He handed a cup to Harry, who took a gulp of the dark liquid.

'It's tough the first time you see Amy, such a shock, but she is better now than she was,' Steve said.

'She didn't respond to me. I could always depend on Ame, and now I can do nothing for her. Nothing.'

'Perhaps I might be able to see her for a moment?' Doug asked. 'I know I'm not family but I'd like to talk to her.'

'Yea, sure,' Steve agreed immediately.

When they left, Steve took up his position at Amy's bedside again. He felt he was living here now. For the last few days the walls of this place had enclosed him. When he left here he couldn't wait to get back to the bustling ICU ward where his darling Amy existed on the brink of life.

He was worn out. Empty. He had faced his addiction yesterday. Glared at it in the face. An evil spirit. He had stood against it. For twenty-two hours, twenty-three hours, and now almost twenty-four hours. Each hour to be faced alone. He curled his hand into a fist. Tight. And vowed to stay away from alcohol. He had taken his last drink.

Chapter Seventy-six

Doug drove to Clifden. On the journey, he couldn't get the sight of Amy lying in that bed out of his head. There had been something haunting about her. Her limbs softly relaxed. Her eyes closed. Dark eyelashes brushed crescents on her cheeks. She had lost weight and her classical bone structure was accentuated. Immediately he had seen Maxine in those features. The woman he had loved all those years. From that very first night when they had met at a cocktail party to the day he had heard that she had died, he had existed in her shadow. So much longing in him. So much love. All those years stifled.

At the house, he turned the key in the front door, and pushed it open. He walked into the hallway and put down the suitcase. There was a strange atmosphere in the house. He wandered around. Everything seemed to be in its place but yet occasionally he saw something which was incongruous and puzzled him.

He called on Brid who told him that the Gardai had been there checking the house.

'When did you last see John?' Doug asked.

'Just over a week, on the day it happened actually. It was at lunch time.'

'How was he?'

'Seemed fine, normal. I can't believe he did such a thing to Amy.' There were tears in her eyes.

Doug shook his head. 'Wonder where he's got to?' He looked out over the sea. At the waves crashing on to the sand. It was high tide, and the wind was strong. The type of day John loved.

'The Gardai asked me to let them know if he came back, and would you call on them as well,' Brid said.

He walked the beach that evening. Had John gone away? Unable to face the obvious inquisition by the authorities. Or had he even committed the felony? Had there been anyone else in the house that night? If there had been any other explanation then he shouldn't have left. He dialled John's phone number again, but the line was dead.

He sat on a broad rock, his fingers twisting a piece of seaweed. The evening sun dipped towards the horizon. Wispy clouds drifted across. Trails of lilac. Silver. Pink. As time passed the glowing orb deepened. It blazed deep orange. Flared. And lit up the vastness of the sky. He felt part of this wonder of nature. Seared by flame.

But lost too. Without John. Tormented with worry. Where had he got to? Why hadn't he confided in him. His friend of so many years. Always together through everything which had happened. Perhaps John hadn't realised how much he had cared for him. They had many an argument over the years, but never enough to drive a rift between them. Doug would have done anything for John. Anything.

But time hung heavy. He was frustrated. Finally, he engaged a private detective to look for John, hoping that he would be able to find him.

Chapter Seventy-seven

'Can I go with you to see Mummy?' Emma asked again. As she had every time she saw him over this interminable week.

He glanced at his own mother.

'Mummy is very ill and they don't allow children into the hospital, but as soon as she is better they will let you come in.' He had discussed the possibility of allowing her in to see Amy with his mother, Babs and Rachel too, but they all felt that the environment of the ICU would be too frightening for Emma.

'The men took her to the hospital in the ambulance? It had a blue light.' Emma crumbled a piece of toast. 'And I was in an ambulance too. There was a lady police with me. She was nice.'

He drank a cup of coffee, but his scrambled eggs were left almost untouched.

'Steve, eat your breakfast,' his mother murmured.

He compressed his lips. Suddenly irritated with her. 'I'm not very hungry.' He felt like he was Emma. He took another forkful. It almost choked him.

Steve opened his eyes. Guilty that he had dozed off in the last few minutes.

A nurse stood by the bedside, and he watched her take Amy's temperature, pulse, and change the drip bags. 'No change, all normal,' she murmured.

'Thanks be to God,' he murmured.

'We'll be moving her up to a ward in a day or two.'

'Is that a good thing?' he asked.

'It means she doesn't need this level of intensive care any longer.'

'It could take a long time then? What do you think? Just give me your personal opinion. Tell me about other people, please? I've no-one to ask who will give me a straight answer. The doctors beat around the bush, or at least it seems that way to me. And you're so experienced you probably know more than they do,' he said, with a grin.

The nurse paused in what she was doing. She smiled at him. 'No two cases are the same, I'm sure you can appreciate that. There was a woman in the hospital who was in coma for over a year, and then there are others who recover within a matter of days, or weeks, after suffering an injury similar to Amy's.'

He nodded.

'I'm sorry I can't be of more help.'

'Thank you, I appreciate it, we appreciate it.' He looked down at Amy, and took her hand. Always so conscious that she might be able to hear their voices. He had to keep that in mind. Amy was there. And just because she couldn't communicate with them, that didn't mean she was unable to understand everything which was going on around her.

Three days later, the medical team decreed that Amy should be transferred out of intensive care. While he was worried about that, he knew immediately that there was one person who would be thrilled to hear the news.

'Tomorrow?' Emma hugged him.

'Yea, in the morning.'

'Can I bring her a present?'

'Sure, what about some flowers?'

'I want to buy them.'

They were all there today to celebrate Amy's move to a regular ward. Steve, Carmel, Emma, Harry, Babs and Rachel. While she didn't respond to their presence, there was a more relaxed atmosphere and much less restrictions.

'Mummy?' Emma ran her finger along Amy's arm. 'Tickle, tickle.'

'She's still asleep,' Steve explained.

'But she always laughs when I tickle.'

He didn't know what to say.

'When will she wake up?'

'We're going to help her wake up by coming in to see her as often as we can. Talking to her. Singing to her. Playing music,' Rachel smiled.

'I can do that too.'

It was decided. They worked out a rota which meant someone was there all the time with Amy. Right around the clock. Although Steve was with her during the night and the day too. Going home only to grab a few hours sleep. Carmel looked after Harry and Emma.

Rachel read to Amy. Poetry. Plays. Prose. Babs talked about music and played their favourite tunes from those days at Trinity. Harry talked about their childhood. Steve talked about those days when they first fell in love. Emma did whatever she felt like doing, less aware of the seriousness of Amy's condition.

'Mummy, look at my drawing, I did it last night, see, you're in it, and Daddy and Gran, you're in bed and you're laughing because I'm tickling,' she giggled. She leaned over Amy. 'Here's another one of us in Clifden and see what I brought today, I'm going to paint your nails like I used to, I know you like pink.' She rooted in her little handbag.

'I'm sorry, Steve, I have to get back to Boston soon, but I'm going to Clifden for a few days,' Harry said. 'Must have a look around for my Dad, Doug is already there.'

He nodded. 'I understand.'

'I wish I could stay longer, man, but it's not possible.'

'You were good to come over. I really appreciate it.'

'She's my sister and I love her. But I feel helpless. I want to find my Dad too, but I'm not sure where to look.'

'Do you think Mummy will like this colour?' Emma waved a small bottle of pink polish at Steve.

'Yea, she will, that's pretty.'

She opened it, and put it on the bedside locker. Then she sat on a chair and lifted Amy's index finger up a little. Slowly, carefully, she painted on the polish.

'I think that looks lovely,' Carmel said. 'But maybe just paint one nail. That can look cool.'

Emma smiled. 'It's the same colour as the flowers.'

'I wish Dad was aware of how Amy is. If he was here, he might be able to help her come out of the coma,' Harry said. 'I can't imagine he would have injured her in any way. There must have been someone else there.'

Steve's teeth ground. He just wanted Harry to shut up about John.

'Look Daddy, look, doesn't Mummy's finger look nice?' Emma raised it up. But the look of lifelessness cut through Steve. The fingers floppy. The skin porcelain white.

The nurse came in. 'Steve, there's a woman outside looking for Harry.'

Harry looked surprised, but went outside and returned a few minutes later. 'Steve, my Mom's arrived - Deborah. I told her about Amy and John, and she decided to fly over. She wants to see you.'

'So you're Steve?' Deborah kissed him on both cheeks. 'It's terrible about Amy, how is she, the poor darling?' She seemed very concerned.

'It's good of you to come over, Deborah, but there's no change really, as I'm sure Harry has told you.'

'I'm devastated.' She dabbed the corner of her eyes with a wisp of lace. 'And John's gone missing. I can't believe it. Have you any idea where he is?'

'We don't know,' Harry put his arm around her shoulders and she leaned into him.

'Can I see Amy?'

'Of course, but don't be shocked, she's just asleep,' Steve warned.

She followed him in, and stood staring at Amy.

'Emma, this is Deborah, your step grandmother.'

'Hello step grandmother.' Emma stopped painting Amy's nail and looked around. 'You're pretty.' She looked up at the woman who was dressed in a white linen suit, her blonde hair in a smooth chignon. Her jewellery glittered. She was utterly chic.

Steve was glad to see her, although he had never met her before. But perhaps her voice might have some affect on Amy, he thought, they hadn't got on well he knew, but maybe that in itself might stir something within his darling. It might make her want to get up and have an argument with her which he remembered was all they did when she was young.

Chapter Seventy-eight

For Steve, life stretched out into a slow pattern. Bound by the weird impersonal environs of the hospital, and odd breaks for sleep at home or at his mother's house. Harry returned to the States. Doug came up occasionally from Clifden. Emma went back to her old school in Sandyford. Rachel and Babs were always there for them, and other friends rallied around.

Christmas loomed. But there was no sense of it without Amy. His mother and the girls made a big effort to celebrate. He helped Emma and his mother put up the tree at her house, and all the decorations. Emma sent her letter to Santa Claus, and her Christmas present list was constantly changed. Everyone had to get a present, especially Amy. And there were decorations put up in her cubicle, and in the main ward, so there was a festive feeling about the place.

The season brought a lot of pressure on Steve. The extra costs meant that he had to rely even more on his mother to support them. But she had a good pension from his Dad's firm, and the old age pension also, and insisted on paying for everything.

The weather was also a problem. The unexpectedly low temperatures and heavy snow which occurred in December hampered transport, and Steve had difficulty getting to the hospital. Although he was lucky to be able to connect with both the Luas and Dart line, there was a lot of walking to make the connections, and it meant that Babs and Rachel were unable to get there as often as they usually did. And some of the time Emma was just too small to travel the journey.

He became very frustrated. The medical opinion had stalled. There was no real prognosis. Amy didn't need full life support now, she could breathe alone. But that was all. He sat with her, but had lost the ability to talk. Heartbroken.

Emma was the one bright star among them. When he could manage to bring her with him, she always raised his spirits.

'Mummy, today we went swimming. I swam the whole length of the pool. And Gran bought me a new swimsuit. I love swimming. I'm putting on lipstick now so that you'll look really nice, and I'm going to take off the old polish.' She spread the lipstick on Amy's lips. 'You look like you're going out with Daddy. To see a movie. What would you like to see, Daddy, can you think of a film to take Mummy to?'

He shook his head.

'But I promised her that we'd go out now that she's all made up.'

'I'll try to think of one.' He bent his head.

'I know, we'll go to *Harry Potter*. Mummy likes his films.' She lifted Amy's finger, and with a removal pad she rubbed off the old polish. Then, with extreme care she painted bright red polish on Amy's finger. Her little face screwed up with concentration.

'Oh, Mummy, you've moved your finger and I've made a mess. I'll have to fix it.' She reached for the pad and wiped the polish. 'Mummy, stop moving, I can't do your nails properly.'

Steve jerked up. His body tense. 'Emma? What did you say?'

'I'm sorry.' She scrubbed with the pad.

'What happened?'

'Mummy moved and I couldn't do it right.'

'She moved?' His heart thumped, and he could feel the hair stand up at the back of his neck. He touched Amy's fingers.

'My God.' He could feel a tremor there. 'My love, can you hear me? Amy?' He kissed her hand.

'Look, Mummy's eyes are opening,' Emma squealed excitedly.

Steve leaned closer. 'We're here, love, Emma and me, just waiting for you, can you see us?'

Amy's eyelashes fluttered.

Steve pressed the bell and kept his finger on it.

Amy's eyes opened a little and then closed again.

'Stay awake, Amy, please, don't go away again on me, I couldn't bear it, stay with us.' He dashed away the tears in his eyes.

The nursing staff arrived followed by a couple of doctors and Steve and Emma had to go outside and let them do their work.

'Daddy, is Mummy going to be all right?' She looked up at him, her face pale, so worried. 'What are they doing?'

'Yes, yes, she is, Emma.' He held her hand tight.

'Is it because I didn't do her nail right?' Her voice trembled.

'No, that was good because she moved her hand. She loved you doing her nails and wanted to tell you. She's coming back to us, I know she is,' he whispered.

Steve spoke with the medical team later.

'There's no change physically, she's still stable.' The doctor explained. 'There is a tremor in her fingers and eyes, but we've found nothing else other than that. Sometimes this can happen but doesn't necessarily mean that she has come out of coma.'

His heart crashed inside him. He had been so sure.

Life continued on again. He had lost track of time. He couldn't always tell the difference between day and night. The only one who didn't realise what was happening was Emma.

'Mummy, I helped Gran in the kitchen today. We made an apple pie. I cut the apples and did the flour and the margarine, my hands got all messy, and there was bits of flour on the counter,' she giggled. 'Then we put it in the dish and I put sugar on the apples, and we broke an egg and I spread it around the top. We cooked it in the oven and I'm going to make one for you. It tasted nice. Daddy liked it.'

Christmas Day came. Turkey and ham, Brussels sprouts, roast potatoes, plum pudding. All the usual fare. While Rachel and Babs visited Amy he ate dinner with his mother and Emma. But he couldn't taste the flavours. The food was bland, like soft cardboard. After that they went into the hospital. The ward was packed with people. All visiting their loved ones on this special day. There was such excitement, he almost couldn't bear it.

'I'll open Mummy's present and show it to her.' Amy ripped open the carefully packaged box. 'I've bought you new nail polish so that we can do your nails beautifully, and there's lipstick too. I hope you like them. And this is Daddy's present and Gran's.' She opened these as well. Perfume from Steve and a cream silk scarf from Carmel.

'Look, isn't the scarf lovely, I helped Gran pick it out and the perfume too.' She squirted some on to Amy's hand. 'It has a lovely smell, I like it.' Carefully, she put it back in its' box and left it on the locker, as she did with the nail polish, and lipstick. She spent some time refolding the scarf neatly. Then she sat looking at Amy for a moment before turning to Steve and Carmel. 'Mummy can't see her presents. Do you think she will wake up today?'

'I don't know, Emma.' He hugged her.

'She knows we're here, Emma, she can hear you talking, and she loves you,' Carmel said softly.

'Do you think so?' Emma touched Amy's hand.

'Give her another kiss. Tell her you love her,' Steve suggested.

She gave Amy a kiss on the cheek. 'I love you, Mummy. This is Christmas. And Santa Claus came and brought me this lovely baby doll. And she cries, and takes her bottle, and I've lovely clothes for her.' She held up the doll for a moment, and then lowered it. 'She can't see her,' she said despondently.

It was the first time that Emma had become disheartened. It made Steve feel even worse, and guilty that she was picking up on his own depression. He still longed for a drink, and managed to stay off alcohol with increasing difficulty. He didn't know how long he could keep it up. The future looked extremely bleak. Would Amy ever come back to them?

Chapter Seventy-nine

Doug stayed on in Clifden. He couldn't have gone home without knowing what had happened to John. He still worked on plans for the film, really just to have something to do. Although he realised now that Amy would probably never be involved. It might be a long time before she recovered. He found it very difficult. Taken back in time to when Maxine died. The loss of the woman he loved never faded. In fact, now it was even worse with the disappearance of John. He had lost them both.

The weather was inclement, so he fished from the shore. It got him out of the house, always hoping that when he got back, John would be there.

The private detective he had engaged to look for John when he had first gone missing had come up with nothing.

To his surprise, Deborah hired a car and was driven down to Clifden. Doug welcomed her, but wondered as to her motivation. The Deborah he knew had only one interest.

'This is such a wild place, Doug, don't know how you stick it.' She stood looking out the big picture window at the stormy sea.

'I love it, and John does too.'

'That whole thing with Amy is very strange isn't it?'

'It's not clear what happened. If we could only find John it might all be sorted but until that happens then we continue to be in the dark.' he sighed.

The Gardai still had a warrant out for John's arrest. He had talked to them, anxious to see what efforts they were making to find him.

'Did you carry out searches in the area? Perhaps he had an accident and could be lying injured somewhere?' he had asked the Garda.

'It isn't a missing persons, it's a felon on the run, sir.'

'But it's strange he hasn't turned up somewhere.'

The Garda shuffled among his papers, and hadn't anything else to say.

'Did John take his passport?' Deborah asked.

'No, nor credit cards.'

'Has money been taken out of his bank account?'

'I can't get access to his personal account. We have a joint company account but nothing has been withdrawn.'

She didn't say anything.

'I've been searching locally. Myself and John have done a lot of walking around here and some of those trails are rough, it's always possible he may have fallen. Do you want to come along?'

'Well, it wouldn't be my thing, and I don't have the gear.' She shook her head. Distaste quite apparent on her face.

'There's jackets and stuff here you could use.' He deliberately tried to make it easy for her, but knew well she wouldn't take the bait.

Doug's searches were organised, and he always told Brid where he was going. So he worked out in spirals from the house into the hinterland. Always carrying his phone, a sandwich and a hot drink in a flask. It gave him a purpose to his day. He kept detailed notes of the various areas he covered, like he was scripting a film.

After he had searched most of the possibilities inland, he went towards the sea. Taking the car, he drove further and further distances and checked every inch of coastline he could access.

It was when he had almost covered the whole local area that he spotted something caught in a rock crevice on the beach nearest the house. It was metal. And attracted the light. He reached down and picked it up. It was a phone, or part of one. Astonishment whipped through him as he stared at it, recognising it immediately. Suddenly, all the uncertainty he had around John's disappearance faded. There had been an accident. He was sure of that now. John would never go anywhere without his phone. He stared out to sea, and a terrible premonition swept through him.

He talked with the Gardai again to try and persuade them to take a different approach. But they didn't consider that the find of the phone to be relevant.

Deborah stayed on, but she found Clifden a very uncomfortable place. One evening as Doug made dinner, he opened a bottle of wine, and decided to try to find out exactly why she was here. Deborah would never choose to live in such a cold climate. And he didn't think for one moment it was all to do with Amy.

'Doug, you're not a bad cook,' she said, slouching across the couch in the living room.

'It's basic, I try.'

'Thanks for cooking dishes to suit me.'

'Salads are not difficult,' he said, smiling.

'I appreciate someone going to the trouble, it's not often that happens.'

'What about Luigi? How does he fare in the kitchen?'

'Bastard.' She swallowed a gulp of white wine.

'Things not going well?'

'You could say that. He lost all our money at the tables in Monte. Now I'm back to square one, living in a hotel again.'

'Sorry to hear that.'

‘I was hoping John would have turned up. I always loved him you know. And he loved me, I know that. And there isn’t a woman in his life, am I right?’ she asked.

‘There isn’t a woman between us, Deborah.’

‘Never say that, Doug,’ she smiled, and sipped in a ladylike fashion. ‘Maybe you and I might get together?’ she moved closer to him.

‘Deborah,’ he laughed.

His phone rang.

‘Excuse me, I must take this,’ he said.

It was the Gardai.

‘The body of a man has been found washed up on Inishbofin Island ...’

Chapter Eighty

The New Year of 2011 was bleak. Ireland was still in recession and the Irish people were unsure of what the future would hold. Steve's hope of finding a job seemed remote and he wondered how long he could depend on his mother for help. The weather continued to be extremely cold, and while there had been a thaw after Christmas, within a few days the temperatures fell again and the grimness of the weather only reflected his own desperation.

Amy had made no visible improvement, and those tiny movements had never happened again. While Steve spent almost all of his time sitting beside her, he had got better at talking. Making one-way conversation and filling in the blanks. Telling her about their daily activities, even who he met on the way to the hospital. When Emma came, she would chat away as if Amy was hearing and responding to her every word.

'Mummy, I brought my baby doll in again. And she can see you. Look at her eyes, they open and close and she can speak to you too.' She pressed a button in her back, and a tinny voice said "I love you". She pressed it again and again and it kept repeating the same words.

'And I love you,' Emma smiled at Amy. 'And Daddy loves you. And Gran loves you. And Grandad loves you. And Joey loves you. And Harry loves you. And Doug loves you. And Rachel loves you. And Babs loves you and all the nurses love you.' All the people in her life were mentioned, and she continued the litany to the tune of a song she had learned in school and often sang with Amy.

Steve watched Amy. The gentle rise and fall of her chest as she breathed. How fragile she was now. She wore a nightdress Emma had chosen. It was pale pink cotton. Her hair had been cut short by the staff. Youth clung like a child. She hardly looked any older than Emma. He felt helpless and looked at his daughter. Wondered if Emma would grow up with a Daddy and no Mummy? Would Amy grow younger each day until she gently faded away?

Anger surged within him. He should have thought of better ideas to spark memories which would draw her back to them. He looked around the cubicle and suddenly realised there was no window. Why hadn't he noticed that before? He had a sudden crazy idea. If there was a window then there would be activity outside. Cars would drive past. The sun would shine in. Birds would sing. Normal every day sounds. She should have a window.

The sounds in here were not every day. Nurses tucked patients up in bed. Checked temperature and blood pressure. Brought bedpans when required. Administered pills. Injections. Discussed cases with doctors. Walked briskly in and out. Always busy. Now a trolley was pushed past the end of the bed. It was time for tea. Poured into cups from the big silver pot. Milked. Sugared. Two biscuits tucked into the saucer.

The tea trolley never stopped at Amy's cubicle.

'I'm going to comb your hair today Mummy, not on the sore side of your head, but on this side.' Emma gently touched the dark hair. Then began to brush it softly. As she did that, she sang her song again.

Steve smiled. He loved her intensely. He leaned back in the chair and stared up at the ceiling. Listened to the sweet voice lilt the tune. It was beautiful.

'Mummy?' The question cut through the tune. 'Are you awake?' Emma asked. 'Do you like my song?'

'Keep singing, Emma, keep singing,' Steve murmured.

'Mummy's eyes are open, look Daddy.' She put her arms around Amy gently, and kissed her cheek.

Steve's heart beat uncomfortably loud. He leaned forward in his chair and looked at Amy's face, still pale and shadowed. And into her eyes which were half open now. A bewildered look in their dark velvet depths.

His eyes filled with tears and he choked, unable to say anything. He thought to himself that he had never seen her more beautiful. Into his mind flashed a sudden image. Of how she had looked just seconds after Emma was born and the baby was put into her arms. A mixture of exhaustion and sheer joy on her face.

'Daddy, kiss Mummy, she's awake,' Emma ordered.

'Amy?' he whispered. He touched her cheek with his fingers.

'Do you want me to sing to you again, Mummy?' Emma asked. 'Do you like your nail polish?' She lifted her hand and began her song again.

Amy's eyes widened, more focussed now. She smiled.

'My love.' Steve drew close to her and kissed her.

He was all around her now.

That scent he knew so well took him to places he thought he would never know again.

'Amy ... Amy.'

THE END

TO MAKE A DONATION TO LAURALYNN HOUSE AT THE CHILDREN'S SUNSHINE HOME

Children's Sunshine Home/LauraLynn A/c.
AIB BANK, Sandyford Business Centre,
Foxrock,
Dublin 18.

A/c No. 32120009
Sort Code: 93-35-70

www.lauralynnhospice.com
www.sunshinehome.ie

CYCLONE COURIERS

Cyclone Couriers – who proudly support LauraLynn House – are the leading supplier of local, national and international courier services in Dublin. Cyclone also supply confidential mobile on-site document shredding and recycling services and secure document storage & records management services through their Cyclone Shredding and Cyclone Archive division.

Cyclone Couriers
The fleet of pushbikes, motorbikes and vans can cater for all your urgent local and national courier requirements.

Cyclone International
Overnight, next day, timed and weekend door-to-door deliveries to destinations within the thirty-two counties of Ireland.
Delivery options to the UK, mainland Europe, USA, and the rest of the world.
A variety of services to all destinations across the globe.

Cyclone Shredding
On-site confidential document and product shredding & recycling service. Destruction and recycling of computers, hard drives, monitors and office electronic equipment.

Cyclone Archive
Secure document & data storage and records management.
Hard copy document storage and tracking – data storage – fireproof media safe – document scanning and upload of document images.

Cyclone Couriers operate from 8, Upper Stephen Street, Dublin 8.

Cyclone Archive, International and Shredding operate from 19-20 North Park, Finglas, Dublin 11.

www.cyclone.ie email: sales@cyclone.ie Tel: 01-4757246

ODDS ON LOVE

Fran O'Brien

Bel and Tom seem to be the perfect couple with successful careers, a beautiful home and all the trappings. But underneath the facade cracks appear and damage the basis of their marriage and the deep love they have shared since that first night they met.

Her longing to have a baby creates problems for Tom, who can't deal with the possibility that her failure to conceive may be his fault. His masculinity is questioned and in attempting to deal with his insecurities he is swept up into something far more insidious and dangerous than he could ever have imagined. Then against all the odds Bel is thrilled to find out she is pregnant. But she is unable to tell Tom the wonderful news as he doesn't come home that night and disappears mysteriously out of her life leaving her to deal with the fall out.

AVAILABLE NOW ONLINE

www.franobrien.net

McGuinness Books

WHO IS FAYE?

CAN THE PAST EVER BE BURIED?

Jenny should be fulfilled. She has a successful career and shares a comfortable life with her husband, Michael, at Ballymoragh Stud.

But increasingly unwelcome memories surface and keep her awake at night.

Is it too late to go back to the source of those fears and confront them?

AVAILABLE ONLINE

www.franobrien.net

McGuinness Books